THE SONG OF ACHILLES

THE SONG OF ACHILLES

MADELINE MILLER

AN IMPRINT OF HARPERCOLLINS PUBLISHERS

HarperCollins books may be purchased for educational, business, or sales promotional use. For information please write: Special Markets Department, HarperCollins Publishers, 10 East 53rd Street, New York, NY 10022.

FIRST EDITION

Library of Congress Cataloging-in-Publication Data has been applied for.

ISBN 978-0-06-206061-7 (hardcover)
ISBN 978-0-06-212612-2 (international edition)

12 13 14 15 16   OV/RRD   10 9 8 7 6 5 4 3 2 1

To my mother, Madeline, and Nathaniel

CHAPTER ONE

MY FATHER WAS A KING AND THE SON OF KINGS. He was a short man, as most of us were, and built like a bull, all shoulders. He married my mother when she was fourteen and sworn by the priestess to be fruitful. It was a good match: she was an only child, and her father's fortune would go to her husband.

He did not find out until the wedding that she was simple. Her father had been scrupulous about keeping her veiled until the ceremony, and my father had humored him. If she was ugly, there were always slave girls and serving boys. When at last they pulled off the veil, they say my mother smiled. That is how they knew she was quite stupid. Brides did not smile.

When I was delivered, a boy, he plucked me from her arms and handed me to a nurse. In pity, the midwife gave my mother a pillow to hold instead of me. My mother hugged it. She did not seem to notice a change had been made.

Quickly, I became a disappointment: small, slight. I was not fast. I was not strong. I could not sing. The best that could be said of me was that I was not sickly. The colds and cramps that seized my peers left me untouched. This only made my father suspicious. Was I a changeling, inhuman? He scowled at me, watching. My hand shook, feeling his gaze. And there was my mother, dribbling wine on herself.

I AM FIVE when it is my father's turn to host the games. Men gather from as far as Thessaly and Sparta, and our storehouses grow rich with their gold. A hundred servants work for twenty days beating out the racing track and clearing it of stones. My father is determined to have the finest games of his generation.

I remember the runners best, nut-brown bodies slicked with oil, stretching on the track beneath the sun. They mix together, broad-shouldered husbands, beardless youths and boys, their calves all thickly carved with muscle.

The bull has been killed, sweating the last of its blood into dust and dark bronze bowls. It went quietly to its death, a good omen for the games to come.

The runners are gathered before the dais where my father and I sit, surrounded by prizes we will give to the winners. There are golden mixing bowls for wine, beaten bronze tripods, ash-wood spears tipped with precious iron. But the real prize is in my hands: a wreath of dusty-green leaves, freshly clipped, rubbed to a shine by my thumb. My father has given it to me grudgingly. He reassures himself: all I have to do is hold it.

The youngest boys are running first, and they wait, shuffling their feet in the sand for the nod from the priest. They're in their first flush of growth, bones sharp and spindly, poking against taut skin. My eye catches on a light head among dozens of dark, tousled crowns. I lean forward to see. Hair lit like honey in the sun, and within it, glints of gold—the circlet of a prince.

He is shorter than the others, and still plump with childhood in a way they are not. His hair is long and tied back with leather; it burns against the dark, bare skin of his back. His face, when he turns, is serious as a man's.

When the priest strikes the ground, he slips past the thickened bodies of the older boys. He moves easily, his heels flashing pink as licking tongues. He wins.

I stare as my father lifts the garland from my lap and crowns him; the leaves seem almost black against the brightness of his hair. His father, Peleus, comes to claim him, smiling and proud. Peleus' kingdom is smaller than ours, but his wife is rumored to be a goddess, and his people love him. My own father watches with envy. His wife is stupid and his son too slow to race in even the youngest group. He turns to me.

"That is what a son should be."

My hands feel empty without the garland. I watch King Peleus embrace his son. I see the boy toss the garland in the air and catch it again. He is laughing, and his face is bright with victory.

BEYOND THIS, I remember little more than scattered images from my life then: my father frowning on his throne, a cunning toy horse I loved, my mother on the beach, her eyes turned towards the Aegean. In this last memory, I am skipping stones for her, *plink, plink, plink,* across the skin of the sea. She seems to like the way the ripples look, dispersing back to glass. Or perhaps it is the sea itself she likes. At her temple a starburst of white gleams like bone, the scar from the time her father hit her with the hilt of a sword. Her toes poke up from the sand where she has buried them, and I am careful not to disturb them as I search for rocks. I choose one and fling it out, glad to be good at this. It is the only memory I have of my mother and so golden that I am almost sure I have made it up. After all, it was unlikely for my father to have allowed us to be alone together, his simple son and simpler wife. And where are we? I do not recognize the beach, the view of coastline. So much has passed since then.

CHAPTER TWO

I WAS SUMMONED TO THE KING. I REMEMBER HATING THIS, the long walk up the endless throne room. At the front, I knelt on stone. Some kings chose to have rugs there for the knees of messengers who had long news to tell. My father preferred not to.

"King Tyndareus' daughter is finally ready for marriage," he said.

I knew the name. Tyndareus was king of Sparta and held huge tracts of the ripest southern lands, the kind my father coveted. I had heard of his daughter too, rumored to be the fairest woman in our countries. Her mother, Leda, was said to have been ravished by Zeus, the king of the gods himself, disguised as a swan. Nine months later, her womb yielded two sets of twins: Clytemnestra and Castor, children of her mortal husband; Helen and Polydeuces, the shining cygnets of the god. But gods were known to be notoriously poor parents; it was expected that Tyndareus would offer patrimony to all.

I did not respond to my father's news. Such things meant nothing to me.

My father cleared his throat, loud in the silent chamber. "We would do well to have her in our family. You will go and put yourself forth as a suitor." There was no one else in the hall, so my startled huff of breath was for his ears alone. But I knew better than to speak my discomfort. My father already knew all that I might say: that I was nine, unsightly, unpromising, uninterested.

We left the next morning, our packs heavy with gifts and food for the journey. Soldiers escorted us, in their finest armor. I don't remember much of the trip—it was overland, through countryside that left no impression. At the head of the column, my father dictated new orders to secretaries and messengers who rode off in every direction. I looked down at the leather reins, smoothed their nap with my thumb. I did not understand my place here. It was incomprehensible, as so much of what my father did was. My donkey swayed, and I swayed with him, glad for even this distraction.

We were not the first suitors to arrive at Tyndareus' citadel. The stables were full of horses and mules, busy with servants. My father seemed displeased with the ceremony afforded us: I saw him rub a hand over the stone of the hearth in our rooms, frowning. I had brought a toy from home, a horse whose legs could move. I lifted one hoof, then the other, imagined that I had ridden him instead of the donkey. A soldier took pity on me and lent me his dice. I clattered them against the floor until they showed all sixes in one throw.

Finally, a day came in which my father ordered me bathed and brushed. He had me change my tunic, then change again. I obeyed, though I saw no difference between the purple with gold or crimson with gold. Neither hid my knobby knees. My father looked powerful and severe, his black beard slashing across his face. The gift that we were presenting to Tyndareus stood ready, a beaten-gold mixing bowl embossed with the story of the princess Danae. Zeus had wooed her in a shower of golden light, and she had borne him Perseus, Gorgon-slayer, second only to Heracles among our heroes. My father handed it to me. "Do not disgrace us," he said.

I heard the great hall before I saw it, the sound of hundreds of voices banging against stone walls, the clatter of goblets and armor. The servants had thrown open the windows to try to dampen the sound; they had hung tapestries, wealth indeed, on every wall. I had never seen so many men inside before. Not men, I corrected myself. Kings.

We were called forward to council, seated on benches draped with cowhide. Servants faded backwards, to the shadows. My father's fingers dug into my collar, warning me not to fidget.

There was violence in that room, with so many princes and heroes and kings competing for a single prize, but we knew how to ape civilization. One by one they introduced themselves, these young men, showing off shining hair and neat waists and expensively dyed clothing. Many were the sons or grandsons of gods. All had a song or two, or more, written of their deeds. Tyndareus greeted each in turn, accepted their gifts in a pile at the center of the room. Invited each to speak and present his suit.

My father was the oldest among them, except for the man who, when his turn came, named himself Philoctetes. "A comrade of Heracles," the man beside us whispered, with an awe I understood. Heracles was the greatest of our heroes, and Philoctetes had been the closest of his companions, the only one still living. His hair was gray, and his thick fingers were all tendon, the sin-

ewy dexterity that marked an archer. And indeed, a moment later
he held up the largest bow I had ever seen, polished yew wood
with a lionskin grip. "The bow of Heracles," Philoctetes named it,
"given to me at his death." In our lands a bow was mocked as the
weapon of cowards. But no one could say such a thing about this
bow; the strength it would take to draw it humbled us all.

The next man, his eyes painted like a woman's, spoke his
name. "Idomeneus, King of Crete." He was lean, and his long hair
fell to his waist when he stood. He offered rare iron, a double-
headed ax. "The symbol of my people." His movements reminded
me of the dancers that my mother liked.

And then Menelaus, son of Atreus, seated beside his hulking,
bearlike brother Agamemnon. Menelaus' hair was a startling
red, the color of fire-forged bronze. His body was strong, stocky
with muscles, vital. The gift he gave was a rich one, beautifully
dyed cloth. "Though the lady needs no adornment," he added,
smiling. This was a pretty bit of speech. I wished I had something as clever to say. I was the only one here under twenty, and
I was not descended from a god. Perhaps Peleus' blond-haired
son would be equal to this, I thought. But his father had kept
him at home.

Man after man, and their names began to blur in my head. My
attention wandered to the dais, where I noticed, for the first time,
the three veiled women seated at Tyndareus' side. I stared at the
white cloth over their faces, as if I might be able to catch some
glimpse of the woman behind it. My father wanted one of them
for my wife. Three sets of hands, prettily adorned with bracelets,
lay quiet in their laps. One of the women was taller than the other
two. I thought I saw a stray dark curl peek from beneath the bot-

tom of her veil. Helen is light haired, I remembered. So that one was not Helen. I had ceased to listen to the kings.

"Welcome, Menoitius." The speaking of my father's name startled me. Tyndareus was looking at us. "I am sorry to hear of the death of your wife."

"My wife lives, Tyndareus. It is my son who comes today to wed your daughter." There was a silence in which I knelt, dizzied by the spin of faces around me.

"Your son is not yet a man." Tyndareus' voice seemed far away. I could detect nothing in it.

"He need not be. I am man enough for both of us." It was the sort of jest our people loved, bold and boasting. But no one laughed.

"I see," said Tyndareus.

The stone floor dug into my skin, yet I did not move. I was used to kneeling. I had never before been glad of the practice in my father's throne room.

My father spoke again, in the silence. "Others have brought bronze and wine, oil and wool. I bring gold, and it is only a small portion of my stores." I was aware of my hands on the beautiful bowl, touching the story's figures: Zeus appearing from the streaming sunlight, the startled princess, their coupling.

"My daughter and I are grateful that you have brought us such a worthy gift, though paltry to you." A murmur, from the kings. There was humiliation here that my father did not seem to understand. My face flushed with it.

"I would make Helen the queen of my palace. For my wife, as you know well, is not fit to rule. My wealth exceeds all of these young men, and my deeds speak for themselves."

"I thought the suitor was your son."

I looked up at the new voice. A man who had not spoken yet. He was the last in line, sitting at ease on the bench, his curling hair gleaming in the light of the fire. He had a jagged scar on one leg, a seam that stitched his dark brown flesh from heel to knee, wrapping around the muscles of the calf and burying itself in the shadow beneath his tunic. It looked like it had been a knife, I thought, or something like it, ripping upwards and leaving behind feathered edges, whose softness belied the violence that must have caused it.

My father was angry. "Son of Laertes, I do not remember inviting you to speak."

The man smiled. "I was not invited. I interrupted. But you need not fear my interference. I have no vested interest in the matter. I speak only as an observer." A small movement from the dais drew my eye. One of the veiled figures had stirred.

"What does he mean?" My father was frowning. "If he is not here for Helen, then for what? Let him go back to his rocks and his goats."

The man's eyebrows lifted, but he said nothing.

Tyndareus was also mild. "If your son is to be a suitor, as you say, then let him present himself."

Even I knew it was my turn to speak. "I am Patroclus, son of Menoitius." My voice sounded high, and scratchy with disuse. "I am here as a suitor for Helen. My father is a king and the son of kings." I had no more to say. My father had not instructed me; he had not thought that Tyndareus would ask me to speak. I stood and carried the bowl to the pile of gifts, placed it where it would not topple. I turned and walked back to my bench. I had not disgraced myself with trembling or tripping, and my words had not been foolish. Still, my face burned with shame. I knew how I must look to these men.

Oblivious, the line of suitors moved on. The man kneeling now was huge, half again as tall as my father, and broad besides. Behind him, two servants braced an enormous shield. It seemed to stand with him as part of his suit, reaching from his heels to his crown; no ordinary man could have carried it. And it was no decoration: scarred and hacked edges bore witness to the battles it had seen. Ajax, son of Telamon, this giant named himself. His speech was blunt and short, claiming his lineage from Zeus and offering his mighty size as proof of his great-grandfather's continuing favor. His gift was a spear, supple wood beautifully cut. The fire-forged point gleamed in the light of the torches.

At last it was the man with the scar's turn. "Well, son of Laertes?" Tyndareus shifted in his seat to face him. "What does a disinterested observer have to say to these proceedings?"

The man leaned back. "I would like to know how you are going to stop the losers from declaring war on you. Or on Helen's lucky new husband. I see half a dozen men here ready to leap at each other's throats."

"You seem amused."

The man shrugged. "I find the folly of men amusing."

"The son of Laertes scorns us!" This was the large man, Ajax, his clenched fist as big as my head.

"Son of Telamon, never."

"Then what, Odysseus? Speak your mind, for once." Tyndareus' voice was as sharp as I'd heard it.

Odysseus shrugged again. "This was a dangerous gamble,

despite the treasure and renown you have won. Each of these men is worthy, and knows it. They will not be so easily put off."

"All this you have said to me in private."

My father stiffened beside me. *Conspiracy.* His was not the only angry face in the hall.

"True. But now I offer you a solution." He held up his hands, empty. "I have brought no gift and do not seek to woo Helen. I am a king, as has been said, of rocks and goats. In return for my solution, I seek from you the prize that I have already named."

"Give me your solution and you shall have it." Again, that slight movement, from the dais. One woman's hand had twitched against her companion's dress.

"Then here it is. I believe that we should let Helen choose." Odysseus paused, to allow for the murmurs of disbelief; women did not have a say in such things. "No one may fault you, then. But she must choose now, at this very moment, so she will not be said to have taken council or instruction from you. And." He held up a finger. "Before she chooses, every man here must swear an oath: to uphold Helen's choice, and to defend her husband against all who would take her from him."

I felt the unrest in the room. *An oath?* And over such an unconventional matter as a woman choosing her husband. The men were suspicious.

"Very well." Tyndareus, his face unreadable, turned to the veiled women. "Helen, do you accept this proposal?"

Her voice was low and lovely, carrying to every corner of the hall. "I do." It was all she said, but I felt the shiver go through the men around me. Even as a child I felt it, and I marveled at the power of this woman who, though veiled, could electrify a room.

Her skin, we suddenly remembered, was rumored to be gilded, her eyes dark and shining as the slick obsidian that we traded our olives for. At that moment she was worth all the prizes in the center of the hall, and more. She was worth our lives.

Tyndareus nodded. "Then I decree that it is so. All those who wish to swear will do so, now."

I heard muttering, a few half-angry voices. But no man left. Helen's voice, and the veil, gently fluttering with her breath, held us all captive.

A swiftly summoned priest led a white goat to the altar. Here, inside, it was a more propitious choice than a bull, whose throat might splash unwholesomely upon the stone floor. The animal died easily, and the man mixed its dark blood with the cypress-ash from the fire. The bowl hissed, loud in the silent room.

"You will be first." Tyndareus pointed to Odysseus. Even a nine-year-old saw how fitting this was. Already Odysseus had shown himself too clever by half. Our ragged alliances prevailed only when no man was allowed to be too much more powerful than another. Around the room, I saw smirks and satisfaction among the kings; he would not be allowed to escape his own noose.

Odysseus' mouth quirked in a half-smile. "Of course. It is my pleasure." But I guessed that it was not so. During the sacrifice I had watched him lean back into the shadows, as if he would be forgotten. He rose now, moved to the altar.

"Now Helen"—Odysseus paused, his arm half-extended to the priest—"remember that I swear only in fellowship, not as a suitor. You would never forgive yourself if you were to choose me." His words were teasing, and drew scattered laughter. We all knew it was not likely that one so luminous as Helen would choose the king of barren Ithaca.

One by one the priest summoned us to the hearth, marking our wrists with blood and ash, binding as chains. I chanted the words of the oath back to him, my arm lifted for all to see.

When the last man had returned to his place, Tyndareus rose. "Choose now, my daughter."

"Menelaus." She spoke without hesitation, startling us all. We had expected suspense, indecision. I turned to the red-haired man, who stood, a huge grin cracking his face. In outsize joy, he clapped his silent brother on the back. Everywhere else was anger, disappointment, even grief. But no man reached for his sword; the blood had dried thick on our wrists.

"So be it." Tyndareus stood also. "I am glad to welcome a second son of Atreus to my family. You shall have my Helen, even as your worthy brother once claimed my Clytemnestra." He gestured to the tallest woman, as though she might stand. She did not move. Perhaps she had not heard.

"What about the third girl?" This shout from a small man, beside the giant Ajax. "Your niece. Can I have her?"

The men laughed, glad for an easing in the tension.

"You're too late, Teucer." Odysseus spoke over the noise. "She's promised to me."

I did not have the chance to hear more. My father's hand seized my shoulder, pulling me angrily off the bench. "We are finished here." We left that very night for home, and I climbed back on my donkey, thick with disappointment: I had not even been allowed to glimpse Helen's fabled face.

My father would never mention the trip again, and once home the events twisted strangely in my memory. The blood and the oath, the room full of kings: they seemed distant and pale, like something a bard had spun, rather than something I lived. Had I really knelt there before them? And what of the oath I had sworn? It seemed absurd even to think of it, foolish and improbable as a dream is by dinner.

CHAPTER THREE

I STOOD IN THE FIELD. IN MY HANDS WERE TWO PAIRS OF dice, a gift. Not from my father, who'd never think of it. Not from my mother, who sometimes did not know me. I could not remember who had given them to me. A visiting king? A favor-currying noble?

They were carved from ivory, inset with onyx, smooth under my thumb. It was late summer, and I was panting with my run from the palace. Since the day of the races I had been appointed a man to train me in all our athletic arts: boxing, sword-and-spear, discus. But I had escaped him, and glowed with the giddy lightness of solitude. It was the first time I had been alone in weeks.

Then the boy appeared. His name was Clysonymus, and he was the son of a nobleman who was often at the palace. Older, larger, and unpleasantly fleshy. His eyes had caught the flash of the dice in my palm. He leered at me, held out his hand. "Let me see them."

"No." I did not want his fingers on them, grubby and thick. And I was the prince, however small. Did I not even have this right? But these noble sons were used to me doing what they wished. They knew my father would not intervene.

"I want them." He didn't bother to threaten me, yet. I hated him for it. I should be worth threatening.

"No."

He stepped forward. "Let me have them."

"They're mine." I grew teeth. I snapped like the dogs who fight for our table scraps.

He reached to take them, and I shoved him backwards. He stumbled, and I was glad. He would not get what was mine.

"Hey!" He was angry. I was so small; I was rumored to be simple. If he backed down now, it would be a dishonor. He advanced on me, face red. Without meaning to, I stepped back.

He smirked then. "Coward."

"I am no coward." My voice rose, and my skin went hot.

"Your father thinks you are." His words were deliberate, as if he were savoring them. "I heard him tell my father so."

"He did not." But I knew he had.

The boy stepped closer. He lifted a fist. "Are you calling me a liar?" I knew that he would hit me now. He was just waiting for an excuse. I could imagine the way my father would have said it. *Coward.* I planted my hands on his chest and shoved, as hard as I could. Our land was one of grass and wheat. Tumbles should not hurt.

I am making excuses. It was also a land of rocks.

His head thudded dully against stone, and I saw the surprised pop of his eyes. The ground around him began to bleed.

I stared, my throat closing in horror at what I had done. I had not seen the death of a human before. Yes, the bulls, and the goats, even the bloodless gasping of fish. And I had seen it in paintings, tapestries, the black figures burned onto our platters. But I had not seen this: the rattle of it, the choke and scrabble. The smell of the flux. I fled.

Sometime later, they found me by the gnarled ankles of an olive tree. I was limp and pale, surrounded by my own vomit. The dice were gone, lost in my flight. My father stared down angrily at me, his lips drawn back to show his yellowing teeth. He gestured, and the servants lifted me and carried me inside.

The boy's family demanded immediate exile or death. They were powerful, and this was their eldest son. They might permit a king to burn their fields or rape their daughters, as long as payment was made. But you did not touch a man's sons. For this, the nobles would riot. We all knew the rules; we clung to them to avoid the anarchy that was always a hairsbreadth away. *Blood feud*. The servants made the sign against evil.

My father had spent his life scrabbling to keep his kingdom, and would not risk losing it over such a son as me, when heirs and the wombs that bore them were so easy to come by. So he agreed: I would be exiled, and fostered in another man's kingdom. In exchange for my weight in gold, they would rear me to manhood. I would have no parents, no family name, no inheritance. In our day, death was preferable. But my father was a practical man. My weight in gold was less than the expense of the lavish funeral my death would have demanded.

This was how I came to be ten, and an orphan. This is how I came to Phthia.

TINY, GEMSTONE-SIZED PHTHIA was the smallest of our countries, set in a northern crook of land between the ridges of Mount

Othrys and the sea. Its king, Peleus, was one of those men whom the gods love: not divine himself, but clever, brave, handsome, and excelling all his peers in piety. As a reward, our divinities offered him a sea-nymph for a wife. It was considered their highest honor. After all, what mortal would not want to bed a goddess and sire a son from her? Divine blood purified our muddy race, bred heroes from dust and clay. And this goddess brought a greater promise still: the Fates had foretold that her son would far surpass his father. Peleus' line would be assured. But, like all the gods' gifts, there was an edge to it; the goddess herself was unwilling.

Everyone, even I, had heard the story of Thetis' ravishment. The gods had led Peleus to the secret place where she liked to sit upon the beach. They had warned him not to waste time with overtures—she would never consent to marriage with a mortal.

They warned him too of what would come once he had caught her: for the nymph Thetis was wily, like her father, Proteus, the slippery old man of the sea, and she knew how to make her skin flow into a thousand different shapes of fur and feather and flesh. And though beaks and claws and teeth and coils and stinging tails would flay him, still Peleus must not let her go.

Peleus was a pious and obedient man and did all that the gods had instructed him to do. He waited for her to emerge from the slate-colored waves, hair black and long as a horse's tail. Then he seized her, holding on despite her violent struggles, squeezing until they were both exhausted, breathless and sand-scraped. The blood from the wounds she had given him mixed with the smears of lost maidenhead on her thighs. Her resistance mattered no longer: a deflowering was as binding as marriage vows.

The gods forced her to swear that she would stay with her

mortal husband for at least a year, and she served her time on earth as the duty it was, silent, unresponsive, and sullen. Now when he clasped her, she did not bother to writhe and twist in protest. Instead she lay stiff and silent, damp and chilled as an old fish. Her reluctant womb bore only a single child. The hour her sentence was finished, she ran out of the house and dove back into the sea.

She would return only to visit the boy, never for any other reason, and never for long. The rest of the time the child was raised by tutors and nurses and overseen by Phoinix, Peleus' most trusted counselor. Did Peleus ever regret the gods' gift to him? An ordinary wife would have counted herself lucky to find a husband with Peleus' mildness, his smile-lined face. But for the sea-nymph Thetis nothing could ever eclipse the stain of his dirty, mortal mediocrity.

I WAS LED through the palace by a servant whose name I had not caught. Perhaps he had not said it. The halls were smaller than at home, as if restrained by the modesty of the kingdom they governed. The walls and floors were local marble, whiter than was found in the south. My feet were dark against its pallor.

I had nothing with me. My few belongings were being carried to my room, and the gold my father sent was on its way to the treasury. I had felt a strange panic as I was parted from it. It had been my companion for the weeks of travel, a reminder of my worth. I knew its contents by heart now: the five goblets with engraved stems, a heavy knobbed scepter, a beaten-gold necklace, two ornamental statues of birds, and a carved lyre, gilded at its tips. This last, I knew, was cheating. Wood was cheap and plentiful and heavy and took up space that should have been used for gold. Yet the lyre was so beautiful no one could object to it; it had been a piece of my mother's dowry. As we rode, I would reach back into my saddlebags to stroke the polished wood.

I guessed that I was being led to the throne room, where I would kneel and pour out my gratitude. But the servant stopped suddenly at a side door. King Peleus was absent, he told me, so I would present myself before his son instead. I was unnerved. This was not what I had prepared myself for, the dutiful words I'd practiced on donkeyback. Peleus' son. I could still remember the dark wreath against his bright hair, the way his pink soles had flashed along the track. *That is what a son should be.*

He was lying on his back on a wide, pillowed bench, balancing a lyre on his stomach. Idly, he plucked at it. He did not hear me enter, or he did not choose to look. This is how I first began to understand my place here. Until this moment I had been a prince, expected and announced. Now I was negligible.

I took another step forward, scuffing my feet, and his head lolled to the side to regard me. In the five years since I had seen him, he had outgrown his babyish roundness. I gaped at the cold shock of his beauty, deep-green eyes, features fine as a girl's. It struck from me a sudden, springing dislike. I had not changed so much, nor so well.

He yawned, his eyes heavy-lidded. "What's your name?"

His kingdom was half, a quarter, an eighth the size of my father's, and I had killed a boy and been exiled and still he did not know me. I ground my jaw shut and would not speak.

He asked again, louder: "What's your name?"

My silence was excusable the first time; perhaps I had not heard him. Now it was not.

"Patroclus." It was the name my father had given me, hopefully but injudiciously, at my birth, and it tasted of bitterness on my tongue. "Honor of the father," it meant. I waited for him to make a joke out of it, some witty jape about my disgrace. He did not. Perhaps, I thought, he is too stupid to.

He rolled onto his side to face me. A stray lock of gold fell half into his eyes; he blew it away. "My name is Achilles."

I jerked my chin up, an inch, in bare acknowledgment. We regarded each other for a moment. Then he blinked and yawned again, his mouth cracked wide as a cat's. "Welcome to Phthia."

I had been raised in a court and knew dismissal when I heard it.

I DISCOVERED THAT AFTERNOON that I was not the only foster child of Peleus. The modest king turned out to be rich in cast-off sons. He had once been a runaway himself, it was rumored, and had a reputation for charity towards exiles. My bed was a pallet in a long barracks-style room, filled with other boys tussling and lounging. A servant showed me where my things had been put. A few boys lifted their heads, stared. I am sure one of them spoke to me, asked my name. I am sure I gave it. They returned to their games. *No one important.* I walked stiff-legged to my pallet and waited for dinner.

We were summoned to eat at dusk by a bell, bronze struck from deep in the palace's turnings. The boys dropped their games and tumbled out into the hallway. The complex was built like a rabbit warren, full of twisting corridors and sudden inner rooms. I nearly tripped over the heels of the boy in front of me, fearful of being left behind and lost.

The room for meals was a long hall at the front of the palace, its windows opening onto Mount Othrys' foothills. It was large enough to feed all of us, many times over; Peleus was a king who liked to host and entertain. We sat on its oakwood benches, at tables that were scratched from years of clattering plates. The food was simple but plentiful—salted fish, and thick bread served with herbed cheese. There was no flesh here, of goats or bulls. That was only for royalty, or festival days. Across the room I caught the flash of bright hair in lamplight. *Achilles.* He sat with a group of boys whose mouths were wide with laughter at something he'd said or done. *That is what a prince should be.* I stared down at my bread, its coarse grains that rubbed rough against my fingers.

After supper we were allowed to do as we liked. Some boys were gathering in a corner for a game. "Do you want to play?" one asked. His hair still hung in childhood curls; he was younger than I was.

"Play?"

"Dice." He opened his hand to show them, carved bone flecked with black dye.

I started, stepped backwards. "No," I said, too loudly.

He blinked in surprise. "All right." He shrugged, and was gone.

That night I dreamed of the dead boy, his skull cracked like an egg against the ground. *He has followed me.* The blood spreads, dark as spilled wine. His eyes open, and his mouth begins to move. I clap my hands over my ears. The voices of the dead were said to have the power to make the living mad. *I must not hear him speak.*

I woke in terror, hoping I had not screamed aloud. The pin-pricks of stars outside the window were the only light; there was no moon I could see. My breathing was harsh in the silence, and the marsh-reed ticking of the mattress crackled softly beneath me, rubbing its thin fingers against my back. The presence of the other boys did not comfort me; our dead come for their vengeance regardless of witnesses.

The stars turned, and somewhere the moon crept across the sky. When my eyes dragged closed again, he was waiting for me still, covered in blood, his face as pale as bone. Of course he was. No soul wished to be sent early to the endless gloom of our underworld. Exile might satisfy the anger of the living, but it did not appease the dead.

I woke sandy-eyed, my limbs heavy and dull. The other boys surged around me, dressing for breakfast, eager for the day. Word had spread quickly of my strangeness, and the younger boy did not approach me again, with dice or anything else. At breakfast, my fingers pushed bread between my lips, and my throat swallowed. Milk was poured for me. I drank it.

Afterwards we were led into the dusty sun of the practice yards for training in spear and sword. Here is where I tasted the full truth of Peleus' kindness: well trained and indebted, we would one day make him a fine army.

I was given a spear, and a callused hand corrected my grip, then corrected it again. I threw and grazed the edge of the oak-tree target. The master blew out a breath and passed me a second spear. My eyes traveled over the other boys, searching for Peleus' son. He was not there. I sighted once more at the oak, its bark pitted and cracked, oozing sap from punctures. I threw.

The sun drove high, then higher still. My throat grew dry and hot, scratched with burning dust. When the masters released us, most of the boys fled to the beach, where small breezes still stirred. There they diced and raced, shouting jokes in the sharp, slanting dialects of the north.

My eyes were heavy in my head, and my arm ached from the morning's exertion. I sat beneath the scrubby shade of an olive tree to stare out over the ocean's waves. No one spoke to me. I was easy to ignore. It was not so very different from home, really.

THE NEXT DAY was the same, a morning of weary exercises, and then long afternoon hours alone. At night, the moon slivered smaller and smaller. I stared until I could see it even when I closed my eyes, the yellow curve bright against the dark of my eyelids. I hoped that it might keep the visions of the boy at bay. Our goddess of the moon is gifted with magic, with power over the dead. She could banish the dreams, if she wished.

She did not. The boy came, night after night, with his staring eyes and splintered skull. Sometimes he turned and showed me the hole in his head, where the soft mass of his brain hung loose. Sometimes he reached for me. I would wake, choking on my horror, and stare at the darkness until dawn.

CHAPTER FOUR

MEALS IN THE VAULTED DINING HALL WERE MY ONLY relief. There the walls did not seem to press in on me so much, and the dust from the courtyard did not clog in my throat. The buzz of constant voices eased as mouths were stuffed full. I could sit with my food alone and breathe again.

It was the only time I saw Achilles. His days were separate, princely, filled with duties we had no part of. But he took each meal with us, circulating among the tables. In the huge hall, his beauty shone like a flame, vital and bright, drawing my eye against my will. His mouth was a plump bow, his nose an aristocratic arrow. When he was seated, his limbs did not skew as mine did, but arranged themselves with perfect grace, as if for a sculptor. Perhaps most remarkable was his unself-consciousness. He did not preen or pout as other handsome children did. Indeed, he seemed utterly unaware of his effect on the boys around him. Though how he was, I could not imagine: they crowded him like dogs in their eagerness, tongues lolling.

I watched all of this from my place at a corner table, bread crumpled in my fist. The keen edge of my envy was like flint, a spark away from fire.

On one of these days he sat closer to me than usual; only a

table distant. His dusty feet scuffed against the flagstones as he ate. They were not cracked and callused as mine were, but pink and sweetly brown beneath the dirt. *Prince*, I sneered inside my head.

He turned, as if he had heard me. For a second our eyes held, and I felt a shock run through me. I jerked my gaze away, and busied myself with my bread. My cheeks were hot, and my skin prickled as if before a storm. When, at last, I ventured to look up again, he had turned back to his table and was speaking to the other boys.

After that, I was craftier with my observation, kept my head down and my eyes ready to leap away. But he was craftier still. At least once a dinner he would turn and catch me before I could feign indifference. Those seconds, half seconds, that the line of our gaze connected, were the only moment in my day that I felt anything at all. The sudden swoop of my stomach, the coursing anger. I was like a fish eyeing the hook.

IN THE FOURTH WEEK of my exile, I walked into the dining hall to find him at the table where I always sat. My table, as I had come to think of it, since few others chose to share it with me. Now, because of him, the benches were full of jostling boys. I froze, caught between flight and fury. Anger won. This was mine, and he would not push me from it, no matter how many boys he brought.

I sat at the last empty space, my shoulders tensed as if for a fight. Across the table the boys postured and prattled, about a spear and a bird that had died on the beach and the spring races.

I did not hear them. His presence was like a stone in my shoe, impossible to ignore. His skin was the color of just-pressed olive oil, and smooth as polished wood, without the scabs and blemishes that covered the rest of us.

Dinner finished, and the plates were cleared. A harvest moon, full and orange, hung in the dusk beyond the dining room's windows. Yet Achilles lingered. Absently, he pushed the hair from his eyes; it had grown longer over the weeks I had been here. He reached for a bowl on the table that held figs and gathered several in his hands.

With a toss of his wrist, he flicked the figs into the air, one, two, three, juggling them so lightly that their delicate skins did not bruise. He added a fourth, then a fifth. The boys hooted and clapped. More, more!

The fruits flew, colors blurring, so fast they seemed not to touch his hands, to tumble of their own accord. Juggling was a trick of low mummers and beggars, but he made it something else, a living pattern painted on the air, so beautiful even I could not pretend disinterest.

His gaze, which had been following the circling fruit, flickered to mine. I did not have time to look away before he said, softly but distinctly, "Catch." A fig leapt from the pattern in a graceful arc towards me. It fell into the cup of my palms, soft and slightly warm. I was aware of the boys cheering.

One by one, Achilles caught the remaining fruits, returned them to the table with a performer's flourish. Except for the last, which he ate, the dark flesh parting to pink seeds under his teeth. The fruit was perfectly ripe, the juice brimming. Without thinking, I brought the one he had thrown me to my lips. Its burst of grainy sweetness filled my mouth; the skin was downy on my tongue. I had loved figs, once.

He stood, and the boys chorused their farewells. I thought he might look at me again. But he only turned and vanished back to his room on the other side of the palace.

THE NEXT DAY Peleus returned to the palace and I was brought before him in his throne room, smoky and sharp from a yew-wood fire. Duly I knelt, saluted, received his famously charitable smile. "Patroclus," I told him, when he asked. I was almost accustomed to it now, the bareness of my name, without my father's behind it. Peleus nodded. He seemed old to me, bent over, but he was no more than fifty, my father's age. He did not look like a man who could have conquered a goddess, or produced such a child as Achilles.

"You are here because you killed a boy. You understand this?"

This was the cruelty of adults. *Do you understand?*

"Yes," I told him. I could have told him more, of the dreams that left me bleary and bloodshot, the almost-screams that scraped my throat as I swallowed them down. The way the stars turned and turned through the night above my unsleeping eyes.

"You are welcome here. You may still make a good man." He meant it as comfort.

LATER THAT DAY, perhaps from him, perhaps from a listening servant, the boys learned at last of the reason for my exile. I should have expected it. I had heard them gossip of others often enough;

rumors were the only coin the boys had to trade in. Still, it took
me by surprise to see the sudden change in them, the fear and fas-
cination blooming on their faces as I passed. Now even the bold-
est of them would whisper a prayer if he brushed against me: bad
luck could be caught, and the *Erinyes*, our hissing spirits of vengeance, were not always particular. The boys watched from a safe
distance, enthralled. *Will they drink his blood, do you think?*

Their whispers choked me, turned the food in my mouth to
ash. I pushed away my plate and sought out corners and spare
halls where I might sit undisturbed, except for the occasional passing servant. My narrow world narrowed further: to the cracks in
the floor, the carved whorls in the stone walls. They rasped softly
as I traced them with my fingertip.

"I HEARD YOU WERE HERE." A clear voice, like ice-melted streams.

My head jerked up. I was in a storeroom, my knees against my
chest, wedged between jars of thick-pressed olive oil. I had been
dreaming myself a fish, silvered by sun as it leapt from the sea.
The waves dissolved, became amphorae and grain sacks again.

It was Achilles, standing over me. His face was serious, the
green of his eyes steady as he regarded me. I prickled with guilt. I
was not supposed to be there and I knew it.

"I have been looking for you," he said. The words were ex-
pressionless; they carried no hint of anything I could read. "You
have not been going to morning drills."

My face went red. Behind the guilt, anger rose slow and dull.
It was his right to chastise me, but I hated him for it.

"How do you know? You aren't there."

"The master noticed, and spoke to my father."

"And he sent you." I wanted to make him feel ugly for his tale-bearing.

"No, I came on my own." Achilles' voice was cool, but I saw his jaw tighten, just a little. "I overheard them speaking. I have come to see if you are ill."

I did not answer. He studied me a moment.

"My father is considering punishment," he said.

We knew what this meant. Punishment was corporal, and usually public. A prince would never be whipped, but I was no longer a prince.

"You are not ill," he said.

"No," I answered, dully.

"Then that will not serve as your excuse."

"What?" In my fear I could not follow him.

"Your excuse for where you have been." His voice was patient. "So you will not be punished. What will you say?"

"I don't know."

"You must say something."

His insistence sparked anger in me. "You are the prince," I snapped.

That surprised him. He tilted his head a little, like a curious bird. "So?"

"So speak to your father, and say I was with you. He will excuse it." I said this more confidently than I felt. If I had spoken to my father for another boy, he would have been whipped out of spite. But I was not Achilles.

The slightest crease appeared between his eyes. "I do not like to lie," he said.

It was the sort of innocence other boys taunted out of you; even if you felt it, you did not say it.

"Then take me with you to your lessons," I said. "So it won't be a lie."

His eyebrows lifted, and he regarded me. He was utterly still, the type of quiet that I had thought could not belong to humans, a stilling of everything but breath and pulse—like a deer, listening for the hunter's bow. I found myself holding my breath.

Then something shifted in his face. A decision.

"Come," he said.

"Where?" I was wary; perhaps now I would be punished for suggesting deceit.

"To my lyre lesson. So, as you say, it will not be a lie. After, we will speak with my father."

"Now?"

"Yes. Why not?" He watched me, curious. *Why not?*

When I stood to follow him, my limbs ached from so long seated on cool stone. My chest trilled with something I could not quite name. Escape, and danger, and hope all at once.

WE WALKED IN SILENCE through the winding halls and came at length to a small room, holding only a large chest and stools for sitting. Achilles gestured to one and I went to it, leather pulled taut over a spare wooden frame. A musician's chair. I had seen them only when bards came, infrequently, to play at my father's fireside.

Achilles opened the chest. He pulled a lyre from it and held it out to me.

"I don't play," I told him.

His forehead wrinkled at this. "Never?"

Strangely, I found myself not wishing to disappoint him. "My father did not like music."

"So? Your father is not here."

I took the lyre. It was cool to the touch, and smooth. I slid my fingers over the strings, heard the humming almost-note; it was the lyre I had seen him with the first day I came.

Achilles bent again into the trunk, pulled out a second instrument, and came to join me.

He settled it on his knees. The wood was carved and golden and shone with careful keeping. It was my mother's lyre, the one my father had sent as part of my price.

Achilles plucked a string. The note rose warm and resonant, sweetly pure. My mother had always pulled her chair close to the bards when they came, so close my father would scowl and the servants would whisper. I remembered, suddenly, the dark gleam of her eyes in the firelight as she watched the bard's hands. The look on her face was like thirst.

Achilles plucked another string, and a note rang out, deeper than the other. His hand reached for a peg, turned it.

That is my mother's lyre, I almost said. The words were in my mouth, and behind them others crowded close. *That is* my *lyre*. But I did not speak. What would he say to such a statement? The lyre was his, now.

I swallowed, my throat dry. "It is beautiful."

"My father gave it to me," he said, carelessly. Only the way his fingers held it, so gently, stopped me from rising in rage.

He did not notice. "You can hold it, if you like."

The wood would be smooth and known as my own skin.

"No," I said, through the ache in my chest. *I will not cry in front of him.*

He started to say something. But at that moment the teacher entered, a man of indeterminate middle age. He had the callused hands of a musician and carried his own lyre, carved of dark walnut.

"Who is this?" he asked. His voice was harsh and loud. A musician, but not a singer.

"This is Patroclus," Achilles said. "He does not play, but he will learn."

"Not on that instrument." The man's hand swooped down to pluck the lyre from my hands. Instinctively, my fingers tightened on it. It was not as beautiful as my mother's lyre, but it was still a princely instrument. I did not want to give it up.

I did not have to. Achilles had caught him by the wrist, mid-reach. "Yes, on that instrument if he likes."

The man was angry but said no more. Achilles released him and he sat, stiffly.

"Begin," he said.

Achilles nodded and bent over the lyre. I did not have time to wonder about his intervention. His fingers touched the strings, and all my thoughts were displaced. The sound was pure and sweet as water, bright as lemons. It was like no music I had ever heard before. It had warmth as a fire does, a texture and weight like polished ivory. It buoyed and soothed at once. A few hairs slipped forward to hang over his eyes as he played. They were fine as lyre strings themselves, and shone.

He stopped, pushed back his hair, and turned to me.

"Now you."

I shook my head, full to spilling. I could not play now. Not ever, if I could listen to him instead. "You play," I said.

Achilles returned to his strings, and the music rose again. This time he sang also, weaving his own accompaniment with a clear, rich treble. His head fell back a little, exposing his throat, supple and fawn-skin soft. A small smile lifted the left corner of his mouth. Without meaning to I found myself leaning forward.

When at last he ceased, my chest felt strangely hollowed. I watched him rise to replace the lyres, close the trunk. He bid farewell to the teacher, who turned and left. It took me a long moment before I came back to myself, to notice he was waiting for me.

"We will go see my father now."

I did not quite trust myself to speak, so I nodded and followed him out of the room and up the twisting hallways to the king.

CHAPTER FIVE

ACHILLES STOPPED ME JUST INSIDE THE BRONZE-STUDDED doors of Peleus' audience chamber. "Wait here," he said.

Peleus was seated on a high-backed chair at the room's other end. An older man, one I had seen before with Peleus, stood near as if the two had been in conference. The fire smoked thickly, and the room felt hot and close.

The walls were hung with deep-dyed tapestries and old weapons kept gleaming by servants. Achilles walked past them and knelt at his father's feet. "Father, I come to ask your pardon."

"Oh?" Peleus lifted an eyebrow. "Speak then." From where I stood his face looked cold and displeased. I was suddenly fearful. We had interrupted; Achilles had not even knocked.

"I have taken Patroclus from his drills." My name sounded strange on his lips; I almost did not recognize it.

The old king's brows drew together. "Who?"

"Menoitiades," Achilles said. *Menoitius' son.*

"Ah." Peleus' gaze followed the carpet back to where I stood, trying not to fidget. "Yes, the boy the arms-master wants to whip."

"Yes. But it is not his fault. I forgot to say I wished him for a companion." *Therapon* was the word he used. A brother-in-arms sworn to a prince by blood oaths and love. In war, these men were his honor guard; in peace, his closest advisers. It was a place of highest esteem, another reason the boys swarmed Peleus' son, showing off; they hoped to be chosen.

Peleus' eyes narrowed. "Come here, Patroclus."

The carpet was thick beneath my feet. I knelt a little behind Achilles. I could feel the king's gaze on me.

"For many years now, Achilles, I have urged companions on you and you have turned them away. Why this boy?"

The question might have been my own. I had nothing to offer such a prince. Why, then, had he made a charity case of me? Peleus and I both waited for his answer.

"He is surprising."

I looked up, frowning. If he thought so, he was the only one.

"Surprising," Peleus echoed.

"Yes." Achilles explained no further, though I hoped he would.

Peleus rubbed his nose in thought. "The boy is an exile with a stain upon him. He will add no luster to your reputation."

"I do not need him to," Achilles said. Not proudly or boastfully. Honestly.

Peleus acknowledged this. "Yet other boys will be envious that you have chosen such a one. What will you tell them?"

"I will tell them nothing." The answer came with no hesitation, clear and crisp. "It is not for them to say what I will do."

I found my pulse beating thickly in my veins, fearing Peleus' anger. It did not come. Father and son met each other's gaze, and the faintest touch of amusement bloomed at the corner of Peleus' mouth.

"Stand up, both of you."

I did so, dizzily.

"I pronounce your sentence. Achilles, you will give your apology to Amphidamas, and Patroclus will give his as well."

"Yes, Father."

"That is all." He turned from us, back to his counselor, in dismissal.

OUTSIDE AGAIN ACHILLES was brisk. "I will see you at dinner," he said, and turned to go.

An hour before I would have said I was glad to be rid of him; now, strangely, I felt stung.

"Where are you going?"

He stopped. "Drills."

"Alone?"

"Yes. No one sees me fight." The words came as if he were used to saying them.

"Why?"

He looked at me a long moment, as if weighing something. "My mother has forbidden it. Because of the prophecy."

"What prophecy?" I had not heard of this.

"That I will be the best warrior of my generation."

It sounded like something a young child would claim, in make-believe. But he said it as simply as if he were giving his name.

The question I wanted to ask was, *And are you the best?* Instead I stuttered out, "When was the prophecy given?"

"When I was born. Just before. Eleithyia came and told it to my mother." Eleithyia, goddess of childbirth, rumored to preside in person over the birth of half-gods. Those whose nativities were too important to be left to chance. I had forgotten. *His mother is a goddess.*

"Is this known?" I was tentative, not wanting to press too far.

"Some know of it, and some do not. But that is why I go alone." But he didn't go. He watched me. He seemed to be waiting.

"Then I will see you at dinner," I said at last.

He nodded and left.

HE WAS ALREADY SEATED when I arrived, wedged at my table amid the usual clatter of boys. I had half-expected him not to be; that I had dreamed the morning. As I sat, I met his eyes, quickly, almost guiltily, then looked away. My face was flushing, I was sure. My hands felt heavy and awkward as they reached for the food. I was aware of every swallow, every expression on my face. The meal was very good that night, roasted fish dressed with lemon and herbs, fresh cheese and bread, and he ate well. The boys were unconcerned by my presence. They had long ago ceased to see me.

"Patroclus." Achilles did not slur my name, as people often did, running it together as if in a hurry to be rid of it. Instead, he rang each syllable: *Pa-tro-clus.* Around us dinner was ending, the servants clearing the plates. I looked up, and the boys quieted, watching with interest. He did not usually address us by name.

"Tonight you're to sleep in my room," he said. I was so shocked that my mouth would have hung open. But the boys were there, and I had been raised with a prince's pride.

"All right," I said.

"A servant will bring your things."

I could hear the thoughts of the staring boys as if they said them. *Why him?* Peleus had spoken true: he had often encouraged Achilles to choose his companions. But in all those years, Achilles showed no special interest in any of the boys, though he was polite to all, as befitted his upbringing. And now he had bestowed the long-awaited honor upon the most unlikely of us, small and ungrateful and probably cursed.

He turned to go and I followed him, trying not to stumble, feeling the eyes of the table on my back. He led me past my old room and the chamber of state with its high-backed throne. Another turn, and we were in a portion of the palace I did not know, a wing that slanted down towards water. The walls were painted with bright patterns that bled to gray as his torch passed them.

His room was so close to the sea that the air tasted of salt. There were no wall pictures here, only plain stone and a single soft rug. The furniture was simple but well made, carved from dark-grained wood I recognized as foreign. Off to one side I saw a thick pallet.

He gestured to it. "That is for you."

"Oh." Saying thank you did not seem the right response.

"Are you tired?" he asked.

"No."

He nodded, as if I had said something wise. "Me neither."

I nodded in turn. Each of us, warily polite, bobbing our head like birds. There was a silence.

"Do you want to help me juggle?"

"I don't know how."

"You don't have to know. I'll show you."

I was regretting saying I was not tired. I did not want to make a fool of myself in front of him. But his face was hopeful, and I felt like a miser to refuse.

"All right."

"How many can you hold?"

"I don't know."

"Show me your hand."

I did, palm out. He rested his own palm against it. I tried not to startle. His skin was soft and slightly sticky from dinner. The plump finger pads brushing mine were very warm.

"About the same. It will be better to start with two, then. Take these." He reached for six leather-covered balls, the type that mummers used. Obediently, I claimed two.

"When I say, throw one to me."

Normally I would chafe at being bossed this way. But somehow the words did not sound like commands in his mouth. He began to juggle the remaining balls. "Now," he said. I let the ball fly from my hand towards him, saw it pulled seamlessly into the circling blur.

"Again," he said. I threw another ball, and it joined the others.

"You do that well," he said.

I looked up, quickly. Was he mocking me? But his face was sincere.

"Catch." A ball came back to me, just like the fig at dinner.

My part took no great skill, but I enjoyed it anyway. We found ourselves smiling at the satisfaction of each smooth catch and throw.

After some time he stopped, yawned. "It's late," he said. I was surprised to see the moon high outside the window; I had not noticed the minutes passing.

I sat on the pallet and watched as he busied himself with the tasks of bed, washing his face with water from a wide-mouthed ewer, untying the bit of leather that bound his hair. The silence brought my uneasiness back. *Why was I here?*

Achilles snuffed out the torch. "Good night," he said.

"Good night." The word felt strange in my mouth, like another language.

Time passed. In the moonlight, I could just make out the shape of his face, sculptor-perfect, across the room. His lips were parted slightly, an arm thrown carelessly above his head. He looked different in sleep, beautiful but cold as moonlight. I found myself wishing he would wake so that I might watch the life return.

THE NEXT MORNING, after breakfast, I went back to the boys' room, expecting to find my things returned. They were not, and I saw that my bed had been stripped of its linens. I checked again after lunch, and after spear practice and then again before bed, but my old place remained empty and unmade. *So. Still.* Warily, I made my way to his room, half-expecting a servant to stop me. None did.

In the doorway of his room, I hesitated. He was within, lounging as I had seen him that first day, one leg dangling.

"Hello," he said. If he had shown any hesitation or surprise, I would have left, gone back and slept on the bare reeds rather than stay here. But he did not. There was only his easy tone and a sharp attention in his eyes.

"Hello," I answered, and went to take my place on the cot across the room.

SLOWLY, I GREW USED TO IT; I no longer startled when he spoke, no longer waited for rebuke. I stopped expecting to be sent away. After dinner, my feet took me to his room out of habit, and I thought of the pallet where I lay as mine.

At night I still dreamed of the dead boy. But when I woke, sweaty and terror-stricken, the moon would be bright on the water outside and I could hear the lick of the waves against the shore. In the dim light I saw his easy breathing, the drowsy tangle of his limbs. In spite of myself, my pulse slowed. There was a vividness to him, even at rest, that made death and spirits seem foolish. After a time, I found I could sleep again. Time after that, the dreams lessened and dropped away.

I learned that he was not so dignified as he looked. Beneath his poise and stillness was another face, full of mischief and faceted like a gem, catching the light. He liked to play games against his own skill, catching things with his eyes closed, setting himself impossible leaps over beds and chairs. When he smiled, the skin at the corners of his eyes crinkled like a leaf held to flame.

He was like a flame himself. He glittered, drew eyes. There was a glamour to him, even on waking, with his hair tousled and his face still muddled with sleep. Up close, his feet looked almost unearthly: the perfectly formed pads of the toes, the tendons that flickered like lyre strings. The heels were callused white over pink from going everywhere barefoot. His father made him rub them with oils that smelled of sandalwood and pomegranate.

He began to tell me the stories of his day before we drifted off
to sleep. At first I only listened, but after time my tongue loosened. I began to tell my own stories, first of the palace, and later
small bits from *before:* the skipping stones, the wooden horse I had
played with, the lyre from my mother's dowry.

"I am glad your father sent it with you," he said.

Soon our conversations spilled out of the night's confinement.
I surprised myself with how much there was to say, about everything, the beach and dinner and one boy or another.

I stopped watching for ridicule, the scorpion's tail hidden in
his words. He said what he meant; he was puzzled if you did not.
Some people might have mistaken this for simplicity. But is it not a
sort of genius to cut always to the heart?

ONE AFTERNOON, as I went to leave him to his private drills
he said, "Why don't you come with me?" His voice was a little
strained; if I had not thought it impossible, I might have said he
was nervous. The air, which had grown comfortable between us,
felt suddenly taut.

"All right," I said.

It was the quiet hours of late afternoon; the palace slept out
the heat and left us alone. We took the longest way, through the
olive grove's twisting path, to the house where the arms were kept.

I stood in the doorway as he selected his practice weapons,
a spear and a sword, slightly blunted at the tip. I reached for my
own, then hesitated.

"Should I—?" He shook his head. *No.*

"I do not fight with others," he told me.

I followed him outside to the packed sand circle. "Never?"

"No."

"Then how do you know that . . ." I trailed off as he took up a stance in the center, his spear in his hand, his sword at his waist.

"That the prophecy is true? I guess I don't."

Divine blood flows differently in each god-born child. Orpheus' voice made the trees weep, Heracles could kill a man by clapping him on the back. Achilles' miracle was his speed. His spear, as he began the first pass, moved faster than my eye could follow. It whirled, flashing forward, reversed, then flashed behind. The shaft seemed to flow in his hands, the dark gray point flickered like a snake's tongue. His feet beat the ground like a dancer, never still.

I could not move, watching. I almost did not breathe. His face was calm and blank, not tensed with effort. His movements were so precise I could almost see the men he fought, ten, twenty of them, advancing on all sides. He leapt, scything his spear, even as his other hand snatched the sword from its sheath. He swung out with them both, moving like liquid, like a fish through the waves.

He stopped, suddenly. I could hear his breaths, only a little louder than usual, in the still afternoon air.

"Who trained you?" I asked. I did not know what else to say.

"My father, a little."

A little. I felt almost frightened.

"No one else?"

"No."

I stepped forward. "Fight me."

He made a sound almost like a laugh. "No. Of course not."

"Fight me." I felt in a trance. He had been trained, a little, by his father. The rest was—what? Divine? This was more of the gods than I had ever seen in my life. He made it look beautiful, this sweating, hacking art of ours. I understood why his father did not let him fight in front of the others. How could any ordinary man take pride in his own skill when there was this in the world?

"I don't want to."

"I dare you."

"You don't have any weapons."

"I'll get them."

He knelt and laid his weapons in the dirt. His eyes met mine. "I will not. Do not ask me again."

"I will ask you again. You cannot forbid me." I stepped forward, defiant. Something burned hot in me now, an impatience, a certainty. I would have this thing. He would give it to me.

His face twisted and, almost, I thought I saw anger. This pleased me. I would goad him, if nothing else. He would fight me then. My nerves sang with the danger of it.

But instead he walked away, his weapons abandoned in the dust.

"Come back," I said. Then louder: "Come back. Are you afraid?"

That strange half-laugh again, his back still turned. "No, I am not afraid."

"You should be." I meant it as a joke, an easing, but it did not sound that way in the still air that hung between us. His back stared at me, unmoving, unmovable.

I will make him look at me, I thought. My legs swallowed up the five steps between us, and I crashed into his back.

He stumbled forward, falling, and I clung to him. We landed, and I heard the quick huff of his breath as it was driven from him. But before I could speak, he was twisting around beneath me, had seized my wrists in his hands. I struggled, not sure what I had meant to do. But here was resistance, and that was something I could fight. "Let me go!" I yanked my wrists against his grip.

"No." In a swift motion, he rolled me beneath him, pinning me, his knees in my belly. I panted, angry but strangely satisfied.

"I have never seen anyone fight the way you do," I told him. Confession or accusation, or both.

"You have not seen much."

I bridled, despite the mildness of his tone. "You know what I mean."

His eyes were unreadable. Over us both, the unripe olives rattled gently.

"Maybe. What do you mean?"

I twisted, hard, and he let go. We sat up, our tunics dusty and stuck to our backs.

"I mean—" I broke off. There was an edge to me now, that familiar keenness of anger and envy, struck to life like flint. But the bitter words died even as I thought them.

"There is no one like you," I said, at last.

He regarded me a moment, in silence. "So?"

Something in the way he spoke it drained the last of my anger from me. I had minded, once. But who was I now, to begrudge such a thing?

As if he heard me, he smiled, and his face was like the sun.

CHAPTER SIX

OUR FRIENDSHIP CAME ALL AT ONCE AFTER THAT, LIKE spring floods from the mountains. Before, the boys and I had imagined that his days were filled with princely instruction, statecraft and spear. But I had long since learned the truth: other than his lyre lessons and his drills, he had no instruction. One day we might go swimming, another we might climb trees. We made up games for ourselves, of racing and tumbling. We would lie on the warm sand and say, "Guess what I'm thinking about."

The falcon we had seen from our window.

The boy with the crooked front tooth.

Dinner.

And as we swam, or played, or talked, a feeling would come. It was almost like fear, in the way it filled me, rising in my chest. It was almost like tears, in how swiftly it came. But it was neither of those, buoyant where they were heavy, bright where they were dull. I had known contentment before, brief snatches of time in which I pursued solitary pleasure: skipping stones or dicing or dreaming. But in truth, it had been less a presence than an absence, a laying aside of dread: my father was not near, nor boys. I was not hungry, or tired, or sick.

This feeling was different. I found myself grinning until my cheeks hurt, my scalp prickling till I thought it might lift off my head. My tongue ran away from me, giddy with freedom. This and this and this, I said to him. I did not have to fear that I spoke too much. I did not have to worry that I was too slender or too slow. This and this and this! I taught him how to skip stones, and he taught me how to carve wood. I could feel every nerve in my body, every brush of air against my skin.

He played my mother's lyre, and I watched. When it was my turn to play, my fingers tangled in the strings and the teacher despaired of me. I did not care. "Play again," I told him. And he played until I could barely see his fingers in the dark.

I saw then how I had changed. I did not mind anymore that I lost when we raced and I lost when we swam out to the rocks and I lost when we tossed spears or skipped stones. For who can be ashamed to lose to such beauty? It was enough to watch him win, to see the soles of his feet flashing as they kicked up sand, or the rise and fall of his shoulders as he pulled through the salt. It was enough.

IT WAS LATE SUMMER, over a year after my exile had begun, when at last I told him of how I had killed the boy. We were in the branches of the courtyard oak, hidden by the patchwork leaves. It was easier here somehow, off the ground, with the solid trunk at my back. He listened silently, and when I had finished, he asked:

"Why did you not say that you were defending yourself?"

It was like him to ask this, the thing I had not thought of before.

"I don't know."

"Or you could have lied. Said you found him already dead."

I stared at him, stunned by the simplicity of it. I could have lied. And then the revelation that followed: *if I had lied, I would still be a prince.* It was not murder that had exiled me, it was my lack of cunning. I understood, now, the disgust in my father's eyes. His moron son, confessing all. I recalled how his jaw had hardened as I spoke. *He does not deserve to be a king.*

"You would not have lied," I said.

"No," he admitted.

"What would you have done?" I asked.

Achilles tapped a finger against the branch he sat on. "I don't know. I can't imagine it. The way the boy spoke to you." He shrugged. "No one has ever tried to take something from me."

"Never?" I could not believe it. A life without such things seemed impossible.

"Never." He was silent a moment, thinking. "I don't know," he repeated, finally. "I think I would be angry." He closed his eyes and rested his head back against a branch. The green oak leaves crowded around his hair, like a crown.

I SAW KING PELEUS often now; we were called to councils sometimes, and dinners with visiting kings. I was allowed to sit at the table beside Achilles, even to speak if I wished. I did not wish; I was happy to be silent and watch the men around me. *Skops,* Peleus took to calling me. Owl, for my big eyes. He was good at this sort of affection, general and unbinding.

After the men were gone, we would sit with him by the fire to hear the stories of his youth. The old man, now gray and faded, told us that he had once fought beside Heracles. When I said that I had seen Philoctetes, he smiled.

"Yes, the bearer of Heracles' great bow. Back then he was a spearman, and much the bravest of us." This was like him too, these sorts of compliments. I understood, now, how his treasury had come to be so full of the gifts of treaty and alliance. Among our bragging, ranting heroes, Peleus was the exception: a man of modesty. We stayed to listen as the servants added one log, and then another, to the flames. It was halfway to dawn before he would send us back to our beds.

THE ONLY PLACE I did not follow was to see his mother. He went late at night, or at dawn before the palace was awake, and returned flushed and smelling of the sea. When I asked about it, he told me freely, his voice strangely toneless.

"It is always the same. She wants to know what I am doing and if I am well. She speaks to me of my reputation among men. At the end she asks if I will come with her."

I was rapt. "Where?"

"The caves under the sea." Where the sea-nymphs lived, so deep the sun did not penetrate.

"Will you go?"

He shook his head. "My father says I should not. He says no mortal who sees them comes back the same."

When he turned away, I made the peasant sign against evil. *Gods avert.* It frightened me a little to hear him speak of a thing so calmly. Gods and mortals never mixed happily in our stories.

But she was his mother, I reassured myself, and he was half-god himself.

In time his visits with her were just another strangeness about him that I became accustomed to, like the marvel of his feet or the inhuman deftness of his fingers. When I heard him climbing back through the window at dawn, I would mumble from my bed, "Is she well?"

And he would answer. "Yes, she is well." And he might add: "The fish are thick today" or "The bay is warm as a bath." And then we would sleep again.

ONE MORNING of my second spring, he came back from his visit with his mother later than usual; the sun was almost out of the water and the goatbells were clanging in the hills.

"Is she well?"

"She is well. She wants to meet you."

I felt a surge of fear, but stifled it. "Do you think I should?" I could not imagine what she would want with me. I knew her reputation for hating mortals.

He did not meet my eyes; his fingers turned a stone he had found over and over. "There is no harm in it. Tomorrow night, she said." I understood now that it was a command. The gods did not make requests. I knew him well enough to see that he was embarrassed. He was never so stiff with me.

"Tomorrow?"

He nodded.

I did not want him to see my fear, though normally we kept nothing from each other. "Should I—should I bring a gift? Honeyed wine?" We poured it over the altars of the gods on festival days. It was one of our richest offerings.

He shook his head. "She doesn't like it."

The next night, when the household slept, I climbed out of our window. The moon was half full, bright enough for me to pick my way over the rocks without a torch. He had said that I was to stand in the surf and she would come. No, he had reassured me, you do not need to speak. She will know.

The waves were warm, and thick with sand. I shifted, watched the small white crabs run through the surf. I was listening, thinking I might hear the splash of her feet as she approached. A breeze blew down the beach and, grateful, I closed my eyes to it. When I opened them again, she was standing before me.

She was taller than I was, taller than any woman I had ever seen. Her black hair was loose down her back, and her skin shone luminous and impossibly pale, as if it drank light from the moon. She was so close I could smell her, seawater laced with dark brown honey. I did not breathe. I did not dare.

"You are Patroclus." I flinched at the sound of her voice, hoarse and rasping. I had expected chimes, not the grinding of rocks in the surf.

"Yes, lady."

Distaste ran over her face. Her eyes were not like a human's; they were black to their center and flecked with gold. I could not bring myself to meet them.

"He will be a god," she said. I did not know what to say, so I said nothing. She leaned forward, and I half-thought she might touch me. But of course she did not.

"Do you understand?" I could feel her breath on my cheek,

not warm at all, but chilled like the depths of the sea. *Do you understand?* He had told me that she hated to be kept waiting.

"Yes."

She leaned closer still, looming over me. Her mouth was a gash of red, like the torn-open stomach of a sacrifice, bloody and oracular. Behind it her teeth shone sharp and white as bone.

"Good." Carelessly, as if to herself, she added, "You will be dead soon enough."

She turned and dove into the sea, leaving no ripples behind her.

I DID NOT GO straight back to the palace. I could not. I went to the olive grove instead, to sit among the twisting trunks and fallen fruits. It was far from the sea. I did not wish to smell the salt now.

You will be dead soon enough. She had said it coldly, as a fact. She did not wish me for his companion, but I was not worth killing. To a goddess, the few decades of human life were barely even an inconvenience.

And she wished him to be a god. She had spoken it so simply, as if it were obvious. A god. I could not imagine him so. Gods were cold and distant, far off as the moon, nothing like his bright eyes, the warm mischief of his smiles.

Her desire was ambitious. It was a difficult thing, to make even a half-god immortal. True, it had happened before, to Heracles and Orpheus and Orion. They sat in the sky now, presiding as constellations, feasting with the gods on ambrosia. But these men had been the sons of Zeus, their sinews strong with the purest ichor that flowed. Thetis was a lesser of the lesser gods, a sea-nymph only. In our stories these divinities had to work by wheedling and flattery, by favors won from stronger gods. They could not do much themselves. Except live, forever.

"WHAT ARE YOU thinking about?" It was Achilles, come to find me. His voice was loud in the quiet grove, but I did not startle. I had half-expected him to come. I had wanted him to.

"Nothing," I said. It was untrue. I guess it always is.

He sat down beside me, his feet bare and dusty.

"Did she tell you that you would die soon?"

I turned to look at him, startled.

"Yes," I said.

"I'm sorry," he said.

The wind blew the gray leaves above us, and somewhere I heard the soft *pat* of an olive fall.

"She wants you to be a god," I told him.

"I know." His face twisted with embarrassment, and in spite of itself my heart lightened. It was such a boyish response. And so human. Parents, everywhere.

But the question still waited to be asked; I could do nothing until I knew the answer.

"Do you want to be—" I paused, struggling, though I had promised myself I wouldn't. I had sat in the grove, practicing this very question, as I waited for him to find me. "Do you want to be a god?"

His eyes were dark in the half-light. I could not make out the gold flecks in the green. "I don't know," he said at last. "I don't know what it means, or how it happens." He looked down at his hands, clasping his knees. "I don't want to leave here. When would it happen anyway? Soon?"

I was at a loss. I knew nothing of how gods were made. I was mortal, only.

He was frowning now, his voice louder. "And is there really a place like that? Olympus? She doesn't even know how she will do it. She pretends she knows. She thinks if I become famous enough . . ." He trailed off.

This at least I could follow. "Then the gods will take you voluntarily."

He nodded. But he had not answered my question.

"Achilles."

He turned to me, his eyes still filled with frustration, with a sort of angry bewilderment. He was barely twelve.

"Do you want to be a god?" It was easier this time.

"Not yet," he said.

A tightness I had not known was there eased a little. I would not lose him yet.

He cupped a hand against his chin; his features looked finer than usual, like carved marble. "I'd like to be a hero, though. I think I could do it. If the prophecy is true. If there's a war. My mother says I am better even than Heracles was."

I did not know what to say to this. I did not know if it was motherly bias or fact. I did not care. *Not yet.*

He was silent a moment. Then turned to me, suddenly. "Would you want to be a god?"

There, among the moss and olives, it struck me as funny. I laughed and, a moment later, he did too.

"I do not think that is likely," I told him.

I stood, put down a hand for him. He took it, pulled himself up. Our tunics were dusty, and my feet tingled slightly with drying sea salt.

"There were figs in the kitchen. I saw them," he said.

We were only twelve, too young to brood.

"I bet I can eat more than you."

"Race you!"

I laughed. We ran.

CHAPTER SEVEN

THE NEXT SUMMER WE TURNED THIRTEEN, HIM FIRST, and then me. Our bodies began to stretch, pulling at our joints till they were aching and weak. In Peleus' shining bronze mirror, I almost did not recognize myself—lanky and gaunt, stork legs and sharpening chin. Achilles was taller still, seeming to tower above me. Eventually we would be of a height, but he came to his maturity sooner, with a startling speed, primed perhaps by the divinity in his blood.

The boys, too, were growing older. Regularly now we heard moans behind closed doors and saw shadows returning to their beds before dawn. In our countries, a man often took a wife before his beard was fully fledged. How much earlier, then, did he take a serving girl? It was expected; very few men came to their marriage beds without having done so. Those who did were unlucky indeed: too weak to compel, too ugly to charm, and too poor to pay.

It was customary for a palace to have a full complement of nobly born women as servants for the mistress of the house. But Peleus had no wife in the palace, and so the women we saw were mostly slaves. They had been bought or taken in warfare, or bred from those who were. During the day they poured wine and scrubbed floors and kept the kitchen. At night they belonged to soldiers or foster boys, to visiting kings or Peleus himself. The swollen bellies that followed were not a thing of shame; they were profit: more slaves. These unions were not always rape; sometimes there was mutual satisfaction and even affection. At least that is what the men who spoke of them believed.

It would have been easy, infinitely easy, for Achilles or me to have bedded one of these girls ourselves. At thirteen we were almost late to do so, especially him, as princes were known for their appetites. Instead, we watched in silence as the foster boys pulled girls onto their laps, or Peleus summoned the prettiest to his room after dinner. Once, I even heard the king offer her to his son. He answered, almost diffidently: *I am tired tonight.* Later, as we walked back to our room, he avoided my eyes.

And I? I was shy and silent with all but Achilles; I could scarcely speak to the other boys, let alone a girl. As a comrade of the prince, I suppose I would not have had to speak; a gesture or a look would have been enough. But such a thing did not occur to me. The feelings that stirred in me at night seemed strangely distant from those serving girls with their lowered eyes and obedience. I watched a boy fumbling at a girl's dress, the dull look on her face as she poured his wine. I did not wish for such a thing.

ONE NIGHT WE had stayed late in Peleus' chamber. Achilles was on the floor, an arm thrown beneath his head for a pillow. I sat more formally, in a chair. It was not just because of Peleus. I did not like the sprawling length of my new limbs.

The old king's eyes were half-closed. He was telling us a story.

"Meleager was the finest warrior of his day, but also the proudest. He expected the best of everything, and because the people loved him, he received it."

My eyes drifted to Achilles. His fingers were stirring, just barely, in the air. He often did this when he was composing a new song. The story of Meleager, I guessed, as his father told it.

"But one day the king of Calydon said, 'Why must we give so much to Meleager? There are other worthy men in Calydon.'"

Achilles shifted, and his tunic pulled tight across his chest. That day, I had overheard a serving girl whispering to her friend: "Do you think the prince looked at me, at dinner?" Her tone was one of hope.

"Meleager heard the words of the king and was enraged."

This morning he had leapt onto my bed and pressed his nose against mine. "Good morning," he'd said. I remembered the heat of him against my skin.

"He said, 'I will not fight for you any longer.' And he went back to his house and sought comfort in the arms of his wife."

I felt a tug on my foot. It was Achilles, grinning at me from the floor.

"Calydon had fierce enemies, and when they heard that Meleager would no longer fight for Calydon—"

I pushed my foot towards him a little, provokingly. His fingers wrapped around my ankle.

"They attacked. And the city of Calydon suffered terrible losses."

Achilles yanked, and I slid half out of the chair. I clung to the wooden frame so I would not be pulled onto the floor.

"So the people went to Meleager, to beg him for his help. And— Achilles, are you listening?"

"Yes, Father."

"You are not. You are tormenting our poor Skops."

I tried to look tormented. But all I felt was the coolness against my ankle, where his fingers had been, a moment before.

"It is just as well, perhaps. I am getting tired. We will finish the story another evening."

We stood and wished the old man good night. But as we turned, he said, "Achilles, you might look for the light-haired girl, from the kitchen. She has been haunting doorways for you, I hear."

It was hard to know if it was the firelight that made his face look so changed.

"Perhaps, Father. I am tired tonight."

Peleus chuckled, as if this were a joke. "I'm sure she could wake you up." He waved us off.

I had to trot, a little, to keep up with him as we walked back to our rooms. We washed our faces in silence, but there was an ache in me, like a rotten tooth. I could not let it be.

"That girl—do you like her?"

Achilles turned to face me from across the room. "Why? Do you?"

"No, no." I flushed. "That is not what I meant." I had not felt so uncertain with him since the earliest days. "I mean, do you want—"

He ran at me, pushed me backwards onto my cot. Leaned over me. "I'm sick of talking about her," he said.

The heat rose up my neck, wrapped fingers over my face. His hair fell around me, and I could smell nothing but him. The grain of his lips seemed to rest a hairsbreadth from mine.

Then, just like that morning, he was gone. Up across the room, and pouring a last cup of water. His face was still, and calm.

"Good night," he said.

AT NIGHT, IN BED, images come. They begin as dreams, trailing caresses in my sleep from which I start, trembling. I lie awake, and still they come, the flicker of firelight on a neck, the curve of a hipbone, drawing downwards. Hands, smooth and strong, reaching to touch me. I know those hands. But even here, behind the darkness of my eyelids, I cannot name the thing I hope for. During the days I grow restless, fidgety. But all my pacing, singing, running does not keep them at bay. They come, and will not be stopped.

IT IS SUMMER, one of the first fine days. We are on the beach after lunch, our backs to a sloping piece of driftwood. The sun is high, and the air warm around us. Beside me, Achilles shifts, and his foot falls open against mine. It is cool, and chafed pink from the sand, soft from a winter indoors. He hums something, a piece of a song he had played earlier.

I turn to look at him. His face is smooth, without the blotches and spots that have begun to afflict the other boys. His features are drawn with a firm hand; nothing awry or sloppy, nothing too large—all precise, cut with the sharpest of knives. And yet the effect itself is not sharp.

He turns and finds me looking at him. "What?" he says.

"Nothing."

I can smell him. The oils that he uses on his feet, pomegranate and sandalwood; the salt of clean sweat; the hyacinths we had walked through, their scent crushed against our ankles. Beneath it all is his own smell, the one I go to sleep with, the one I wake up to. I cannot describe it. It is sweet, but not just. It is strong but not too strong. Something like almond, but that still is not right. Sometimes, after we have wrestled, my own skin smells like it.

He puts a hand down, to lean against. The muscles in his arms curve softly, appearing and disappearing as he moves. His eyes are deep green on mine.

My pulse jumps, for no reason I can name. He has looked at me a thousand thousand times, but there is something different in this gaze, an intensity I do not know. My mouth is dry, and I can hear the sound of my throat as I swallow.

He watches me. It seems that he is waiting.

I shift, an infinitesimal movement, towards him. It is like the leap from a waterfall. I do not know, until then, what I am going to do. I lean forward and our lips land clumsily on each other. They are like the fat bodies of bees, soft and round and giddy with pollen. I can taste his mouth—hot and sweet with honey from dessert. My stomach trembles, and a warm drop of pleasure spreads beneath my skin. *More.*

The strength of my desire, the speed with which it flowers, shocks me; I flinch and startle back from him. I have a moment, only a moment, to see his face framed in the afternoon light, his lips slightly parted, still half-forming a kiss. His eyes are wide with surprise.

I am horrified. What have I done? But I do not have time to apologize. He stands and steps backwards. His face has closed over, impenetrable and distant, freezing the explanations in my mouth. He turns and races, the fastest boy in the world, up the beach and away.

My side is cold with his absence. My skin feels tight, and my face, I know, is red and raw as a burn.

Dear gods, I think, *let him not hate me.*

I should have known better than to call upon the gods.

WHEN I TURNED THE CORNER onto the garden path, she was there, sharp and knife-bright. A blue dress clung to her skin as if damp. Her dark eyes held mine, and her fingers, chill and unearthly pale, reached for me. My feet knocked against each other as she lifted me from the earth.

"I have seen," she hissed. The sound of waves breaking on stone.

I could not speak. She held me by the throat.

"He is leaving." Her eyes were black now, dark as sea-wet rocks, and as jagged. "I should have sent him long ago. Do not try to follow."

I could not breathe now. But I did not struggle. That much, at least, I knew. She seemed to pause, and I thought she might speak again. She did not. Only opened her hand and released me, boneless, to the ground.

A mother's wishes. In our countries, they were not worth much. But she was a goddess, first and always.

When I returned to the room, it was already dark. I found Achilles sitting on his bed, staring at his feet. His head lifted, almost hopefully, as I came to the doorway. I did not speak; his mother's black eyes still burned in front of me, and the sight of his heels, flashing up the beach. *Forgive me, it was a mistake.* This is what I might have dared to say then, if it had not been for her.

I came into the room, sat on my own bed. He shifted, his eyes flicking to mine. He did not resemble her the way that children normally look like a parent, a tilt of chin, the shape of an eye. It was something in his movements, in his luminous skin. Son of a goddess. What had I thought would happen?

Even from where I sat I could smell the sea on him.

"I'm supposed to leave tomorrow," he said. It was almost an accusation.

"Oh," I said. My mouth felt swollen and numb, too thick to form words.

"I'm going to be taught by Chiron." He paused, then added. "He taught Heracles. And Perseus."

Not yet, he had said to me. But his mother had chosen differently.

He stood and pulled off his tunic. It was hot, full summer, and we were accustomed to sleeping naked. The moon shone on his belly, smooth, muscled, downed with light brown hairs that darkened as they ran below his waist. I averted my eyes.

The next morning, at dawn, he rose and dressed. I was awake; I had not slept. I watched him through the fringes of my eyelids, feigning sleep. From time to time he glanced at me; in the dim half-light his skin glowed gray and smooth as marble. He slung his bag over his shoulder and paused, a last time, at the door. I remember him there, outlined in the stone frame, his hair falling loose, still untidy from sleep. I closed my eyes, and a moment passed. When I opened them again, I was alone.

CHAPTER EIGHT

BY BREAKFAST, EVERYONE KNEW HE WAS GONE. THEIR glances and whispers followed me to the table, lingered as I reached for food. I chewed and swallowed, though the bread sat like a stone in my stomach. I yearned to be away from the palace; I wanted the air.

I walked to the olive grove, the earth dry beneath my feet. I half-wondered if I was expected to join the boys, now that he was gone. I half-wondered if anyone would notice whether I did. I half-hoped they would. *Whip me*, I thought.

I could smell the sea. It was everywhere, in my hair, in my clothes, in the sticky damp of my skin. Even here in the grove, amidst the must of leaves and earth, the unwholesome salty decay still found me. My stomach heaved a moment, and I leaned against the scabbed trunk of a tree. The rough bark pricked my forehead, steadying me. *I must get away from this smell*, I thought.

I walked north, to the palace road, a dusty strip worn smooth by wagon wheels and horses' hooves. A little beyond the palace yard it divided. One half ran south and west, through grass and rocks and low hills; that was the way I had come, three years ago. The other half twisted northwards, towards Mount Othrys and then beyond, to Mount Pelion. I traced it with my eyes. It skirted the wooded foothills for some time before disappearing within them.

The sun bore down on me, hot and hard in the summer sky, as if it would drive me back to the palace. Yet I lingered. I had heard they were beautiful, our mountains—pears and cypress and streams of just-melted ice. It would be cool there and shaded. Far away from the diamond-bright beaches, and the flashing of the sea.

I could leave. The thought was sudden, arresting. I had come to the road meaning only to escape the sea. But the path lay before me, and the mountains. *And Achilles.* My chest rose and fell rapidly, as if trying to keep pace with my thoughts. I had nothing that belonged to me, not a tunic, not a sandal; they were Peleus' all. *I do not need to pack, even.*

Only my mother's lyre, kept in the wooden chest within the inner room, stayed me. I hesitated a moment, thinking I might try to go back, to take it with me. But it was already midday. I had only the afternoon to travel, before they would discover my absence—so I flattered myself—and send after me. I glanced back at the palace and saw no one. The guards were elsewhere. *Now. It must be now.*

I ran. Away from the palace, down the path towards the woods, feet stinging as they slapped the heat-baked ground. As I ran, I promised myself that if I ever saw him again, I would keep my thoughts behind my eyes. I had learned, now, what it would cost me if I did not. The ache in my legs, the knifing heaves of my chest felt clean and good. I ran.

Sweat slicked my skin, fell upon the earth beneath my feet. I grew dirty, then dirtier. Dust and broken bits of leaves clung to my legs. The world around me narrowed to the pounding of my feet and the next dusty yard of road.

Finally, after an hour? Two? I could go no farther. I bent over in pain, the bright afternoon sun wavering to black, the rush of blood deafening in my ears. The path was heavily wooded now, on both sides, and Peleus' palace was a long way behind me. To my right loomed Othrys, with Pelion just beyond it. I stared at its peak and tried to guess how much farther. Ten thousand paces? Fifteen? I began to walk.

Hours passed. My muscles grew wobbly and weak, my feet jumbled together. The sun was well across the zenith now, hanging low in the western sky. I had four, perhaps five, hours until dark, and the peak was as far as ever. Suddenly, I understood: I would not reach Pelion by nightfall. I had no food, nor water, nor hope of shelter. I had nothing but the sandals on my feet and the soaked tunic on my back.

I would not catch up to Achilles, I was sure of that now. He had left the road and his horse long ago, was now moving up the slopes on foot. A good tracker would have observed the woods beside the road, could have seen where the bracken was bent or torn, where a boy had made a path. But I was not a good tracker, and the scrub by the road looked all the same to me. My ears buzzed dully— with cicadas, with the shrill calls of birds, with the rasp of my own breath. There was an ache in my stomach, like hunger or despair.

And then there was something else. The barest sound, just at the limit of hearing. But I caught it, and my skin, even in the heat, went cold. I knew that sound. It was the sound of stealth, of a man attempting silence. It had been just the smallest misstep, the giving way of a single leaf, but it had been enough.

I strained to listen, fear jumping in my throat. Where had it come from? My eyes tracked the woods on either side. I dared not move; any sound would echo loudly up the slopes. I had not thought of dangers as I ran, but now my mind tumbled with them: soldiers, sent by Peleus or Thetis herself, white hands cold as sand on my throat. Or bandits. I knew that they waited by roads, and I remembered stories of boys taken and kept until they died of misuse. My fingers pinched themselves white as I tried to still all breath, all movement, to give nothing away. My gaze caught on a thick clutch of blooming yarrow that could hide me. *Now. Go.*

There was movement from the woods at my side, and I jerked my head towards it. Too late. Something—someone—struck me from behind, throwing me forward. I landed heavily, facedown on the ground, with the person already on top of me. I closed my eyes and waited for a knife.

There was nothing. Nothing but silence and the knees that pinned my back. A moment passed, and it came to me that the knees were not so very heavy and were placed so that their pressure did not hurt.

"Patroclus." *Pa-tro-clus.*

I did not move.

The knees lifted, and hands reached down to turn me, gently, over. Achilles was looking down at me.

"I hoped that you would come," he said. My stomach rolled, awash with nerves and relief at once. I drank him in, the bright hair, the soft curve of his lips upwards. My joy was so sharp I did not dare to breathe. I do not know what I might have said then. I'm sorry, perhaps. Or perhaps something more. I opened my mouth.

"Is the boy hurt?"

A deep voice spoke from behind us both. Achilles' head turned. From where I was, beneath him, I could see only the legs of the man's horse—chestnut, fetlocks dulled with dust.

The voice again, measured and deliberate. "I am assuming, Achilles Pelides, that this is why you have not yet joined me on the mountain?"

My mind groped towards understanding. Achilles had not gone to Chiron. He had waited, here. For me.

"Greetings, Master Chiron, and my apologies. Yes, it is why I have not come." He was using his prince's voice.

"I see."

I wished that Achilles would get up. I felt foolish here, on the ground beneath him. And I was also afraid. The man's voice showed no anger, but it showed no kindness, either. It was clear and grave and dispassionate.

"Stand up," it said.

Slowly, Achilles rose.

I would have screamed then, if my throat had not closed over with fear. Instead I made a noise like a half-strangled yelp and scrambled backwards.

The horse's muscular legs ended in flesh, the equally muscular torso of a man. I stared—at that impossible suture of horse and human, where smooth skin became a gleaming brown coat.

Beside me Achilles bowed his head. "Master Centaur," he said. "I am sorry for the delay. I had to wait for my companion." He knelt, his clean tunic in the dusty earth. "Please accept my apologies. I have long wished to be your student."

The man's—centaur's—face was serious as his voice. He was older, I saw, with a neatly trimmed black beard.

He regarded Achilles a moment. "You do not need to kneel to me, Pelides. Though I appreciate the courtesy. And who is this companion that has kept us both waiting?"

Achilles turned back to me and reached a hand down. Unsteadily, I took it and pulled myself up.

"This is Patroclus."

There was a silence, and I knew it was my turn to speak.

"My lord," I said. And bowed.

"I am not a lord, Patroclus Menoitiades."

My head jerked up at the sound of my father's name.

"I am a centaur, and a teacher of men. My name is Chiron."

I gulped and nodded. I did not dare to ask how he knew my name.

His eyes surveyed me. "You are overtired, I think. You need water and food, both. It is a long way to my home on Pelion, too long for you to walk. So we must make other arrangements."

He turned then, and I tried not to gawk at the way his horse legs moved beneath him.

"You will ride on my back," the centaur said. "I do not usually offer such things on first acquaintance. But exceptions must be made." He paused. "You have been taught to ride, I suppose?"

We nodded, quickly.

"That is unfortunate. Forget what you learned. I do not like to be squeezed by legs or tugged at. The one in front will hold on to my waist, the one behind will hold on to him. If you feel that you are going to fall, speak up."

Achilles and I exchanged a look, quickly.

He stepped forward.

"How should I—?"

"I will kneel." His horse legs folded themselves into the dust. His back was broad and lightly sheened with sweat. "Take my arm for balance," the centaur instructed. Achilles did, swinging his leg over and settling himself.

It was my turn. At least I would not be in front, so close to that place where skin gave way to chestnut coat. Chiron offered me his arm, and I took it. It was muscled and large, thickly covered with black hair that was nothing like the color of his horse half. I seated myself, my legs stretched across that wide back, almost to discomfort.

Chiron said, "I will stand now." The motion was smooth, but still I grabbed for Achilles. Chiron was half as high again as a normal horse, and my feet dangled so far above the ground it made me dizzy. Achilles' hands rested loosely on Chiron's trunk. "You will fall, if you hold so lightly," the centaur said.

My fingers grew damp with sweat from clutching Achilles' chest. I dared not relax them, even for a moment. The centaur's gait was less symmetrical than a horse's, and the ground was uneven. I slipped alarmingly upon the sweat-slick horsehair.

There was no path I could see, but we were rising swiftly upwards through the trees, carried along by Chiron's sure, unslowing steps. I winced every time a jounce caused my heels to kick into the centaur's sides.

As we went, Chiron pointed things out to us, in that same steady voice.

There is Mount Othrys.

The cypress trees are thicker here, on the north side, you can see.

This stream feeds the Apidanos River that runs through Phthia's lands.

Achilles twisted back to look at me, grinning.

We climbed higher still, and the centaur swished his great black tail, swatting flies for all of us.

CHIRON STOPPED SUDDENLY, and I jerked forward into Achilles' back. We were in a small break in the woods, a grove of sorts, half encircled by a rocky outcrop. We were not quite at the peak, but we were close, and the sky was blue and glowing above us.

"We are here." Chiron knelt, and we stepped off his back, a bit unsteadily.

In front of us was a cave. But to call it that is to demean it, for it was not made of dark stone, but pale rose quartz.

"Come," the centaur said. We followed him through the entrance, high enough so that he did not need to stoop. We blinked, for it was shadowy inside, though lighter than it should have been, because of the crystal walls. At one end was a small spring that seemed to drain away inside the rock.

On the walls hung things I did not recognize: strange bronze implements. Above us on the cave's ceiling, lines and specks of dye shaped the constellations and the movements of the heavens. On carved shelves were dozens of small ceramic jars covered with slanted markings. Instruments hung in one corner, lyres and flutes, and next to them tools and cooking pots.

There was a single human-sized bed, thick and padded with

animal skins, made up for Achilles. I did not see where the centaur slept. Perhaps he did not.

"Sit now," he said. It was pleasantly cool inside, perfect after the sun, and I sank gratefully onto one of the cushions Chiron indicated. He went to the spring and filled cups, which he brought to us. The water was sweet and fresh. I drank as Chiron stood over me. "You will be sore and tired tomorrow," he told me. "But it will be better if you eat."

He ladled out stew, thick with chunks of vegetables and meat, from a pot simmering over a small fire at the back of the cave. There were fruits, too, round red berries that he kept in a hollowed outcropping of rock. I ate quickly, surprised at how hungry I was. My eyes kept returning to Achilles, and I tingled with the giddy buoyancy of relief. *I have escaped.*

With my new boldness, I pointed to some of the bronze tools on the wall. "What are those?"

Chiron sat across from us, his horse-legs folded beneath him. "They are for surgery," he told me.

"Surgery?" It was not a word I knew.

"Healing. I forget the barbarities of the low countries." His voice was neutral and calm, factual. "Sometimes a limb must go. Those are for cutting, those for suturing. Often by removing some, we may save the rest." He watched me staring at them, taking in the sharp, saw-toothed edges. "Do you wish to learn medicine?"

I flushed. "I don't know anything about it."

"You answer a different question than the one I asked."

"I'm sorry, Master Chiron." I did not want to anger him. *He will send me back.*

"There is no need to be sorry. Simply answer."

I stammered a little. "Yes. I would like to learn. It seems useful, does it not?"

"It is very useful," Chiron agreed. He turned to Achilles, who had been following the conversation.

"And you, Pelides? Do you also think medicine is useful?"

"Of course," Achilles said. "Please do not call me Pelides. Here I am—I am just Achilles."

Something passed through Chiron's dark eyes. A flicker that was almost amusement.

"Very well. Do you see anything you wish to know of?"

"Those." Achilles was pointing to the musical instruments, the lyres and flutes and seven-stringed kithara. "Do you play?"

Chiron's gaze was steady. "I do."

"So do I," said Achilles. "I have heard that you taught Heracles and Jason, thick-fingered though they were. Is it true?"

"It is."

I felt a momentary unreality: he knew Heracles and Jason. Had known them as children.

"I would like you to teach me."

Chiron's stern face softened. "That is why you have been sent here. So that I may teach you what I know."

IN THE LATE AFTERNOON LIGHT, Chiron guided us through the ridges near the cave. He showed us where the mountain lions had their dens, and where the river was, slow and sun-warm, for us to swim.

"You may bathe, if you like." He was looking at me. I had forgotten how grimy I was, sweat-stained and dusty from the road. I ran a hand through my hair and felt the grit.

"I will too," Achilles said. He pulled off his tunic and, a moment after, I followed. The water was cool in the depths, but not unpleasantly so. From the bank Chiron taught still: "Those are loaches, do you see? And perch. That is a vimba, you will not find it farther south. You may know it by the upturned mouth and silver belly."

His words mingled with the sound of the river over its rocks, soothing any strangeness there might have been between Achilles and me. There was something in Chiron's face, firm and calm and imbued with authority, that made us children again, with no world beyond this moment's play and this night's dinner. With him near us, it was hard to remember what might have happened on the day by the beach. Even our bodies felt smaller beside the centaur's bulk. How had we thought we were grown?

We emerged from the water sweet and clean, shaking our hair in the last of the sun. I knelt by the bank and used stones to scrub the dirt and sweat from my tunic. I would have to be naked until it dried, but so far did Chiron's influence stretch that I thought nothing of it.

We followed Chiron back to the cave, our wrung-dry tunics draped over our shoulders. He stopped occasionally, to point out the trails of hare and corncrakes and deer. He told us we would hunt for them, in days to come, and learn to track. We listened, questioning him eagerly. At Peleus' palace there had been only the dour lyre-master for a teacher, or Peleus himself, half-drowsing as he spoke. We knew nothing of forestry or the other skills Chiron had spoken of. My mind went back to the implements on the cave's wall, the herbs and tools of healing. *Surgery* was the word he had used.

It was almost full dark when we reached the cave again. Chiron gave us easy tasks, gathering wood and kindling the fire in the clearing at the cave's mouth. After it caught, we lingered by the flames, grateful for their steady warmth in the cooling air. Our bodies were pleasantly tired, heavy from our exertions, and our legs and feet tangled comfortably as we sat. We talked about where we'd go tomorrow, but lazily, our words fat and slow with contentment. Dinner was more stew, and a thin type of bread that Chiron cooked on bronze sheets over the fire. For dessert, berries with mountain-gathered honey.

As the fire dwindled, my eyes closed in half-dreaming. I was warm, and the ground beneath me was soft with moss and fallen leaves. I could not believe that only this morning I had woken in Peleus' palace. This small clearing, the gleaming walls of the cave within, were more vivid than the pale white palace had ever been.

Chiron's voice, when it came, startled me. "I will tell you that your mother has sent a message, Achilles."

I felt the muscles of Achilles' arm tense against me. I felt my own throat tighten.

"Oh? What did she say?" His words were careful, neutral.

"She said that should the exiled son of Menoitius follow you, I was to bar him from your presence."

I sat up, all drowsiness gone.

Achilles' voice swung carelessly in the dark. "Did she say why?"

"She did not."

I closed my eyes. At least I would not be humiliated before Chiron, the tale of the day at the beach told. But it was bare comfort.

Chiron continued, "I assume you knew of her feelings on the matter. I do not like to be deceived."

My face flushed, and I was glad of the darkness. The centaur's voice sounded harder than it had before.

I cleared my throat, rusty and suddenly dry. "I'm sorry," I heard myself say. "It is not Achilles' fault. I came on my own. He did not know that I would. I did not think—" I stopped myself. "I hoped she would not notice."

"That was foolish of you." Chiron's face was deep in shadow.

"Chiron—" Achilles began, bravely.

The centaur held up a hand. "As it happens, the message came this morning, before either of you arrived. So despite your foolishness, I was not deceived."

"You knew?" This was Achilles. I would never have spoken so boldly. "Then you have decided? You will disregard her message?"

Chiron's voice held a warning of displeasure. "She is a goddess, Achilles, and your mother besides. Do you think so little of her wishes?"

"I honor her, Chiron. But she is wrong in this." His hands were balled so tightly I could see the tendons, even in the low light.

"And why is she wrong, Pelides?"

I watched him through the darkness, my stomach clenching. I did not know what he might say.

"She feels that—" He faltered a moment, and I almost did not breathe. "That he is a mortal and not a fit companion."

"Do you think he is?" Chiron asked. His voice gave no hint of the answer.

"Yes."

My cheeks warmed. Achilles, his jaw jutting, had thrown the word back with no hesitation.

"I see." The centaur turned to me. "And you, Patroclus? You are worthy?"

I swallowed. "I do not know if I am worthy. But I wish to stay." I paused, swallowed again. "Please."

There was silence. Then Chiron said, "When I brought you both here, I had not decided yet what I would do. Thetis sees many faults, some that are and some that are not."

His voice was unreadable again. Hope and despair flared and died in me by turns.

"She is also young and has the prejudices of her kind. I am older and flatter myself that I can read a man more clearly. I have no objection to Patroclus as your companion."

My body felt hollow in its relief, as if a storm had gone through.

"She will not be pleased, but I have weathered the anger of gods before." He paused. "And now it is late, and time for you to sleep."

"Thank you, Master Chiron." Achilles' voice, earnest and vigorous. We stood, but I hesitated.

"I just want—" My fingers twitched towards Chiron. Achilles understood and disappeared into the cave.

I turned to face the centaur. "I will leave, if there will be trouble."

There was a long silence, and I almost thought he had not heard me. At last, he said: "Do not let what you gained this day be so easily lost."

Then he bade me good night, and I turned to join Achilles in the cave.

CHAPTER NINE

THE NEXT MORNING I WOKE TO THE SOFT SOUNDS OF Chiron getting breakfast ready. The pallet was thick beneath me; I had slept well, and deeply. I stretched, startling a little when my limbs bumped against Achilles, still asleep beside me. I watched him a moment, rosy cheeks and steady breaths. Something tugged at me, just beneath my skin, but then Chiron lifted a hand in greeting from across the cave, and I lifted one shyly in return, and it was forgotten.

That day, after we ate, we joined Chiron for his chores. It was easy, pleasurable work: collecting berries, catching fish for dinner, setting quail snares. The beginning of our studies, if it is possible to call them that. For Chiron liked to teach, not in set lessons, but in opportunities. When the goats that wandered the ridges took ill, we learned how to mix purgatives for their bad stomachs, and when they were well again, how to make a poultice that repelled their ticks. When I fell down a ravine, fracturing my arm and tearing open my knee, we learned how to set splints, clean wounds, and what herbs to give against infection.

On a hunting trip, after we had accidentally flushed a corncrake from its nest, he taught us how to move silently and how to read the scuffles of tracks. And when we had found the animal, the best way to aim a bow or sling so that death was quick.

If we were thirsty and had no waterskin, he would teach us about the plants whose roots carried beads of moisture. When a mountain-ash fell, we learned carpentry, splitting off the bark, sanding and shaping the wood that was left. I made an axe handle, and Achilles the shaft of a spear; Chiron said that soon we would learn to forge the blades for such things.

Every evening and every morning we helped with meals, churning the thick goat's milk for yogurt and cheese, gutting fish. It was work we had never been allowed to do before, as princes, and we fell upon it eagerly. Following Chiron's instructions, we watched in amazement as butter formed before our eyes, at the way pheasant eggs sizzled and solidified on fire-warmed rocks.

After a month, over breakfast, Chiron asked us what else we wished to learn. "Those." I pointed to the instruments on the wall. *For surgery*, he had said. He took them down for us, one by one.

"Careful. The blade is very sharp. It is for when there is rot in the flesh that must be cut. Press the skin around the wound, and you will hear a crackle."

Then he had us trace the bones in our own bodies, running a hand over the ridging vertebrae of each other's backs. He pointed with his fingers, teaching the places beneath the skin where the organs lodged.

"A wound in any of them will eventually be fatal. But death is quickest here." His finger tapped the slight concavity of Achilles' temple. A chill went through me to see it touched, that place where Achilles' life was so slenderly protected. I was glad when we spoke of other things.

At night we lay on the soft grass in front of the cave, and Chiron showed us the constellations, telling their stories—Andromeda, cowering before the sea monster's jaws, and Perseus poised to rescue her; the immortal horse Pegasus, aloft on his wings, born from the severed neck of Medusa. He told us too of Heracles, his labors, and the madness that took him. In its grip he had not recognized his wife and children, and had killed them for enemies.

Achilles asked, "How could he not recognize his wife?"

"That is the nature of madness," Chiron said. His voice sounded deeper than usual. He had known this man, I remembered. Had known the wife.

"But why did the madness come?"

"The gods wished to punish him," Chiron answered.

Achilles shook his head, impatiently. "But this was a greater punishment for her. It was not fair of them."

"There is no law that gods must be fair, Achilles," Chiron said. "And perhaps it is the greater grief, after all, to be left on earth when another is gone. Do you think?"

"Perhaps," Achilles admitted.

I listened and did not speak. Achilles' eyes were bright in the firelight, his face drawn sharply by the flickering shadows. I would know it in dark or disguise, I told myself. I would know it even in madness.

"Come," said Chiron. "Have I told you the legend of Aesclepius, and how he came to know the secrets of healing?"

He had, but we wanted to hear it again, the story of how the hero, son of Apollo, had spared a snake's life. The snake had licked his ears clean in gratitude, so that he might hear her whisper the secrets of herbs to him.

"But you were the one who really taught him healing," Achilles said.

"I was."

"You do not mind that the snake gets all the credit?"

Chiron's teeth showed through his dark beard. A smile. "No, Achilles, I do not mind."

Later Achilles would play the lyre, as Chiron and I listened. My mother's lyre. He had brought it with him.

"I wish I had known," I said the first day, when he had showed it to me. "I almost did not come, because I did not want to leave it."

He smiled. "Now I know how to make you follow me everywhere."

The sun sank below Pelion's ridges, and we were happy.

TIME PASSED QUICKLY on Mount Pelion, days slipping by in idyll. The mountain air was cold now in the mornings when we woke, and warmed only reluctantly in the thin sunlight that filtered through the dying leaves. Chiron gave us furs to wear, and hung animal skins from the cave's entrance to keep the warmth in. During the days we collected wood for winter fires, or salted meat for preserving. The animals had not yet gone to their dens, but they would soon, Chiron said. In the mornings, we marveled at the frost-etched leaves. We knew of snow from bards and stories; we had never seen it.

One morning, I woke to find Chiron gone. This was not unusual. He often rose before we did, to milk the goats or pick fruits for breakfast. I left the cave so that Achilles might sleep, and sat to wait for Chiron in the clearing. The ashes of last night's fire were white and cold. I stirred them idly with a stick, listening to the woods around me. A quail muttered in the underbrush, and a mourning dove called. I heard the rustle of groundcover, from the wind or an animal's careless weight. In a moment I would get more wood and rekindle the fire.

The strangeness began as a prickling of my skin. First the quail went silent, then the dove. The leaves stilled, and the breeze died, and no animals moved in the brush. There was a quality to the silence like a held breath. Like the rabbit beneath the hawk's shadow. I could feel my pulse striking my skin.

Sometimes, I reminded myself, Chiron did small magics, tricks of divinity, like warming water or calming animals.

"Chiron?" I called. My voice wavered, thinly. "Chiron?"

"It is not Chiron."

I turned. Thetis stood at the edge of the clearing, her bone-white skin and black hair bright as slashes of lightning. The dress she wore clung close to her body and shimmered like fish-scale. My breath died in my throat.

"You were not to be here," she said. The scrape of jagged rocks against a ship's hull.

She stepped forward, and the grass seemed to wilt beneath her feet. She was a sea-nymph, and the things of earth did not love her.

"I'm sorry," I managed, my voice a dried leaf, rattling in my throat.

"I warned you," she said. The black of her eyes seemed to seep into me, fill my throat to choking. I could not have cried out if I'd dared to.

A noise behind me, and then Chiron's voice, loud in the quiet. "Greetings, Thetis."

Warmth surged back into my skin, and breath returned. I almost ran to him. But her gaze held me there, unwavering. I did not doubt she could reach me if she wished.

"You are frightening the boy," Chiron said.

"He does not belong here," she said. Her lips were red as newly spilled blood.

Chiron's hand landed firmly on my shoulder. "Patroclus," he said. "You will return to the cave now. I will speak with you later."

I stood, unsteadily, and obeyed.

"You have lived too long with mortals, Centaur," I heard her say before the animal skins closed behind me. I sagged against the cave's wall; my throat tasted brackish and raw.

"Achilles," I said.

His eyes opened, and he was beside me before I could speak again.

"Are you all right?"

"Your mother is here," I said.

I saw the tightening of muscle beneath his skin.

"She did not hurt you?"

I shook my head. I did not add that I thought she wanted to. That she might have, if Chiron had not come.

"I must go," he said. The skins whispered against each other as they parted for him, then slipped shut again.

I could not hear what was said in the clearing. Their voices were low, or perhaps they had gone to speak elsewhere. I waited, tracing spirals in the packed earth floor. I did not worry, any longer, for myself. Chiron meant to keep me, and he was older than she was, full grown when the gods still rocked in their cradles, when she had been only an egg in the womb of the sea. But there was something else, less easy to name. A loss, or lessening, that I feared her presence might bring.

It was almost midday when they returned. My gaze went to Achilles' face first, searching his eyes, the set of his mouth. I saw nothing but perhaps a touch of tiredness. He threw himself onto the pallet beside me. "I'm hungry," he said.

"As well you should be," Chiron said. "It is much past lunch." He was already preparing food for us, maneuvering in the cave's space easily despite his bulk.

Achilles turned to me. "It is all right," he said. "She just wanted to speak to me. To see me."

"She will come to speak with him again," Chiron said. And as if he knew what I thought, he added, "As is proper. She is his mother."

She is a goddess first, I thought.

Yet as we ate, my fears eased. I had half-worried she might have told Chiron of the day by the beach, but he was no different towards either of us, and Achilles was the same as he always was. I went to bed, if not at peace, at least reassured.

She came more often after that day, as Chiron had said she would. I learned to listen for it—a silence that dropped like a curtain—and knew to stay close to Chiron then, and the cave. The intrusion was not much, and I told myself I did not begrudge her. But I was always glad when she was gone again.

WINTER CAME, and the river froze. Achilles and I ventured onto it, feet slipping. Later, we cut circles from it and dropped lines for

fishing. It was the only fresh meat we had; the forests were empty
of all but mice and the occasional marten.

Snows came, as Chiron had promised they would. We lay
on the ground and let the flakes cover us, blowing them with our
breath till they melted. We had no boots, nor cloaks other than
Chiron's furs, and were glad of the cave's warmth. Even Chiron
donned a shaggy overshirt, sewed from what he said was bear-
skin.

We counted the days after the first snowfall, marking them off
with lines on a stone. "When you reach fifty," Chiron said, "the
river's ice will begin to crack." The morning of the fiftieth day we
heard it, a strange sound, like a tree falling. A seam had split the
frozen surface nearly from bank to bank. "Spring will come soon
now," Chiron said.

It was not long after that the grass began to grow again, and
the squirrels emerged lean and whip-thin from their burrows. We
followed them, eating our breakfasts in the new-scrubbed spring
air. It was on one of these mornings that Achilles asked Chiron if
he would teach us to fight.

I do not know what made him think of this then. A winter
indoors, with not enough exercise perhaps, or the visit from his
mother, the week before. Perhaps neither.

Will you teach us to fight?

There was a pause so brief I almost might have imagined it,
before Chiron answered, "If you wish it, I will teach you."

Later that day, he took us to a clearing, high on a ridge. He
had spear-hafts and two practice swords for us, taken from stor-
age in some corner of the cave. He asked us each to perform
the drills that we knew. I did, slowly, the blocks and strikes and

footwork I had learned in Phthia. To my side, just at the corner of my vision, Achilles' limbs blurred and struck. Chiron had brought a bronze-banded staff, and he interposed it occasionally into our passes, probing with it, testing our reactions.

It seemed to go on for a long time, and my arms grew sore with lifting and placing the point of the sword. At last Chiron called a stop. We drank deep from waterskins and lay back on the grass. My chest was heaving. Achilles' was steady.

Chiron was silent, standing in front of us.

"Well, what do you think?" Achilles was eager, and I remembered that Chiron was only the fourth person to have ever seen him fight.

I did not know what I expected the centaur to say. But it was not what followed.

"There is nothing I can teach you. You know all that Heracles knew, and more. You are the greatest warrior of your generation, and all the generations before."

A flush stained Achilles' cheeks. I could not tell if it was embarrassment or pleasure or both.

"Men will hear of your skill, and they will wish for you to fight their wars." He paused. "What will you answer?"

"I do not know," Achilles said.

"That is an answer for now. It will not be good enough later," Chiron said.

There was a silence then, and I felt the tightness in the air around us. Achilles' face, for the first time since we had come, looked pinched and solemn.

"What about me?" I asked.

Chiron's dark eyes moved to rest on mine. "You will never gain fame from your fighting. Is this surprising to you?"

His tone was matter-of-fact, and somehow that eased the sting of it.

"No," I said truthfully.

"Yet it is not beyond you to be a competent soldier. Do you wish to learn this?"

I thought of the boy's dulled eyes, how quickly his blood had soaked the ground. I thought of Achilles, the greatest warrior of his generation. I thought of Thetis who would take him from me, if she could.

"No," I said.

And that was the end of our lessons in soldiery.

SPRING PASSED INTO SUMMER, and the woods grew warm and abundant, lush with game and fruit. Achilles turned fourteen, and messengers brought gifts for him from Peleus. It was strange to see them here, in their uniforms and palace colors. I watched their eyes, flickering over me, over Achilles, over Chiron most of all. Gossip was dear in the palace, and these men would be received like kings when they returned. I was glad to see them shoulder their empty trunks and be gone.

The gifts were welcome—new lyre strings and fresh tunics, spun from the finest wool. There was a new bow as well, and arrows tipped with iron. We fingered their metal, the keen-edged points that would bring down our dinners in days to come.

Some things were less useful—cloaks stiff with inlaid gold

that would give the owner's presence away at fifty paces, and a jewel-studded belt, too heavy to wear for anything practical. There was a horsecoat as well, thickly embroidered, meant to adorn the mount of a prince.

"I hope that is not for me," Chiron said, lifting an eyebrow. We tore it up for compresses and bandages and scrub cloths; the rough material was perfect for pulling up crusted dirt and food.

That afternoon, we lay on the grass in front of the cave. "It has been almost a year since we came," Achilles said. The breeze was cool against our skin.

"It does not feel so long," I answered. I was half-sleepy, my eyes lost in the tilting blue of the afternoon sky.

"Do you miss the palace?"

I thought of his father's gifts, the servants and their gazes, the whispering gossip they would bring back to the palace.

"No," I said.

"I don't either," he said. "I thought I might, but I don't."

The days turned, and the months, and two years passed.

CHAPTER TEN

IT WAS SPRING, AND WE WERE FIFTEEN. THE WINTER ICE HAD lasted longer than usual, and we were glad to be outside once more, beneath the sun. Our tunics were discarded, and our skin prickled in the light breeze. I had not been so naked all winter; it had been too cold to take off our furs and cloaks, beyond quick washes in the hollowed-out rock that served as our bath. Achilles was stretching, rolling limbs that were stiff from too long indoors. We had spent the morning swimming and chasing game through the forest. My muscles felt wearily content, glad to be used again.

I watched him. Other than the unsteady surface of the river, there were no mirrors on Mount Pelion, so I could only measure myself by the changes in Achilles. His limbs were still slender, but I could see the muscles in them now, rising and falling beneath his skin as he moved. His face, too, was firmer, and his shoulders broader than they had been.

"You look older," I said.

He stopped, turned to me. "I do?"

"Yes." I nodded. "Do I?"

"Come over here," he said. I stood, walked to him. He regarded me a moment. "Yes," he said.

"How?" I wanted to know. "A lot?"

"Your face is different," he said.

"Where?"

He touched my jaw with his right hand, drew his fingertips along it. "Here. Your face is wider than it once was." I reached up with my own hand, to see if I could feel this difference, but it was all the same to me, bone and skin. He took my hand and brought it down to my collarbone. "You are wider here also," he said. "And this." His finger touched, gently, the soft bulb that had emerged from my throat. I swallowed, and felt his fingertip ride against the motion.

"Where else?" I asked.

He pointed to the trail of fine, dark hair that ran down my chest and over my stomach.

He paused, and my face grew warm.

"That's enough," I said, more abruptly than I meant to. I sat again on the grass, and he resumed his stretches. I watched the breeze stir his hair; I watched the sun fall on his golden skin. I leaned back and let it fall on me as well.

After some time, he stopped and came to sit beside me. We watched the grass, and the trees, and the nubs of new buds, just growing.

His voice was remote, almost careless. "You would not be displeased, I think. With how you look now."

My face grew warm, again. But we spoke no more of it.

WE WERE ALMOST SIXTEEN. Soon Peleus' messengers would come with gifts; soon the berries would ripen, the fruits would

blush and fall into our hands. Sixteen was our last year of childhood, the year before our fathers named us men, and we would
begin to wear not just tunics but capes and chitons as well. A marriage would be arranged for Achilles, and I might take a wife, if I
wished to. I thought again of the serving girls with their dull eyes.
I remembered the snatches of conversation I had overheard from
the boys, the talk of breasts and hips and coupling.

She's like cream, she's that soft.

Once her thighs are around you, you'll forget your own name.

The boys' voices had been sharp with excitement, their color
high. But when I tried to imagine what they spoke of, my mind
slid away, like a fish who would not be caught.

Other images came in their stead. The curve of a neck bent
over a lyre, hair gleaming in firelight, hands with their flickering tendons. We were together all day, and I could not escape:
the smell of the oils he used on his feet, the glimpses of skin as he
dressed. I would wrench my gaze from him and remember the day
on the beach, the coldness in his eyes and how he ran from me.
And, always, I remembered his mother.

I began to go off by myself, early in the mornings, when
Achilles still slept, or in the afternoons, when he would practice
his spear thrusts. I brought a flute with me, but rarely played it. Instead I would find a tree to lean against and breathe the sharp drift
of cypress-scent, blown from the highest part of the mountain.

Slowly, as if to escape my own notice, my hand would move to
rest between my thighs. There was shame in this thing that I did,
and a greater shame still in the thoughts that came with it. But it
would be worse to think them inside the rose-quartz cave, with
him beside me.

It was difficult sometimes, after, to return to the cave. "Where were you?" he'd ask.

"Just—" I'd say, and point vaguely.

He'd nod. But I knew he saw the flush that colored my cheeks.

THE SUMMER GREW HOTTER, and we sought the river's shade, its water that threw off arcs of light as we splashed and dove. The rocks of the bottom were mossy and cool, rolling beneath my toes as I waded. We shouted, and frightened the fish, who fled to their muddy holes or quieter waters upstream. The rushing ice melt of spring was gone; I lay on my back and let the dozy current carry me. I liked the feel of the sun on my stomach and the cool depths of the river beneath me. Achilles floated beside me or swam against the slow tug of the river's flow.

When we tired of this, we would seize the low-hanging branches of the osiers and hoist ourselves half-out of the water. On this day we kicked at each other, our legs tangling, trying to dislodge the other, or perhaps climb onto their branch. On an impulse, I released my branch and seized him around his hanging torso. He let out an *ooph* of surprise. We struggled that way for a moment, laughing, my arms wrapped around him. Then there was a sharp cracking sound, and his branch gave way, plunging us into the river. The cool water closed over us, and still we wrestled, hands against slippery skin.

When we surfaced, we were panting and eager. He leapt for me, bearing me down through the clear water. We grappled, emerged to gasp air, then sank again.

At length, our lungs burning, our faces red from too long underwater, we dragged ourselves to the bank and lay there amidst the sedge-grass and marshy weeds. Our feet sank into the cool mud of the water's edge. Water still streamed from his hair, and I watched it bead, tracing across his arms and the lines of his chest.

ON THE MORNING of his sixteenth birthday I woke early. Chiron had showed me a tree on Pelion's far slope that had figs just ripening, the first of the season. Achilles did not know of it, the centaur assured me. I watched them for days, their hard green knots swelling and darkening, growing gravid with seed. And now I would pick them for his breakfast.

It wasn't my only gift. I had found a seasoned piece of ash and began to fashion it secretly, carving off its soft layers. Over nearly two months a shape had emerged—a boy playing the lyre, head raised to the sky, mouth open, as if he were singing. I had it with me now, as I walked.

The figs hung rich and heavy on the tree, their curved flesh pliant to my touch—two days later and they would be too ripe. I gathered them in a carved-wood bowl and bore them carefully back to the cave.

Achilles was sitting in the clearing with Chiron, a new box from Peleus resting unopened at his feet. I saw the quick widening of his eyes as he took in the figs. He was on his feet, eagerly reaching into the bowl before I could even set it down beside him. We ate until we were stuffed, our fingers and chins sticky with sweetness.

The box from Peleus held more tunics and lyre strings, and this time, for his sixteenth birthday, a cloak dyed with the expensive purple from the *murex*'s shell. It was the cape of a prince, of a future king, and I saw that it pleased him. It would look good on him, I knew, the purple seeming richer still beside the gold of his hair.

Chiron, too, gave presents—a staff for hiking, and a new belt-knife. And last, I passed him the statue. He examined it, his fingertips moving over the small marks my knife had left behind.

"It's you," I said, grinning foolishly.

He looked up, and there was bright pleasure in his eyes.

"I know," he said.

ONE EVENING, not long after, we stayed late beside the fire's embers. Achilles had been gone for much of the afternoon—Thetis had come and kept him longer even than usual. Now he was playing my mother's lyre. The music was quiet and bright as the stars over our heads.

Next to me, I heard Chiron yawn, settle more deeply onto his folded legs. A moment later the lyre ceased, and Achilles' voice came loud in the darkness. "Are you weary, Chiron?"

"I am."

"Then we will leave you to your rest."

He was not usually so quick to go, nor to speak for me, but I was tired myself and did not object. He rose and bade Chiron good night, turning for the cave. I stretched, soaked up a few more moments of firelight, and followed.

Inside the cave, Achilles was already in bed, his face damp from a wash at the spring. I washed too, the water cool across my forehead.

He said, "You didn't ask me about my mother's visit yet."

I said, "How is she?"

"She is well." This was the answer he always gave. It was why I sometimes did not ask him.

"Good." I lifted a handful of water, to rinse the soap off my face. We made it from the oil of olives, and it still smelled faintly of them, rich and buttery.

Achilles spoke again. "She says she cannot see us here."

I had not been expecting him to say more. "Hmmm?"

"She cannot see us here. On Pelion."

There was something in his voice, a strain. I turned to him. "What do you mean?"

His eyes studied the ceiling. "She says—I asked her if she watches us here." His voice was high. "She says, she does not."

There was silence in the cave. Silence, but for the sound of the slowly draining water.

"Oh," I said.

"I wished to tell you. Because—" He paused. "I thought you would wish to know. She—" He hesitated again. "She was not pleased that I asked her."

"She was not pleased," I repeated. I felt dizzy, my mind turning and turning through his words. *She cannot see us.* I realized that I was standing half-frozen by the water basin, the towel still raised to my chin. I forced myself to put down the cloth, to move to the bed. There was a wildness in me, of hope and terror.

I pulled back the covers and lay down on bedding already warm from his skin. His eyes were still fixed on the ceiling.

"Are you—pleased with her answer?" I said, finally.

"Yes," he said.

We lay there a moment, in that strained and living silence. Usually at night we would tell each other jokes or stories. The ceiling above us was painted with the stars, and if we grew tired of talking, we would point to them. "Orion," I would say, following his finger. "The Pleiades."

But tonight there was nothing. I closed my eyes and waited, long minutes, until I guessed he was asleep. Then I turned to look at him.

He was on his side, watching me. I had not heard him turn. *I never hear him.* He was utterly motionless, that stillness that was his alone. I breathed, and was aware of the bare stretch of dark pillow between us.

He leaned forward.

Our mouths opened under each other, and the warmth of his sweetened throat poured into mine. I could not think, could not do anything but drink him in, each breath as it came, the soft movements of his lips. It was a miracle.

I was trembling, afraid to put him to flight. I did not know what to do, what he would like. I kissed his neck, the span of his chest, and tasted the salt. He seemed to swell beneath my touch, to ripen. He smelled like almonds and earth. He pressed against me, crushing my lips to wine.

He went still as I took him in my hand, soft as the delicate velvet of petals. I knew Achilles' golden skin and the curve of his neck, the crooks of his elbows. I knew how pleasure looked on him. Our bodies cupped each other like hands.

The blankets had twisted around me. He shucked them from us both. The air over my skin was a shock, and I shivered. He was outlined against the painted stars; Polaris sat on his shoulder. His hand slipped over the quickened rise and fall of my belly's breathing. He stroked me gently, as though smoothing finest cloth, and my hips lifted to his touch. I pulled him to me, and trembled and trembled. He was trembling, too. He sounded as though he had been running far and fast.

I said his name, I think. It blew through me; I was hollow as a reed hung up for the wind to sound. There was no time that passed but our breaths.

I found his hair between my fingers. There was a gathering inside me, a beat of blood against the movement of his hand. His face was pressed against me, but I tried to clutch him closer still. Do not stop, I said.

He did not stop. The feeling gathered and gathered till a hoarse cry leapt from my throat, and the sharp flowering drove me, arching, against him.

It was not enough. My hand reached, found the place of his pleasure. His eyes closed. There was a rhythm he liked, I could feel it, the catch of his breath, the yearning. My fingers were cease-less, following each quickening gasp. His eyelids were the color of the dawn sky; he smelled like earth after rain. His mouth opened in an inarticulate cry, and we were pressed so close that I felt the spurt of his warmth against me. He shuddered, and we lay still.

Slowly, like dusk-fall, I became aware of my sweat, the damp-ness of the covers, and the wetness that slid between our bellies. We separated, peeling away from each other, our faces puffy and half-bruised from kisses. The cave smelled hot and sweet, like fruit beneath the sun. Our eyes met, and we did not speak. Fear rose in me, sudden and sharp. This was the moment of truest peril, and I tensed, fearing his regret.

He said, "I did not think—" And stopped. There was nothing in the world I wanted more than to hear what he had not said.

"What?" I asked him. *If it is bad, let it be over quickly.*

"I did not think that we would ever—" He was hesitating over every word, and I could not blame him.

"I did not think so either," I said.

"Are you sorry?" The words were quickly out of him, a single breath.

"I am not," I said.

"I am not either."

There was silence then, and I did not care about the damp pallet or how sweaty I was. His eyes were unwavering, green flecked with gold. A surety rose in me, lodged in my throat. *I will never leave him. It will be this, always, for as long as he will let me.*

If I had had words to speak such a thing, I would have. But there were none that seemed big enough for it, to hold that swelling truth.

As if he had heard me, he reached for my hand. I did not need to look; his fingers were etched into my memory, slender and petal-veined, strong and quick and never wrong.

"Patroclus," he said. He was always better with words than I.

THE NEXT MORNING I awoke light-headed, my body woozy with warmth and ease. After the tenderness had come more passion; we had been slower then, and lingering, a dreamy night that stretched on and on. Now, watching him stir beside me, his hand resting on my stomach, damp and curled as a flower at dawn, I was nervous again. I remembered in a rush the things I had said and done, the noises I had made. I feared that the spell was broken, that the light that crept through the cave's entrance would turn it all to stone.

But then he was awake, his lips forming a half-sleepy greeting, and his hand was already reaching for mine. We lay there, like that, until the cave was bright with morning, and Chiron called.

We ate, then ran to the river to wash. I savored the miracle of being able to watch him openly, to enjoy the play of dappled light on his limbs, the curving of his back as he dove beneath the water. Later, we lay on the riverbank, learning the lines of each other's bodies anew. This, and this and this. We were like gods at the dawning of the world, and our joy was so bright we could see nothing else but the other.

IF CHIRON NOTICED a change, he did not speak of it. But I could not help worrying.

"Do you think he will be angry?"

We were by the olive grove on the north side of the mountain. The breezes were sweetest here, cool and clean as springwater.

"I don't think he will." He reached for my collarbone, the line he liked to draw his finger down.

"But he might. Surely he must know by now. Should we say something?"

It was not the first time I had wondered this. We had discussed it often, eager with conspiracy.

"If you like." That is what he had said before.

"You don't think he will be angry?"

He paused now, considering. I loved this about him. No matter how many times I had asked, he answered me as if it were the first time.

"I don't know." His eyes met mine. "Does it matter? I would

not stop." His voice was warm with desire. I felt an answering flush across my skin.

"But he could tell your father. *He* might be angry."

I said it almost desperately. Soon my skin would grow too warm, and I would no longer be able to think.

"So what if he is?" The first time he had said something like this, I had been shocked. That his father might be angry and Achilles would still do as he wished—it was something I did not understand, could barely imagine. It was like a drug to hear him say it. I never tired of it.

"What about your mother?"

This was the trinity of my fears—Chiron, Peleus, and Thetis.

He shrugged. "What could she do? Kidnap me?"

She could kill me, I thought. But I did not say this. The breeze was too sweet, and the sun too warm for a thought like that to be spoken.

He studied me a moment. "Do you care if they are angry?"

Yes. I would be horrified to find Chiron upset with me. Disapproval had always burrowed deep in me; I could not shake it off as Achilles did. But I would not let it separate us, if it came to that. "No," I told him.

"Good," he said.

I reached down to stroke the wisps of hair at his temple. He closed his eyes. I watched his face, tipped up to meet the sun. There was a delicacy to his features that sometimes made him look younger than he was. His lips were flushed and full.

His eyes opened. "Name one hero who was happy."

I considered. Heracles went mad and killed his family; Theseus lost his bride and father; Jason's children and new wife were murdered by his old; Bellerophon killed the Chimera but was crippled by the fall from Pegasus' back.

"You can't." He was sitting up now, leaning forward.

"I can't."

"I know. They never let you be famous *and* happy." He lifted an eyebrow. "I'll tell you a secret."

"Tell me." I loved it when he was like this.

"I'm going to be the first." He took my palm and held it to his. "Swear it."

"Why me?"

"Because you're the reason. Swear it."

"I swear it," I said, lost in the high color of his cheeks, the flame in his eyes.

"I swear it," he echoed.

We sat like that a moment, hands touching. He grinned.

"I feel like I could eat the world raw."

A trumpet blew, somewhere on the slopes beneath us. It was abrupt and ragged, as if sounded in warning. Before I could speak or move, he was on his feet, his dagger out, slapped up from the sheath on his thigh. It was only a hunting knife, but in his hands it would be enough. He stood poised, utterly still, listening with all of his half-god senses.

I had a knife, too. Quietly, I reached for it and stood. He had placed himself between me and the sound. I did not know if I should go to him, stand beside him with my own weapon lifted. In the end, I did not. It had been a soldier's trumpet, and battle, as Chiron had so bluntly said, was his gift, not mine.

The trumpet sounded again. We heard the swish of underbrush, tangled by a pair of feet. *One man.* Perhaps he was lost, perhaps in danger. Achilles took a step towards the sound. As if in answer, the trumpet came again. Then a voice bawled up the mountain, "Prince Achilles!"

We froze.

"Achilles! I am here for Prince Achilles!"

Birds burst from the trees, fleeing the clamor.

"From your father," I whispered. Only a royal herald would have known where to call for us.

Achilles nodded, but seemed strangely reluctant to answer. I imagined how hard his pulse would be beating; he had been prepared to kill a moment ago.

"We are here!" I shouted into the cupped palms of my hand. The noise stopped for a moment.

"Where?"

"Can you follow my voice?"

He could, though poorly. It was some time before he stepped forward into the clearing. His face was scratched, and he had sweated through his palace tunic. He knelt with ill grace, resentfully. Achilles had lowered the knife, though I saw how tightly he still held it.

"Yes?" His voice was cool.

"Your father summons you. There is urgent business at home."

I felt myself go still, as still as Achilles had been a moment before. If I stayed still enough, perhaps we would not have to go.

"What sort of business?" Achilles asked.

The man had recovered himself, somewhat. He remembered he was speaking to a prince.

"My lord, your pardon, I do not know all of it. Messengers came to Peleus from Mycenae with news. Your father plans to speak tonight to the people, and wishes you to be there. I have horses for you below."

There was a moment of silence. Almost, I thought Achilles would decline. But at last he said, "Patroclus and I will need to pack our things."

On the way back to the cave and Chiron, Achilles and I speculated about the news. Mycenae was far to our south, and its king was Agamemnon, who liked to call himself a lord of men. He was said to have the greatest army of all our kingdoms.

"Whatever it is, we'll only be gone for a night or two," Achilles told me. I nodded, grateful to hear him say it. *Just a few days.*

Chiron was waiting for us. "I heard the shouts," the centaur said. Achilles and I, knowing him well, recognized the disapproval in his voice. He did not like the peace of his mountain disturbed.

"My father has summoned me home," Achilles said, "just for tonight. I expect I will be back soon."

"I see," Chiron said. He seemed larger than usual, standing there, hooves dull against the bright grass, his chestnut-colored flanks lit by the sun. I wondered if he would be lonely without us. I had never seen him with another centaur. We asked him about them once, and his face had gone stiff. "Barbarians," he'd said.

We gathered our things. I had almost nothing to bring with me, some tunics, a flute. Achilles had only a few possessions more, his clothes, and some spearheads he had made, and the statue I had carved for him. We placed them in leather bags and went to say our farewells to Chiron. Achilles, always bolder, embraced the centaur, his arms encircling the place where the horse flank gave way to flesh. The messenger, waiting behind me, shifted.

"Achilles," Chiron said, "do you remember when I asked you what you would do when men wanted you to fight?"

"Yes," said Achilles.

"You should consider your answer," Chiron said. A chill went through me, but I did not have time to think on it. Chiron was turning to me.

"Patroclus," he said, a summons. I walked forward, and he placed his hand, large and warm as the sun, on my head. I breathed in the scent that was his alone, horse and sweat and herbs and forest.

His voice was quiet. "You do not give things up so easily now as you once did," he said.

I did not know what to say to this, so I said, "Thank you."

A trace of smile. "Be well." Then his hand was gone, leaving my head chilled in its absence.

"We will be back soon," Achilles said, again.

Chiron's eyes were dark in the slanting afternoon light. "I will look for you," he said.

We shouldered our bags and left the cave's clearing. The sun was already past the meridian, and the messenger was impatient. We moved quickly down the hill and climbed on the horses that waited for us. A saddle felt strange after so many years on foot, and the horses unnerved me. I half-expected them to speak, but of course they could not. I twisted in my seat to look back at Pelion. I hoped that I might be able to see the rose-quartz cave, or maybe Chiron himself. But we were too far. I turned to face the road and allowed myself to be led to Phthia.

CHAPTER ELEVEN

THE LAST BIT OF SUN WAS FLARING ON THE WESTERN horizon as we passed the boundary stone that marked the palace grounds. We heard the cry go up from the guards, and an answering trumpet. We crested the hill, and the palace lay before us; behind it brooded the sea.

And there on the house's threshold, sudden as lightning-strike, stood Thetis. Her hair shone black against the white marble of the palace. Her dress was dark, the color of an uneasy ocean, bruising purples mixed with churning grays. Somewhere beside her there were guards, and Peleus, too, but I did not look at them. I saw only her, and the curved knife's blade of her jaw.

"Your mother," I whispered to Achilles. I could have sworn her eyes flashed over me as if she had heard. I swallowed and forced myself onward. *She will not hurt me; Chiron has said she will not.*

It was strange to see her among mortals; she made all of them, guards and Peleus alike, look bleached and wan, though it was her skin that was pale as bone. She stood well away from them, spearing the sky with her unnatural height. The guards lowered their eyes in fear and deference.

Achilles swung down from his horse, and I followed. Thetis drew him into an embrace, and I saw the guards shifting their feet.

They were wondering what her skin felt like; they were glad they did not know.

"Son of my womb, flesh of my flesh, Achilles," she said. The words were not spoken loudly but they carried through the courtyard. "Be welcome home."

"Thank you, Mother," Achilles said. He understood that she was claiming him. We all did. It was proper for a son to greet his father first; mothers came second, if at all. But she was a goddess. Peleus' mouth had tightened, but he said nothing.

When she released him, he went to his father. "Be welcome, son," Peleus said. His voice sounded weak after his goddess-wife's, and he looked older than he had been. Three years we had been away.

"And be welcome also, Patroclus."

Everyone turned to me, and I managed a bow. I was aware of Thetis' gaze, raking over me. It left my skin stinging, as if I had gone from the briar patch to the ocean. I was glad when Achilles spoke.

"What is the news, Father?"

Peleus eyed the guards. Speculation and rumor must be racing down every corridor.

"I have not announced it, and I do not mean to until everyone is gathered. We were waiting on you. Come and let us begin."

We followed him into the palace. I wanted to speak to Achilles but did not dare to; Thetis walked right behind us. Servants skittered from her, huffing in surprise. *The goddess.* Her feet made no sound as they moved over the stone floors.

THE GREAT DINING HALL was crammed full of tables and benches. Servants hurried by with platters of food or lugged mixing bowls brimming with wine. At the front of the room was a dais, raised. This is where Peleus would sit, beside his son and wife. Three places. My cheeks went red. What had I expected?

Even amidst the noise of the preparations Achilles' voice seemed loud. "Father, I do not see a place for Patroclus." My blush went even deeper.

"Achilles," I began in a whisper. *It does not matter*, I wanted to say. *I will sit with the men; it is all right.* But he ignored me.

"Patroclus is my sworn companion. His place is beside me." Thetis' eyes flickered. I could feel the heat in them. I saw the refusal on her lips.

"Very well," Peleus said. He gestured to a servant and a place was added for me, thankfully at the opposite side of the table from Thetis. Making myself as small as I could, I followed Achilles to our seats.

"She'll hate me now," I said.

"She already hates you," he answered, with a flash of smile.

This did not reassure me. "Why has she come?" I whispered. Only something truly important would have drawn her here from her caves in the sea. Her loathing for me was nothing to what I saw on her face when she looked at Peleus.

He shook his head. "I do not know. It is strange. I have not seen them together since I was a boy."

I remembered Chiron's parting words to Achilles: *you should consider your answer.*

"Chiron thinks the news will be war."

Achilles frowned. "But there is always war in Mycenae. I do not see why we should have been called."

Peleus sat, and a herald blew three short blasts upon his trumpet. The signal for the meal to begin. Normally it took several minutes for the men to gather, dawdling on the practice fields, drawing out the last bit of whatever they were doing. But this time they came like a flood after the breaking of the winter's ice. Quickly, the room was swollen with them, jostling for seats and gossiping. I heard the edge in their voices, a rising excitement. No one bothered to snap at a servant or kick aside a begging dog. There was nothing on their minds but the man from Mycenae and the news he had brought.

Thetis was seated also. There was no plate for her, no knife: the gods lived on ambrosia and nectar, on the savor of our burnt offerings, and the wine we poured over their altars. Strangely, she was not so visible here, so blazing as she had been outside. The bulky, ordinary furniture seemed to diminish her, somehow.

Peleus stood. The room quieted, out to the farthest benches. He lifted his cup.

"I have received word from Mycenae, from the sons of Atreus, Agamemnon and Menelaus." The final stirrings and murmurs ceased, utterly. Even the servants stopped. I did not breathe. Beneath the table, Achilles pressed his leg to mine.

"There has been a crime." He paused again, as if he were weighing what he would say. "The wife of Menelaus, Queen Helen, has been abducted from the palace in Sparta."

Helen! The hushed whisper of men to their neighbors. Since her marriage the tales of her beauty had grown still greater. Menelaus had built around her palace walls thick with double-layered rock; he had trained his soldiers for a decade to defend it. But, for all his care, she had been stolen. *Who had done it?*

"Menelaus welcomed an embassy sent from King Priam of Troy. At its head was Priam's son, the prince Paris, and it is he who is responsible. He stole the queen of Sparta from her bed-chamber while the king slept."

A rumble of outrage. Only an Easterner would so dishonor the kindness of his host. Everyone knew how they dripped with perfume, were corrupt from soft living. A real hero would have taken her outright, with the strength of his sword.

"Agamemnon and Mycenae appeal to the men of Hellas to sail to the kingdom of Priam for her rescue. Troy is rich and will be easily taken, they say. All who fight will come home wealthy and renowned."

This was well worded. Wealth and reputation were the things our people had always killed for.

"They have asked me to send a delegation of men from Phthia, and I have agreed." He waited for the murmuring to settle before adding, "Though I will not take any man who does not wish to go. And I will not lead the army myself."

"Who will lead it?" someone shouted.

"That is not yet determined," Peleus said. But I saw his eyes flicker to his son.

No, I thought. My hand tightened on the edge of the chair. *Not yet.* Across from me Thetis' face was cool and still, her eyes distant. *She knew this was coming,* I realized. *She wants him to go.* Chiron and the rose cave seemed impossibly far away; a child-ish idyll. I understood, suddenly, the weight of Chiron's words: war was what the world would say Achilles was born for. That

his hands and swift feet were fashioned for this alone—the cracking of Troy's mighty walls. They would throw him among thousands of Trojan spears and watch with triumph as he stained his
fair hands red.

Peleus gestured to Phoinix, his oldest friend, at one of the
first tables. "Lord Phoinix will note the names of all who wish to
fight."

There was a movement at the benches, as men started to rise.
But Peleus held up his hand.

"There is more." He lifted a piece of linen, dark with dense
markings. "Before Helen's betrothal to King Menelaus, she had
many suitors. It seems these suitors swore an oath to protect her,
whosoever might win her hand. Agamemnon and Menelaus now
charge these men to fulfill their oath and bring her back to her
rightful husband." He handed the linen sheet to the herald.

I stared. *An oath.* In my mind, the sudden image of a brazier,
and the spill of blood from a white goat. A rich hall, filled with
towering men.

The herald lifted the list. The room seemed to tilt, and my
eyes would not focus. He began to read.

Antenor.

Eurypylus.

Machaon.

I recognized many of the names; we all did. They were the
heroes and kings of our time. But they were more to me than that.
I had seen them, in a stone chamber heavy with fire-smoke.

Agamemnon. A memory of a thick black beard; a brooding
man with narrowed, watchful eyes.

Odysseus. The scar that wrapped his calf, pink as gums.

Ajax. Twice as large as any man in the room, with his huge shield behind him.

Philoctetes, the bowman.

Menoitiades.

The herald paused a moment, and I heard the murmur: *who?* My father had not distinguished himself in the years since my exile. His fame had diminished; his name was forgotten. And those who did know him had never heard of a son. I sat frozen, afraid to move lest I give myself away. *I am bound to this war.*

The herald cleared his throat.

Idomeneus.

Diomedes.

"Is that you? You were there?" Achilles had turned back to face me. His voice was low, barely audible, but still I feared that someone might hear it.

I nodded. My throat was too dry for words. I had thought only of Achilles' danger, of how I would try to keep him here, if I could. I had not even considered myself.

"Listen. It is not your name anymore. Say nothing. We will think what to do. We will ask Chiron." Achilles never spoke like that, each word cutting off the next in haste. His urgency brought me back to myself, a little, and I took heart from his eyes on mine. I nodded again.

The names kept coming, and memories came with them. Three women on a dais, and one of them Helen. A pile of treasure, and my father's frown. The stone beneath my knees. I had thought I dreamt it. I had not.

When the herald had finished, Peleus dismissed the men. They stood as one, benches scraping, eager to get to Phoinix to enlist. Peleus turned to us. "Come. I would speak further with you both." I looked to Thetis, to see if she would come too, but she was gone.

WE SAT BY PELEUS' FIRESIDE; he had offered us wine, barely watered. Achilles refused it. I took a cup, but did not drink. The king was in his old chair, the one closest to the fire, with its cushions and high back. His eyes rested on Achilles.

"I have called you home with the thought that you might wish to lead this army."

It was spoken. The fire popped; its wood was green.

Achilles met his father's gaze. "I have not finished yet with Chiron."

"You have stayed on Pelion longer than I did, than any hero before."

"That does not mean I must run to help the sons of Atreus every time they lose their wives."

I thought Peleus might smile at that, but he did not. "I do not doubt that Menelaus rages at the loss of his wife, but the messenger came from Agamemnon. He has watched Troy grow rich and ripe for years, and now thinks to pluck her. The taking of Troy is a feat worthy of our greatest heroes. There may be much honor to be won from sailing with him."

Achilles' mouth tightened. "There will be other wars."

Peleus did not nod, exactly. But I saw him register the truth of it. "What of Patroclus, then? He is called to serve."

"He is no longer the son of Menoitius. He is not bound by the oath."

Pious Peleus raised an eyebrow. "There is some shuffling there."

"I do not think so." Achilles lifted his chin. "The oath was un-done when his father disowned him."

"I do not wish to go," I said, softly.

Peleus regarded us both for a moment. Then he said, "Such a thing is not for me to decide. I will leave it to you."

I felt the tension slide from me a little. He would not expose me.

"Achilles, men are coming here to speak with you, kings sent by Agamemnon."

Outside the window, I heard the ocean's steady whisper against the sand. I could smell the salt.

"They will ask me to fight," Achilles said. It was not a question.

"They will."

"You wish me to give them audience."

"I do."

There was quiet again. Then Achilles said, "I will not dis-honor them, or you. I will hear their reasons. But I say to you that I do not think they will convince me."

I saw that Peleus was surprised, a little, by his son's certainty, but not displeased. "That is also not for me to decide," he said mildly.

The fire popped again, spitting out its sap.

Achilles knelt, and Peleus placed one hand on his head. I was used to seeing Chiron do this, and Peleus' hand looked with-ered by comparison, threaded with trembling veins. It was hard to remember, sometimes, that he had been a warrior, that he had walked with gods.

ACHILLES' ROOM was as we had left it, except for the cot, which had been removed in our absence. I was glad; it was an easy excuse, in case anyone asked why we shared a bed. We reached for each other, and I thought of how many nights I had lain awake in this room loving him in silence.

Later, Achilles pressed close for a final, drowsy whisper. "If you have to go, you know I will go with you." We slept.

CHAPTER TWELVE

I WOKE TO THE RED OF MY EYELIDS STRAINING OUT THE SUN. I was cold, my right shoulder exposed to the breezes of the window, the one that faced the sea. The space beside me on the bed was empty, but the pillow still held the shape of him, and the sheets smelled of us both.

I had spent so many mornings alone in this room, as he visited his mother, I did not think it was strange to find him gone. My eyes closed, and I sank again into the trailing thoughts of dreams. Time passed, and the sun came hot over the windowsill. The birds were up, and the servants, and even the men. I heard their voices from the beach and the practice hall, the rattle and bang of chores. I sat up. His sandals were overturned beside the bed, forgotten. It was not unusual; he went barefoot most places.

He had gone to breakfast, I guessed. He was letting me sleep. Half of me wanted to stay in the room until his return, but that was cowardice. I had a right to a place by his side now, and I would not let the eyes of the servants drive me away. I pulled on my tunic and left to find him.

HE WAS NOT IN the great hall, busy with servants removing the same platters and bowls there had always been. He was not in Peleus' council chamber, hung with purple tapestry and the weapons of former Phthian kings. And he was not in the room where we used to play the lyre. The trunk that had once kept our instruments sat forlorn in the room's center.

He was not outside, either, in the trees he and I had climbed. Or by the sea, on the jutting rocks where he waited for his mother. Nor on the practice field where men sweated through drills, clacking their wooden swords.

I do not need to say that my panic swelled, that it became a live thing, slippery and deaf to reason. My steps grew hurried; the kitchen, the basement, the storerooms with their amphorae of oil and wine. And still I did not find him.

It was midday when I sought out Peleus' room. It was a sign of the size of my unease that I went at all: I had never spoken to the old man alone before. The guards outside stopped me when I tried to enter. The king was at rest, they said. He was alone and would see no one.

"But is Achilles—" I gulped, trying not to make a spectacle of myself, to feed the curiosity I saw in their eyes. "Is the prince with him?"

"He is alone," one of them repeated.

I went to Phoinix next, the old counselor who had looked after Achilles when he was a boy. I was almost choking with fear as I walked to his stateroom, a modest square chamber at the palace's heart. He had clay tablets in front of him, and on them the men's marks from the night before, angular and crisscrossing, pledging their arms to the war against Troy.

"The prince Achilles—" I said. I spoke haltingly, my voice thick with panic. "I cannot find him."

He looked up with some surprise. He had not heard me come in the room; his hearing was poor, and his eyes when they met mine were rheumy and opaque with cataract.

"Peleus did not tell you then." His voice was soft.

"No." My tongue was like a stone in my mouth, so big I could barely speak around it.

"I'm sorry," he said kindly. "His mother has him. She took him last night as he was sleeping. They are gone, no one knows where."

Later I would see the red marks where my nails had dug through my palms. *No one knows where.* To Olympus perhaps, where I could never follow. To Africa, or India. To some village where I would not think to look.

Phoinix's gentle hands guided me back to my room. My mind twisted desperately from thought to thought. I would return to Chiron and seek counsel. I would walk the countryside, calling his name. She must have drugged him, or tricked him. He would not have gone willingly.

As I huddled in our empty room, I imagined it: the goddess leaning over us, cold and white beside the warmth of our sleeping bodies. Her fingernails prick into his skin as she lifts him, her neck is silvery in the window's moonlight. His body lolls on her shoulder, sleeping or spelled. She carries him from me as a soldier might carry a corpse. She is strong; it takes only one of her hands to keep him from falling.

I did not wonder why she had taken him. I knew. She had wanted to separate us, the first chance she had, as soon as we were out of the mountains. I was angry at how foolish we had been. Of course she would do this; why had I thought we would be safe? That Chiron's protection would extend here, where it never had before.

She would take him to the caves of the sea and teach him contempt for mortals. She would feed him with the food of the gods and burn his human blood from his veins. She would shape him into a figure meant to be painted on vases, to be sung of in songs, to fight against Troy. I imagined him in black armor, a dark helmet that left him nothing but eyes, bronze greaves that covered his feet. He stands with a spear in each hand and does not know me.

Time folded in on itself, closed over me, buried me. Outside my window, the moon moved through her shapes and came up full again. I slept little and ate less; grief pinned me to the bed like an anchor. It was only my pricking memory of Chiron that finally drove me forth. *You do not give up so easily as you once did.*

I went to Peleus. I knelt before him on a wool rug, woven bright with purple. He started to speak, but I was too quick for him. One of my hands went to clasp his knees, the other reached upwards, to seize his chin with my hand. The pose of supplication. It was a gesture I had seen many times, but had never made myself. I was under his protection now; he was bound to treat me fairly, by the law of the gods.

"Tell me where he is," I said.

He did not move. I could hear the muffled batter of his heart against his chest. I had not realized how intimate supplication was, how closely we would be pressed. His ribs were sharp beneath my cheek; the skin of his legs was soft and thin with age.

"I do not know," he said, and the words echoed down the chamber, stirring the guards. I felt their eyes on my back. Suppliants were rare in Phthia; Peleus was too good a king for such desperate measures.

I pulled at his chin, tugging his face to mine. He did not resist.

"I do not believe you," I said.

A moment passed.

"Leave us," he said. The words were for the guards. They shuffled their feet, but obeyed. We were alone.

He leaned forward, down to my ear. He whispered, "Scyros."

A place, an island. Achilles.

When I stood, my knees ached, as if I had been kneeling a long time. Perhaps I had. I do not know how many moments passed between us in that long hall of Phthian kings. Our eyes were level now, but he would not meet my gaze. He had answered me because he was a pious man, because I had asked him as a suppliant, because the gods demanded it. He would not have otherwise. There was a dullness in the air between us, and something heavy, like anger.

"I will need money," I told him. I do not know where these words came from. I had never spoken so before, to anyone. But I had nothing left to lose.

"Speak to Phoinix. He will give it to you."

I nodded my head, barely. I should have done much more. I should have knelt again and thanked him, rubbed my forehead on his expensive rug. I didn't. Peleus moved to stare out the open window; the sea was hidden by the house's curve, but we could both hear it, the distant hiss of waves against sand.

"You may go," he told me. He meant it to be cold, I think, and dismissive; a displeased king to his subject. But all I heard was his weariness.

I nodded once more and left.

THE GOLD THAT Phoinix gave me would have carried me to Scyros and back twice over. The ship's captain stared when I handed it to him. I saw his eyes flicking over it, weighing its worth, counting what it could buy him.

"You will take me?"

My eagerness displeased him. He did not like to see desperation in those who sought passage; haste and a free hand spoke of hidden crimes. But the gold was too much for him to object. He made a noise, grudging, of acceptance, and sent me to my berth.

I had never been at sea before and was surprised at how slow it was. The boat was a big-bellied trader, making its lazy rounds of the islands, sharing the fleece, oil, and carved furniture of the mainland with the more isolated kingdoms. Every night we put in at a different port to refill our water pots and unload our stores. During the days I stood at the ship's prow, watching the waves fall away from our black-tarred hull, waiting for the sight of land. At another time I would have been enchanted with it all: the names of the ship's parts, halyard, mast, stern; the color of the water; the scrubbed-clean smell of the winds. But I barely noticed these things. I thought only of the small island flung out somewhere in front of me, and the fair-haired boy I hoped I would find there.

THE BAY OF SCYROS was so small that I did not see it until we had swung around the rocky island's southern rim and were almost upon it. Our ship narrowly squeezed between its extending arms, and the sailors leaned over the sides to watch the rocks slide by, holding their breath. Once we were inside, the water was utterly calm, and the men had to row us the rest of the way. The confines were difficult to maneuver; I did not envy the captain's voyage out.

"We are here," he told me, sullenly. I was already walking for the gangway.

The cliff face rose sharply in front of me. There was a path of steps carved into the rock, coiling up to the palace, and I took them. At their top were scrubby trees and goats, and the palace, modest and dull, made half from stone and half from wood. If it had not been the only building in sight, I might not have known it for the king's home. I went to the door and entered.

The hall was narrow and dim, the air dingy with the smell of old dinners. At the far end two thrones sat empty. A few guards idled at tables, dicing. They looked up.

"Well?" one asked me.

"I am here to see King Lycomedes," I said. I lifted my chin, so they would know I was a man of some importance. I had worn the finest tunic I could find—one of Achilles'.

"I'll go," another one said to his fellows. He dropped his dice with a clatter and slumped out of the hall. Peleus would never have allowed such disaffection; he kept his men well and expected much from them in return. Everything about the room seemed threadbare and gray.

The man reappeared. "Come," he said. I followed him, and

my heart picked up. I had thought long about what I would say. I was ready.

"In here." He gestured to an open door, then turned to go back to his dice.

I stepped through the doorway. Inside, seated before the wispy remains of a fire, sat a young woman.

"I am the princess Deidameia," she announced. Her voice was bright and almost childishly loud, startling after the dullness of the hall. She had a tipped-up nose and a sharp face, like a fox. She was pretty, and she knew it.

I summoned my manners and bowed. "I am a stranger, come for a kindness from your father."

"Why not a kindness from me?" She smiled, tilting her head. She was surprisingly small; I guessed she would barely be up to my chest if she stood. "My father is old and ill. You may address your petition to me, and I will answer it." She affected a regal pose, carefully positioned so the window lit her from behind.

"I am looking for my friend."

"Oh?" Her eyebrow lifted. "And who is your friend?"

"A young man," I said, carefully.

"I see. We do have some of those here." Her tone was playful, full of itself. Her dark hair fell down her back in thick curls. She tossed her head a little, making it swing, and smiled at me again. "Perhaps you'd like to start with telling me your name?"

"Chironides," I said. *Son of Chiron.*

She wrinkled her nose at the name's strangeness.

"Chironides. And?"

"I am seeking a friend of mine, who would have arrived here perhaps a month ago. He is from Phthia."

Something flashed in her eyes, or maybe I imagined it did. "And why do you seek him?" she asked. I thought that her tone was not so light as it had been.

"I have a message for him." I wished very much that I had been led to the old and ill king, rather than her. Her face was like quicksilver, always racing to something new. She unsettled me.

"Hmmm. A message." She smiled coyly, tapped her chin with a painted fingertip. "A message for a friend. And why should I tell you if I know this young man or not?"

"Because you are a powerful princess, and I am your humble suitor." I knelt.

This pleased her. "Well, perhaps I do know such a man, and perhaps I do not. I will have to think on it. You will stay for dinner and await my decision. If you are lucky, I may even dance for you, with my women." She cocked her head, suddenly. "You have heard of Deidameia's women?"

"I am sorry to say that I have not."

She made a moue of displeasure. "All the kings send their daughters here for fostering. Everyone knows that but you."

I bowed my head, sorrowfully. "I have spent my time in the mountains and have not seen much of the world."

She frowned a little. Then flicked her hand at the door. "Till dinner, Chironides."

I spent the afternoon in the dusty courtyard grounds. The palace sat on the island's highest point, held up against the blue of the sky, and the view was pretty, despite the shabbiness. As I sat, I tried to remember all that I had heard of Lycomedes. He was known to be kind enough, but a weak king, of limited resources. Euboia to the west and Ionia to the east had long eyed his lands;

soon enough one of them would bring war, despite the inhospi-
table shoreline. If they heard a woman ruled here, it would be all
the sooner.

When the sun had set, I returned to the hall. Torches had been
lit, but they only seemed to increase the gloom. Deidameia, a gold
circlet gleaming in her hair, led an old man into the room. He was
hunched over, and so draped with furs that I could not tell where
his body began. She settled him on a throne and gestured grandly
to a servant. I stood back, among the guards and a few other men
whose function was not immediately apparent. Counselors? Cousins? They had the same worn appearance as everything else in the
room. Only Deidameia seemed to escape it, with her blooming
cheeks and glossy hair.

A servant motioned to the cracked benches and tables, and I
sat. The king and the princess did not join us; they remained on
their thrones at the hall's other end. Food arrived, hearty enough,
but my eyes kept returning to the front of the room. I could not
tell if I should make myself known. Had she forgotten me?

But then she stood and turned her face towards our tables.
"Stranger from Pelion," she called, "you will never again be able
to say that you have not heard of Deidameia's women." Another
gesture, with a braceleted hand. A group of women entered, perhaps two dozen, speaking softly to each other, their hair covered
and bound back in cloth. They stood in the empty central area
that I saw now was a dancing circle. A few men took out flutes and
drums, one a lyre. Deidameia did not seem to expect a response
from me, or even to care if I had heard. She stepped down from
the throne's dais and went to the women, claiming one of the taller
ones as a partner.

The music began. The steps were intricate, and the girls moved through them featly. In spite of myself, I was impressed. Their dresses swirled, and jewelry swung around their wrists and ankles as they spun. They tossed their heads as they whirled, like high-spirited horses.

Deidameia was the most beautiful, of course. With her golden crown and unbound hair, she drew the eye, flashing her wrists prettily in the air. Her face was flushed with pleasure, and as I watched her, I saw her brightness grow brighter still. She was beaming at her partner, almost flirting. Now she would duck her eyes at the woman, now step close as if to tease with her touch. Curious, I craned my head to see the woman she danced with, but the crowd of white dresses obscured her.

The music trilled to an end, and the dancers finished. Deidameia led them forward in a line to receive our praise. Her partner stood beside her, head bowed. She curtsied with the rest and looked up.

I made some sort of sound, the breath jumping in my throat. It was quiet, but it was enough. The girl's eyes flickered to me.

Several things happened at once then. Achilles—for it was Achilles—dropped Deidameia's hand and flung himself joyously at me, knocking me backwards with the force of his embrace. Deidameia screamed "Pyrrha!" and burst into tears. Lycomedes, who was not so far sunk into dotage as his daughter had led me to believe, stood.

"Pyrrha, what is the meaning of this?"

I barely heard. Achilles and I clutched each other, almost incoherent with relief.

"My mother," he whispered, "my mother, she—"

"Pyrrha!" Lycomedes' voice carried the length of the hall, rising over his daughter's noisy sobs. He was talking to Achilles, I realized. *Pyrrha*. Fire-hair.

Achilles ignored him; Deidameia wailed louder. The king, showing a judiciousness that surprised me, threw his eye upon the rest of his court, women and men both. "Out," he ordered. They obeyed reluctantly, trailing their glances behind them.

"Now." Lycomedes came forward, and I saw his face for the first time. His skin was yellowed, and his graying beard looked like dirty fleece; yet his eyes were sharp enough. "Who is this man, Pyrrha?"

"No one!" Deidameia had seized Achilles' arm, was tugging at it.

At the same time, Achilles answered coolly, "My husband."

I closed my mouth quickly, so I did not gape like a fish.

"He is not! That's not true!" Deidameia's voice rose high, startling the birds roosting in the rafters. A few feathers wafted down to the floor. She might have said more, but she was crying too hard to speak clearly.

Lycomedes turned to me as if for refuge, man to man. "Sir, is this true?"

Achilles was squeezing my fingers.

"Yes," I said.

"No!" the princess shrieked.

Achilles ignored her pulling at him, and gracefully inclined his head at Lycomedes. "My husband has come for me, and now I may leave your court. Thank you for your hospitality." Achilles curtsied. I noted with an idle, dazed part of my mind that he did it remarkably well.

Lycomedes held up a hand to prevent us. "We should consult your mother first. It was she who gave you to me to foster. Does she know of this husband?"

"No!" Deidameia said again.

"Daughter!" This was Lycomedes, frowning in a way that was not unlike his daughter's habit. "Stop this scene. Release Pyrrha."

Her face was blotchy and swollen with tears, her chest heaving. "No!" She turned to Achilles. "You are lying! You have betrayed me! Monster! *Apathes!*" *Heartless*.

Lycomedes froze. Achilles' fingers tightened on mine. In our language, words come in different genders. She had used the masculine form.

"What was that?" said Lycomedes, slowly.

Deidameia's face had gone pale, but she lifted her chin in defiance, and her voice did not waver.

"He is a *man*," she said. And then, "We are married."

"What!" Lycomedes clutched his throat.

I could not speak. Achilles' hand was the only thing that kept me to earth.

"Do not do this," Achilles said to her. "Please."

It seemed to enrage her. "I *will* do it!" She turned to her father. "You are a fool! I'm the only one who knew! I knew!" She struck her chest in emphasis. "And now I'll tell everyone. Achilles!" She screamed as if she would force his name through the stout stone walls, up to the gods themselves. "Achilles! Achilles! I'll tell everyone!"

"You will not." The words were cold and knife-sharp; they parted the princess's shouts easily.

I know that voice. I turned.

Thetis stood in the doorway. Her face glowed, the white-blue of the flame's center. Her eyes were black, gashed into her skin, and she stood taller than I had ever seen her. Her hair was as sleek as it always was, and her dress as beautiful, but there was something about her that seemed wild, as if an invisible wind whipped around her. She looked like a Fury, the demons that come for men's blood. I felt my scalp trying to climb off my head; even Deidameia dropped into silence.

We stood there a moment, facing her. Then Achilles reached up and tore the veil from his hair. He seized the neckline of his dress and ripped it down the front, exposing his chest beneath. The firelight played over his skin, warming it to gold.

"No more, Mother," he said.

Something rippled beneath her features, a spasm of sorts. I was half afraid she would strike him down. But she only watched him with those restless black eyes.

Achilles turned then, to Lycomedes. "My mother and I have deceived you, for which I offer my apologies. I am the prince Achilles, son of Peleus. She did not wish me to go to war and hid me here, as one of your foster daughters."

Lycomedes swallowed and did not speak.

"We will leave now," Achilles said gently.

The words shook Deidameia from her trance. "No," she said, voice rising again. "You cannot. Your mother said the words over us, and we are married. You are my husband."

Lycomedes' breath rasped loudly in the chamber; his eyes were for Thetis alone. "Is this true?" he asked.

"It is," the goddess answered.

Something fell from a long height in my chest. Achilles turned to me, as if he would speak. But his mother was faster.

"You are bound to us now, King Lycomedes. You will continue to shelter Achilles here. You will say nothing of who he is. In return, your daughter will one day be able to claim a famous husband." Her eyes went to a point above Deidameia's head, then back. She added, "It is better than she would have done."

Lycomedes rubbed at his neck, as if he would smooth its wrinkles. "I have no choice," he said. "As you know."

"What if I will not be silent?" Deidameia's color was high. "You have ruined me, you and your son. I have lain with him, as you told me to, and my honor is gone. I will claim him now, before the court, as recompense."

I have lain with him.

"You are a foolish girl," Thetis said. Each word fell like an axe blade, sharp and severing. "Poor and ordinary, an expedient only. You do not deserve my son. You will keep your peace or I will keep it for you."

Deidameia stepped backwards, her eyes wide, her lips gone white. Her hands were trembling. She lifted one to her stomach and clutched the fabric of her dress there, as if to steady herself. Outside the palace, beyond the cliffs, we could hear huge waves breaking on the rocks, dashing the shoreline to pieces.

"I am pregnant," the princess whispered.

I was watching Achilles when she said it, and I saw the horror on his face. Lycomedes made a noise of pain.

My chest felt hollowed, and egg-shell thin. *Enough.* Perhaps I said it, perhaps I only thought it. I let go of Achilles' hand and strode to the door. Thetis must have moved aside for me; I would have run into her if she had not. Alone, I stepped into the darkness.

"WAIT!" ACHILLES SHOUTED. It took him longer to reach me than it should have, I noted with detachment. *The dress must be tangling his legs.* He caught up to me, seized my arm.

"Let go," I said.

"Please, wait. Please, let me explain. I did not want to do it. My mother—" He was breathless, almost panting. I had never seen him so upset.

"She led the girl to my room. She made me. I did not want to. My mother said—she said—" He was stumbling over his words. "She said that if I did as she said, she would tell you where I was."

What had Deidameia thought would happen, I wondered, when she had her women dance for me? Had she really thought I would not know him? I could recognize him by touch alone, by smell; I would know him blind, by the way his breaths came and his feet struck the earth. I would know him in death, at the end of the world.

"Patroclus." He cupped my cheek with his hand. "Do you hear me? Please, say something."

I could not stop imagining her skin beside his, her swelling breasts and curving hips. I remembered the long days I grieved for him, my hands empty and idle, plucking the air like birds peck at dry earth.

"Patroclus?"

"You did it for nothing."

He flinched at the emptiness of my voice. But how else was I to sound?

"What do you mean?"

"Your mother did not tell me where you were. It was Peleus."

His face had gone pale, bled dry. "She did not tell you?"

"No. Did you truly expect she would?" My voice cut harder than I meant it to.

"Yes," he whispered.

There were a thousand things I might have said, to reproach him for his naïveté. He had always trusted too easily; he had had so little in his life to fear or suspect. In the days before our friendship, I had almost hated him for this, and some old spark of that flared in me, trying to relight. Anyone else would have known that Thetis acted for her own purposes only. How could he be so foolish? The angry words pricked in my mouth.

But when I tried to speak them, I found I could not. His cheeks were flushed with shame, and the skin beneath his eyes was weary. His trust was a part of him, as much as his hands or his miraculous feet. And despite my hurt, I would not wish to see it gone, to see him as uneasy and fearful as the rest of us, for any price.

He was watching me closely, reading my face over and over, like a priest searching the auguries for an answer. I could see the slight line in his forehead that meant utmost concentration.

Something shifted in me then, like the frozen surface of the Apidanos in spring. I had seen the way he looked at Deidameia; or rather the way he did not. It was the same way he had looked at the boys in Phthia, blank and unseeing. He had never, not once, looked at me that way.

"Forgive me," he said again. "I did not want it. It was not you. I did not—I did not like it."

Hearing it soothed the last of the jagged grief that had begun when Deidameia shouted his name. My throat was thick with the beginning of tears. "There is nothing to forgive," I said.

LATER THAT EVENING we returned to the palace. The great hall was dark, its fire burned to embers. Achilles had repaired his dress as best he could, but it still gaped to the waist; he held it closed in case we met a lingering guard.

The voice came from the shadows, startling us.

"You have returned." The moonlight did not quite reach the thrones, but we saw the outline of a man there, thick with furs. His voice seemed deeper than it had before, heavier.

"We have," Achilles said. I could hear the slight hesitation before he answered. He had not expected to face the king again so soon.

"Your mother is gone, I do not know where." The king paused, as if awaiting a response.

Achilles said nothing.

"My daughter, your wife, is in her room crying. She hopes you will come to her."

I felt the flinch of Achilles' guilt. His words came out stiffly; it was not a feeling he was used to.

"It is unfortunate that she hopes for this."

"It is indeed," Lycomedes said.

We stood in silence a moment. Then Lycomedes drew a weary breath. "I suppose that you want a room for your friend?"

"If you do not mind," Achilles said, carefully.

Lycomedes let out a soft laugh. "No, Prince Achilles, I do not mind." There was another silence. I heard the king lift a goblet, drink, replace it on the table.

"The child must have your name. You understand this?" This is what he had waited in the dark to say, beneath his furs, by the dying fire.

"I understand it," Achilles said quietly.

"And you swear it?"

There was a hairsbreadth of a pause. I pitied the old king. I was glad when Achilles said, "I swear it."

The old man made a sound like a sigh. But his words, when they came, were formal; he was a king again.

"Good night to you both."

We bowed and left him.

In the bowels of the palace, Achilles found a guard to show us to the guest quarters. The voice he used was high and fluting, his girl's voice. I saw the guard's eyes flicker over him, lingering on the torn edges of the dress, his disheveled hair. He grinned at me with all his teeth.

"Right away, mistress," he said.

IN THE STORIES, the gods have the power to delay the moon's course if they wish, to spin a single night the length of many. Such was this night, a bounty of hours that never ran dry. We drank deeply, thirsty for all that we had missed in the weeks we were separated. It was not until the sky began to blanch at last to gray that I remembered what he had said to Lycomedes in the hall. It had been forgotten amidst Deidameia's pregnancy, his marriage, our reunion.

"Your mother was trying to hide you from the war?"

He nodded. "She does not want me to go to Troy."

"Why?" I had always thought she wanted him to fight.

"I don't know. She says I'm too young. Not yet, she says."

"And it was her idea—?" I gestured at the remnants of the dress.

"Of course. I wouldn't have done it myself." He made a face and yanked at his hair, hanging still in its womanly curls. An irritant, but not a crippling shame, as it would have been to another boy. He did not fear ridicule; he had never known it. "Anyway, it is only until the army leaves."

My mind struggled with this.

"So, truly, it was not because of me? That she took you?"

"Deidameia was because of you, I think." He stared at his hands a moment. "But the rest was the war."

CHAPTER THIRTEEN

THE NEXT DAYS PASSED QUIETLY. WE TOOK MEALS IN our room and spent long hours away from the palace, exploring the island, seeking what shade there was beneath the scruffy trees. We had to be careful; Achilles could not be seen moving too quickly, climbing too skillfully, holding a spear. But we were not followed, and there were many places where he could safely let his disguise drop.

On the far side of the island there was a deserted stretch of beach, rock-filled but twice the size of our running tracks. Achilles made a sound of delight when he saw it, and tore off his dress I watched him race across it, as swiftly as if the beach had been flat. "Count for me," he shouted, over his shoulder. I did, tapping against the sand to keep the time.

"How many?" he called, from the beach's end.

"Thirteen," I called back.

"I'm just warming up," he said.

The next time it was eleven. The last time it was nine. He sat down next to me, barely winded, his cheeks flushed with joy. He had told me of his days as a woman, the long hours of enforced tedium, with only the dances for relief. Free now, he stretched his muscles like one of Pelion's mountain cats, luxuriant in his own strength.

In the evenings, though, we had to return to the great hall. Reluctant, Achilles would put on his dress and smooth back his hair. Often he bound it up in cloth, as he had that first night; golden hair was uncommon enough to be remarked upon by the sailors and merchants who passed through our harbor. If their tales found the ears of someone clever enough—I did not like to think of it.

A table was set for us at the front of the hall near the thrones. We ate there, the four of us, Lycomedes, Deidameia, Achilles, and I. Sometimes we were joined by a counselor or two, sometimes not. These dinners were mostly silent; they were for form, to quell gossip and maintain the fiction of Achilles as my wife and the king's ward. Deidameia's eyes darted eagerly towards him, hoping he would look at her. But he never did. "Good evening," he would say, in his proper girl's voice, as we sat, but nothing more. His indifference was a palpable thing, and I saw her pretty face flinch through emotions of shame and hurt and anger. She kept looking to her father, as if she hoped he might intervene. But Lycomedes put bite after bite in his mouth and said nothing.

Sometimes she saw me watching her; her face would grow hard then, and her eyes would narrow. She put a hand on her belly, possessively, as if to ward off some spell I might cast. Perhaps she thought I was mocking her, flourishing my triumph. Perhaps she thought I hated her. She did not know that I almost asked him, a hundred times, to be a little kinder to her. *You do not have to humiliate her so thoroughly*, I thought. But it was not kindness he lacked; it was interest. His gaze passed over her as if she were not there.

Once she tried to speak to him, her voice trembling with hope. "Are you well, Pyrrha?"

He continued eating, in his elegant swift bites. He and I had planned to take spears to the far side of the island after dinner and catch fish by moonlight. He was eager to be gone. I had to nudge him, beneath the table.

"What is it?" he asked me.

"The princess wants to know if you are well."

"Oh." He glanced at her briefly, then back to me. "I am well," he said.

AS THE DAYS WORE ON, Achilles took to waking early, so that he might practice with spears before the sun rose high. We had hidden weapons in a distant grove, and he would exercise there before returning to womanhood in the palace. Sometimes he might visit his mother afterwards, sitting on one of Scyros' jagged rocks, dangling his feet into the sea.

It was one of these mornings, when Achilles was gone, that there was a loud rap on my door.

"Yes?" I called. But the guards were already stepping inside. They were more formal than I had ever seen them, carrying spears and standing at attention. It was strange to see them without their dice.

"You're to come with us," one of them said.

"Why?" I was barely out of bed and still bleary with sleep.

"The princess ordered it." A guard took each of my arms

and towed me to the door. When I stuttered a protest, the first guard leaned towards me, his eyes on mine. "It will be better if you go quietly." He drew his thumb over his spearpoint in theatrical menace.

I did not really think they would hurt me, but neither did I want to be dragged through the halls of the palace. "All right," I said.

THE NARROW CORRIDORS where they led me I had never visited before. They were the women's quarters, twisting off from the main rooms, a beehive of narrow cells where Deidameia's foster sisters slept and lived. I heard laughter from behind the doors, and the endless *shush-shush* of the shuttle. Achilles said that the sun did not come through the windows here, and there was no breeze. He had spent nearly two months in them; I could not imagine it.

At last we came to a large door, cut from finer wood than the rest. The guard knocked on it, opened it, and pushed me through. I heard it close firmly behind me.

Inside, Deidameia was seated primly on a leather-covered chair, regarding me. There was a table beside her, and a small stool at her feet; otherwise the room was empty.

She must have planned this, I realized. She knew that Achilles was away.

There was no place for me to sit, so I stood. The floor was cold stone, and my feet were bare. There was a second, smaller door; it led to her bedroom, I guessed.

She watched me looking, her eyes bright as a bird's. There was nothing clever to say, so I said something foolish.

"You wanted to speak with me."

She sniffed a little, with contempt. "Yes, Patroclus. I wanted to speak with you."

I waited, but she said nothing more, only studied me, a finger tapping the arm of her chair. Her dress was looser than usual; she did not have it tied across the waist as she often did, to show her figure. Her hair was unbound and held back at the temples with carved ivory combs. She tilted her head and smiled at me.

"You are not even handsome, that is the funny thing. You are quite ordinary."

She had her father's way of pausing as if she expected a reply. I felt myself flushing. *I must say something.* I cleared my throat.

She glared at me. "I have not given you leave to speak." She held my gaze a moment, as if to make sure that I would not disobey, then continued. "I think it's funny. Look at you." She rose, and her quick steps ate up the space between us. "Your neck is short. Your chest is thin as a boy's." She gestured at me with disdainful fingers. "And your face." She grimaced. "Hideous. My women quite agree. Even my father agrees." Her pretty red lips parted to show her white teeth. It was the closest I had ever been to her. I could smell something sweet, like acanthus flower; close up, I could see that her hair was not just black, but shot through with shifting colors of rich brown.

"Well? What do you say?" Her hands were on her hips.

"You have not given me leave to speak," I said.

Anger flashed over her face. "Don't be an idiot," she spat at me.

"I wasn't—"

She slapped me. Her hand was small but carried surprising force. It turned my head to the side roughly. The skin stung, and my lip throbbed sharply where she had caught it with a ring. I had not been struck like this since I was a child. Boys were not usually slapped, but a father might do it to show contempt. Mine had. It shocked me; I could not have spoken even if I had known what to say.

She bared her teeth at me, as if daring me to strike her in return. When she saw I would not, her face twisted with triumph. "Coward. As craven as you are ugly. And half-moron besides, I hear. I do not understand it! It makes no sense that he should—" She stopped abruptly, and the corner of her mouth tugged down, as if caught by a fisherman's hook. She turned her back to me and was silent. A moment passed. I could hear the sound of her breaths, drawn slowly, so I would not guess she was crying. I knew the trick. I had done it myself.

"I hate you," she said, but her voice was thick and there was no force in it. A sort of pity rose in me, cooling the heat of my cheeks. I remembered how hard a thing indifference was to bear.

I heard her swallow, and her hand moved swiftly to her face, as if to wipe away tears. "I'm leaving tomorrow," she said. "That should make you happy. My father wants me to begin my confinement early. He says it would bring shame upon me for the pregnancy to be seen, before it was known I was married."

Confinement. I heard the bitterness in her voice when she said it. Some small house, at the edge of Lycomedes' land. She would not be able to dance or speak with companions there. She would be alone, with a servant and her growing belly.

"I'm sorry," I said.

She did not answer. I watched the soft heaving of her back beneath the white gown. I took a step towards her, then stopped. I had thought to touch her, to smooth her hair in comfort. But it would not be comfort, from me. My hand fell back to my side.

We stood there like that for some time, the sound of our breaths filling the chamber. When she turned, her face was ruddy from crying.

"Achilles does not regard me." Her voice trembled a little. "Even though I bear his child and am his wife. Do you—know why this is so?"

It was a child's question, like why the rain falls or why the sea's motion never ceases. I felt older than her, though I was not.

"I do not know," I said softly.

Her face twisted. "That's a lie. You're the reason. You will sail with him, and I will be left here."

I knew something of what it was to be alone. Of how another's good fortune pricked like a goad. But there was nothing I could do.

"I should go," I said, as gently as I could.

"No!" She moved quickly to block my way. Her words tumbled out. "You cannot. I will call the guards if you try. I will—I will say you attacked me."

Sorrow for her dragged at me, bearing me down. Even if she called them, even if they believed her, they could not help her. I was the companion of Achilles and invulnerable.

My feelings must have shown on my face; she recoiled from me as if stung, and the heat sparked in her again.

"You were angry that he married me, that he lay with me. You were jealous. You should be." Her chin lifted, as it used to. "It was not just once."

It was twice. Achilles had told me. She thought that she had power to drive a wedge between us, but she had nothing.

"I'm sorry," I said again. I had nothing better to say. He did not love her; he never would.

As if she heard my thought, her face crumpled. Her tears fell on the floor, turning the gray stone black, drop by drop.

"Let me get your father," I said. "Or one of your women."

She looked up at me. "Please—" she whispered. "Please do not leave."

She was shivering, like something just born. Always before, her hurts had been small, and there had been someone to offer her comfort. Now there was only this room, the bare walls and single chair, the closet of her grief.

Almost unwillingly, I stepped towards her. She gave a small sigh, like a sleepy child, and drooped gratefully into the circle of my arms. Her tears bled through my tunic; I held the curves of her waist, felt the warm, soft skin of her arms. He had held her just like this, perhaps. But Achilles seemed a long way off; his brightness had no place in this dull, weary room. Her face, hot as if with fever, pressed against my chest. All I could see of her was the top of her head, the whorl and tangle of her shining dark hair, the pale scalp beneath.

After a time, her sobs subsided, and she drew me closer. I felt her hands stroking my back, the length of her body pressing to mine. At first I did not understand. Then I did.

"You do not want this," I said. I made to step back, but she held me too tightly.

"I do." Her eyes had an intensity to them that almost frightened me.

"Deidameia." I tried to summon the voice I had used to make Peleus yield. "The guards are outside. You must not—"

But she was calm now, and sure. "They will not disturb us."

I swallowed, my throat dry with panic. "Achilles will be looking for me."

She smiled sadly. "He will not look here." She took my hand. "Come," she said. And drew me through her bedroom's door.

Achilles had told me about their nights together when I asked. It had not been awkward for him to do so—nothing was forbidden between us. Her body, he said, was soft and small as a child's. She had come to his cell at night with his mother and lain beside him on the bed. He had feared he would hurt her; it had been swift, and neither spoke. He floundered as he tried to describe the heavy, thick smell, the wetness between her legs. "Greasy," he said, "like oil." When I pressed him further, he shook his head. "I cannot remember, really. It was dark, and I could not see. I wanted it to be over." He stroked my cheek. "I missed you."

The door closed behind us, and we were alone in a modest room. The walls were hung with tapestries, and the floor was thick with sheepskin rugs. There was a bed, pushed against the window, to catch the hint of breeze.

She pulled her dress over her head, and dropped it on the floor. "Do you think I am beautiful?" she asked me.

I was grateful for a simple answer. "Yes," I said. Her body was small and delicately made, with just the barest rise of belly where the child grew. My eyes were drawn down to what I had never seen before, a small furred area, the dark hairs spreading lightly upwards. She saw me looking. Reaching for my hand she guided me to that place, which radiated heat like the embers of a fire.

The skin that slipped against my fingers was warm and delicate, so fragile I was almost afraid I would tear it with my touch.

My other hand reached up to stroke her cheek, to trace the softness beneath her eyes. The look in them was terrible to see: there
was no hope or pleasure, only determination.

Almost, I fled. But I could not bear to see her face broken open
with more sorrow, more disappointment—another boy who could
not give her what she wanted. So I allowed her hands, fumbling
a little, to draw me to the bed, to guide me between her thighs,
where tender skin parted, weeping slow warm drops. I felt resistance and would have drawn back, but she shook her head sharply.
Her small face was tight with concentration, her jaw set as if
against pain. It was a relief for us both when at last the skin eased,
gave way. When I slipped into that sheathing warmth within her.

I will not say I was not aroused. A slow climbing tension
moved through me. It was a strange, drowsy feeling, so different
from my sharp, sure desires for Achilles. She seemed hurt by this,
my heavy-lidded repose. *More indifference.* And so I let myself
move, made sounds of pleasure, pressed my chest against hers as if
in passion, flattening her soft, small breasts beneath me.

She was pleased then, suddenly fierce, pulling and pushing me
harder and faster, her eyes lighting in triumph at the changes in
my breath. And then, at the slow rising of tide inside me, her legs,
light but firm, wrapped around my back, bucking me into her,
drawing out the spasm of my pleasure.

Afterwards we lay breathless, side by side but not touching.
Her face was shadowed and distant, her posture strangely stiff. My
mind was still muddied from climax, but I reached to hold her. I
could offer her this, at least.

But she drew away from me and stood, her eyes wary; the skin
beneath them was dark as bruises. She turned to dress, and her

round heart-shaped buttocks stared at me like a reproach. I did not understand what she had wanted; I only knew I had not given it. I stood and pulled on my tunic. I would have touched her, stroked her face, but her eyes warned me away, sharp and full. She held open the door. Hopelessly, I stepped over the threshold.

"Wait." Her voice sounded raw. I turned. "Tell him good-bye," she said. And then closed the door, dark and thick between us.

WHEN I FOUND ACHILLES again, I pressed myself to him in relief at the joy between us, at being released from her sadness and hurt.

Later, I almost convinced myself it had not happened, that it had been a vivid dream, drawn from his descriptions and too much imagination. But that is not the truth.

CHAPTER FOURTEEN

D
EIDAMEIA LEFT THE NEXT MORNING, AS SHE HAD SAID she would. "She is visiting an aunt," Lycomedes told the court at breakfast, his voice flat. If there were questions, no one dared to ask them. She would be gone until the child was born, and Achilles could be named as father.

The weeks that passed now felt curiously suspended. Achilles and I spent as much time as possible away from the palace, and our joy, so explosive at our reunion, had been replaced with impatience. We wanted to leave, to return to our lives on Pelion, or in Phthia. We felt furtive and guilty with the princess gone; the court's eyes on us had sharpened, grown uncomfortable. Lycomedes frowned whenever he saw us.

And then there was the war. Even here, in far-off, forgotten Scyros, news came of it. Helen's former suitors had honored their vow, and Agamemnon's army was rich with princely blood. It was said that he had done what no man before him could: united our fractious kingdoms with common cause. I remembered him—a grim-faced shadow, shaggy as a bear. To my nine-year-old self, his brother Menelaus had been much the more memorable of the two, with his red hair and merry voice. But Agamemnon was older, and his armies the larger; he would lead the expedition to Troy.

It was morning, and late winter, though it did not seem it. So far south, the leaves did not fall and no frost pinched the morning air. We lingered in a rock cleft that looked over the span of horizon, watching idly for ships or the gray flash of dolphin back. We hurled pebbles from the cliff, leaning over to watch them skitter down the rock-face. We were high enough that we could not hear the sound of them breaking on the rocks below.

"I wish I had your mother's lyre," he said.

"Me too." But it was in Phthia, left behind with everything else. We were silent a moment, remembering the sweetness of its strings.

He leaned forward. "What is that?"

I squinted. The sun sat differently on the horizon now that it was winter, seeming to slant into my eyes from every angle.

"I cannot tell." I stared at the haze where the sea vanished into the sky. There was a distant smudge that might have been a ship, or a trick of the sun on the water. "If it's a ship, there will be news," I said, with a familiar clutch in my stomach. Each time I feared word would come of a search for the last of Helen's suitors, the oath-breaker. I was young then; it did not occur to me that no leader would wish it known that some had not obeyed his summons.

"It is a ship, for certain," Achilles said. The smudge was closer now; the ship must be moving very quickly. The bright colors of the sail resolved themselves moment by moment out of the sea's blue-gray.

"Not a trader," Achilles commented. Trading ships used white sails only, practical and cheap; a man needed to be rich indeed to waste his dye on sailcloth. Agamemnon's messengers had crimson and purple sails, symbols stolen from eastern royalty. This ship's sails were yellow, whorled with patterns of black.

"Do you know the design?" I asked.

Achilles shook his head.

We watched the ship skirt the narrow mouth of Scyros' bay and beach itself on the sandy shore. A rough-cut stone anchor was heaved overboard, the gangway lowered. We were too far to see much of the men on its deck, beyond dark heads.

We had stayed longer than we should have. Achilles stood and tucked his wind-loosened hair back beneath its kerchief. My hands busied themselves with the folds of his dress, settling them more gracefully across his shoulders, fastening the belts and laces; it was barely strange anymore to see him in it. When we were finished, Achilles bent towards me for a kiss. His lips on mine were soft, and stirred me. He caught the expression in my eyes and smiled. "Later," he promised me, then turned and went back down the path to the palace. He would go to the women's quarters and wait there, amidst the looms and the dresses, until the messenger was gone.

The hairline cracks of a headache were beginning behind my eyes; I went to my bedroom, cool and dark, its shutters barring the midday sun, and slept.

A knock woke me. A servant perhaps, or Lycomedes. My eyes still closed, I called, "Come in."

"It's rather too late for that," a voice answered. The tone was amused, dry as driftwood. I opened my eyes and sat up. A man stood inside the open door. He was sturdy and muscular, with a close-cropped philosopher's beard, dark brown tinged with faintest red. He smiled at me, and I saw the lines where other smiles had been. It was an easy motion for him, swift and practiced. Something about it tugged at my memory.

"I'm sorry if I disturbed you." His voice was pleasant, well modulated.

"It's all right," I said, carefully.

"I was hoping I might have a word with you. Do you mind if I sit?" He gestured towards a chair with a wide palm. The request was politely made; despite my unease, I could find no reason to refuse him.

I nodded, and he drew the chair to him. His hands were callused and rough; they would not have looked out of place holding a plow, yet his manner bespoke nobility. To stall I stood and opened the shutters, hoping my brain would shake off its sleepy fog. I could think of no reason that any man would want a moment of my time. Unless he had come to claim me for my oath. I turned to face him.

"Who are you?" I asked.

The man laughed. "A good question. I've been terribly rude, barging into your room like this. I am one of the great king Agamemnon's captains. I travel the islands and speak to promising young men, such as yourself"—he inclined his head towards me—"about joining our army against Troy. Have you heard of the war?"

"I have heard of it," I said.

"Good." He smiled and stretched his feet in front of him. The fading light fell on his legs, revealing a pink scar that seamed the brown flesh of his right calf from ankle to knee. *A pink scar.* My stomach dropped as if I leaned over Scyros' highest cliff, with nothing beneath me but the long fall to the sea. He was older now, and larger, come into the full flush of his strength. *Odysseus.*

He said something, but I did not hear it. I was back in Tyndareus' hall, remembering his clever dark eyes that missed nothing. Did he know me? I stared at his face, but saw only a slightly puzzled expectation. *He is waiting for an answer.* I forced down my fear.

"I'm sorry," I said. "I did not hear you. What?"

"Are you interested? In joining us to fight?"

"I don't think you'd want me. I'm not a very good soldier."

His mouth twisted wryly. "It's funny—no one seems to be, when I come calling." His tone was light; it was a shared joke, not a reproach. "What's your name?"

I tried to sound as casual as he. "Chironides."

"Chironides," he repeated. I watched him for disbelief, but saw none. The tension in my muscles ebbed a little. Of course he did not recognize me. I had changed much since I was nine.

"Well, Chironides, Agamemnon promises gold and honor for all who fight for him. The campaign looks to be short; we will have you back home by next fall. I will be here for a few days, and I hope you will consider it." He dropped his hands to his knees with finality, and stood.

"That's it?" I had expected persuasion and pressure, a long evening of it.

He laughed, almost affectionately. "Yes, that's it. I assume I will see you at dinner?"

I nodded. He made as if to go, then stopped. "You know, it's funny; I keep thinking I've seen you before."

"I doubt it," I said quickly. "I don't recognize you."

He studied me a moment, then shrugged, giving up. "I must be confusing you with another young man. You know what they say. The older you get, the less you remember." He scratched his beard thoughtfully. "Who's your father? Perhaps it's him I know."

"I am an exile."

He made a sympathetic face. "I'm sorry to hear it. Where were you from?"

"The coast."

"North or south?"

"South."

He shook his head ruefully. "I would have sworn you were from the north. Somewhere near Thessaly, say. Or Phthia. You have the same roundness to your vowels that they do."

I swallowed. In Phthia, the consonants were harder than elsewhere, and the vowels wider. It had sounded ugly to me, until I heard Achilles speak. I had not realized how much of it I had adopted.

"I—did not know that," I mumbled. My heart was beating very fast. If only he would leave.

"Useless information is my curse, I'm afraid." He was amused again, that slight smile. "Now don't forget to come find me if you decide you want to join us. Or if you happen to know of any other likely young men I should speak to." The door snicked shut behind him.

THE DINNER BELL had rung and the corridors were busy with servants carrying platters and chairs. When I stepped into the hall, my visitor was already there, standing with Lycomedes and another man.

"Chironides," Lycomedes acknowledged my arrival. "This is Odysseus, ruler of Ithaca."

"Thank goodness for hosts," Odysseus said. "I realized after I left that I never told you my name."

And I did not ask because I knew. It had been a mistake but was not irreparable. I widened my eyes. "You're a king?" I dropped to a knee, in my best startled obeisance.

"Actually, he's only a prince," a voice drawled. "I'm the one who's a king." I looked up to meet the third man's eyes; they were a brown so light it was almost yellow, and keen. His beard was short and black, and it emphasized the slanting planes of his face.

"This is Lord Diomedes, King of Argos," Lycomedes said. "A comrade of Odysseus." And another suitor of Helen's, though I remembered no more than his name.

"Lord." I bowed to him. I did not have time to fear recognition—he had already turned away.

"Well." Lycomedes gestured to the table. "Shall we eat?"

For dinner we were joined by several of Lycomedes' counselors, and I was glad to vanish among them. Odysseus and Diomedes largely ignored us, absorbed in talk with the king.

"And how is Ithaca?" Lycomedes asked politely.

"Ithaca is well, thank you," Odysseus answered. "I left my wife and son there, both in good health."

"Ask him about his wife," Diomedes said. "He loves to talk about her. Have you heard how he met her? It's his favorite story." There was a goading edge to his voice, barely sheathed. The men around me stopped eating, to watch.

Lycomedes looked between the two men, then ventured, "And how did you meet your wife, Prince of Ithaca?"

If Odysseus felt the tension, he did not show it. "You are kind to ask. When Tyndareus sought a husband for Helen, suitors came from every kingdom. I'm sure you remember."

"I was married already," Lycomedes said. "I did not go."

"Of course. And these were too young, I'm afraid." He tossed a smile at me, then turned back to the king.

"Of all these men, I was fortunate to arrive first. The king invited me to dine with the family: Helen; her sister, Clytemnestra; and their cousin Penelope."

"Invited," Diomedes scoffed. "Is that what they call crawling through the bracken to spy upon them?"

"I'm sure the prince of Ithaca would not do such a thing." Lycomedes frowned.

"Unfortunately I did just that, though I appreciate your faith in me." He offered Lycomedes a genial smile. "It was Penelope who caught me, actually. Said she had been watching me for over an hour and thought she should step in before I hit the thornbush. Naturally, there was some awkwardness about it, but Tyndareus eventually came around and asked me to stay. In the course of dinner, I came to see that Penelope was twice as clever as her cousins and just as beautiful. So—"

"As beautiful as Helen?" Diomedes interrupted. "Is that why she was twenty and unmarried?"

Odysseus' voice was mild. "I'm sure you would not ask a man to compare his wife unfavorably to another woman," he said.

Diomedes rolled his eyes and settled back to pick his teeth with the point of his knife.

Odysseus returned to Lycomedes. "So, in the course of our conversation, when it became clear that the Lady Penelope favored me—"

"Not for your looks, certainly," Diomedes commented.

"Certainly not," Odysseus agreed. "She asked me what wedding present I would make to my bride. A wedding bed, I said, rather gallantly, of finest holm-oak. But this answer did not please her. 'A wedding bed should not be made of dead, dry wood, but something green and living,' she told me. 'And what if I can make such a bed?' I said. 'Will you have me?' And she said—"

The king of Argos made a noise of disgust. "I'm sick to death of this tale about your marriage bed."

"Then perhaps you shouldn't have suggested I tell it."

"And perhaps you should get some new stories, so I don't fucking kill myself of boredom."

Lycomedes looked shocked; obscenity was for back rooms and practice fields, not state dinners. But Odysseus only shook his head sadly. "Truly, the men of Argos get more and more barbaric with each passing year. Lycomedes, let us show the king of Argos a bit of civilization. I was hoping for a glimpse of the famous dancers of your isle."

Lycomedes swallowed. "Yes," he said. "I had not thought—" He stopped himself, then began again, with the most kingly voice he could summon. "If you wish."

"We do." This was Diomedes.

"Well." Lycomedes' eyes darted between the two men. Thetis had ordered him to keep the women away from visitors, but to refuse would be suspicious. He cleared his throat, decided. "Well, let us call them, then." He gestured sharply at a servant, who turned and ran from the hall. I kept my eyes on my plate, so they would not see the fear in my face.

The women had been surprised by the summons and were still making small adjustments of clothes and hair as they entered the hall. Achilles was among them, his head carefully covered, his gaze modestly down. My eyes went anxiously to Odysseus and Diomedes, but neither even glanced at him.

The girls took their places, and the music was struck. We watched as they began the complicated series of steps. It was beautiful, though lessened by Deidameia's absence; she had been the best of them.

"Which one is your daughter?" Diomedes asked.

"She is not here, King of Argos. She is visiting family."

"Too bad," Diomedes said. "I hoped it was that one." He pointed to a girl on the end, small and dark; she did look something like Deidameia, and her ankles were particularly lovely, flashing beneath the whirling hem of her dress.

Lycomedes cleared his throat. "Are you married, my lord?"

Diomedes half-smiled. "For now." His eyes never left the women.

When the dance had finished, Odysseus stood, his voice raised for all to hear. "We are truly honored by your performance; not everyone can say that they have seen the dancers of Scyros. As tokens of our admiration we have brought gifts for you and your king."

A murmur of excitement. Luxuries did not come often to Scyros; no one here had the money to buy them.

"You are too kind." Lycomedes' face was flushed with genuine pleasure; he had not expected this generosity. The servants

brought trunks forth at Odysseus' signal and began unloading
them on the long tables. I saw the glitter of silver, the shine of
glass and gems. All of us, men and women both, leaned towards
them, eager to see.

"Please, take what you would like," Odysseus said. The girls
moved swiftly to the tables, and I watched them fingering the
bright trinkets: perfumes in delicate glass bottles stoppered with
a bit of wax; mirrors with carved ivory for handles; bracelets of
twisted gold; ribbons dyed deep in purples and reds. Among these
were a few things I assumed were meant for Lycomedes and his
counselors: leather-bound shields, carved spear hafts, and silvered
swords with supple kidskin sheaths. Lycomedes' eyes had caught
on one of these, like a fish snagged by a line. Odysseus stood near,
presiding benevolently.

Achilles kept to the back, drifting slowly along the tables.
He paused to dab some perfume on his slender wrists, stroke the
smooth handle of a mirror. He lingered a moment over a pair of
earrings, blue stones set in silver wire.

A movement at the far end of the hall caught my eye. Diomedes had crossed the chamber and was speaking with one of his
servants, who nodded and left through the large double doors.
Whatever it was could not be important; Diomedes seemed half-
asleep, his eyes heavy-lidded and bored.

I looked back to Achilles. He was holding the earrings up to
his ears now, turning them this way and that, pursing his lips,
playing at girlishness. It amused him, and the corner of his mouth
curved up. His eyes flicked around the hall, catching for a moment
on my face. I could not help myself. I smiled.

A trumpet blew, loud and panicked. It came from outside, a

sustained note, followed by three short blasts: our signal for utmost, impending disaster. Lycomedes lurched to his feet, the guards' heads jerked towards the door. Girls screamed and clung to each other, dropping their treasures to the ground in tinkles of breaking glass.

All the girls but one. Before the final blast was finished, Achilles had swept up one of the silvered swords and flung off its kidskin sheath. The table blocked his path to the door; he leapt it in a blur, his other hand grabbing a spear from it as he passed. He landed, and the weapons were already lifted, held with a deadly poise that was like no girl, nor no man either. *The greatest warrior of his generation.*

I yanked my gaze to Odysseus and Diomedes and was horrified to see them smiling. "Greetings, Prince Achilles," Odysseus said. "We've been looking for you."

I stood helpless as the faces of Lycomedes' court registered Odysseus' words, turned towards Achilles, stared. For a moment Achilles did not move. Then, slowly, he lowered the weapons.

"Lord Odysseus," he said. His voice was remarkably calm. "Lord Diomedes." He inclined his head politely, one prince to another. "I am honored to be the subject of so much effort." It was a good answer, full of dignity and the slightest twist of mockery. It would be harder for them to humiliate him now.

"I assume you wish to speak with me? Just a moment, and I will join you." He placed the sword and spear carefully on the table. With steady fingers he untied the kerchief, drew it off. His hair, revealed, gleamed like polished bronze. The men and women of Lycomedes' court whispered to one another in muted scandal; their eyes clung to his figure.

"Perhaps this will help?" Odysseus had claimed a tunic from some bag or box. He tossed it to Achilles, who caught it.

"Thank you," Achilles said. The court watched, hypnotized, as he unfolded it, stripped to the waist, and drew it over himself.

Odysseus turned to the front of the room. "Lycomedes, may we borrow a room of state, please? We have much to discuss with the prince of Phthia."

Lycomedes' face was a frozen mask. I knew he was thinking of Thetis, and punishment. He did not answer.

"Lycomedes." Diomedes' voice was sharp, cracking like a blow.

"Yes," Lycomedes croaked. I pitied him. I pitied all of us. "Yes. Just through there." He pointed.

Odysseus nodded. "Thank you." He moved towards the door, confidently, as if never doubting but that Achilles would follow.

"After you," Diomedes smirked. Achilles hesitated, and his eyes went to me, just the barest glance.

"Oh yes," Odysseus called over his shoulder. "You're welcome to bring Patroclus along, if you like. We have business with him, as well."

CHAPTER FIFTEEN

THE ROOM HAD A FEW THREADBARE TAPESTRIES AND four chairs. I forced myself to sit straight against the stiff wood back, as a prince should. Achilles' face was tight with emotion, and his neck flushed.

"It was a trick," he accused.

Odysseus was unperturbed. "You were clever in hiding yourself; we had to be cleverer still in finding you."

Achilles lifted an eyebrow in princely hauteur. "Well? You've found me. What do you want?"

"We want you to come to Troy," Odysseus said.

"And if I do not want to come?"

"Then we make this known." Diomedes lifted Achilles' discarded dress.

Achilles flushed as if he'd been struck. It was one thing to wear a dress out of necessity, another thing for the world to know of it. Our people reserved their ugliest names for men who acted like women; lives were lost over such insults.

Odysseus held up a restraining hand. "We are all noble men here and it should not have to come to such measures. I hope we can offer you happier reasons to agree. Fame, for instance. You will win much of it, if you fight for us."

"There will be other wars."

"Not like this one," said Diomedes. "This will be the greatest war of our people, remembered in legend and song for generations. You are a fool not to see it."

"I see nothing but a cuckolded husband and Agamemnon's greed."

"Then you are blind. What is more heroic than to fight for the honor of the most beautiful woman in the world, against the mightiest city of the East? Perseus cannot say he did so much, nor Jason. Heracles would kill his wife again for a chance to come along. We will master Anatolia all the way to Araby. We will carve ourselves into stories for ages to come."

"I thought you said it would be an easy campaign, home by next fall," I managed. I had to do something to stop the relentless roll of their words.

"I lied." Odysseus shrugged. "I have no idea how long it will be. Faster if we have you." He looked at Achilles. His dark eyes pulled like the tide, however you swam against it. "The sons of Troy are known for their skill in battle, and their deaths will lift your name to the stars. If you miss it, you will miss your chance at immortality. You will stay behind, unknown. You will grow old, and older in obscurity."

Achilles frowned. "You cannot know that."

"Actually, I can." He leaned back in his chair. "I am fortunate to have some knowledge of the gods." He smiled as if at a memory of some divine mischief. "And the gods have seen fit to share with me a prophecy about you."

I should have known that Odysseus would not come with tawdry blackmail as his only coin. The stories named him *polutropos,* the man of many turnings. Fear stirred in me like ash.

"What prophecy?" Achilles asked, slowly.

"That if you do not come to Troy, your godhead will wither in you, unused. Your strength will diminish. At best, you will be like Lycomedes here, moldering on a forgotten island with only daughters to succeed him. Scyros will be conquered soon by a nearby state; you know this as well as I. They will not kill him; why should they? He can live out his years in some corner eating the bread they soften for him, senile and alone. When he dies, people will say, *who?*"

The words filled the room, thinning the air until we could not breathe. Such a life was a horror.

But Odysseus' voice was relentless. "He is known now only because of how his story touches yours. If you go to Troy, your fame will be so great that a man will be written into eternal legend just for having passed a cup to you. You will be—"

The doors blew open in a fury of flying splinters. Thetis stood in the doorway, hot as living flame. Her divinity swept over us all, singeing our eyes, blackening the broken edges of the door. I could feel it pulling at my bones, sucking at the blood in my veins as if it would drink me. I cowered, as men were made to do.

Odysseus' dark beard was dusted with fine debris from the door's ruin. He stood. "Greetings, Thetis."

Her gaze went to him as a snake's to her prey, and her skin glowed. The air around Odysseus seemed to tremble slightly, as if with heat or a breeze. Diomedes, on the ground, edged away. I closed my eyes, so I would not have to see the explosion.

A silence, into which at last I opened my eyes. Odysseus stood unharmed. Thetis' fists were strangling themselves white. It no longer burned to look at her.

"The gray-eyed maiden has ever been kind to me," Odysseus said, almost apologetically. "She knows why I am here; she blesses and guards my purpose."

It was as if I had missed a step of their conversation. I struggled now to follow. The gray-eyed maiden—goddess of war and its arts. She was said to prize cleverness above all.

"Athena has no child to lose." The words grated from Thetis' throat, hung in the air.

Odysseus did not try to answer, only turned to Achilles. "Ask her," he said. "Ask your mother what she knows."

Achilles swallowed, loud in the silent chamber. He met his mother's black eyes. "Is it true, what he says?"

The last of her fire was gone; only marble remained. "It is true. But there is more, and worse that he has not said." The words came tonelessly, as a statue would speak them. "If you go to Troy, you will never return. You will die a young man there."

Achilles' face went pale. "It is certain?"

This is what all mortals ask first, in disbelief, shock, fear. *Is there no exception for me?*

"It is certain."

If he had looked at me then, I would have broken. I would have begun to weep and never stopped. But his eyes were fixed on his mother. "What should I do?" he whispered.

The slightest tremor, over the still water of her face. "Do not ask me to choose," she said. And vanished.

I CANNOT REMEMBER what we said to the two men, how we left them, or how we came to our room. I remember his face, skin drawn tightly over his cheeks, the dulled pallor of his brow. His shoulders, usually so straight and fine, seemed fallen. Grief swelled inside me, choking me. *His death.* I felt as if I was dying just to think of it, plummeting through a blind, black sky.

You must not go. I almost said it, a thousand times. Instead I held his hands fast between mine; they were cold, and very still.

"I do not think I could bear it," he said, at last. His eyes were closed, as if against horrors. I knew he spoke not of his death, but of the nightmare Odysseus had spun, the loss of his brilliance, the withering of his grace. I had seen the joy he took in his own skill, the roaring vitality that was always just beneath the surface. Who was he if not miraculous and radiant? Who was he if not destined for fame?

"I would not care," I said. The words scrabbled from my mouth. "Whatever you became. It would not matter to me. We would be together."

"I know," he said quietly, but did not look at me.

He knew, but it was not enough. The sorrow was so large it threatened to tear through my skin. When he died, all things swift and beautiful and bright would be buried with him. I opened my mouth, but it was too late.

"I will go," he said. "I will go to Troy."

The rosy gleam of his lip, the fevered green of his eyes. There was not a line anywhere on his face, nothing creased or graying;

all crisp. He was spring, golden and bright. Envious Death would drink his blood, and grow young again.

He was watching me, his eyes as deep as earth.

"Will you come with me?" he asked.

The never-ending ache of love and sorrow. Perhaps in some other life I could have refused, could have torn my hair and screamed, and made him face his choice alone. But not in this one. He would sail to Troy and I would follow, even into death. "*Yes,*" I whispered. "*Yes.*"

Relief broke in his face, and he reached for me. I let him hold me, let him press us length to length so close that nothing might fit between us.

Tears came, and fell. Above us, the constellations spun and the moon paced her weary course. We lay stricken and sleepless as the hours passed.

WHEN DAWN CAME, he rose stiffly. "I must go tell my mother," he said. He was pale, and his eyes were shadowed. He looked older already. Panic rose in me. *Don't go,* I wanted to say. But he drew on a tunic and was gone.

I lay back and tried not to think of the minutes passing. Just yesterday we had had a wealth of them. Now each was a drop of heartsblood lost.

The room turned gray, then white. The bed felt cold without him, and too large. I heard no sounds, and the stillness frightened me. *It is like a tomb.* I rose and rubbed my limbs, slapped them awake, trying to ward off a rising hysteria. *This is what it will be, every day, without him.* I felt a wild-eyed tightness in my chest, like a scream. *Every day, without him.*

I left the palace, desperate to shut out thought. I came to the cliffs, Scyros' great rocks that beetled over the sea, and began to climb. The winds tugged at me, and the stones were slimy with spray, but the strain and danger steadied me. I arrowed upwards, towards the most treacherous peak, where before I would have been too fearful to go. My hands were cut almost to blood by jagged shards of rock. My feet left stains where they stepped. The pain was welcome, ordinary and clean. So easy to bear it was laughable.

I reached the summit, a careless heap of boulders at the cliff's edge, and stood. An idea had come to me as I climbed, fierce and reckless as I felt.

"Thetis!" I screamed it into the snatching wind, my face towards the sea. "Thetis!" The sun was high now; their meeting had ended long ago. I drew a third breath.

"Do not speak my name again."

I whirled to face her and lost my balance. The rocks jumbled under my feet, and the wind tore at me. I grabbed at an outcrop, steadied myself. I looked up.

Her skin was paler even than usual, the first winter's ice. Her lips were drawn back, to show her teeth.

"You are a fool," she said. "Get down. Your halfwit death will not save him."

I was not so fearless as I thought; I flinched from the malice in her face. But I forced myself to speak, to ask the thing I had to know of her. "How much longer will he live?"

She made a noise in her throat, like the bark of a seal. It took me a moment to understand that it was laughter. "Why? Would you prepare yourself for it? Try to stop it?" Contempt spilled across her face.

"Yes," I answered. "If I can."

The sound again.

"Please." I knelt. "Please tell me."

Perhaps it was because I knelt. The sound ceased, and she considered me a moment. "Hector's death will be first," she said. "This is all I am given to know."

Hector. "Thank you," I said.

Her eyes narrowed, and her voice hissed like water poured on coals. "Do not presume to thank me. I have come for another reason."

I waited. Her face was white as splintered bone.

"It will not be so easy as he thinks. The Fates promise fame, but how much? He will need to guard his honor carefully. He is too trusting. The men of Greece"—she spat the words—"are dogs over a bone. They will not simply give up preeminence to another. I will do what I can. And you." Her eyes flickered over my long arms and skinny knees. "You will not disgrace him. Do you understand?"

Do you understand?

"Yes," I said. And I did. His fame must be worth the life he paid for it. The faintest breath of air touched her dress's hem, and I knew she was about to leave, to vanish back to the caves of the sea. Something made me bold.

"Is Hector a skilled soldier?"

"He is the best," she answered. "But for my son."

Her gaze flickered to the right, where the cliff dropped away. "He is coming," she said.

ACHILLES CRESTED THE RISE and came to where I sat. He looked at my face and my bloodied skin. "I heard you talking," he said.

"It was your mother," I said.

He knelt and took my foot in his lap. Gently, he picked the fragments of rock from the wounds, brushing off dirt and chalky dust. He tore a strip from his tunic's hem and pressed it tight to stanch the blood.

My hand closed over his. "You must not kill Hector," I said.

He looked up, his beautiful face framed by the gold of his hair. "My mother told you the rest of the prophecy."

"She did."

"And you think that no one but me can kill Hector."

"Yes," I said.

"And you think to steal time from the Fates?"

"Yes."

"Ah." A sly smile spread across his face; he had always loved defiance. "Well, why should I kill him? He's done nothing to me."

For the first time then, I felt a kind of hope.

WE LEFT THAT AFTERNOON; there was no reason to linger. Ever dutiful to custom, Lycomedes came to bid us farewell. The three of us stood together stiffly; Odysseus and Diomedes had gone ahead to the ship. They would escort us back to Phthia, where Achilles would muster his own troops.

There was one more thing to be done here, and I knew Achilles did not wish to do it.

"Lycomedes, my mother has asked me to convey her desires to you."

The faintest tremor crossed the old man's face, but he met his son-in-law's gaze. "It is about the child," he said.

"It is."

"And what does she wish?" the king asked, wearily.

"She wishes to raise him herself. She—" Achilles faltered before the look on the old man's face. "The child will be a boy, she says. When he is weaned, she will claim him."

Silence. Then Lycomedes closed his eyes. I knew he was thinking of his daughter, arms empty of both husband and child. "I wish you had never come," he said.

"I'm sorry," Achilles said.

"Leave me," the old king whispered. We obeyed.

THE SHIP WE SAILED ON was yare, tightly made and well manned. The crew moved with a competent fleetness, the ropes gleamed with new fibers, and the masts seemed fresh as living trees. The prow piece was a beauty, the finest I had ever seen: a woman, tall, with dark hair and eyes, her hands clasped in front of her as if in contemplation. She was beautiful, but quietly so—an elegant jaw, and upswept hair showing a slender neck. She had been lovingly painted, each darkness or lightness perfectly rendered.

"You are admiring my wife, I see." Odysseus joined us at the railing, leaning on muscular forearms. "She refused at first, wouldn't let the artist near her. I had to have him follow her in secret. I think it turned out rather well, actually."

A marriage for love, rare as cedars from the East. It almost made me want to like him. But I had seen his smiles too often now.

Politely, Achilles asked, "What is her name?"

"Penelope," he said.

"Is the ship new?" I asked. If he wanted to speak of his wife, I wanted to speak of something else.

"Very. Every last timber of it, from the best wood that Ithaca has." He slapped the railing with his large palm, as one might the flank of a horse.

"Bragging about your new ship again?" Diomedes had joined us. His hair was lashed back with a strip of leather, and it made his face look sharper even than usual.

"I am."

Diomedes spat into the water.

"The king of Argos is unusually eloquent today," Odysseus commented.

Achilles had not seen their game before, as I had. His eyes went back and forth between the two men. A small smile curled at the corner of his mouth.

"Tell me," Odysseus continued. "Do you think such quick wit comes from your father having eaten that man's brains?"

"What?" Achilles' mouth hung open.

"You don't know the tale of Mighty Tydeus, king of Argos, eater of brains?"

"I've heard of him. But not about the—brains."

"I was thinking of having the scene painted on our plates," Diomedes said.

In the hall, I had taken Diomedes for Odysseus' dog. But there was a keenness that hummed between the two men, a pleasure in their sparring that could come only from equals. I remembered that Diomedes was rumored to be a favorite of Athena as well.

Odysseus made a face. "Remind me not to dine in Argos any time soon."

Diomedes laughed. It was not a pleasant sound.

The kings were inclined to talk and lingered by the rail with us. They passed stories back and forth: of other sea voyages, of wars, of contests won in games long past. Achilles was an eager audience, with question after question.

"Where did you get this?" He was pointing to the scar on Odysseus' leg.

"Ah," Odysseus rubbed his hands together. "That is a tale worth telling. Though I should speak to the captain first." He gestured to the sun, hanging ripe and low over the horizon. "We'll need to stop soon for camp."

"I'll go." Diomedes stood from where he leaned against the rail. "I've heard this one almost as many times as that sickening bed story."

"Your loss," Odysseus called after him. "Don't mind him. His wife's a hellhound bitch, and that would sour anyone's temper. Now, my wife—"

"I swear." Diomedes' voice carried back up the length of the ship. "If you finish that sentence, I will throw you over the side and you can swim to Troy."

"See?" Odysseus shook his head. "Sour." Achilles laughed, delighted by them both. He seemed to have forgiven their part in his unmasking, and all that came after.

"Now what was I saying?"

"The scar," Achilles said, eagerly.

"Yes, the scar. When I was thirteen—"

I watched him hang on the other man's words. *He is too trusting.* But I would not be the raven on his shoulder all the time, predicting gloom.

The sun slid lower in the sky, and we drew close to the dark shadow of land where we would make camp. The ship found the harbor, and the sailors drew her up on the shore for the night. Supplies were unloaded—food and bedding and tents for the princes.

We stood by the campsite that had been laid for us, a small fire and pavilion. "Is all well here?" Odysseus had come to stand with us.

"Very well," Achilles said. He smiled, his easy smile, his honest one. "Thank you."

Odysseus smiled in return, teeth white against his dark beard. "Excellent. One tent's enough, I hope? I've heard that you prefer to share. Rooms and bedrolls both, they say."

Heat and shock rushed through my face. Beside me, I heard Achilles' breath stop.

"Come now, there's no need for shame—it's a common enough thing among boys." He scratched his jaw, contemplated. "Though you're not really boys any longer. How old are you?"

"It's not true," I said. The blood in my face fired my voice. It rang loudly down the beach.

Odysseus raised an eyebrow. "True is what men believe, and they believe this of you. But perhaps they are mistaken. If the rumor concerns you, then leave it behind when you sail to war."

Achilles' voice was tight and angry. "It is no business of yours, Prince of Ithaca."

Odysseus held up his hands. "My apologies if I have offended. I merely came to wish you both good night and ensure that all was satisfactory. Prince Achilles. Patroclus." He inclined his head and turned back to his own tent.

Inside the tent there was quietness between us. I had wondered when this would come. As Odysseus said, many boys took each other for lovers. But such things were given up as they grew older, unless it was with slaves or hired boys. Our men liked conquest; they did not trust a man who was conquered himself.

Do not disgrace him, the goddess had said. And this is some of what she had meant.

"Perhaps he is right," I said.

Achilles' head came up, frowning. "You do not think that."

"I do not mean—" I twisted my fingers. "I would still be with you. But I could sleep outside, so it would not be so obvious. I do not need to attend your councils. I—"

"No. The Phthians will not care. And the others can talk all they like. I will still be *Aristos Achaion.*" *Best of the Greeks.*

"Your honor could be darkened by it."

"Then it is darkened." His jaw shot forward, stubborn. "They are fools if they let my glory rise or fall on this."

"But Odysseus—"

His eyes, green as spring leaves, met mine. "Patroclus. I have given enough to them. I will not give them this."

After that, there was nothing more to say.

THE NEXT DAY, with the southern wind caught in our sail, we found Odysseus by the prow.

"Prince of Ithaca," Achilles said. His voice was formal; there were none of the boyish smiles from the day before. "I wish to hear you speak of Agamemnon and the other kings. I would know the men I am to join, and the princes I am to fight."

"Very wise, Prince Achilles." If Odysseus noticed a change, he did not comment on it. He led us to the benches at the base of the mast, below the big-bellied sail. "Now, where to begin?" Almost absently, he rubbed the scar on his leg. It was starker in daylight, hairless and puckered. "There is Menelaus, whose wife we go to retrieve. After Helen picked him for her husband—Patroclus can tell you about that—he became king of Sparta. He is known as a good man, fearless in battle and well liked in the world. Many kings have rallied to his cause, and not just those who are bound to their oaths."

"Such as?" Achilles asked.

Odysseus counted them off on his large farmer's hands. "Meriones, Idomeneus, Philoctetes, Ajax. Both Ajaxes, larger and lesser." One was the man I remembered from Tyndareus' hall, a huge man with a shield; the other I did not know.

"Old King Nestor of Pylos will be there as well." I'd heard the name—he had sailed with Jason in his youth, to find the Golden Fleece. He was long past his fighting days now, but brought his sons to war, and his counsel, too.

Achilles' face was intent, his eyes dark. "And the Trojans?"

"Priam, of course. King of Troy. The man is said to have fifty sons, all raised with a sword in their hands."

"Fifty sons?"

"And fifty daughters. He's known to be pious and much loved by the gods. His sons are famous in their own right—Paris, of course, beloved of the goddess Aphrodite, and much noted for his beauty. Even the youngest, who's barely ten, is supposed to be ferocious. Troilus, I think. They have a god-born cousin who fights for them, too. Aeneas, his name is, a child of Aphrodite herself."

"What about Hector?" Achilles' eyes never left Odysseus.

"Priam's oldest son and heir, favorite of the god Apollo. Troy's mightiest defender."

"What does he look like?"

Odysseus shrugged. "I don't know. They say he is large, but that is said of most heroes. You'll meet him before I do, so you'll have to tell me."

Achilles narrowed his eyes. "Why do you say that?"

Odysseus made a wry face. "As I'm sure Diomedes will agree, I am a competent soldier but no more; my talents lie elsewhere. If I were to meet Hector in battle, I would not be bringing back news of him. You, of course, are a different matter. You will win the greatest fame from his death."

My skin went cold.

"Perhaps I would, but I see no reason to kill him." Achilles answered coolly. "He's done nothing to me."

Odysseus chuckled, as if a joke had been made. "If every soldier killed only those who'd personally offended him, Pelides, we'd have no wars at all." He lifted an eyebrow. "Though maybe it's not such a bad idea. In that world, perhaps I'd be *Aristos Achaion*, instead of you."

Achilles did not answer. He had turned to look over the ship's side at the waves beyond. The light fell upon his cheek, lit it to glowing. "You have told me nothing of Agamemnon," he said.

"Yes, our mighty king of Mycenae." Odysseus leaned back again. "Proud scion of the house of Atreus. His great-grandfather Tantalus was a son of Zeus. Surely you've heard his story."

All knew of Tantalus' eternal torment. To punish his contempt for their powers, the gods had thrown him into the deepest pit of the underworld. There they afflicted the king with perpetual thirst and hunger, while food and drink sat just out of his reach.

"I've heard of him. But I never knew what his crime was," Achilles said.

"Well. In the days of King Tantalus, all our kingdoms were the same size, and the kings were at peace. But Tantalus grew dissatisfied with his portion, and began to take his neighbors' lands by force. His holdings doubled, then doubled again, but still Tantalus was not satisfied. His success had made him proud, and having bested all men who came before him, he sought next to best the gods themselves. Not with weapons, for no man may match the gods in battle. But in trickery. He wished to prove that the gods do not know all, as they say they do.

"So he called his son to him, Pelops, and asked him if he wanted to help his father. 'Of course,' Pelops said. His father smiled and drew his sword. With a single blow he slit his son's throat clean across. He carved the body into careful pieces and spitted them over the fire."

My stomach heaved at the thought of the iron skewer through the boy's dead flesh.

"When the boy was cooked, Tantalus called to his father Zeus on Olympus. 'Father!' he said. 'I have prepared a feast to honor

you and all your kin. Hurry, for the meat is tender still, and fresh.'
The gods love such feasting and came quickly to Tantalus' hall.
But when they arrived, the smell of the cooking meat, normally
so dear, seemed to choke them. At once Zeus knew what had been
done. He seized Tantalus by the legs and threw him into Tartarus,
to suffer his eternal punishment."

The sky was bright, and the wind brisk, but in the spell of
Odysseus' story I felt that we were by a fireside, with night pressing all around.

"Zeus then drew the pieces of the boy back together and
breathed a second life into him. Pelops, though only a boy, became king of Mycenae. He was a good king, distinguished in
piety and wisdom, yet many miseries afflicted his reign. Some
said that the gods had cursed Tantalus' line, condemning them
all to violence and disaster. Pelops' sons, Atreus and Thyestes,
were born with their grandfather's ambition, and their crimes
were dark and bloody, as his had been. A daughter raped by her
father, a son cooked and eaten, all in their bitter rivalry for the
throne.

"It is only now, by the virtue of Agamemnon and Menelaus,
that their family fortune has begun to change. The days of civil
war are gone, and Mycenae prospers under Agamemnon's upright
rule. He has won just renown for his skill with a spear and the
firmness of his leadership. We are fortunate to have him as our
general."

I had thought Achilles was no longer listening. But he turned
now, frowning. "We are each generals."

"Of course," Odysseus agreed. "But we are all going to fight
the same enemy, are we not? Two dozen generals on one battle-

field will be chaos and defeat." He offered a grin. "You know how well we all get along—we'd probably end up killing each other instead of the Trojans. Success in such a war as this comes only through men sewn to a single purpose, funneled to a single spear thrust rather than a thousand needle-pricks. You lead the Phthians, and I the Ithacans, but there must be someone who uses us each to our abilities"—he tipped a gracious hand towards Achilles —"however great they may be."

Achilles ignored the compliment. The setting sun cut shadows into his face; his eyes were flat and hard. "I come of my free will, Prince of Ithaca. I will take Agamemnon's counsel, but not his orders. I would have you understand this."

Odysseus shook his head. "Gods save us from ourselves. Not even in battle yet, and already worrying over honors."

"I am not—"

Odysseus waved a hand. "Believe me, Agamemnon understands your great worth to his cause. It was he who first wished you to come. You will be welcomed to our army with all the pomp you could desire."

It was not what Achilles had meant, exactly, but it was close enough. I was glad when the lookout shouted landfall up ahead.

THAT EVENING, when we had set aside our dinners, Achilles lay back on the bed. "What do you think of these men we will meet?"

"I don't know."

"I am glad Diomedes is gone, at least."

"Me too." We had let the king off at Euboia's northern tip, to wait for his army from Argos. "I do not trust them."

"I suppose we will know soon enough what they are like," he said.

We were silent a moment, thinking of that. Outside, we could hear the beginnings of rain, soft, barely sounding on the tent roof.

"Odysseus said it would storm tonight."

An Aegean storm, quickly here and quickly gone. Our boat was safely beached, and tomorrow would be clear again.

Achilles was looking at me. "Your hair never quite lies flat here." He touched my head, just behind my ear. "I don't think I've ever told you how I like it."

My scalp prickled where his fingers had been. "You haven't," I said.

"I should have." His hand drifted down to the vee at the base of my throat, drew softly across the pulse. "What about this? Have I told you what I think of this, just here?"

"No," I said.

"This surely, then." His hand moved across the muscles of my chest; my skin warmed beneath it. "Have I told you of this?"

"That you have told me." My breath caught a little as I spoke.

"And what of this?" His hand lingered over my hips, drew down the line of my thigh. "Have I spoken of it?"

"You have."

"And this? Surely, I would not have forgotten this." His cat's smile. "Tell me I did not."

"You did not."

"There is this, too." His hand was ceaseless now. "I know I have told you of this."

I closed my eyes. "Tell me again," I said.

LATER, ACHILLES SLEEPS next to me. Odysseus' storm has come, and the coarse fabric of the tent wall trembles with its force. I hear the stinging slap, over and over, of waves reproaching the shore. He stirs and the air stirs with him, bearing the musk-sweet smell of his body. I think: *This is what I will miss.* I think: *I will kill myself rather than miss it.* I think: *How long do we have?*

CHAPTER SIXTEEN

WE ARRIVED IN PHTHIA THE NEXT DAY. THE SUN WAS just over the meridian, and Achilles and I stood looking at the rail.

"Do you see that?"

"What?" As always, his eyes were sharper than mine.

"The shore. It looks strange."

As we drew closer we saw why. It was thick with people, jostling impatiently, craning their necks towards us. And the sound: at first it seemed to come from the waves, or the ship as it cut them, a rushing roar. But it grew louder with each stroke of our oars, until we understood that it was voices, then words. Over and over, it came. *Prince Achilles! Aristos Achaion!*

As our ship touched the beach, hundreds of hands threw themselves into the air, and hundreds of throats opened in a cheer. All other noises, the wood of the gangplank banging down on rock, the sailors' commands, were lost to it. We stared, in shock.

It was that moment, perhaps, that our lives changed. Not before in Scyros, nor before that still, on Pelion. But here, as we began to understand the grandness, now and always, that would follow him wherever he went. He had chosen to become a legend, and this was the beginning. He hesitated, and I touched my hand to his, where the crowd could not see it. "Go," I urged him. "They are waiting for you."

Achilles stepped forward onto the gangplank, his arm lifted in greeting, and the crowd screamed itself hoarse. I half-feared they would swarm onto the ship, but soldiers pushed forward and lined the gangway, making a path straight through the crush.

Achilles turned back to me, said something. I could not hear it, but I understood. *Come with me.* I nodded, and we began to walk. On either side of us, the crowd surged against the soldiers' barrier. At the aisle's end was Peleus, waiting for us. His face was wet, and he made no attempt to wipe aside the tears. He drew Achilles to him, held him long before he let him go.

"Our prince has returned!" His voice was deeper than I remembered, resonant and carrying far, over the noise of the crowd. They quieted, to hear the words of their king.

"Before you all I offer welcome to my most beloved son, sole heir to my kingdom. He will lead you to Troy in glory; he will return home in triumph."

Even there beneath the bright sun, I felt my skin go cold. *He will not come home at all.* But Peleus did not know this, yet.

"He is a man grown, and god born. *Aristos Achaion!*"

There was no time to think of it now. The soldiers were beating on their shields with their spears; the women screamed; the men howled. I caught sight of Achilles' face; the look on it was stunned, but not displeased. He was standing differently, I noticed, shoulders back and legs braced. He looked older, somehow, taller even. He leaned over to say something in his father's ear, but I could not hear what he said. A chariot was waiting; we stepped into it and watched the crowd stream behind us up the beach.

Inside the palace, attendants and servants buzzed around us. We were given a moment to eat and drink what was pressed into our hands. Then we were led to the palace courtyard, where twenty-five hundred men waited for us. At our approach they lifted their square shields, shining like carapace, in salute to their new general. This, out of all of it, was perhaps the strangest: that he was their commander now. He would be expected to know them all, their names and armor and stories. *He no longer belongs to me alone.*

If he was nervous, even I could not tell. I watched as he greeted them, spoke ringing words that made them stand up straighter. They grinned, loving every inch of their miraculous prince: his gleaming hair, his deadly hands, his nimble feet. They leaned towards him, like flowers to the sun, drinking in his luster. It was as Odysseus had said: he had light enough to make heroes of them all.

WE WERE NEVER ALONE. Achilles was always needed for something—his eye on draft sheets and figures, his advice on food supplies and levy lists. Phoinix, his father's old counselor, would be accompanying us, but there were still a thousand questions for Achilles to answer—how many? how much? who will be your captains? He did what he could, then announced, "I defer all the rest of such matters to the experience of Phoinix." I heard a servant girl sigh behind me. Handsome and gracious, both.

He knew that I had little to do here. His face, when he turned to me, was increasingly apologetic. He was always sure to place the tablets where I could see them too, to ask my opinion. But

I did not make it easy for him, standing in the back, listless and silent.

Even there, I could not escape. Through every window came the constant clatter of soldiers, bragging and drilling and sharpening their spears. The Myrmidons, they had begun calling themselves, *ant-men,* an old nickname of honor. Another thing Achilles had had to explain to me: the legend of Zeus creating the first Phthians from ants. I watched them marching, rank on cheerful rank. I saw them dreaming of the plunder they would bring home, and the triumph. There was no such dream for us.

I began to slip away. I would find a reason to linger behind as the attendants ushered him forward: an itch, or a loose strap of my shoe. Oblivious, they hurried on, turned a corner, and left me suddenly, blessedly, alone. I took the twisting corridors I had learned so many years ago and came gratefully to our empty room. There I lay on the cool stone of the floor and closed my eyes. I could not stop imagining how it would end—spear-tip or swordpoint, or smashed by a chariot. The rushing, unending blood of his heart.

One night in the second week, as we lay half-drowsing, I asked him: "How will you tell your father? About the prophecy?"

The words were loud in the silence of midnight. For a moment he was still. Then he said, "I do not think I will."

"Never?"

He shook his head, just the barest shadow. "There is nothing he can do. It would only bring him grief."

"What about your mother? Won't she tell him?"

"No," he said. "It was one of the things I asked her to promise me, that last day on Scyros."

I frowned. He had not told me this before. "What were the other things?"

I saw him hesitate. But we did not lie to each other; we never had. "I asked her to protect you," he said. "After."

I stared at him, dry-mouthed. "What did she say?"

Another silence. Then, so quietly I could imagine the dull red shame of his cheeks, he answered, "She said no."

Later, when he slept, and I lay wakeful and watching under the stars, I thought of this. Knowing that he had asked warmed me—it chased away some of the coldness of the days here in the palace, when he was wanted every moment and I was not.

As for the goddess's answer, I did not care. I would have no need of her. I did not plan to live after he was gone.

SIX WEEKS PASSED—the six weeks that it took to organize soldiers, to equip a fleet, to pack up food and clothing to last the length of the war—a year perhaps, or two. Sieges were always long.

Peleus insisted that Achilles take only the best. He paid for a small fortune in armor, more than six men would need. There were hammered-bronze breastplates, graven with lions and a rising phoenix, stiff leather greaves with gold bands, horsehair plumed helms, a silver-forged sword, dozens of spearheads, and two light-wheeled chariots. With this came a four-horse team, including the pair given to Peleus by the gods at his wedding. Xanthos and Balios, they were called: Golden and Dapple, and their eyes rolled white with impatience whenever they were not free to run. He gave us also a charioteer, a boy younger than we were, but sturdily built and said to be skilled with headstrong horses. Automedon, his name was.

Finally, last of all: a long spear, ash sapling peeled of bark and polished until it glowed like gray flame. From Chiron, Peleus said, handing it to his son. We bent over it, our fingers trailing its surface as if to catch the centaur's lingering presence. Such a fine gift would have taken weeks of Chiron's deft shaping; he must have begun it almost the day that we left. Did he know, or only guess at Achilles' destiny? As he lay alone in his rose-colored cave, had some glimmer of prophecy come to him? Perhaps he simply assumed: a bitterness of habit, of boy after boy trained for music and medicine, and unleashed for murder.

Yet this beautiful spear had been fashioned not in bitterness, but love. Its shape would fit no one's hand but Achilles', and its heft could suit no one's strength but his. And though the point was keen and deadly, the wood itself slipped under our fingers like the slender oiled strut of a lyre.

AT LAST THE DAY for our departure came. Our ship was a beauty, finer even than Odysseus'—sleek and slim as a knifepoint, meant to cut the sea. It rode low in the water, heavy with stores of food and supplies.

And that was only the flagship. Beside it, forty-nine others, a city of wood, rolled gently in the waters of Phthia's harbor. Their bright prow-pieces were a bestiary of animals and nymphs and creatures half in between, and their masts stood as tall as the trees they had been. At the front of each of these ships, one of our new-minted captains stood at attention, saluting as we walked up the ramp to our vessel.

Achilles went first, his purple cloak stirring in the breeze from the sea, then Phoinix, and me with a new cloak of my own, holding the old man's arm to steady his steps. The people cheered for us and for our soldiers, filing onto their own ships. All around us final promises were shouted: of glory, of the gold that would be stripped and brought home from Priam's rich city.

Peleus stood at the shore's edge, one hand raised in farewell. True to his word, Achilles had not told him of the prophecy, merely hugged him tightly, as if to soak the old man into his skin. I had embraced him too, those thin, wiry limbs. I thought, *This is what Achilles will feel like when he is old*. And then I remembered: he will never be old.

The ship's boards were still sticky with new resin. We leaned over the railing to wave our last farewell, the sun-warm wood pressed against our bellies. The sailors heaved up the anchor, square and chalky with barnacles, and loosened the sails. Then they took their seats at the oars that fringed the boat like eyelashes, waiting for the count. The drums began to beat, and the oars lifted and fell, taking us to Troy.

CHAPTER SEVENTEEN

B UT FIRST, TO AULIS. AULIS, A JUTTING FINGER OF LAND with enough shoreline to beach all our ships at once. Agamemnon had wanted his mighty force assembled in a single place before it sailed. A symbol perhaps: the visible power of Greece Offended.

After five days churning through the rough waters of the Euboean coast, we came around the last hitch of the winding straight, and Aulis was there. It appeared all at once, as if a veil had been yanked off: shoreline thick with vessels in every size and color and shape, its beach covered in a shifting carpet of thousands upon thousands of men. Beyond them the canvas tops of tents stretched out to the horizon, bright pennants marking the kings' pavilions. Our men strove at their oars, guiding us towards the last empty place on the crowded shore—big enough for our whole fleet. Anchors dropped from fifty sterns.

Horns blew. The Myrmidons from the other ships were already wading ashore. They stood now at the water's edge, surrounding us, white tunics billowing. At a signal we could not see they began to chant their prince's name, twenty-five hundred men speaking as one. *A-chil-les!* All along the shore, heads turned—Spartans, Argives, Mycenaeans, and all the rest. The news went rippling through them, passing one to another. *Achilles is here.*

As the sailors lowered the gangway we watched them gather, kings and conscripts both. I could not see the princely faces from the distance, but I recognized the pennants that their squires carried before them: the yellow banner of Odysseus, the blue of Diomedes, and then the brightest, the biggest—a lion on purple, the symbol of Agamemnon and Mycenae.

Achilles looked to me, drew in a breath; the screaming crowd at Phthia was nothing compared to this. But he was ready. I saw it in the way he lifted his chest, in the fierce green of his eyes. He walked to the gangway and stood at its top. The Myrmidons kept up their shouts, and they were not alone now; others in the crowd had joined them. A broad-chested Myrmidon captain cupped his hands around his mouth. "Prince Achilles, son of King Peleus and the goddess Thetis. *Aristos Achaion!*"

As if in answer, the air changed. Bright sunlight broke and poured over Achilles, went rolling down his hair and back and skin, turning him to gold. He seemed suddenly larger, and his tunic, wrinkled from travel, straightened until it shone white and clean as a sail. His hair caught the light like buoyant flame.

Gasps amongst the men; new cheers burst forth. *Thetis,* I thought. It could be no one else. She was pulling his divinity forth, mantling it like cream on every inch of his skin. Helping her son make the most of his dearly bought fame.

I could see the tug of a smile at the corner of his mouth. He was enjoying it, licking the crowd's worship off his lips. He did not know, he told me later, what was happening. But he did not question it; it did not seem strange to him.

A pathway had been left open for him, straight through the crowd's heart to where the kings gathered. Each arriving prince was to present himself before his peers and new commander; now it was Achilles' turn. He strode down the plank and past the jostling ranks of men, stopping perhaps ten feet from the kings. I was a few paces farther behind.

Agamemnon was waiting for us. His nose was curved and sharp like an eagle's beak, and his eyes glittered with a greedy intelligence. He was solid and broad across his chest, firmly planted in his feet. He looked seasoned, but also worn—older than the forty years we knew him to be. At his right side, a place of honor, stood Odysseus and Diomedes. On his left was his brother, Menelaus—king of Sparta, cause of war. The vivid red hair that I remembered from Tyndareus' hall was touched now with threading gray. Like his brother he was tall and square, his shoulders strong as a yoke-ox. His family's dark eyes and curving nose seemed softer on him, more temperate. His face was smile-lined and handsome where his brother's was not.

The only other king that I could identify with any surety was Nestor—the old man, chin barely covered by a sparse white beard, eyes sharp in his age-whittled face. He was the oldest man living, it was rumored, the canny survivor of a thousand scandals and battles and coups. He ruled the sandy strip of Pylos, whose throne he still clutched stubbornly, disappointing dozens of sons who grew old and then older, even as he bred new ones from his famed and well-worn loins. It was two of these sons who held his arms steady now, shouldering other kings aside for a place at the front. As he watched us his mouth hung open, breath puffing his threadbare beard with excitement. He loved a commotion.

Agamemnon stepped forward. He opened his hands in a gesture of welcome and stood regally expectant, waiting for the bows, obeisance, and oaths of loyalty he was owed. It was Achilles' place to kneel and offer them.

He did not kneel. He did not call out a greeting to the great king, or incline his head or offer a gift. He did nothing but stand straight, chin proudly lifted, before them all.

Agamemnon's jaw tightened; he looked silly like that, with his arms out, and he knew it. My gaze caught on Odysseus and Diomedes; their eyes were sending sharp messages. Around us the uneasy silence spread. Men exchanged glances.

My hands clutched each other behind my back as I watched Achilles and the game he played. His face seemed cut from stone as he stared his warning at the king of Mycenae—*You do not command me.* The silence went on and on, painful and breathless, like a singer overreaching to finish a phrase.

Then, just as Odysseus moved forward to intervene, Achilles spoke. "I am Achilles, son of Peleus, god-born, best of the Greeks," he said. "I have come to bring you victory." A second of startled silence, then the men roared their approval. Pride became us—heroes were never modest.

Agamemnon's eyes went flat. And then Odysseus was there, his hand hard on Achilles' shoulder, wrinkling the fabric as his voice smoothed the air.

"Agamemnon, Lord of Men, we have brought the prince Achilles to pledge his allegiance to you." His look warned Achilles —*it is not too late.* But Achilles simply smiled and stepped forward so that Odysseus' hand fell off him.

"I come freely to offer my aid to your cause," he said loudly.

Then turning to the crowd around him, "I am honored to fight with so many noble warriors of our kingdoms."

Another cheer, loud and long, taking what felt like minutes to die. Finally, from the deep crag of his face, Agamemnon spoke, with patience that had been hard won, hard practiced.

"Indeed, I have the finest army in the world. And I welcome you to it, young prince of Phthia." His smile cut sharply. "It is a pity you were so slow to come."

There was implication here, but Achilles had no chance to answer. Agamemnon was already speaking again, his voice lifted over us all: "Men of Greece, we have delayed long enough. We leave for Troy tomorrow. Repair to your camps and make yourselves ready." Then he turned with finality and strode up the beach.

The kings of Agamemnon's innermost circle followed him, dispersing back to their ships—Odysseus, Diomedes, Nestor, Menelaus, more. But others lingered to meet the new hero: Thessalian Eurypylus and Antilochus of Pylos, Meriones of Crete and the physician Podalerius. Men drawn here for glory or bound by their oath, from every far-flung crag of our countries. Many had been here for months, waiting as the rest of the army straggled together. After such tedium, they said, looking slyly at Achilles, they welcomed any harmless entertainment. Particularly at the expense of—

"Prince Achilles," interrupted Phoinix. "Please excuse my intrusion. I thought you would wish to know that your camp is being prepared." His voice was stiff with disapproval; but here, in front of the others, he would not chide.

"Thank you, worthy Phoinix," Achilles said. "If you'll pardon us—?"

Yes, yes, of course they would. They'd come by later, or tomorrow. They'd bring their best wine and we'd broach it together. Achilles clasped hands with them, promised it would be so.

IN CAMP, Myrmidons streamed around us hefting baggage and food, poles and canvas. A man in livery approached and bowed—one of Menelaus' heralds. His king could not come in person, he regretted, but had sent the herald here in his place to welcome us. Achilles and I exchanged a glance. This was clever diplomacy—we had not made a friend in his brother, so Menelaus did not come himself. Yet, some welcome was due to the best of the Greeks. "A man who plays both sides of the fence," I whispered to Achilles.

"A man who cannot afford to offend me if he wants his wife returned," he whispered back.

Would we accept a tour? the herald asked. Yes, we said, in our best princely manner. We would.

The main encampment was a dizzying chaos, a bedlam of motion—the constant fluttering of pennants, laundry on lines, tent walls, the hurrying bodies of thousands and thousands of men. Beyond this was the river, with its old watermark from when the armies had first arrived, a foot higher on the bank. Then the marketplace center, the agora, with its altar and makeshift podium. Last, the latrines—long, open ditches, busy with men.

Wherever we went, we were observed. I watched Achilles closely, waiting to see if Thetis would again make his hair brighter or his muscles bigger. If she did, I did not notice; all the grace I saw then was his own: simple, unadorned, glorious. He waved to the men who stared at him; he smiled and greeted them as he passed. I heard the words, whispered from behind beards and broken teeth and callused hands: *Aristos Achaion*. Was he as Odysseus and Diomedes had promised? Did they believe those slender limbs could hold against an army of Trojans? Could a boy of sixteen really be our greatest warrior? And everywhere, as I watched the questions, I saw also the answers. Yes, they nodded to each other, yes, yes.

CHAPTER EIGHTEEN

I WOKE THAT NIGHT GASPING. I WAS SWEAT-SOAKED, AND THE
tent felt oppressively warm. Beside me Achilles slept, his skin
as damp as mine.

I stepped outside, eager for a breeze off the water. But here,
too, the air was heavy and humid. It was quiet, strangely so. I
heard no flapping of canvas, no jingle of an unsecured harness.
Even the sea was silent, as if the waves had ceased to fall against
the shore. Out beyond the breakers it was flat as a polished bronze
mirror.

There was no wind, I realized. That was the strangeness. The
air that hung around me did not stir, even with the faintest whisper of current. I remember thinking: if it keeps up like this we
won't be able to sail tomorrow.

I washed my face, glad of the water's coolness, then returned
to Achilles and restless, turning sleep.

THE NEXT MORNING is the same. I wake in a pool of sweat, my skin
puckered and parched. Gratefully I gulp the water that Automedon
brings us. Achilles wakes, draws a hand over his soaked forehead.
He frowns, goes outside, returns.

"There is no wind."

I nod.

"We will not leave today." Our men are strong oarsmen, but even they cannot power a full day's journey. We need the wind to take us to Troy.

It does not come. Not that day, or that night, or the next day either. Agamemnon is forced to stand in the marketplace and announce further delay. As soon as the wind returns, we will leave, he promises us.

But the wind does not return. We are hot all the time, and the air feels like the blasts off a fire, scorching our lungs. We had never noticed how scalding the sand could be, how scratchy our blankets. Tempers fray, and fights break out. Achilles and I spend all our time in the sea, seeking the meager comfort it offers.

The days pass and our foreheads crease with worry. Two weeks with no wind is unnatural, yet Agamemnon does nothing. At last Achilles says, "I will speak to my mother." I sit in the tent sweating and waiting while he summons her. When he returns, he says, "It is the gods." But his mother will not—cannot—say who.

We go to Agamemnon. The king's skin is red with heat-rash, and he is angry all the time—at the wind, at his restless army, at anyone who will give him an excuse for it. Achilles says, "You know my mother is a goddess."

Agamemnon almost snarls his answer. Odysseus lays a restraining hand on his shoulder.

"She says the weather is not natural. That it is a message from the gods."

Agamemnon is not pleased to hear it; he glowers and dismisses us.

A month passes, a weary month of feverish sleep and swelter-
ing days. Men's faces are heavy with anger, but there are no more
fights—it is too hot. They lie in the dark and hate each other.

Another month. We are all, I think, going to go mad, suffo-
cated by the weight of the motionless air. How much longer can
this go on? It is terrible: the glaring sky that pins down our host,
the choking heat we suck in with every breath. Even Achilles and
I, alone in our tent with the hundred games we make for each
other, feel winnowed and bare. When will it end?

Finally, word comes. Agamemnon has spoken with the chief
priest, Calchas. We know him—he is small, with a patchy brown
beard. An ugly man, with a face sharp like a weasel and a habit
of running a flickering tongue over his lips before he speaks. But
most ugly of all are his eyes: blue, bright blue. When people see
them, they flinch. Such things are freakish. He is lucky he was not
killed at birth.

Calchas believes it is the goddess Artemis we have offended,
though he does not say why. He gives the usual prescription: an
enormous sacrifice. Dutifully, the cattle are gathered, and the
honey-wine mixed. At our next camp meeting, Agamemnon announces that he has invited his daughter to help preside over the
rites. She is a priestess of Artemis, and the youngest woman ever
to have been so anointed; perhaps she can soothe the raging goddess.

Then we hear more—this daughter is being brought from
Mycenae not just for the ceremony, but for marriage to one of the
kings. Weddings are always propitious, pleasing to the gods; perhaps this too will help.

Agamemnon summons Achilles and me to his tent. His face

looks rumpled and swollen, the skin of a man who has not been sleeping. His nose is still red with rash. Beside him sits Odysseus, cool as ever.

Agamemnon clears his throat. "Prince Achilles. I have called you here with a proposition. Perhaps you have heard that—" He stops, clears his throat again. "I have a daughter, Iphigenia. I would wish her to be your wife."

We stare. Achilles' mouth opens, closes.

Odysseus says, "Agamemnon offers you a great honor, Prince of Phthia."

Achilles stutters, a rare clumsiness. "Yes, and I thank him." His eyes go to Odysseus, and I know that he is thinking: What of Deidameia? Achilles is already married, as Odysseus well knows.

But the king of Ithaca nods, slight so that Agamemnon will not see. We are to pretend that the princess of Scyros does not exist.

"I am honored that you would think of me," Achilles says, hesitating still. His eyes flicker to me, in a question.

Odysseus sees, as he sees everything. "Sadly, you will only have a night together before she must leave again. Though of course, much may happen in a night." He smiles. No one else does.

"It will be good, I believe, a wedding," Agamemnon's words come slowly. "Good for our families, good for the men." He does not meet our gaze.

Achilles is watching for my answer; he will say no if I wish it. Jealousy pricks, but faintly. *It will only be a night,* I think. *It will win him status and sway, and make peace with Agamemnon. It will mean nothing.* I nod, slight, as Odysseus had.

Achilles offers his hand. "I accept, Agamemnon. I will be proud to name you father-in-law."

Agamemnon takes the younger man's hand. I watch his eyes as he does—they are cold and almost sad. Later, I will remember this.

He clears his throat, a third time. "Iphigenia," he says, "is a good girl."

"I am sure she is," Achilles says. "I will be honored to have her as my wife."

Agamemnon nods, a dismissal, and we turn to go. *Iphigenia.* A tripping name, the sound of goat hooves on rock, quick, lively, lovely.

A FEW DAYS LATER, she arrived with a guard of stern Mycenaeans —older men, the ones not fit for war. As her chariot rattled over the stony road to our camp, soldiers came out to stare. It had been long now, since many of them had seen a woman. They feasted on the curve of her neck, a flash of ankle, her hands prettily smoothing the skirt of her bridal gown. Her brown eyes were lit with excitement; she was coming to marry the best of the Greeks.

The wedding would take place in our makeshift marketplace, the square wooden platform with a raised altar behind it. The chariot drew closer, past the thronging, gathered men. Agamemnon stood on the dais, flanked by Odysseus and Diomedes; Calchas too was near. Achilles waited, as grooms do, at the dais's side.

Iphigenia stepped delicately out of her chariot and onto the raised wood floor. She was very young, not yet fourteen, caught between priestess poise and childlike eagerness. She threw her arms around her father's neck, laced her hands through his hair. She whispered something to him and laughed. I could not see his face, but his hands on her slender shoulders seemed to tighten.

Odysseus and Diomedes moved forward all smiles and bows, offering their greetings. Her responses were gracious, but impatient. Her eyes were already searching for the husband she had been promised. She found him easily, her gaze catching on his golden hair. She smiled at what she saw.

At her look, Achilles stepped forward to meet her, standing now just at the platform's edge. He could have touched her then, and I saw him start to, reach towards her tapered fingers, fine as sea-smoothed shells.

Then the girl stumbled. I remember Achilles frowning. I remember him shift, to catch her.

But she wasn't falling. She was being dragged backwards, to the altar behind her. No one had seen Diomedes move, but his hand was on her now, huge against her slender collarbone, bearing her down to the stone surface. She was too shocked to struggle, to know even what was happening. Agamemnon yanked something from his belt. It flashed in the sun as he swung it.

The knife's edge fell onto her throat, and blood spurted over the altar, spilled down her dress. She choked, tried to speak, could not. Her body thrashed and writhed, but the hands of the king pinned her down. At last her struggles grew weaker, her kicking less; at last she lay still.

Blood slicked Agamemnon's hands. He spoke into the silence: "The goddess is appeased."

Who knows what might have happened then? The air was close with the iron-salt smell of her death. Human sacrifice was an abomination, driven from our lands long ago. And his own daughter. We were horrified and angry, and there was violence in us.

Then, before we could move: something on our cheeks. We paused, unsure, and it came again. Soft and cool and smelling of the sea. A murmur went through the men. *Wind. The wind has come.* Jaws unclenched, and muscles loosened. *The goddess is appeased.*

Achilles seemed frozen, fixed to his spot beside the dais. I took his arm and pulled him through the crowd towards our tent. His eyes were wild, and his face was spattered with her blood. I wet a cloth and tried to clean it away, but he caught my hand. "I could have stopped them," he said. The skin of his face was very pale; his voice was hoarse. "I was close enough. I could have saved her."

I shook my head. "You could not have known."

He buried his face in his hands and did not speak. I held him and whispered all the bits of broken comfort I could find.

AFTER HE HAD WASHED his stained hands and changed his bloodied clothes, Agamemnon called us all back to the marketplace. Artemis, he said, had been displeased with the bloodshed this huge army intended. She demanded payment for it, in advance, in kind. Cows were not enough. A virgin priestess was required, human blood for human blood; the leader's eldest daughter would be best.

Iphigenia had known, he said, had agreed to do it. Most men had not been close enough to see the startled panic in her eyes. Gratefully, they believed their general's lie.

They burned her that night on cypress wood, the tree of our darkest gods. Agamemnon broached a hundred casks of wine for celebration; we were leaving for Troy on the morning's tide. Inside our tent Achilles fell into exhausted sleep, his head in my lap. I stroked his forehead, watching the trembles of his dreaming face. In the corner lay his bloodied groom's tunic. Looking at it, at him, my chest felt hot and tight. It was the first death he had ever witnessed. I eased his head off my lap and stood.

Outside, men sang and shouted, drunk and getting drunker. On the beach the pyre burned high, fed by the breeze. I strode past campfires, past lurching soldiers. I knew where I was going.

There were guards outside his tent, but they were slumping, half-asleep. "Who are you?" one asked, starting up. I stepped past him and threw open the tent's door.

Odysseus turned. He had been standing at a small table, his finger to a map. There was a half-finished dinner plate beside it.

"Welcome, Patroclus. It's all right, I know him," he added to the guard stuttering apologies behind me. He waited until the man was gone. "I thought you might come."

I made a noise of contempt. "You would say that whatever you thought."

He half-smiled. "Sit, if you like. I'm just finishing my dinner."

"You let them murder her." I spat the words at him.

He drew a chair to the table. "What makes you think I could have stopped them?"

"You would have, if it had been your daughter." I felt like my eyes were throwing off sparks. I wanted him burnt.

"I don't have a daughter." He tore a piece of bread, sopped it into gravy. Ate.

"Your wife then. What if it had been your wife?"

He looked up at me. "What do you wish me to say? That I would not have done it?"

"Yes."

"I would not have. But perhaps that is why Agamemnon is king of Mycenae, and I rule only Ithaca."

Too easily his answers came to him. His patience enraged me.

"Her death is on your head."

A wry twist of his mouth. "You give me too much credit. I am a counselor only, Patroclus. Not a general."

"You lied to us."

"About the wedding? Yes. It was the only way Clytemnestra would let the girl come." *The mother, back in Argos.* Questions rose in me, but I knew this trick of his. I would not let him divert me from my anger. My finger stabbed the air.

"You dishonored him." Achilles had not thought of this yet— he was too grieved with the girl's death. But I had. They had tainted him with their deceit.

Odysseus waved a hand. "The men have already forgotten he was part of it. They forgot it when the girl's blood spilled."

"It is convenient for you to think so."

He poured himself a cup of wine, drank. "You are angry, and not without reason. But why come to me? I did not hold the knife, or the girl."

"There was blood," I snarled. "All over him, his face. In his mouth. Do you know what it did to him?"

"He grieves that he did not prevent it."

"Of course," I snapped. "He could barely speak."

Odysseus shrugged. "He has a tender heart. An admirable

quality, surely. If it helps his conscience, tell him I placed Diomedes where he was on purpose. So Achilles would see too late."

I hated him so much I could not speak.

He leaned forward in his chair. "May I give you some advice? If you are truly his friend, you will help him leave this soft heart behind. He's going to Troy to kill men, not rescue them." His dark eyes held me like swift-running current. "He is a weapon, a killer. Do not forget it. You can use a spear as a walking stick, but that will not change its nature."

The words drove breath from me, left me stuttering. "He is not—"

"But he is. The best the gods have ever made. And it is time he knew it, and you did too. If you hear nothing else I say, hear that. I do not say it in malice."

I was no match for him and his words that lodged like quills and would not be shaken loose.

"You are wrong," I said. He did not answer me, only watched me turn and flee from him in silence.

CHAPTER NINETEEN

WE LEFT THE NEXT DAY, EARLY, WITH THE REST OF the fleet. From the stern of our ship, Aulis's beach looked strangely bare. Only the gouges of the latrines and the ash-white ruins of the girl's pyre were left to mark our passage. I had woken him this morning with Odysseus' news—that he could not have seen Diomedes in time. He heard me out dully, his eyes bruised despite how long he had slept. Then he said, "She is dead, all the same."

Now he paced the deck behind me. I tried to point things out to him—the dolphins that ran beside us, the rain-swelled clouds on the horizon—but he was listless and only half-listening. Later I caught him standing alone, practicing drill-steps and sword-swings and frowning to himself.

Each night we put in at a different port; our boats were not built for long journeys, for day after day of submersion. The only men we saw were our own Phthians, and Diomedes' Argives. The fleet split so that each island would not be forced to give landfall to the entire army. I was sure it was no coincidence that the king of Argos was paired with us. *Do they think we will run away?* I did my best to ignore him, and he seemed content to leave us in peace.

The islands looked all the same to me—high cliffs bleached

white, pebbled beaches that scratched the underside of our ships with their chalky fingernails. They were frequently scrubby, brush struggling up beside olives and cypresses. Achilles barely noticed any of it. He bent over his armor, polishing it till it shone bright as flame.

On the seventh day we came to Lemnos, just across from the Hellespont's narrow mouth. It was lower than most of our islands, full of swamps and stagnant ponds choking with water lilies. We found a pool some distance from the camp and sat by it. Bugs shivered on its surface, and bulbous eyes peered from amidst the weeds. We were only two days from Troy.

"What was it like when you killed that boy?"

I looked up. His face was in shadow, the hair falling around his eyes.

"Like?" I asked.

He nodded, staring at the water, as if to read its depths. "What did it look like?"

"It's hard to describe." He had taken me by surprise. I closed my eyes to conjure it. "The blood came quickly, I remember that. And I couldn't believe how much there was. His head was split, and his brains showed a little." I fought down the nausea that gripped me, even now. "I remember the sound his head made against the rock."

"Did he twitch? Like animals do?"

"I did not stay long enough to watch."

He was silent a moment. "My father told me once to think of them like animals. The men I kill."

I opened my mouth to speak, then closed it again. He did not look up from his vigil over the water's surface.

"I do not think I can do it," he said. Simply, as was his way.

Odysseus' words pressed in on me, weighed down my tongue. *Good*, I wanted to say. But what did I know? I did not have to win my immortality with war. I held my peace.

"I cannot stop seeing it," he said softly. "Her death." I could not either; the gaudy spray of blood, the shock and pain in her eyes.

"It will not always be like that," I heard myself say. "She was a girl and innocent. These will be men that you fight, warriors who will kill you if you do not strike first."

He turned to look at me, his gaze intent.

"But you will not fight, even if they strike at you. You hate it." If it had been any other man, the words would have been an insult.

"Because I don't have the skill," I said.

"I don't think that is the only reason," he said.

His eyes were green and brown as forest, and even in the dim light I could see the gold.

"Perhaps not," I said, at last.

"But you will forgive me?"

I reached for his hand and took it. "I have no need to forgive you. You cannot offend me." They were rash words, but I said them with all the conviction of my heart.

He looked down a moment at where our hands sat joined. Then his hand ripped itself from mine and blurred past me so swiftly I could not follow it. He stood, something limp and long as a piece of wet rope dangling from his fingers. My eyes stared at it, uncomprehending.

"*Hydros*," Achilles said. Water-snake. It was dun gray, and its flat head hung brokenly to the side. Its body still trembled a little, dying.

Weakness sluiced through me. Chiron had made us memorize their homes and colors. Brown-gray, by water. Quick to anger. Deadly bite.

"I did not even see it," I managed. He threw the thing aside, to lie blunt-nosed and brown among the weeds. He had broken its neck.

"You did not have to," he said. "I saw it."

HE WAS EASIER AFTER THAT, no longer pacing the deck and staring. But I knew that Iphigenia still weighed on him. On both of us. He took to carrying one of his spears with him always. He would toss it into the air and catch it, over and over again.

Slowly, the fleet straggled back together. Some had gone the long way around, south by the island of Lesbos. Others, taking the most direct route, already waited near Sigeum, northwest of Troy. Still others had come as we did, along the Thracian coast. United again, we massed by Tenedos, the island just off of Troy's wide beach. Shouting from ship to ship, we passed word of Agamemnon's plan: the kings would take the front line, their men fanned out behind them. Maneuvering into place was chaos; there were three collisions, and everyone chipped oars on someone else's hull.

At last we were set, with Diomedes on our left and Meriones on our right. The drums began to beat and the line of ships thrust forward, stroke by stroke. Agamemnon had given the order to go slowly, to hold the line and keep pace as one. But our kings were green still at following another man's orders, and each wanted the honor of being first to Troy. Sweat streamed from the faces of the rowers as their leaders lashed them on.

We stood at the prow with Phoinix and Automedon, watching the shore draw closer. Idly, Achilles tossed and caught his spear. The oarsmen had begun to set their strokes by it, the steady, repetitive slap of wood against his palm.

Closer, we started to see distinction on the shore: tall trees and mountains resolving out of the blurring green-brown land. We had edged ahead of Diomedes and were a whole ship length in front of Meriones.

"There are men on the beach," Achilles said. He squinted. "With weapons."

Before I could respond, a horn blew from somewhere in the fleet, and others answered it. The alarm. On the wind came the faint echo of shouts. We had thought we would surprise the Trojans, but they knew we were coming. They were waiting for us.

All along the line, rowers jammed their oars into the water to slow our approach. The men on the beach were undoubtedly soldiers, all dressed in the dark crimson of the house of Priam. A chariot flew along their ranks, churning up sand. The man in it wore a horsehair helmet, and even from a distance we could see the strong lines of his body. He was large, yes, but not as large as Ajax or Menelaus. His power came from his carriage, his perfectly squared shoulders, the straight line of his back arrowing up to heaven. This was no slouchy prince of wine halls and debauchery, as Easterners were said to be. This was a man who moved like the gods were watching; every gesture he made was upright and correct. There was no one else it could be but Hector.

He leapt from the chariot, shouting to his men. We saw spears hoisted and arrows nocked. We were still too far away for their bows, but the tide was dragging us in despite our oars, and the anchors were not catching. Shouts came down the line, in confusion. Agamemnon had no orders; hold position; do not make landfall.

"We are almost in range of their arrows," Achilles commented. He did not seem alarmed by it, though around us there was panic and the sound of feet pounding the deck.

I stared at the shore coming closer. Hector was gone now, back up the beach to a different part of his army. But there was another man before us, a captain, in leather armor and a full helmet that covered all but his beard. He pulled back the string of his bow as the line of ships drew closer. It was not as big a weapon as Philoctetes', but it was not far off. He sighted along the shaft and prepared to kill his first Greek.

He never had the chance. I did not see Achilles move, but I heard it: the whistle of air, and his soft exhalation. The spear was out of his hand and flying across the water that separated our deck from the beach. It was a gesture only. No spearman could throw half so far as an arrow could fly. It would fall well short.

It did not. Its black head pierced the bowman's chest, drove him backwards and over. His arrow twanged harmlessly into the air, shot wild from nerveless fingers. He fell to the sand and did not rise.

From the ships beside us, those who had seen, there were shouts and triumphant horns. The news flared along the line of Greek ships, in either direction: first blood was ours, spilt by the god-like prince of Phthia.

Achilles' face was still, almost peaceful. He did not look like a man who had performed a miracle. On the shore, the Trojans shook their weapons and shouted strange, harsh words. There was a group of them kneeling around the fallen man. Behind me

I heard Phoinix whisper something to Automedon, who ran off. A moment later he reappeared with a handful of spears. Achilles took one without looking, hefted it, and threw. I watched him this time, the graceful curve of his arm, the lift of his chin. He did not pause, as most men did, to aim or sight. He knew where it would go. On the shore another man fell.

We were close now, and arrows began to fly on both sides. Many hit the water, others stuck in masts and hulls. A few men cried out along our line; a few men fell along theirs. Achilles calmly took a shield from Automedon. "Stand behind me," he said. I did. When an arrow came close, he brushed it aside with the shield. He took another spear.

The soldiers grew wilder—their overeager arrows and spears littered the water. Somewhere down the line Protesilaus, Prince of Phylace, leapt laughing from the bow of his ship and began to swim to shore. Perhaps he was drunk; perhaps his blood was fired with hopes of glory; perhaps he wished to outdo the prince of Phthia. A spinning spear, from Hector himself, hit him, and the surf around him flushed red. He was the first of the Greeks to die.

Our men slid down ropes, lifted huge shields to cover themselves from arrows, and began to stream to shore. The Trojans were well marshaled, but the beach offered no natural defense and we outnumbered them. At a command from Hector they seized their fallen comrades and relinquished the beach. Their point had been made: they would not be so easy to kill.

CHAPTER TWENTY

WE GAINED THE BEACH, AND PULLED THE FIRST SHIPS onto the sand. Scouts were sent ahead to watch for further Trojan ambush, and guards were posted. Hot though it was, no one took off his armor.

Quickly, while ships still clogged the harbor behind us, lots were drawn for the placement of each kingdom's camp. The spot assigned to the Phthians was at the farthest end of the beach, away from where the marketplace would be, away from Troy and all the other kings. I spared a quick glance at Odysseus; it was he who had chosen the lots. His face was mild and inscrutable as always.

"How do we know how far to go?" Achilles asked. He was shading his eyes and looking north. The beach seemed to stretch on forever.

"When the sand ends," Odysseus said.

Achilles gestured our ships up the beach, and the Myrmidon captains began unsnarling themselves from the other fleet lines to follow. The sun beat down on us—it seemed brighter here, but perhaps that was only the whiteness of the sand. We walked until we came to a grassy rise springing from the beach. It was crescent-shaped, cradling our future camp at the side and back. At its top was a forest that spread east towards a glinting river. To the south, Troy was a smudge on the horizon. If the pick had been Odysseus' design, we owed him our thanks—it was the best of the camps by far, offering green and shade and quiet.

We left the Myrmidons under Phoinix's direction and made our way back to the main camp. Every place we walked buzzed with the same activities: dragging ships onto the shore, setting tents, unloading supplies. There was a hectic energy to the men, a manic purpose. We were here, at last.

Along the way we passed the camp of Achilles' famous cousin, towering Ajax, king of the isle of Salamis. We had seen him from afar at Aulis and heard the rumors: he cracked the deck of the ship when he walked, he had borne a bull a mile on his back. We found him lifting huge bags out of his ship's hold. His muscles looked large as boulders.

"Son of Telamon," Achilles said.

The huge man turned. Slowly, he registered the unmistakable boy before him. His eyes narrowed, and then stiff politeness took over. "Pelides," he said thickly. He put down his burden and offered a hand knobbed with calluses big as olives. I pitied Ajax, a little. He would be *Aristos Achaion*, if Achilles were not.

Back in the main camp, we stood on the hill that marked the boundary between sand and grass, and regarded the thing we had come for. Troy. It was separated from us by a flat expanse of grass and framed by two wide, lazy rivers. Even so far away, its stone walls caught the sharp sun and gleamed. We fancied we could see the metallic glint of the famous Scaean gate, its brazen hinges said to be tall as a man.

Later, I would see those walls up close, their sharp squared stones perfectly cut and fitted against each other, the work of the god Apollo, it was said. And I would wonder at them—at how, ever, the city could be taken. For they were too high for siege towers, and too strong for catapults, and no sane person would ever try to climb their sheer, divinely smoothed face.

WHEN THE SUN HUNG LOW in the sky, Agamemnon called the first council meeting. A large tent had been set up and filled with a few rows of chairs in a ragged semicircle. At the front of the room sat Agamemnon and Menelaus, flanked by Odysseus and Diomedes. The kings came in and took their seats one by one. Trained from birth in hierarchy, the lesser kings took the lesser places, leaving the front rows for their more famous peers. Achilles, with no hesitation, took a seat in the first row and motioned me to sit beside him. I did so, waiting for someone to object, to ask for my removal. But then Ajax arrived with his bastard half-brother Teucer, and Idomeneus brought his squire and charioteer. Apparently the best were allowed their indulgences.

Unlike those meetings we had heard complaints of at Aulis (pompous, pointless, endless), this was all business—latrines, food supplies, and strategy. The kings were divided between attack and diplomacy—should we not perhaps try to be civilized first? Surprisingly, Menelaus was the loudest voice in favor of a parley. "I will gladly go myself to treat with them," he said. "It is my office."

"What have we come all this way for, if you intend to talk them into surrender?" Diomedes complained. "I could have stayed at home."

"We are not savages," Menelaus said stubbornly. "Perhaps they will hear reason."

"But likely not. Why waste the time?"

"Because, dear King of Argos, if war comes after some diplomacy or delay, we do not seem so much the villains." This was Odysseus. "Which means the cities of Anatolia will not feel so much duty to come to Troy's aid."

"You are for it then, Ithaca?" Agamemnon asked.

Odysseus shrugged. "There are many ways to start a war. I always think raiding makes a good beginning. It accomplishes almost the same thing as diplomacy, but with greater profit."

"Yes! Raiding!" brayed Nestor. "We must have a show of strength before anything else!"

Agamemnon rubbed his chin and swung his gaze over the room of kings. "I think Nestor and Odysseus are correct. Raids first. Then perhaps we will send an embassy. We begin tomorrow."

He needed to give no further instructions. Raiding was typical siege warfare—you would not attack the city, but the lands that surrounded it that supplied it with grain and meat. You would kill those who resisted, make serfs of those who did not. All their food went now to you, and you held their daughters and wives as hostages to their loyalty. Those who escaped would flee to the city for sanctuary. Quarters would quickly grow crowded and mutinous; disease would arise. Eventually, the gates would have to open—out of desperation, if not honor.

I hoped that Achilles might object, declare that there was no glory in killing farmers. But he only nodded, as if this were his hundredth siege, as if he had done nothing but lead raids his whole life.

"One final thing—if there is an attack, I do not want chaos.

We must have lines, and companies." Agamemnon shifted in his chair, seemed almost nervous. Well he might be; our kings were prickly, and this was the first distribution of honor: the place in the line. If there was a rebellion against his authority, now would be the time. The very thought of it seemed to anger him, and his voice grew rougher. This was a frequent fault of his: the more precarious his position, the more unlikable he became.

"Menelaus and I will take the center, of course." There was a faint ripple of discontent at that, but Odysseus spoke over it.

"Very wise, King of Mycenae. Messengers will be able to find you easily."

"Exactly so." Agamemnon nodded briskly, as if that had indeed been the reason. "To my brother's left will be the prince of Phthia. And to my right, Odysseus. The wings will be Diomedes and Ajax." All of these were the most dangerous positions, the places where the enemy would seek to flank or punch through. They were therefore the most important to hold at all costs, and the most prestigious.

"The rest shall be determined by lot." When the murmur had died, Agamemnon stood. "It is settled. We begin tomorrow. Raids, at sun-up."

The sun was just setting as we walked back up the beach to our camp. Achilles was well pleased. One of the greatest places of primacy was his, and without a fight. It was too soon for dinner, so we climbed the grassy hill that lay just beyond our camp, a thin thrust of land emerging from the woods. We stopped there a moment, surveying the new camp and the sea beyond. The dying light was in his hair, and his face was sweet with evening.

A question had burned in me since the battle on the ships, but there had been no time before now to ask it.

"Did you think of them as animals? As your father said?"

He shook his head. "I did not think at all."

Over our heads the gulls screamed and wheeled. I tried to imagine him bloodied and murderous after his first raid tomorrow.

"Are you frightened?" I asked. The first call of a nightingale in the trees at our backs.

"No," he answered. "This is what I was born for."

I WOKE NEXT MORNING to the sound of Trojan waves against the Trojan shore. Achilles still drowsed beside me, so I left the tent to let him sleep. Outside the sky was as cloudless as the day before: the sun bright and piercing, the sea throwing off great sheets of light. I sat and felt the drops of sweat prick and pool against my skin.

In less than an hour the raid would begin. I had fallen asleep thinking of it; I had woken with it. We had discussed, already, that I would not go. Most of the men would not. This was a king's raid, picked to grant first honors to the best warriors. It would be his first real kill.

Yes, there had been the men on the shore, the previous day. But that had been a distant thing, with no blood that we could see. They had fallen almost comically, from too far away to see their faces or pain.

Achilles emerged from the tent, already dressed. He sat beside me and ate the breakfast that was waiting for him. We said little.

There were no words to speak to him of how I felt. Our world was one of blood, and the honor it won; only cowards did not fight. For a prince there was no choice. You warred and won, or warred and died. Even Chiron had sent him a spear.

Phoinix was already up and marshaling the Myrmidons who would accompany him down by the water's edge. It was their first fight, and they wanted their master's voice. Achilles stood, and I watched as he strode towards them—the way the bronze buckles on his tunic threw off fire flashes, the way his dark purple cape brightened his hair to sun's gold. He seemed so much the hero, I could barely remember that only the night before we had spit olive pits at each other, across the plate of cheeses that Phoinix had left for us. That we had howled with delight when he had landed one, wet and with bits of fruit still hanging from it, in my ear.

He held up his spear as he spoke, and shook its gray tip, dark as stone or stormy water. I felt sorry for other kings who had to fight for their authority or wore it poorly, their gestures jagged and rough. With Achilles it was graceful as a blessing, and the men lifted their faces to it, as they would to a priest.

After, he came to bid me farewell. He was life-size again and held his spear loosely, almost lazily.

"Will you help me put the rest of my armor on?"

I nodded and followed him into the cool of the tent, past the heavy cloth door that fell closed like a lamp blown out. I handed him bits of leather and metal as he gestured for them, coverings for his upper thighs, his arms, his belly. I watched him strap these things on, one by one, saw the stiff leather dig into his soft flesh, skin that only last night I had traced with my finger. My hand twitched towards him, longing to pull open the tight buckles, to release him. But I did not. The men were waiting.

I handed him the last piece, his helmet, bristling with horse-hair, and watched as he fitted it over his ears, leaving only a thin strip of his face open. He leaned towards me, framed by bronze, smelling of sweat and leather and metal. I closed my eyes, felt his lips on mine, the only part of him still soft. Then he was gone.

Without him the tent seemed suddenly much smaller, close and smelling of the hides that hung on the walls. I lay on our bed and listened to his shouted orders, then the stamps and snorts of horses. Last of all, the creaking of his chariot wheels as they bore him off. At least I had no fears for his safety. As long as Hector lived he could not die. I closed my eyes and slept.

I WOKE TO HIS NOSE on mine, pressing insistently against me as I struggled from the webbing of my dreams. He smelled sharp and strange, and for a moment I was almost revolted at this creature that clung to me and shoved its face against mine. But then he sat back on his heels and was Achilles again, his hair damp and darkened, as if all the morning's sun had been poured out of it. It stuck to his face and ears, flattened and wet from the helmet.

He was covered in blood, vivid splashes not yet dried to rust. My first thought was terror—that he was wounded, bleeding to death. "Where are you hurt?" I asked. My eyes raked him for the source of the blood. But the spatters seemed to come from no-where. Slowly, my sleep-stupid brain understood. It was not his.

"They could not get close enough to touch me," he said. There was a sort of wondering triumph in his voice. "I did not know how easy it would be. Like nothing. You should have seen it. The men cheered me afterwards." His words were almost dreamy. "I cannot miss. I wish you had seen."

"How many?" I asked.

"Twelve."

Twelve men with nothing at all to do with Paris or Helen or any of us.

"Farmers?" There was a bitterness to my voice that seemed to bring him back to himself.

"They were armed," he said, quickly. "I would not kill an unarmed man."

"How many will you kill tomorrow, do you think?" I asked.

He heard the edge in my voice and looked away. The pain on his face struck me, and I was ashamed. Where was my promise that I would forgive him? I knew what his destiny was, and I had chosen to come to Troy anyway. It was too late for me to object simply because my conscience had begun to chafe.

"I'm sorry," I said. I asked him to tell me what it was like, all of it, as we had always spoken to each other. And he did, everything, how his first spear had pierced the hollow of a man's cheek, carrying flesh with it as it came out the other side. How the second man had fallen struck through the chest, how the spear had caught against his ribcage when Achilles tried to retrieve it. The village had smelled terrible when they left it, muddy and metallic, with the flies already landing.

I listened to every word, imagining it was a story only. As if it were dark figures on an urn he spoke of instead of men.

AGAMEMNON POSTED GUARDS to watch Troy every hour of every day. We were all waiting for something—an attack, or an embassy, or a demonstration of power. But Troy kept her gates shut, and so the raids continued. I learned to sleep through the day so that I would not be tired when he returned; he always needed to talk then, to tell me down to the last detail about the faces and the wounds and the movements of men. And I wanted to be able to listen, to digest the bloody images, to paint them flat and un-remarkable onto the vase of posterity. To release him from it and make him Achilles again.

CHAPTER TWENTY-ONE

WITH THE RAIDS CAME THE DISTRIBUTION. THIS WAS a custom of ours, the awarding of prizes, the claiming of war spoils. Each man was allowed to keep what he personally won—armor that he stripped from a dead soldier, a jewel he tore from the widow's neck. But the rest, ewers and rugs and vases, were carried to the dais and piled high for distribution.

It was not so much about the worth of any object as about honor. The portion you were given was equal to your standing in the army. First allotment went usually to the army's best soldier, but Agamemnon named himself first and Achilles second. I was surprised that Achilles only shrugged. "Everyone knows I am better. This only makes Agamemnon look greedy." He was right, of course. And it made it all the sweeter when the men cheered for us, tottering beneath our pile of treasure, and not for Agamemnon. Only his own Mycenaeans applauded him.

After Achilles came Ajax, then Diomedes and Menelaus, and then Odysseus and on and away until Cebriones was left with only wooden helmets and chipped goblets. Sometimes, though, if a man had done particularly well that day, the general might award him something particularly fine, before even the first man's turn. Thus, even Cebriones was not without hope.

IN THE THIRD WEEK, a girl stood on the dais amidst the swords and woven rugs and gold. She was beautiful, her skin a deep brown, her hair black and gleaming. High on her cheekbone was a spreading bruise where a knuckle had connected. In the twilight, her eyes seemed bruised as well, shadowed as if with Egyptian kohl. Her dress was torn at the shoulder and stained with blood. Her hands were bound.

The men gathered eagerly. They knew what her presence meant—Agamemnon was giving us permission for camp followers, for spear-wives and bed slaves. Until now, the women had simply been forced in the fields and left. In your own tent was a much more convenient arrangement.

Agamemnon mounted the dais, and I saw his eyes slide over the girl, a slight smile on his lips. He was known—all the house of Atreus was—for his appetites. I do not know what came over me then. But I seized Achilles' arm and spoke into his ear.

"Take her."

He turned to me, his eyes wide with surprise.

"Take her as your prize. Before Agamemnon does. Please."

He hesitated, but only a second.

"Men of Greece." He stepped forward, still in the day's armor, still smeared with blood. "Great King of Mycenae."

Agamemnon turned to face him, frowning. "Pelides?"

"I would have this girl as my war-prize."

At the back of the dais Odysseus raised an eyebrow. The men around us murmured. His request was unusual, but not unreasonable; in any other army, first choice would have been his anyway. Irritation flashed in Agamemnon's eyes. I saw the thoughts turn across his face: he did not like Achilles, yet it was not worth it, here, already, to be churlish. She was beautiful, but there would be other girls.

"I grant your wish, Prince of Phthia. She is yours."

The crowd shouted its approval—they liked their commanders generous, their heroes bold and lusty.

Her eyes had followed the exchange with bright intelligence. When she understood that she was to come with us, I saw her swallow, her gaze darting over Achilles.

"I will leave my men here, for the rest of my belongings. The girl will come with me now."

Appreciative laughter and whistles from the men. The girl trembled all over, very slightly, like a rabbit checked by a hawk overhead. "Come," Achilles commanded. We turned to go. Head down, she followed.

BACK IN OUR CAMP, Achilles drew his knife, and her head jerked a little with fear. He was still bloody from the day's battle; it had been her village he had plundered.

"Let me," I said. He handed me the knife and backed away, almost embarrassed.

"I am going to free you," I said.

Up close I saw how dark her eyes were, brown as richest earth, and large in her almond-shaped face. Her gaze flickered from the blade to me. I thought of frightened dogs I had seen, backed small and sharp into corners.

"No, no," I said quickly. "We will not hurt you. I am going to free you."

She looked at us in horror. The gods knew what she thought I was saying. She was an Anatolian farm-girl, with no reason to have ever heard Greek before. I stepped forward to put a hand her arm, to reassure. She flinched as if expecting a blow. I saw the fear in her eyes, of rape and worse.

I could not bear it. There was only one thing I could think of. I turned to Achilles and seized the front of his tunic. I kissed him.

When I let go again, she was staring at us. Staring and staring.

I gestured to her bonds and back to the knife. "All right?"

She hesitated a moment. Then slowly offered her hands.

ACHILLES LEFT TO SPEAK to Phoinix about procuring another tent. I took her to the grass-sided hill and had her sit while I made a compress for her bruised face. Gingerly, eyes downcast, she took it. I pointed to her leg—it was torn open, a long cut along her shin.

"May I see?" I asked, gesturing. She made no response, but reluctantly let me take her leg, dress the wound, and tie it closed with bandages. She followed every movement of my hands and never met my gaze.

After, I took her to her new-pitched tent. She seemed startled by it, almost afraid to enter. I threw open the flap and gestured— food, blankets, an ewer of water, and some clean cast-off clothes.

Hesitating, she stepped inside, and I left her there, eyes wide, staring at it all.

THE NEXT DAY Achilles went raiding again. I trailed around the camp, collecting driftwood, cooling my feet in the surf. All the time I was aware of the new tent in the camp's corner. We had seen nothing of her yet; the flap was shut tight as Troy. A dozen times I almost went to call through the fabric.

At last, at midday, I saw her in the doorway. She was watching me, half-hidden behind the folds. When she saw that I had noticed her, she turned quickly and went to leave.

"Wait!" I said.

She froze. The tunic she wore—one of mine—hung past her knees and made her look very young. How old was she? I did not even know.

I walked up to her. "Hello." She stared at me with those wide eyes. Her hair had been drawn back, revealing the delicate bones of her cheeks. She was very pretty.

"Did you sleep well?" I do not know why I kept talking to her. I thought it might comfort her. I had once heard Chiron say that you talked to babies to soothe them.

"Patroclus," I said, pointing at myself. Her eyes flickered to me, then away.

"Pa-tro-clus." I repeated slowly. She did not answer, did not move; her fingers clutched the cloth of the tent flap. I felt ashamed then. I was frightening her.

"I will leave you," I said. I inclined my head and made to go.

She spoke something, so low I could not hear it. I stopped.

"What?"

"Briseis," she repeated. She was pointing to herself.

"Briseis?" I said. She nodded, shyly.

That was the beginning.

IT TURNED OUT that she did know a little Greek. A few words that her father had picked up and taught her when he heard the army was coming. *Mercy* was one. *Yes* and *please* and *what do you want?* A father, teaching his daughter how to be a slave.

During the days, the camp was nearly empty but for us. We would sit on the beach and halt through sentences with each other. I grew to understand her expressions first, the thoughtful quiet of her eyes, the flickering smiles she would hide behind her hand. We could not talk of much, in those early days, but I did not mind. There was a peace in sitting beside her, the waves rolling companionably over our feet. Almost, it reminded me of my mother, but Briseis' eyes were bright with observation as hers had never been.

Sometimes in the afternoons we would walk together around the camp, pointing to each thing she did not know the name of yet. Words piled on each other so quickly that soon we needed elaborate pantomimes. *Cook dinner, have a bad dream.* Even when my sketches were clumsy, Briseis understood and translated it into a series of gestures so precise that I could smell the meat cooking. I laughed often at her ingenuity, and she would grant me her secret smile.

THE RAIDING CONTINUED. Every day Agamemnon would climb the dais amidst the day's plunder and say, "No news." No news meant no soldiers, no signals, no sounds from the city. It sat stubbornly on the horizon and made us wait.

The men consoled themselves in other ways. After Briseis there was a girl or two on the dais nearly every day. They were all farm girls with callused hands and burnt noses, used to hard work in the sun. Agamemnon took his share, and the other kings as well. You saw them everywhere now, weaving between tents, slopping buckets of water onto their long wrinkled dresses—what they had happened to be wearing the day they were taken. They served fruit and cheese and olives, carved meat, and filled wine-cups. They polished armor, wedging the carapaces between their legs as they sat on the sand. Some of them even wove, spinning threads from tangled clots of sheepswool, animals we had stolen in our raids.

At night they served in other ways, and I cringed at the cries that reached even our corner of the camp. I tried not to think of their burnt villages and dead fathers, but it was difficult to banish. The raids were stamped on every one of the girls' faces, large smears of grief that kept their eyes as wobbling and sloppy as the buckets that swung into their legs. And bruises too, from fists or elbows, and sometimes perfect circles—spear butts, to the forehead or temple.

I could barely watch these girls as they stumbled into camp to be parceled off. I sent Achilles out to ask for them, to seek as many as he could, and the men teased him about his voraciousness, his endless priapism. "Didn't even know you liked girls," Diomedes joked.

Each new girl went first to Briseis, who would speak comfort to her in soft Anatolian. She would be allowed to bathe and be given new clothes, and then would join the others in the tent. We put up a new one, larger, to fit them all: eight, ten, eleven girls. Mostly it was Phoinix and I who spoke to them; Achilles stayed away. He knew that they had seen him killing their brothers and lovers and fathers. Some things could not be forgiven.

Slowly, they grew less frightened. They spun, and talked in their own language, sharing the words they picked up from us— helpful words, like cheese, or water, or wool. They were not as quick as Briseis was, but they patched together enough that they could speak to us.

It was Briseis' idea for me to spend a few hours with them each day, teaching them. But the lessons were more difficult than I thought: the girls were wary, their eyes darting to each other; they were not sure what to make of my sudden appearance in their lives. It was Briseis again who eased their fears and let our lessons grow more elaborate, stepping in with a word of explanation or a clarifying gesture. Her Greek was quite good now, and more and more I simply deferred to her. She was a better teacher than I, and funnier too. Her mimes brought us all to laughter: a sleepy-eyed lizard, two dogs fighting. It was easy to stay with them long and late, until I heard the creaking of the chariot, and the distant banging of bronze, and returned to greet my Achilles.

It was easy, in those moments, to forget that the war had not yet really begun.

CHAPTER TWENTY-TWO

A S TRIUMPHANT AS THE RAIDS WERE, THEY WERE ONLY raids. The men who died were farmers, tradesmen, from the vast network of villages that supported the mighty city—not soldiers. In councils Agamemnon's jaw grew increasingly tight, and the men were restive: where was the fight we were promised?

Close, Odysseus said. He pointed out the steady flood of refugees into Troy. The city must be near to bursting now. Hungry families would be spilling into the palace, makeshift tents would clog the city's streets. It was only a matter of time, he told us.

As if conjured by his prophecy, a flag of parley flew above Troy's walls the very next morning. The soldier on watch raced down the beach to tell Agamemnon: King Priam was willing to receive an embassy.

The camp was afire with the news. One way or another now, something would happen. They would return Helen, or we would get to fight for her properly, in the field.

The council of kings sent Menelaus and Odysseus, the obvious choices. The two men left at first light on their high-stepping horses, brushed to a shine and jingling with ornament. We watched them cross the grass of Troy's wide plain, then vanish into the blur of the dark gray walls.

Achilles and I waited in our tents, wondering. Would they see Helen? Paris could hardly dare to keep her from her husband, and he could hardly dare to show her either. Menelaus had gone conspicuously unarmed; perhaps he did not trust himself.

"Do you know why she chose him?" Achilles asked me.

"Menelaus? No." I remembered the king's face in Tyndareus' hall, glowing with health and good humor. He had been handsome, but not the handsomest man there. He had been powerful, but there were many men with more wealth and greater deeds to their name. "He brought a generous gift. And her sister was already married to his brother, maybe that was part of it."

Achilles considered this, arm folded behind his head. "Do you think she went with Paris willingly?"

"I think if she did, she will not admit it to Menelaus."

"Mmm." He tapped a finger against his chest, thinking. "She must have been willing, though. Menelaus' palace is like a fortress. If she had struggled or cried out, someone would have heard. She knew he must come after her, for his honor if nothing else. And that Agamemnon would seize this opportunity and invoke the oath."

"I would not have known that."

"You are not married to Menelaus."

"So you think she did it on purpose? To cause the war?" This shocked me.

"Maybe. She used to be known as the most beautiful woman in our kingdoms. Now they say she's the most beautiful woman in the world." He put on his best singer's falsetto. "A thousand ships have sailed for her."

A thousand was the number Agamemnon's bards had started using; one thousand, one hundred and eighty-six didn't fit well in a line of verse.

"Maybe she really fell in love with Paris."

"Maybe she was bored. After ten years shut up in Sparta, I'd want to leave too."

"Maybe Aphrodite made her."

"Maybe they'll bring her back with them."

We considered this.

"I think Agamemnon would attack anyway."

"I think so too. They never even mention her anymore."

"Except in speeches to the men."

We were silent a moment.

"So which of the suitors would you have picked?"

I shoved him, and he laughed.

THEY RETURNED AT NIGHTFALL, alone. Odysseus reported to the council, while Menelaus sat silent. King Priam had welcomed them warmly, feasted them in his hall. Then he had stood before them, flanked by Paris and Hector, with his other forty-eight sons arrayed behind. "We know why you have come," he said. "But the lady herself does not wish to return, and has put herself under our protection. I have never refused a woman's defense, and I will not begin now."

"Clever," said Diomedes. "They have found a way around their guilt."

Odysseus continued, "I told them that if they were so resolved, there was no more to say."

Agamemnon rose, his voice ringing grandly. "Indeed there is not. We have tried diplomacy and been rebuffed. Our only honorable course is war. Tomorrow you go to win the glory you deserve, every last man of you."

There was more, but I did not hear it. *Every last man.* Fear sluiced through me. How could I not have thought of this? Of course I would be expected to fight. We were at war now, and all had to serve. Especially the closest companion of *Aristos Achaion.*

That night I barely slept. The spears that leaned against the walls of our tent seemed impossibly tall, and my mind scrambled to remember a few lessons—how to heft them, how to duck. The Fates had said nothing about me—nothing about how long I would live. I woke Achilles, in panic.

"I will be there," he promised me.

IN THE DARK just before dawn, Achilles helped me arm. Greaves, gauntlets, a leather cuirass and bronze breastplate over it. It all seemed more of a hindrance than protection, knocking against my chin when I walked, confining my arms, weighing me down. He assured me that I would get used to it. I did not believe him. Walking out of the tent into the morning's sun I felt foolish, like someone trying on an older brother's clothing. The Myrmidons were waiting, jostling each other with excitement. Together we began the long trip down the beach to the enormous, massing army. Already my breaths were shallow and swift.

We could hear the army before we saw it; boasting, clattering weapons, blowing horns. Then the beach unkinked and revealed a bristling sea of men laid out in neat squares. Each was marked with a pennant that declared its king. Only one square was empty still: a place of primacy, reserved for Achilles and his Myrmidons. We marched forward and arrayed ourselves, Achilles out in front, then a line of captains to either side of me. Behind us, rank upon gleaming rank of proud Phthians.

Before us was the wide flat plain of Troy, ending in the massive gates and towers of the city. At its base a roiling morass was ranged up against us, a blur of dark heads and polished shields that caught the sun and flashed. "Stay behind me," Achilles turned to say. I nodded, and the helmet shook around my ears. Fear was twisting inside of me, a wobbling cup of panic that threatened each moment to spill. The greaves dug into the bones of my feet; my spear weighed down my arm. A trumpet blew and my chest heaved. Now. It was now.

In a clanking, clattering mass, we lurched into a run. This is how we fought—a dead-run charge that met the enemy in the middle. With enough momentum you could shatter their ranks all at once.

Our lines went quickly ragged as some outstripped others in their speed, glory-hungry, eager to be the first to kill a real Trojan. By halfway across the plain we were no longer in ranks, or even kingdoms. The Myrmidons had largely passed me, drifting in a cloud off to the left, and I mingled among Menelaus' long-haired Spartans, all oiled and combed for battle.

I ran, armor banging. My breath came thickly, and the ground shook with the pounding of feet, a rumbling roar growing louder. The dust kicked up by the charge was almost blinding. I could not see Achilles. I could not see the man beside me. I could do nothing but grip my shield and run.

The front lines collided in an explosion of sound, a burst of spraying splinters and bronze and blood. A writhing mass of men and screams, sucking up rank after rank like Charybdis. I saw the mouths of men moving but could not hear them. There was only the crash of shields against shields, of bronze against shattering wood.

A Spartan beside me dropped suddenly, transfixed through the chest by a spear. My head jerked around, looking for the man who had thrown it, but saw nothing but a jumble of bodies. I knelt by the Spartan to close his eyes, to say a quick prayer, then almost vomited when I saw that he was still alive, wheezing at me in beseeching terror.

A crash next to me—I startled and saw Ajax using his giant shield like a club, smashing it into faces and bodies. In his wake, the wheels of a Trojan chariot creaked by, and a boy peered over the side, showing his teeth like a dog. Odysseus pounded past, running to capture its horses. The Spartan clutched at me, his blood pouring over my hands. The wound was too deep; there was nothing to be done. A dull relief when the light faded from his eyes at last. I closed them with gritty, trembling fingers.

I staggered dizzily to my feet; the plain seemed to slew and pound like surf before me. My eyes would not focus; there was too much movement, flashes of sun and armor and skin.

Achilles appeared from somewhere. He was blood-splattered and breathless, his face flushed, his spear smeared red up to the grip. He grinned at me, then turned and leapt into a clump of Trojans. The ground was strewn with bodies and bits of armor, with spear-shafts and chariot wheels, but he never stumbled, not once. He was the only thing on the battlefield that didn't pitch feverishly, like the salt-slicked deck of a ship, until I was sick with it.

I did not kill anyone, or even attempt to. At the end of the morning, hours and hours of nauseating chaos, my eyes were sun blind, and my hand ached with gripping my spear—though I had used it more often to lean on than threaten. My helmet was a boulder crushing my ears slowly into my skull.

It felt like I had run for miles, though when I looked down I saw that my feet had beaten the same circle over and over again, flattening the same dry grass as if preparing a dancing field. Constant terror had siphoned and drained me, even though somehow I always seemed to be in a lull, a strange pocket of emptiness into which no men came, and I was never threatened.

It was a measure of my dullness, my dizziness, that it took me until midafternoon to see that this was Achilles' doing. His gaze was on me always, preternaturally sensing the moment when a soldier's eyes widened at the easy target I presented. Before the man drew another breath, he would cut him down.

He was a marvel, shaft after shaft flying from him, spears that he wrenched easily from broken bodies on the ground to toss at new targets. Again and again I saw his wrist twist, exposing its pale underside, those flute-like bones thrusting elegantly forward. My spear sagged forgotten to the ground as I watched. I could not even see the ugliness of the deaths anymore, the brains, the shattered bones that later I would wash from my skin and hair. All I saw was his beauty, his singing limbs, the quick flickering of his feet.

DUSK CAME AT LAST and released us, limping and exhausted, back to our tents, dragging the wounded and dead. A good day, our kings said, clapping each other on the back. An auspicious beginning. Tomorrow we will do it again.

We did it again, and again. A day of fighting became a week, then a month. Then two.

It was a strange war. No territory was gained, no prisoners were taken. It was for honor only, man against man. With time, a mutual rhythm emerged: we fought a civilized seven days out of ten, with time off for festivals and funerals. No raids, no surprise attacks. The leaders, once buoyant with hopes of swift victory, grew resigned to a lengthy engagement. The armies were remarkably well matched, could tussle on the field day after day with no side discernibly stronger. This was due in part to the soldiers who poured in from all over Anatolia to help the Trojans and make their names. Our people were not the only ones greedy for glory.

Achilles flourished. He went to battle giddily, grinning as he fought. It was not the killing that pleased him—he learned quickly that no single man was a match for him. Nor any two men, nor three. He took no joy in such easy butchery, and less than half as many fell to him as might have. What he lived for were the charges, a cohort of men thundering towards him. There, amidst twenty stabbing swords he could finally, truly *fight*. He gloried in his own strength, like a racehorse too long penned, allowed at last to run. With a fevered impossible grace he fought off ten, fifteen, twenty-five men. *This, at last, is what I can really do.*

I did not have to go with him as often as I had feared. The longer the war dragged on, the less it seemed important to roust every Greek from his tent. I was not a prince, with honor at stake.

I was not a soldier, bound to obedience, or a hero whose skill would be missed. I was an exile, a man with no status or rank. If Achilles saw fit to leave me behind, that was his business alone.

My visits to the field faded to five days, then three, then once every week. Then only when Achilles asked me. This was not often. Most days he was content to go alone, to wade out and perform only for himself. But from time to time he would grow sick of the solitude and beg me to join him, to strap on the leather stiffened with sweat and blood and clamber over bodies with him. To bear witness to his miracles.

Sometimes, as I watched him, I would catch sight of a square of ground where soldiers did not go. It would be near to Achilles, and if I stared at it, it would grow light, then lighter. At last it might reluctantly yield its secret: a woman, white as death, taller than the men who toiled around her. No matter how the blood sprayed, it did not fall on her pale-gray dress. Her bare feet did not seem to touch the earth. She did not help her son; she did not need to. Only watched, as I did, with her huge black eyes. I could not read the look on her face; it might have been pleasure, or grief, or nothing at all.

Except for the time she turned and saw me. Her face twisted in disgust, and her lips pulled back from her teeth. She hissed like a snake, and vanished.

In the field beside him, I steadied, got my sea legs. I was able to discern other soldiers whole, not just body parts, pierced flesh, bronze. I could even drift, sheltered in the harbor of Achilles' protection, along the battle lines, seeking out the other kings. Closest to us was Agamemnon skilled-at-the-spear, always behind the bulk of his well-ranked Mycenaeans. From such safety he would shout orders and hurl spears. It was true enough that he was skilled at it: he had to be to clear the heads of twenty men.

Diomedes, unlike his commander, was fearless. He fought like a feral, savage animal, leaping forward, teeth bared, in quick strikes that did not so much puncture flesh as tear it. After, he would lean wolfishly over the body to strip it, tossing the bits of gold and bronze onto his chariot before moving on.

Odysseus carried a light shield and faced his foes crouched like a bear, spear held low in his sun-browned hand. He would watch the other man with glittering eyes, tracking the flicker of his muscles for where and how the spear would come. When it had passed harmlessly by, he would run forward and spit him at close quarters, like a man spearing fish. His armor was always soaked with blood by the day's end.

I began to know the Trojans, too: Paris, loosing careless arrows from a speeding chariot. His face, even strapped and compressed by the helmet, was cruelly beautiful—bones fine as Achilles' fingers. His slim hips lounged against the sides of his chariot in habitual hauteur, and his red cloak fell around him in rich folds. No wonder he was Aphrodite's favorite: he seemed as vain as she.

From far off, glimpsed only quickly through the corridors of shifting men, I saw Hector. He was always alone, strangely solitary in the space the other men gave him. He was capable and steady and thoughtful, every movement considered. His hands were large and work-roughened, and sometimes, as our army withdrew, we would see him washing the blood from them, so he could pray without pollution. A man who still loved the gods, even as his brothers and cousins fell because of them; who fought fiercely for his family rather than the fragile ice-crust of fame. Then the ranks would close, and he would be gone.

I never tried to get closer to him, and neither did Achilles, who carefully turned from his glimpsed figure to face other Trojans, to wade off to other shoals. Afterwards, when Agamemnon would ask him when he would confront the prince of Troy, he would smile his most guileless, maddening smile. "What has Hector ever done to me?"

CHAPTER TWENTY-THREE

ONE FESTIVAL DAY, SOON AFTER OUR LANDING AT Troy, Achilles rose at dawn. "Where are you going?" I asked him.

"My mother," he said, then slipped through the tent flap before I could speak again.

His mother. Some part of me had hoped, foolishly, that she would not follow us here. That her grief would keep her away, or the distance. But of course they did not. The shore of Anatolia was no more inconvenient than the shore of Greece. And her grief only made her visits longer. He would leave at dawn, and the sun would be nearly at its peak before he would return. I would wait, pacing and unsettled. What could she possibly have to say to him for so long? Some divine disaster, I feared. Some celestial dictate that would take him from me.

Briseis came often to wait with me. "Do you want to walk up to the woods?" she would say. Just the low sweetness of her voice, the fact that she wished to comfort me, helped take me out of myself. And a trip with her to the woods always soothed me. She seemed to know all its secrets, just as Chiron had—where the mushrooms hid, and the rabbits had their burrows. She had even begun to teach me the native names of the plants and trees.

When we were finished, we would sit on the ridge, looking over the camp, so I could watch for his return. On this day, she had picked a small basket of coriander; the fresh green-leaf smell was all around us.

"I am sure he will be back soon," she said. Her words were like new leather, still stiff and precise, not yet run together with use. When I did not answer, she asked, "Where does he stay so long?"

Why shouldn't she know? It wasn't a secret.

"His mother is a goddess," I said. "A sea-nymph. He goes to see her."

I had expected her to be startled or frightened, but she only nodded. "I thought that he was—something. He does not—" She paused. "He does not move like a human."

I smiled then. "What does a human move like?"

"Like you," she said.

"Clumsy, then."

She did not know the word. I demonstrated, thinking to make her laugh. But she shook her head, vehemently. "No. You are not like that. That is not what I meant."

I never heard what she meant, for at that moment Achilles crested the hill.

"I thought I'd find you here," he said. Briseis excused herself, and returned to her tent. Achilles threw himself down on the ground, hand behind his head.

"I'm starving," he said.

"Here." I gave him the rest of the cheese we had brought for lunch. He ate it, gratefully.

"What did you talk about with your mother?" I was almost

nervous to ask. Those hours with her were not forbidden to me, but they were always separate.

His breath blew out, not quite a sigh. "She is worried about me," he said.

"Why?" I bristled at the thought of her fretting over him; that was mine to do.

"She says that there is strangeness among the gods, that they are fighting with each other, taking sides in the war. She fears that the gods have promised me fame, but not how much."

This was a new worry I had not considered. But of course: our stories had many characters. Great Perseus or modest Peleus. Heracles or almost-forgotten Hylas. Some had a whole epic, others just a verse.

He sat up, wrapping his arms around his knees. "I think she is afraid that someone else is going to kill Hector. Before me."

Another new fear. Achilles' life suddenly cut shorter than it already was. "Who does she mean?"

"I don't know. Ajax has tried and failed. Diomedes, too. They are the best after me. There is no one else I can think of."

"What about Menelaus?"

Achilles shook his head. "Never. He is brave and strong, but that is all. He would break against Hector like water on a rock. So. It is me, or no one."

"You will not do it." I tried not to let it sound like begging.

"No." He was quiet a moment. "But I can see it. That's the strange thing. Like in a dream. I can see myself throwing the spear, see him fall. I walk up to the body and stand over it."

Dread rose in my chest. I took a breath, forced it away. "And then what?"

"That's the strangest of all. I look down at his blood and know my death is coming. But in the dream I do not mind. What I feel, most of all, is relief."

"Do you think it can be prophecy?"

The question seemed to make him self-conscious. He shook his head. "No. I think it is nothing at all. A daydream."

I forced my voice to match his in lightness. "I'm sure you're right. After all, Hector hasn't done anything to you."

He smiled then, as I had hoped he would. "Yes," he said. "I've heard that."

DURING THE LONG HOURS of Achilles' absence, I began to stray from our camp, seeking company, something to occupy myself. Thetis' news had disturbed me; quarrels among the gods, Achilles' mighty fame endangered. I did not know what to make of it, and my questions chased themselves around my head until I was half-crazy. I needed a distraction, something sensible and real. One of the men pointed me towards the white physicians' tent. "If you're looking for something to do, they always need help," he said. I remembered Chiron's patient hands, the instruments hung on rose-quartz walls. I went.

The tent's interior was dim, the air dark and sweet and musky, heavy with the metallic scent of blood. In one corner was the physician Machaon, bearded, square-jawed, pragmatically bare-chested, an old tunic tied carelessly around his waist. He was darker than most Greeks, despite the time he spent inside, and his hair was cropped short, practical again, to keep it from his eyes. He bent now over a wounded man's leg, his finger gently probing an embedded arrow point. On the other side of the tent his brother Podalerius finished strapping on his armor. He tossed an offhand word to Machaon before shouldering past me out the door. It was well known that he preferred the battlefield to the surgeon's tent, though he served in both.

Machaon did not look up as he spoke: "You can't be very wounded if you can stand for so long."

"No," I said. "I'm here—" I paused as the arrowhead came free in Machaon's fingers, and the soldier groaned in relief.

"Well?" His voice was business-like but not unkind.

"Do you need help?"

He made a noise I guessed was assent. "Sit down and hold the salves for me," he said, without looking. I obeyed, gathering up the small bottles strewn on the floor, some rattling with herbs, some heavy with ointment. I sniffed them and remembered: garlic and honey salve against infection, poppy for sedation, and yarrow to make the blood clot. Dozens of herbs that brought the centaur's patient fingers back to me, the sweet green smell of the rose-colored cave.

I held out the ones he needed and watched his deft application —a pinch of sedative on the man's upper lip for him to nose and nibble at, a swipe of salve to ward off infection, then dressings to pack and bind and cover. Machaon smoothed the last layer of creamy, scented beeswax over the man's leg and looked up wearily. "Patroclus, yes? And you studied with Chiron? You are welcome here."

A clamor outside the tent, raised voices and cries of pain. He nodded towards it. "They've brought us another—you take him."

The soldiers, Nestor's men, hoisted their comrade onto the

empty pallet in the tent's corner. He had been shot with an arrow, barbed at the tip, through the right shoulder. His face was foamy with sweat-scum, and he'd bitten his lip almost in half with trying not to scream. His breath came now in muffled, explosive pants, and his panicked eyes rolled and trembled. I resisted the urge to call for Machaon—busy with another man who had started to wail—and reached for a cloth to wipe his face.

The arrow had pierced through the thickest part of his shoulder and was threaded half in and half out, like a terrible needle. I would have to break off the fletching and pull the end through him, without further tearing the flesh or leaving splinters that might fester.

Quickly, I gave him the draught that Chiron had taught me: a mix of poppy and willow bark that made the patient light-headed and blunted to pain. He could not hold the cup, so I held it for him, lifting and cradling his head so he would not choke, feeling his sweat and foam and blood seep into my tunic.

I tried to look reassuring, tried not to show the panic I was feeling. He was, I saw, only a year or so older than I. One of Nestor's sons, Antilochus, a sweet-faced young man who doted on his father. "It will be all right," I said, over and over, to myself or him I did not know.

The problem was the arrow shaft; normally a doctor would snap off one end, before pulling it through. But there was not enough of it sticking out of his chest to do it without tearing the flesh further. I could not leave it, nor drag the fletching through the wound. What then?

Behind me one of the soldiers who had brought him stood fidgeting in the doorway. I gestured to him over my shoulder.

"A knife, quickly. Sharp as you can find." I surprised myself with the brisk authority in my voice, the instant obedience it provoked. He returned with a short, finely honed blade meant for cutting meat, still rusty with dried blood. He cleaned it on his tunic before handing it to me.

The boy's face was slack now, his tongue flopping loose in his mouth. I leaned over him and held the arrow shaft, crushing the fletching into my damp palm. With my other hand, I began sawing, cutting through the wood a flake at a time, as lightly as possible, so as not to jar the boy's shoulder. He snuffled and muttered, lost in the fog of the draught.

I sawed and braced and sawed. My back ached, and I berated myself for leaving his head on my knees, for not choosing a better position. Finally the feathered end snapped off, leaving only one long splinter that the knife quickly cut through. At last.

Then, just as difficult: to draw the shaft out the other side of his shoulder. In a moment of inspiration, I grabbed a salve for infection and carefully coated the wood, hoping it would ease the journey and ward off corruption. Then, a little at a time, I began to work the arrow through. After what felt like hours, the splintered end emerged, soaked with blood. With the last of my wits, I wrapped and packed the wound, binding it in a sort of sling across his chest.

Later Podalerius would tell me that I was insane to have done what I did, to have cut so slowly, at such an angle—a good wrench, he said, and the end would have broken. Jarred wound and splinters inside be damned, there were other men who needed tending. But Machaon saw how well the shoulder healed, with no

infection and little pain, and next time there was an arrow wound
he called me over and passed me a sharp blade, looking at me expectantly.

IT WAS A STRANGE TIME. Over us, every second, hung the terror
of Achilles' destiny, while the murmurs of war among the gods
grew louder. But even I could not fill each minute with fear. I have
heard that men who live by a waterfall cease to hear it—in such
a way did I learn to live beside the rushing torrent of his doom.
The days passed, and he lived. The months passed, and I could go
a whole day without looking over the precipice of his death. The
miracle of a year, then two.

The others seemed to feel a similar softening. Our camp began
to form a sort of family, drawn together around the flames of the
dinner fire. When the moon rose and the stars pricked through
the sky's darkness, we would all find our way there: Achilles and
I, and old Phoinix, and then the women—originally only Briseis,
but now a small clump of bobbing faces, reassured by the welcome
she had received. And still one more—Automedon, the youngest of us, just seventeen. He was a quiet young man, and Achilles
and I had watched his strength and deftness grow as he learned
to drive Achilles' difficult horses, to wheel around the battlefield
with the necessary flourish.

It was a pleasure for Achilles and me to host our own hearth,
playing the adults we did not quite feel like, as we passed the meat
and poured the wine. As the fire died down, we would wipe the
juice of the meal from our faces and clamor for stories from Phoi-

nix. He would lean forward in his chair to oblige. The firelight made the bones of his face look significant, Delphic, something that augurs might try to read.

Briseis told stories too, strange and dreamlike—tales of enchantment, of gods spellbound by magic and mortals who blundered upon them unawares; the gods were strange, half man and half animal: rural deities, not the high gods that the city worshipped. They were beautiful, these tales, told in her low singsong voice. Sometimes they were funny too—her imitations of a Cyclops, or the snuffling of a lion seeking out a hidden man.

Later, when we were alone, Achilles would repeat little snatches of them, lifting his voice, playing a few notes on the lyre. It was easy to see how such lovely things might become songs. And I was pleased, because I felt that he had seen her, had understood why I spent my days with her when he was gone. She was one of us now, I thought. A member of our circle, for life.

IT WAS ON ONE OF THESE NIGHTS that Achilles asked her what she knew of Hector.

She had been leaning back on her hands, the inner flush of her elbows warmed by the fire. But at his voice, she startled a little and sat up. He did not speak directly to her often, nor she to him. A remnant, perhaps, of what had happened in her village.

"I do not know much," she said. "I have never seen him, nor any of Priam's family."

"But you have heard things." Achilles was sitting forward now himself.

"A little. I know more of his wife."

"Anything," Achilles said.

She nodded, cleared her throat softly as she often did before a story. "Her name is Andromache, and she is the only daughter of King Eetion of Cilicia. Hector is said to love her above all things.

"He first saw her when he came to her father's kingdom for tribute. She welcomed him, and entertained him at the feast that evening. At the night's end, Hector asked her father for her hand."

"She must have been very beautiful."

"People say she is fair, but not the fairest girl Hector might have found. She is known for a sweet temper and gentle spirit. The country people love her because she often brings them food and clothes. She was pregnant, but I have not heard what became of the child."

"Where is Cilicia?" I asked.

"It is to the south, along the coast, not far from here by horse."

"Near Lesbos," Achilles said. Briseis nodded.

Later, when all the rest had gone, he said, "We raided Cilicia. Did you know?"

"No."

He nodded. "I remember that man, Eetion. He had eight sons. They tried to hold us off."

I could tell by the quietness of his voice.

"You killed them." An entire family, slaughtered.

He caught the look on my face though I tried to hide it. But he did not lie to me, ever.

"Yes."

I knew he killed men every day; he came home wet with their blood, stains he scrubbed from his skin before dinner. But there were moments, like now, when that knowledge overwhelmed me.

When I would think of all the tears that he had made fall, in all the years that had passed. And now Andromache, too, and Hector grieved because of him. He seemed to sit across the world from me then, though he was so close I could feel the warmth rising from his skin. His hands were in his lap, spear-callused but beautiful still. No hands had ever been so gentle, or so deadly.

Overhead, the stars were veiled. I could feel the air's heaviness. There would be a storm tonight. The rain would be soaking, filling up the earth till she burst her seams. It would gush down from the mountaintops, gathering strength to sweep away what stood in its path: animals and houses and men.

He is such a flood, I thought.

His voice broke the silence of my thoughts. "I left one son alive," he said. "The eighth son. So that their line would not die."

Strange that such a small kindness felt like grace. And yet, what other warrior would have done as much? Killing a whole family was something to boast of, a glorious deed that proved you powerful enough to wipe a name from the earth. This surviving son would have children; he would give them his family's name and tell their story. They would be preserved, in memory if not in life.

"I am glad," I said, my heart full.

The logs in the fire grew white with ash. "It is strange," he said. "I have always said that Hector's done nothing to offend me. But he cannot say the same, now."

CHAPTER TWENTY-FOUR

YEARS PASSED AND A SOLDIER, ONE OF AJAX'S, BEGAN TO complain about the war's length. At first he was ignored; the man was hideously ugly and known to be a scoundrel. But he grew eloquent. Four years, he said, and nothing to show for it. Where is the treasure? Where is the woman? When will we leave? Ajax clouted him on the head, but the man would not be silenced. See how they treat us?

Slowly, his discontent spread from one camp to the next. It had been a bad season, particularly wet, and miserable for fighting. Injuries abounded, rashes and mud-turned ankles and infections. The biting flies had settled so thickly over parts of the camp they looked like clouds of smoke.

Sullen and scratching, men began to loiter around the agora. At first they did nothing but collect in small groups, whispering. Then the soldier who had begun it joined them, and their voices grew louder.

Four years!

How do we know she's even in there? Has anyone seen her?

Troy will never submit to us.

We should all just stop fighting.

When Agamemnon heard, he ordered them whipped. The next day there were twice as many; not a few were Mycenaeans.

Agamemnon sent an armed force to disperse them. The men slunk off, then returned when the force was gone. In answer, Agamemnon ordered a phalanx to guard the agora all day. But this was frustrating duty—in full sun, where the flies were most numerous. By the end of the day, the phalanx was ragged from desertion and the number of mutineers had swollen.

Agamemnon used spies to report on those who complained; these men were then seized and whipped. The next morning, several hundred men refused to fight. Some gave illness as an excuse, some gave no excuse at all. Word spread, and more men took suddenly ill. They threw their swords and shields onto the dais in a heap and blocked the agora. When Agamemnon tried to force his way through, they folded their arms and would not budge.

Denied in his own agora, Agamemnon grew red in the face, then redder. His fingers went white on the scepter he held, stout wood banded with iron. When the man in front of him spat at his feet, Agamemnon lifted the scepter and brought it down sharply on his head. We all heard the crack of breaking bone. The man dropped.

I do not think Agamemnon meant to hit him so hard. He seemed frozen, staring at the body at his feet, unable to move. Another man knelt to roll the body over; half the skull was caved in from the force of the blow. The news hissed through the men with a sound like a fire lighting. Many drew their knives. I heard Achilles murmur something; then he was gone from my side.

Agamemnon's face was filled with the growing realization of his mistake. He had recklessly left his loyal guards behind. He was surrounded now; help could not reach him even if it wanted to. I held my breath, sure I was about to see him die.

"Men of Greece!"

Startled faces turned to the shout. Achilles stood atop a pile of shields on the dais. He looked every inch the champion, beautiful and strong, his face serious.

"You are angry," he said.

This caught their attention. They *were* angry. It was unusual for a general to admit that his troops might feel such a thing.

"Speak your grievance," he said.

"We want to leave!" The voice came from the back of the crowd. "The war is hopeless!"

"The general lied to us!"

A surging murmur of agreement.

"It has been four years!" This last was the angriest of all. I could not blame them. For me these four years had been an abundance, time that had been wrested from the hands of miserly fates. But for them it was a life stolen: from children and wives, from family and home.

"It is your right to question such things," Achilles said. "You feel misled; you were promised victory."

"Yes!"

I caught a glimpse of Agamemnon's face, curdled with anger. But he was stuck in the crowd, unable to free himself or speak without causing a scene.

"Tell me," Achilles said. "Do you think *Aristos Achaion* fights in hopeless wars?"

The men did not answer.

"Well?"

"No," someone said.

Achilles nodded, gravely. "No. I do not, and I will swear so on any oath. I am here because I believe that we will win. I am staying until the end."

"That is fine for you." A different voice. "But what of those who wish to go?"

Agamemnon opened his mouth to answer. I could imagine what he might have said. No one leaves! Deserters will be executed! But he was lucky that Achilles was swifter.

"You're welcome to leave whenever you like."

"We are?" The voice was dubious.

"Of course." He paused, and offered his most guileless, friendly smile. "But I get your share of the treasure when we take Troy."

I felt the tension in the air ease, heard a few huffs of appreciative laughter. The prince Achilles spoke of treasure to be won, and where there was greed there was hope.

Achilles saw the change in them. He said, "It is past time to take the field. The Trojans will start to think we are afraid." He drew his flashing sword and held it in the air. "Who dares to show them otherwise?"

There were shouts of agreement, followed by a general clanging as men reclaimed their armor, seized their spears. They hoisted the dead man and carried him off; everyone agreed that he had always been troublesome. Achilles leapt down from the dais and passed Agamemnon with a formal nod. The king of Mycenae said nothing. But I watched his eyes follow Achilles for a long time after that.

IN THE AFTERMATH of the almost-rebellion, Odysseus devised a project to keep the men too busy for further unrest: a giant palisade, built around the entire camp. Ten miles, he wanted it to run, protecting our tents and our ships from the plain beyond. At its base would be a ditch, bristling with spikes.

When Agamemnon announced the project, I was sure the men would know it for the ploy it was. In all the years of the war, the camp and ships had never been in danger, whatever reinforcements came. After all, who could get past Achilles?

But then Diomedes stepped forward, praising the plan and frightening the men with visions of night raids and burning ships. This last was particularly effective—without the ships, we could not get home again. By the end of it, the men's eyes were bright and eager. As they went cheerfully off to the woods with their hatchets and levels, Odysseus found the original trouble-causing soldier—Thersites, his name was—and had him beaten quietly into unconsciousness.

That was the end of mutinies at Troy.

THINGS CHANGED AFTER THAT, whether because of the joint venture of the wall or the relief of violence averted. All of us, from the lowest foot soldier to the general himself, began to think of Troy as a sort of home. Our invasion became an occupation. Before now we had lived as scavengers off the land and the villages that we raided. Now we began to build, not just the wall, but the things of a town: a forge, and a pen for the cattle that we stole from the neighboring farms, even a potter's shed. In this last, amateur artisans labored to replace the cracking ceramics we had brought with us, most of them leaking or broken from hard camp use. Everything we owned now was makeshift, scrounged, having lived at least two lives before as something else. Only the kings' personal armors remained untouched, insignias polished and pure.

The men too became less like dozens of different armies, and more like countrymen. These men, who had left Aulis as Cretans and Cypriots and Argives, now were simply Greeks—cast into the same pot by the otherness of the Trojans, sharing food and women and clothing and battle stories, their distinctions blurred away. Agamemnon's boast of uniting Greece was not so idle after all. Even years later this camaraderie would remain, a fellow-feeling so uncharacteristic of our fiercely warring kingdoms. For a generation, there would be no wars among those of us who had fought at Troy.

EVEN I WAS NOT EXEMPT. During this time—six, seven years in which I spent more and more hours in Machaon's tent and fewer with Achilles in the field—I got to know the other men well. Everyone eventually made their way there, if only for smashed toes or ingrown nails. Even Automedon came, covering the bleeding remnants of a savaged boil with his hand. Men doted on their slave women and brought them to us with swollen bellies. We delivered their children in a steady, squalling stream, then fixed their hurts as they grew older.

And it was not just the common soldiery: in time, I came to know the kings as well. Nestor with his throat syrup, honeyed and warmed, that he wanted at the end of a day; Menelaus and the opiate he took for his headaches; Ajax's acid stomach. It moved me to see how much they trusted me, turned hopeful faces towards me for comfort; I grew to like them, no matter how difficult they were in council.

I developed a reputation, a standing in the camp. I was asked for, known for my quick hands and how little pain I caused. Less and less often Podalerius took his turn in the tent—I was the one who was there when Machaon was not.

I began to surprise Achilles, calling out to these men as we walked through the camp. I was always gratified at how they would raise a hand in return, point to a scar that had healed over well.

After they were gone, Achilles would shake his head. "I don't know how you remember them all. I swear they look the same to me."

I would laugh and point them out again. "That's Sthenelus, Diomedes' charioteer. And that's Podarces, whose brother was the first to die, remember?"

"There are too many of them," he said. "It's simpler if they just remember me."

THE FACES AROUND OUR HEARTH began to dwindle, as one woman after another quietly took a Myrmidon for her lover, and then husband. They no longer needed our fire; they had their own. We were glad. Laughter in the camp, and voices raised in pleasure at night, and even the swelling of bellies—Myrmidons grinning with satisfaction—were things that we welcomed, the golden stitch of their happiness like a fretted border around our own.

After a time, only Briseis was left. She never took a lover, despite her beauty and the many Myrmidons who pursued her. Instead she grew into a kind of aunt—a woman with sweets and love potions and soft fabrics for the drying of eyes. This is how I think of us, when I remember our nights at Troy: Achilles and I beside each other, and Phoinix smiling, and Automedon stuttering through the punch lines of jokes, and Briseis with her secret eyes and quick, spilling laughter.

I WOKE BEFORE DAWN and felt the first twinging cold of fall in the air. It was a festival day, the harvest of first-fruits to the god Apollo. Achilles was warm beside me, his naked body heavy with sleep. The tent was very dark, but I could just see the features of his face, the strong jaw and gentle curves of his eyes. I wanted to wake him and see those eyes open. A thousand thousand times I had seen it, but I never tired of it.

My hand slid lightly over his chest, stroking the muscles beneath. We were both of us strong now, from days in the white tent and in the field; it shocked me sometimes to catch sight of myself. I looked like a man, broad as my father had been, though much leaner.

He shivered beneath my hand, and I felt desire rise in me. I drew back the covers so that I might see all of him. I bent and pressed my mouth to him, in soft kisses that trailed down his stomach.

Dawn stole through the tent flap. The room lightened. I saw the moment he woke and knew me. Our limbs slid against one another, on paths that we had traced so many times before, yet still were not old.

Some time later, we rose and took our breakfast. We had thrown open the tent flap to let in the air; it ruffled pleasantly over our damp skin. Through the doorway we watched the crisscrossing of Myrmidons about their chores. We saw Automedon race down to the sea for a swim. We saw the sea itself, inviting and warm from a summer of sun. My hand sat familiarly on his knee.

She did not come through the door. She was simply there, in the tent's center, where a moment before there had been empty space. I gasped, and yanked my hand from where it rested on him. I knew it was foolish, even as I did it. She was a goddess; she could see us whenever she wished.

"Mother," he said, in greeting.

"I have received a warning." The words were snapped off, like an owl biting through a bone. The tent was dim, but Thetis' skin burned cold and bright. I could see each slicing line of her face, each fold of her shimmering robe. It had been a long time since I had seen her so close, since Scyros. I had changed since then. I had gained strength and size, and a beard that grew if I did not shave it away. But she was the same. Of course she was.

"Apollo is angry and looks for ways to move against the Greeks. You will sacrifice to him today?"

"I will," Achilles said. We always observed the festivals, dutifully slitting the throats and roasting the fat.

"You must," she said. Her eyes were fixed on Achilles; they did not seem to see me at all. "A hecatomb." Our grandest offering, a hundred head of sheep or cattle. Only the richest and most powerful men could afford such an extravagance of piety. "Whatever the others do, do this. The gods have chosen sides, and you must not draw their anger."

It would take us most of the day to slaughter them all, and the camp would smell like a charnel house for a week. But Achilles nodded. "We will do it," he promised.

Her lips were pressed together, two red slashes like the edge of a wound.

"There is more," she said.

Even without her gaze upon me, she frightened me. She brought the whole urgent universe wherever she went, portents and angry deities and a thousand looming perils.

"What is it?"

She hesitated, and fear knotted my throat. What could make a goddess pause was terrifying indeed.

"A prophecy," she said. "That the best of the Myrmidons will die before two more years have passed."

Achilles' face was still; utterly still. "We have known it was coming," he said.

A curt shake of her head. "No. The prophecy says you will still be alive when it happens."

Achilles frowned. "What do you think it means?"

"I do not know," she said. Her eyes were very large; the black pools opened as if they would drink him, pull him back into her. "I fear a trick." The Fates were well known for such riddles, unclear until the final piece had fallen. Then, bitterly clear.

"Be watchful," she said. "You must take care."

"I will," he said.

She had not seemed to know I was there, but now her eyes found me, and her nose wrinkled, as if at a rising stench. She looked back to him. "He is not worthy of you," she said. "He has never been."

"We disagree on this," Achilles answered. He said it as if he had said it many times before. Probably he had.

She made a low noise of contempt, then vanished. Achilles turned to me. "She is afraid."

"I know," I said. I cleared my throat, trying to release the clot of dread that had formed there.

"Who is the best of the Myrmidons, do you think? If I am excluded."

I cast my mind through our captains. I thought of Automedon, who had become Achilles' valuable second on the battlefield. But I would not call him best.

"I don't know," I said.

"Do you think it means my father?" he asked.

Peleus, home in Phthia, who had fought with Heracles and Perseus. A legend in his own time for piety and courage, even if not in times to come. "Maybe," I admitted.

We were silent a moment. Then he said, "I suppose we will know soon enough."

"It is not you," I said. "At least there is that."

That afternoon we performed the sacrifice his mother had commanded. The Myrmidons built the altar fires high, and I held bowls for the blood while Achilles cut throat after throat. We burned the rich thigh-pieces with barley and pomegranate, poured our best wine over the coals. *Apollo is angry,* she had said. One of our most powerful gods, with his arrows that could stop a man's heart, swift as rays of sun. I was not known for my piety, but that day I praised Apollo with an intensity that could have rivaled Peleus himself. And whoever the best of the Myrmidons was, I sent the gods a prayer for him as well.

BRISEIS ASKED ME to teach her medicine and promised in return a knowledge of the area's herbs, indispensable to Machaon's dwindling supply. I agreed, and passed many contented days with her in the forest, parting low-hanging branches, reaching underneath rotting logs for mushrooms as delicate and soft as the ear of a baby.

Sometimes on those days her hand would accidentally brush mine, and she would look up and smile, water drops hanging from her ears and hair like pearls. Her long skirt was tied practically around her knees, revealing feet that were sturdy and sure.

One of these days we had stopped for lunch. We feasted on cloth-wrapped bread and cheese, strips of dried meat, and water scooped with our hands from the stream. It was spring, and we were surrounded by the profusion of Anatolian fertility. For three weeks the earth would paint herself in every color, burst every bud, unfurl each rioting petal. Then, the wild flush of her excitement spent, she would settle down to the steady work of summer. It was my favorite time of year.

I should have seen it coming. Perhaps you will think me stupid that I did not. I was telling her a story—something about Chiron, I think—and she was listening, her eyes dark like the earth on which we sat. I finished, and she was quiet. This was nothing unusual; she was often quiet. We were sitting close to each other, heads together as if in conspiracy. I could smell the fruit she had eaten; I could smell the rose oils she pressed for the other girls, still staining her fingers. She was so dear to me, I thought. Her serious face and clever eyes. I imagined her as a girl, scraped with tree-climbing, skinny limbs flying as she ran. I wished that I had known her then, that she had been with me at my father's house, had skipped stones with my mother. Almost, I could imagine her there, hovering just at the edge of my remembrance.

Her lips touched mine. I was so surprised I did not move. Her mouth was soft and a little hesitant. Her eyes were sweetly closed. Of habit, of its own accord, my mouth parted. A moment passed like this, the ground beneath us, the breeze sifting flower scents. Then she drew back, eyes down, waiting for judgment. My pulse sounded in my ears, but it was not as Achilles made it sound. It was something more like surprise, and fear that I would hurt her. I put my hand to hers.

She knew, then. She felt it in the way I took her hand, the way my gaze rested on her. "I'm sorry," she whispered.

I shook my head, but could not think of what more to say.

Her shoulders crept up, like folded wings. "I know that you love him," she said, hesitating a little before each word. "I know But I thought that—some men have wives and lovers both."

Her face looked very small, and so sad that I could not be silent.

"Briseis," I said. "If I ever wished to take a wife, it would be you."

"But you do not wish to take a wife."

"No," I said, as gently as I could.

She nodded, and her eyes dropped again. I could hear her slow breaths, the faint tremor in her chest.

"I'm sorry," I said.

"Do you not ever want children?" she asked.

The question surprised me. I still felt half a child myself, though most my age were parents several times over.

"I don't think I would be much of a parent," I said.

"I do not believe that," she said.

"I don't know," I said. "Do you?"

I asked it casually, but it seemed to strike deep, and she hesitated. "Maybe," she said. And then I understood, too late, what she had really been asking me. I flushed, embarrassed at my thoughtlessness. And humbled, too. I opened my mouth to say something. To thank her, perhaps.

But she was already standing, brushing off her dress. "Shall we go?"

There was nothing to do but rise and join her.

THAT NIGHT I could not stop thinking of it: Briseis' and my child. I saw stumbling legs, and dark hair and the mother's big eyes. I saw us by the fire, Briseis and I, and the baby, playing with some bit of wood I had carved. Yet there was an emptiness to the scene, an ache of absence. Where was Achilles? Dead? Or had he never existed? I could not live in such a life. *But Briseis had not asked me to.* She had offered me all of it, herself and the child and Achilles, too.

I shifted to face Achilles. "Did you ever think of having children?" I asked.

His eyes were closed, but he was not sleeping. "I have a child," he answered.

It shocked me anew each time I remembered it. His child with Deidameia. A boy, Thetis had told him, called Neoptolemus. *New*

War. Nicknamed Pyrrhus, for his fiery red hair. It disturbed me to think of him—a piece of Achilles wandering through the world. "Does he look like you?" I had asked Achilles once. Achilles had shrugged. "I didn't ask."

"Do you wish you could see him?"

Achilles shook his head. "It is best that my mother raise him. He will be better with her."

I did not agree, but this was not the time to say so. I waited a moment, for him to ask me if I wished to have a child. But he did not, and his breathing grew more even. He always fell asleep before I did.

"Achilles?"

"Mmm?"

"Do you like Briseis?"

He frowned, his eyes still closed. "Like her?"

"Enjoy her," I said. "You know."

His eyes opened, more alert than I had expected. "What does this have to do with children?"

"Nothing." But I was obviously lying.

"Does she wish to have a child?"

"Maybe," I said.

"With me?" he said.

"No," I said.

"That is good," he said, eyelids drooping once more. Moments passed, and I was sure he was asleep. But then he said, "With you. She wants to have a child with you."

My silence was his answer. He sat up, the blanket falling from his chest. "Is she pregnant?" he asked.

There was a tautness to his voice I had not heard before.

"No," I said.

His eyes dug into mine, sifting them for answers.

"Do you want to?" he asked. I saw the struggle on his face. Jealousy was strange to him, a foreign thing. He was hurt, but did not know how to speak of it. I felt cruel, suddenly, for bringing it up.

"No," I said. "I don't think so. No."

"If you wanted it, it would be all right." Each word was carefully placed; he was trying to be fair.

I thought of the dark-haired child again. I thought of Achilles.

"It is all right now," I said.

The relief on his face filled me with sweetness.

THINGS WERE STRANGE for some time after that. Briseis would have avoided me, but I called on her as I used to, and we went for our walks as we always had. We talked of camp gossip and medicine. She did not mention wives, and I was careful not to mention children. I still saw the softness in her eyes when she looked at me. I did my best to return it as I could.

CHAPTER TWENTY-FIVE

O NE DAY IN THE NINTH YEAR, A GIRL MOUNTED THE dais. There was a bruise on her cheek, spreading like spilled wine down the side of her face. Ribbons fluttered from her hair—ceremonial fillets that marked her as servant to a god. A priest's daughter, I heard someone say. Achilles and I exchanged a glance.

She was beautiful, despite her terror: large hazel eyes set in a round face, soft chestnut hair loose around her ears, a slender girlish frame. As we watched, her eyes filled, dark pools that brimmed their banks, spilling down her cheeks, falling from her chin to the ground. She did not wipe them away. Her hands were tied behind her back.

As the men gathered, her eyes lifted, seeking the sky in mute prayer. I nudged Achilles, and he nodded; but before he could claim her, Agamemnon stepped forward. He rested one hand on her slight, bowed shoulder. "This is Chryseis," he said. "And I take her for myself." Then he pulled her from the dais, leading her roughly to his tent. I saw the priest Calchas frowning, his mouth half-open as if he might object. But then he closed it, and Odysseus finished the distribution.

IT WAS BARELY A MONTH after that the girl's father came, walking down the beach with a staff of gold-studded wood, threaded with garlands. He wore his beard long in the style of Anatolian priests, his hair unbound but decorated with bits of ribbon to match his staff. His robe was banded with red and gold, loose with fabric that billowed and flapped around his legs. Behind him, silent underpriests strained to heft the weight of huge wooden chests. He did not slow for their faltering steps but strode relentlessly onwards.

The small procession moved past the tents of Ajax, and Diomedes, and Nestor—closest to the agora—and then onto the dais itself. By the time Achilles and I had heard, and run, weaving around slower soldiers, he had planted himself there, staff strong. When Agamemnon and Menelaus mounted the dais to approach him, he did not acknowledge them, only stood there proud before his treasure and the heaving chests of his underlings. Agamemnon glowered at the presumption, but held his tongue.

Finally, when enough soldiers had gathered, drawn from every corner by breathless rumor, he turned to survey them all, his eyes moving across the crowd, taking in kings and common. Landing, at last, on the twin sons of Atreus who stood before him.

He spoke in a voice resonant and grave, made for leading prayers. He gave his name, Chryses, and identified himself, staff raised, as a high priest of Apollo. Then he pointed to the chests, open now to show gold and gems and bronze catching the sun.

"None of this tells us why you have come, Priest Chryses." Menelaus' voice was even, but with an edge of impatience. Trojans did not climb the dais of the Greek kings and make speeches.

"I have come to ransom my daughter, Chryseis," he said. "Taken unlawfully by the Greek army from our temple. A slight girl, and young, with fillets in her hair."

The Greeks muttered. Suppliants seeking ransom knelt and begged, they did not speak like kings giving sentence in court. Yet he was a high priest, not used to bending to anyone but his god, and allowances could be made. The gold he offered was generous, twice what the girl was worth, and a priest's favor was never something to scorn. That word, *unlawful*, had been sharp as a drawn sword, but we could not say that he was wrong to use it. Even Diomedes and Odysseus were nodding, and Menelaus drew a breath as if to speak.

But Agamemnon stepped forward, broad as a bear, his neck muscles twisting in anger.

"Is this how a man begs? You are lucky I do not kill you where you stand. I am this army's commander," he spat. "And you have no leave to speak before my men. Here is your answer: no. There will be no ransom. She is my prize, and I will not give her up now or ever. Not for this trash, or any other you can bring." His fingers clenched, only inches from the priest's throat. "You will depart now, and let me not ever catch you in my camps again, *priest*, or even your garlands will not save you."

Chryses' jaw was clamped down on itself, though whether from fear or biting back a reply we could not tell. His eyes burned with bitterness. Sharply, without a word, he turned and stepped from the dais and strode back up the beach. Behind him trailed his underpriests with their clinking boxes of treasure.

Even after Agamemnon left and the men had exploded into

gossip around me, I watched the shamed priest's distant, retreating figure. Those at the end of the beach said that he was crying out and shaking his staff at the sky.

That night, slipping among us like a snake, quick and silent and flickering, the plague began.

WHEN WE WOKE the next morning, we saw the mules drooping against their fences, breaths shallow and bubbling with yellow mucus, eyes rolling. Then by midday it was the dogs—whining and snapping at the air, tongues foaming a red-tinged scum. By the late afternoon, every one of these beasts was dead, or dying, shuddering on the ground in pools of bloody vomit.

Machaon and I, and Achilles too, burned them as fast as they fell, ridding the camp of their bile-soaked bodies, their bones that rattled as we tossed them onto the pyres. When we went back to the camp that night, Achilles and I scrubbed ourselves in the harsh salt of the sea, and then with clean water from the stream in the forest. We did not use the Simois or the Scamander, the big meandering Trojan rivers that the other men washed in and drank from.

In bed, later, we speculated in hushed whispers, unable to help but listen for the hitch in our own breath, the gathering of mucus in our throats. But we heard nothing except our voices repeating the remedies Chiron had taught us like murmured prayers.

THE NEXT MORNING it was the men. Dozens pierced with illness, crumpling where they stood, their eyes bulging and wet, lips cracking open and bleeding fine red threads down their chins. Machaon and Achilles and Podalerius and I, and even, eventually, Briseis, ran to drag away each newly dropped man—downed as suddenly as if by a spear or arrow.

At the edge of the camp a field of sick men bloomed. Ten and twenty and then fifty of them, shuddering, calling for water, tearing off their clothes for respite from the fire they claimed raged in them. Finally, in the later hours, their skin broke apart, macerating like holes in a worn blanket, shredding to pus and pulpy blood. At last their violent trembling ceased, and they lay puddling in the swamp of their final torrent: the dark emptying of their bowels, clotted with blood.

Achilles and I built pyre after pyre, burning every scrap of wood we could find. Finally we abandoned dignity and ritual for necessity, throwing onto each fire not one, but a heap of bodies. We did not even have time to stand watch over them as their flesh and bone mingled and melted together.

Eventually most of the kings joined us— Menelaus first, then Ajax, who split whole trees with a single stroke, fuel for fire after fire. As we worked, Diomedes went among the men and discovered the few who still lay concealed in their tents, shaking with fever and vomit, hidden by their friends who did not want, yet, to send them to the death grounds. Agamemnon did not leave his tent.

Another day then, and another, and every company, every king, had lost dozens of soldiers. Although strangely, Achilles and I noted, our hands pulling closed eyelid after eyelid, none of them were kings. Only minor nobles and foot soldiers. None of them were women; this too we noticed. Our eyes found each other's, full of suspicions that grew as men dropped suddenly with a cry,

hands clutching their chests where the plague had struck them like
the quick shaft of an arrow.

IT WAS THE NINTH NIGHT of this—of corpses, and burning, and
our faces streaked with pus. We stood in our tent gasping with ex-
haustion, stripping off the tunics we had worn, throwing them aside
for the fire. Our suspicions tumbled out, confirmed in a thousand
ways, that this was not a natural plague, not the creeping spread of
haphazard disease. It was something else, sudden and cataclysmic
as the snuffing of Aulis' winds. A god's displeasure.

We remembered Chryses and his righteous outrage at Agamemnon's blasphemy, his disregard for the codes of war and fair
ransom. And we remembered, too, which god he served. The divinity of light and medicine and plague.

Achilles slipped out of the tent when the moon was high. He
came back some time later, smelling of the sea.

"What does she say?" I asked, sitting up in bed.

"She says we are right."

ON THE TENTH DAY of the plague, with the Myrmidons at our
backs, we strode up the beach to the agora. Achilles mounted the
dais and cupped his hands to help his voice carry. Shouting over
the roar of pyres and the weeping of women and the groans of the
dying, he called for every man in camp to gather.

Slowly, fearfully, men staggered forward, blinking in the sun.
They looked pale and hunted, fearful of the plague arrows that
sank in chests like stones into water, spreading their rot as ripples

in a pond. Achilles watched them come, armor buckled around him, sword strapped to his side, his hair gleaming like water poured over bright bronze. It was not forbidden for someone other than the general to call a meeting, but it had never been done in our ten years at Troy.

Agamemnon shouldered through the crowd with his Mycenaeans to mount the dais. "What is this?" he demanded.

Achilles greeted him politely. "I have gathered the men to speak of the plague. Do I have your leave to address them?"

Agamemnon's shoulders were hunched forward with shame-sprung rage; he should have called this meeting himself long ago, and he knew it. He could hardly rebuke Achilles for doing it now, especially not with the men watching. The contrast between the two had never seemed more sharp: Achilles relaxed and in control, with an ease that denied the funeral pyres and sunken cheeks; Agamemnon with his face tight as a miser's fist, louring over us all.

Achilles waited until the men had assembled, kings and common both. Then he stepped forward and smiled. "Kings," he said, "Lords, Men of the Greek Kingdoms, how can we fight a war when we are dying of plague? It's time—past time—that we learn what we have done to deserve a god's anger."

Swift whispers and murmurs; men had suspected the gods. Was not all great evil and good sent from their hands? But to hear Achilles say so openly was a relief. His mother was a goddess, and he would know.

Agamemnon's lips were pulled back to show his teeth. He stood too close to Achilles, as if he would crowd him off the dais. Achilles did not seem to notice. "We have a priest here, among us, a man close to the gods. Should we not ask him to speak?"

A hopeful ripple of assent went through the men. I could hear the creaking of metal, Agamemnon's grip on his own wrist, the slow strangle of his buckled gauntlet.

Achilles turned to the king. "Is this not what you recommended to me, Agamemnon?"

Agamemnon's eyes narrowed. He did not trust generosity; he did not trust anything. He stared at Achilles a moment, waiting for the trap. At last, ungratefully, he said, "Yes. I did." He gestured roughly to his Mycenaeans. "Bring me Calchas."

They towed the priest forward, out of the crowd. He was uglier than ever, with his beard that never quite filled in, his hair scraggly and rank with sour sweat. He had a habit of darting his tongue across cracked lips before he spoke.

"High King and Prince Achilles, you catch me unprepared. I did not think that—" Those freakish blue eyes flickered between the two men. "That is, I did not expect I would be asked to speak here before so many." His voice wheedled and ducked, like a weasel escaping the nest.

"Speak," Agamemnon commanded.

Calchas seemed at a loss; his tongue swiped his lips again and again.

Achilles' clear voice prompted him. "You have done sacrifices surely? You have prayed?"

"I—have, of course I have. But . . ." The priest's voice trembled. "I am afraid that what I say might anger someone here. Someone who is powerful and does not forget insult easily."

Achilles squatted to reach a hand out to the grimed shoulder of the flinching priest, clasping it genially. "Calchas, we are dying. This is not the time for such fears. What man among us would hold your words against you? I would not, even if you named me as the cause. Would any of you?" He looked at the men before him. They shook their heads.

"You see? No sane man would ever harm a priest."

Agamemnon's neck went taut as ship ropes. I was suddenly aware of how strange it was to see him standing alone. Always his brother or Odysseus or Diomedes was near him. But those men waited on the side, with the rest of the princes.

Calchas cleared his throat. "The auguries have shown that it is the god Apollo who is angry." Apollo. The name went through the host like wind in summer wheat.

Calchas' eyes flickered to Agamemnon, then back to Achilles. He swallowed. "He is offended, it seems, so the omens say, at the treatment of his dedicated servant. Chryses."

Agamemnon's shoulders were rigid.

Calchas stumbled on. "To appease him, the girl Chryseis must be returned without ransom, and High King Agamemnon must offer prayers and sacrifices." He stopped, his last word gulped down suddenly, as if he had run out of air.

Agamemnon's face had broken into dark red blotches of shock. It seemed like the greatest arrogance or stupidity not to have guessed he might be at fault, but he had not. The silence was so profound I felt I could hear the grains of sand falling against each other at our feet.

"Thank you, Calchas," Agamemnon said, his voice splintering the air. "Thank you for always bringing good news. Last time it was my daughter. Kill her, you said, because you have angered the goddess. Now you seek to humiliate me before my army."

He wheeled on the men, his face twisted in rage. "Am I not your general? And do I not see you fed and clothed and honored? And are my Mycenaeans not the largest part of this army? The girl is mine, given to me as a prize, and I will not give her up. Have you forgotten who I am?"

He paused, as if he hoped the men might shout *No! No!* But none did.

"King Agamemnon." Achilles stepped forward. His voice was easy, almost amused. "I don't think anyone has forgotten that you are leader of this host. But you do not seem to remember that we are kings in our own right, or princes, or heads of our families. We are allies, not slaves." A few men nodded; more would have liked to.

"Now, while we die, you complain about the loss of a girl you should have ransomed long ago. You say nothing of the lives you have taken, or the plague you have started."

Agamemnon made an inarticulate noise, his face purple with rage. Achilles held up a hand.

"I do not mean to dishonor you. I only wish to end the plague. Send the girl to her father and be done."

Agamemnon's cheeks were creased with fury. "I understand you, Achilles. You think because you're the son of a sea-nymph you have the right to play high prince wherever you go. You have never learned your place among men."

Achilles opened his mouth to answer.

"You will be silent," Agamemnon said, words lashing like a whip. "You will not speak another word or you will be sorry."

"Or I will be sorry?" Achilles' face was very still. The words were quiet, but distinctly audible. "I do not think, High King, that you can afford to say such things to me."

"Do you threaten me?" Agamemnon shouted. "Did you not hear him threaten me?"

"It is not a threat. What is your army without me?"

Agamemnon's face was clotted with malice. "You have always thought too much of yourself," he sneered. "We should have left you where we found you, hiding behind your mother's skirts. In a skirt yourself."

The men frowned in confusion, whispered to each other.

Achilles' hands were fisted at his sides; he hung on to his composure, barely. "You say this to turn attention away from yourself. If I had not called this council, how long would you have let your men die? Can you answer that?"

Agamemnon was already roaring over him. "When all of these brave men came to Aulis, they knelt to offer me their loyalty. All of them but you. I think we have indulged your arrogance long enough. It is time, past time"—he mimicked Achilles—"that you swore the oath."

"I do not need to prove myself to you. To any of you." Achilles' voice was cold, his chin lifted in disdain. "I am here of my own free will, and you are lucky that it is so. I am not the one who should kneel."

It was too far. I felt the men shift around me. Agamemnon seized upon it, like a bird bolting a fish. "Do you hear his pride?" He turned to Achilles. "You will not kneel?"

Achilles' face was like stone. "I will not."

"Then you are a traitor to this army, and will be punished like one. Your war prizes are hostage, placed in my care until you offer your obedience and submission. Let us start with that girl. Briseis, is her name? She will do as penance for the girl you have forced me to return."

The air died in my lungs.

"She is mine," Achilles said. Each word fell sharp, like a butcher cutting meat. "Given to me by all the Greeks. You cannot take her. If you try, your life is forfeit. Think on that, King, before you bring harm to yourself."

Agamemnon's answer came quickly. He could never back down in front of a crowd. Never.

"I do not fear you. I will have her." He turned to his Mycenaeans. "Bring the girl."

Around me were the shocked faces of kings. Briseis was a war prize, a living embodiment of Achilles' honor. In taking her, Agamemnon denied Achilles the full measure of his worth. The men muttered, and I hoped they might object. But no one spoke.

Because he was turned, Agamemnon did not see Achilles' hand go to his sword. My breath caught. I knew that he was capable of this, a single thrust through Agamemnon's cowardly heart. I saw the struggle on his face. I still do not know why he stopped himself; perhaps he wanted greater punishment for the king than death.

"Agamemnon," he said. I flinched from the roughness of his voice. The king turned, and Achilles drove a finger into his chest. The high king could not stop the *huff* of surprise. "Your words today have caused your own death, and the death of your men. I will fight for you no longer. Without me, your army will fall. Hector will grind you to bones and bloody dust, and I will watch it and laugh. You will come, crying for mercy, but I will give none. They will all die, Agamemnon, for what you have done here."

He spat, a huge wet smack between Agamemnon's feet. And then he was before me, and past me, and I was dizzied as I turned to follow him, feeling the Myrmidons behind me—hundreds of men shouldering their way through the crowd, storming off to their tents.

POWERFUL STRIDES TOOK HIM swiftly up the beach. His anger was incandescent, a fire under his skin. His muscles were pulled so taut I was afraid to touch him, fearing they would snap like bowstrings. He did not stop once we reached the camp. He did not turn and speak to the men. He seized the extra tent flap covering our door and ripped it free as he passed.

His mouth was twisted, ugly and tight as I had ever seen it. His eyes were wild. "I will kill him," he swore. "I will kill him." He grabbed a spear and broke it in half with an explosion of wood. The pieces fell to the floor.

"I almost did it there," he said. "I should have done it. How *dare* he?" He flung a ewer aside, and it shattered against a chair. "The cowards! You saw how they bit their lips and did not dare to speak. I hope he takes all their prizes. I hope he swallows them one by one."

A voice, tentative, outside. "Achilles?"

"Come in," Achilles snarled.

Automedon was breathless and stuttering. "I am sorry to disturb you. Phoinix told me to stay, so I could listen and tell you what happened."

"And?" Achilles demanded.

Automedon flinched. "Agamemnon asked why Hector still lived. He said that they do not need you. That perhaps you are not —what you say you are." Another spear shaft shattered in Achilles' fingers. Automedon swallowed. "They are coming, now, for Briseis."

Achilles had his back to me; I could not see his face. "Leave us," he told his charioteer. Automedon backed away, and we were alone.

They were coming for Briseis. I stood, my hands balled. I felt strong, unbending, like my feet pierced through the earth to the other side of the world.

"We must do something," I said. "We can hide her. In the woods or—"

"He will pay, now," Achilles said. There was fierce triumph in his voice. "Let him come for her. He has doomed himself."

"What do you mean?"

"I must speak to my mother." He started from the tent.

I seized his arm. "We don't have time. They will have taken her by the time you are back. We must do something now!"

He turned. His eyes looked strange, the pupils huge and dark, swallowing his face. He seemed to be looking a long way off. "What are you talking about?"

I stared at him. "Briseis."

He stared back. I could not follow the flicker of emotion in his eyes. "I can do nothing for her," he said at last. "If Agamemnon chooses this path, he must bear the consequences."

A feeling, as if I were falling into ocean depths, weighted with stones.

"You are not going to let him take her."

He turned away; he would not look at me. "It is his choice. I told him what would happen if he did."

"You know what he will do to her."

"It is his choice," he repeated. "He would deprive me of my honor? He would punish me? I will let him." His eyes were lit with an inner fire.

"You will not help her?"

"There is nothing I can do," he said with finality.

A tilting vertigo, as if I were drunk. I could not speak, or think. I had never been angry with him before; I did not know how.

"She is one of us. How can you just let him take her? Where is your honor? How can you let him defile her?"

And then, suddenly, I understood. Nausea seized me. I turned to the door.

"Where are you going?" he asked.

My voice was scraped and savage. "I have to warn her. She has a right to know what you have chosen."

I STAND OUTSIDE her tent. It is small, brown with hides, set back. "Briseis," I hear myself say.

"Come in!" Her voice is warm and pleased. We have had no time to speak during the plague, beyond necessities.

Inside, she is seated on a stool, mortar and pestle in her lap. The air smells sharply of nutmeg. She is smiling.

I feel wrung dry with grief. How can I tell her what I know?

"I—" I try to speak, stop. She sees my face, and her smile vanishes. Swiftly, she is on her feet and by my side.

"What is it?" She presses the cool skin of her wrist to my forehead. "Are you ill? Is Achilles all right?" I am sick with shame. But there is no space for my self-pity. They are coming.

"Something has happened," I say. My tongue thickens in my mouth; my words do not come out straight. "Achilles went today to speak to the men. The plague is Apollo's."

"We thought so." She nods, her hand resting gently on mine, in comfort. I almost cannot go on.

"Agamemnon did not—he was angry. He and Achilles quarreled. Agamemnon wants to punish him."

"Punish him? How?"

Now she sees something in my eyes. Her face goes quiet, pulling into itself. Bracing. "What is it?"

"He is sending men. For you."

I see the flare of panic, though she tries to hide it. Her fingers tighten on mine. "What will happen?"

My shame is caustic, searing every nerve. It is like a nightmare; I expect, each moment, to wake to relief. But there is no waking. It is true. He will not help.

"He—" I cannot say more.

It is enough. She knows. Her right hand clutches at her dress, chapped and raw from the rough work of the past nine days. I force out stuttering words meant to be a comfort, of how we will get her back, and how it will be all right. Lies, all of it. We both know what will happen to her in Agamemnon's tent. Achilles knows, too, and sends her anyway.

My mind is filled with cataclysm and apocalypse: I wish for

earthquakes, eruptions, flood. Only that seems large enough to hold all of my rage and grief. I want the world overturned like a bowl of eggs, smashed at my feet.

A trumpet blows outside. Her hand goes to her cheek, swipes away tears. "Go," she whispers. "Please."

CHAPTER TWENTY-SIX

I N THE DISTANCE TWO MEN ARE WALKING TOWARDS US UP the long stretch of beach, wearing the bright purple of Agamemnon's camp, stamped with the symbol of heralds. I know them—Talthybius and Eurybates, Agamemnon's chief messengers, honored as men of discretion close to the high king's ear. Hate knots my throat. I want them dead.

They are close now, passing the glaring Myrmidon guards, who rattle their armor threateningly. They stop ten paces from us—enough, perhaps they think, to be able to escape Achilles if he were to lose his temper. I indulge myself in vicious images: Achilles leaping up to snap their necks, leaving them limp as dead rabbits in a hunter's hand.

They stutter out a greeting, feet shifting, eyes down. Then: "We have come to take custody of the girl."

Achilles answers them—cold and bitter, but wryly so, his anger banked and shielded. He is giving a show, I know, of grace, of tolerance, and my teeth clench at the calmness in his tone. He likes this image of himself, the wronged young man, stoically accepting the theft of his prize, a martyrdom for the whole camp to see. I hear my name and see them looking at me. I am to get Briseis.

She is waiting for me. Her hands are empty; she is taking

nothing with her. "I'm sorry," I whisper. She does not say it is all right; it is not. She leans forward, and I can smell the warm sweetness of her breath. Her lips graze mine. Then she steps past me and is gone.

Talthybius takes one side of her, Eurybates the other. Their fingers press, not gently, into the skin of her arm. They tow her forward, eager to be away from us. She is forced to move, or fall. Her head turns back to look at us, and I want to break at the desperate hope in her eyes. I stare at him, will him to look up, to change his mind. He does not.

They are out of our camp now, moving quickly. After a moment I can barely distinguish them from the other dark figures that move against the sand—eating and walking and gossiping intently about their feuding kings. Anger sweeps through me like brushfire.

"How can you let her go?" I ask, my teeth hard against one another.

His face is blank and barren, like another language, impenetrable. He says, "I must speak with my mother."

"Go then," I snarl.

I watch him leave. My stomach feels burned to cinders; my palms ache where my nails have cut into them. *I do not know this man,* I think. He is no one I have ever seen before. My rage towards him is hot as blood. I will never forgive him. I imagine tearing down our tent, smashing the lyre, stabbing myself in the stomach and bleeding to death. I want to see his face broken with grief and regret. I want to shatter the cold mask of stone that has slipped down over the boy I knew. He has given her to Agamemnon knowing what will happen.

Now he expects that I will wait here, impotent and obedient. I have nothing to offer Agamemnon for her safety. I cannot bribe him, and I cannot beg him. The king of Mycenae has waited too long for this triumph. He will not let her go. I think of a wolf, guarding its bone. There were such wolves on Pelion, who would hunt men if they were hungry enough. "If one of them is stalking you," Chiron said, "you must give it something it wants more than you."

There is only one thing that Agamemnon wants more than Briseis. I yank the knife from my belt. I have never liked blood, but there is no help for that, now.

THE GUARDS SEE me belatedly and are too surprised to lift their weapons. One has the presence of mind to seize me, but I dig my nails into his arm, and he lets go. Their faces are slow and stupid with shock. Am I not just Achilles' pet rabbit? If I were a warrior, they would fight me, but I am not. By the time they think they should restrain me, I am inside the tent.

The first thing I see is Briseis. Her hands have been tied, and she is shrinking in a corner. Agamemnon stands with his back to the entrance, speaking to her.

He turns, scowling at the interruption. But when he sees me, his face goes slick with triumph. I have come to beg, he thinks. I am here to plead for mercy, as Achilles' ambassador. Or perhaps I will rage impotently, for his entertainment.

I lift the knife, and Agamemnon's eyes widen. His hand goes to the knife at his own belt, and his mouth opens to call the guards. He does not have time to speak. I slash the knife down at my left wrist. It scores the skin but does not bite deep enough. I slash again, and this time I find the vein. Blood spurts in the enclosed space. I hear Briseis' noise of horror. Agamemnon's face is spattered with drops.

"I swear that the news I bring is truth," I say. "I swear it on my blood."

Agamemnon is taken aback. The blood and the oath stay his hand; he has always been superstitious.

"Well," he says curtly, trying for dignity, "speak your news then."

I can feel the blood draining down my wrist, but I do not move to stanch it.

"You are in the gravest danger," I say.

He sneers. "Are you threatening me? Is this why he has sent you?"

"No. He has not sent me at all."

His eyes narrow, and I see his mind working, fitting tiles into the picture. "Surely you come with his blessing."

"No," I say.

He is listening, now.

"He knows what you intend towards the girl," I say.

Out of the corner of my eye I can see Briseis following our conversation, but I do not dare to look at her directly. My wrist throbs dully, and I can feel the warm blood filling my hand, then emptying again. I drop the knife and press my thumb onto the vein to slow the steady draining of my heart.

"And?"

"Do you not wonder why he did not prevent you from taking her?" My voice is disdainful. "He could have killed your men, and all your army. Do you not think he could have held you off?"

Agamemnon's face is red. But I do not allow him to speak.

"He let you take her. He knows you will not resist bedding her, and this will be your downfall. She is his, won through fair service. The men will turn on you if you violate her, and the gods as well."

I speak slowly, deliberately, and the words land like arrows, each in its target. It is true what I say, though he has been too blinded by pride and lust to see it. She is in Agamemnon's custody, but she is Achilles' prize still. To violate her is a violation of Achilles himself, the gravest insult to his honor. Achilles could kill him for it, and even Menelaus would call it fair.

"You are at your power's limit even in taking her. The men allowed it because he was too proud, but they will not allow more." We obey our kings, but only within reason. If *Aristos Achaion*'s prize is not safe, none of ours are. Such a king will not be allowed to rule for long.

Agamemnon has not thought of any of this. The realizations come like waves, drowning him. Desperate, he says, "My counselors have said nothing of this."

"Perhaps they do not know what you intend. Or perhaps it serves their own purposes." I pause to let him consider this. "Who will rule if you fall?"

He knows the answer. Odysseus, and Diomedes, together, with Menelaus as figurehead. He begins to understand, at last, the size of the gift I have brought him. He has not come so far by being a fool.

"You betray him by warning me."

It is true. Achilles has given Agamemnon a sword to fall upon, and I have stayed his hand. The words are thick and bitter. "I do."

"Why?" he asks.

"Because he is wrong," I say. My throat feels raw and broken, as though I have drunk sand and salt.

Agamemnon considers me. I am known for my honesty, for my kindheartedness. There is no reason to disbelieve me. He smiles. "You have done well," he says. "You show yourself loyal to your true master." He pauses, savoring this, storing it up. "Does he know what you have done?"

"Not yet," I say.

"Ah." His eyes half-close, imagining it. I watch the bolt of his triumph sliding home. He is a connoisseur of pain. There is nothing that could cause Achilles greater anguish than this: being betrayed to his worst enemy by the man he holds closest to his heart.

"If he will come and kneel for pardon, I swear I will release her. It is only his own pride that keeps his honor from him, not I. Tell him."

I do not answer. I stand, and walk to Briseis. I cut the rope that binds her. Her eyes are full; she knows what this has cost me. "Your wrist," she whispers. I cannot answer her. My head is a confusion of triumph and despair. The sand of the tent is red with my blood.

"Treat her well," I say.

I turn and leave. She will be all right now, I tell myself. He is feasting fat on the gift I have given him. I tear a strip from my tunic to bind my wrist. I am dizzy, though I do not know if it is with loss of blood or what I have done. Slowly, I begin the long walk back up the beach.

HE IS STANDING OUTSIDE the tent when I return. His tunic is damp from where he knelt in the sea. His face is wrapped closed, but there is a weariness to its edges, like fraying cloth; it matches mine.

"Where have you been?"

"In the camp." I am not ready yet, to tell him. "How is your mother?"

"She is well. You are bleeding."

The bandage has soaked through.

"I know," I say.

"Let me look at it." I follow him obediently into the tent. He takes my arm and unwraps the cloth. He brings water to rinse the wound clean and packs it with crushed yarrow and honey.

"A knife?" he asks.

"Yes."

We know the storm is coming; we are waiting as long as we can. He binds the wound with clean bandages. He brings me watered wine, and food as well. I can tell by his face that I look ill and pale.

"Will you tell me who hurt you?"

I imagine saying, *You*. But that is nothing more than childishness.

"I did it to myself."

"Why?"

"For an oath." There is no waiting any longer. I look at him, full in the face. "I went to Agamemnon. I told him of your plan."

"My plan?" His words are flat, almost detached.

"To let him rape Briseis, so that you might revenge yourself on him." Saying it out loud is more shocking than I thought it would be.

He rises, half-turning so I cannot see his face. I read his shoulders instead, their set, the tension of his neck.

"So you warned him?"

"I did."

"You know if he had done it, I could have killed him." That same flat tone. "Or exiled him. Forced him from the throne. The men would have honored me like a god."

"I know," I say.

There is a silence, a dangerous one. I keep waiting for him to turn on me. To scream, or strike out. And he does turn, to face me, at last.

"Her safety for my honor. Are you happy with your trade?"

"There is no honor in betraying your friends."

"It is strange," he says, "that you would speak against betrayal."

There is more pain in those words, almost, than I can bear. I force myself to think of Briseis. "It was the only way."

"You chose her," he says. "Over me."

"Over your pride." The word I use is *hubris*. Our word for arrogance that scrapes the stars, for violence and towering rage as ugly as the gods.

His fists tighten. Now, perhaps, the attack will come.

"My life is my reputation," he says. His breath sounds ragged. "It is all I have. I will not live much longer. Memory is all I can hope for." He swallows, thickly. "You know this. And would you let Agamemnon destroy it? Would you help him take it from me?"

"I would not," I say. "But I would have the memory be worthy of the man. I would have you be yourself, not some tyrant remembered for his cruelty. There are other ways to make Agamemnon pay. We will do it. I will help you, I swear. But not like this. No fame is worth what you did today."

He turns away again and is silent. I stare at his unspeaking back. I memorize each fold in his tunic, each bit of drying salt and sand stuck to his skin.

When he speaks at last, his voice is weary, and defeated. He doesn't know how to be angry with me, either. We are like damp wood that won't light.

"It is done then? She is safe? She must be. You would not have come back, otherwise."

"Yes. She is safe."

A tired breath. "You are a better man than I."

The beginning of hope. We have given each other wounds, but they are not mortal. Briseis will not be harmed and Achilles will remember himself and my wrist will heal. There will be a moment after this, and another after that.

"No," I say. I stand and walk to him. I put my hand to the warmth of his skin. "It is not true. You left yourself today. And now you are returned."

His shoulders rise and fall on a long breath. "Do not say that," he says, "until you have heard the rest of what I have done."

CHAPTER TWENTY-SEVEN

THERE ARE THREE SMALL STONES ON THE RUGS OF OUR
tent, kicked in by our feet or crept in on their own. I pick
them up. They are something to hold on to.

His weariness has faded as he speaks. " . . . I will fight for him
no longer. At every turn he seeks to rob me of my rightful glory.
To cast me into shadow and doubt. He cannot bear another man to
be honored over him. But he will learn. I will show him the worth
of his army without *Aristos Achaion*."

I do not speak. I can see the temper rising in him. It is like
watching a storm come, when there is no shelter.

"The Greeks will fall without me to defend them. He will be
forced to beg, or die."

I remember how he looked when he went to see his mother.
Wild, fevered, hard as granite. I imagine him kneeling before her,
weeping with rage, beating his fists on the jagged sea rocks. They
have insulted him, he says to her. They have dishonored him.
They have ruined his immortal reputation.

She listens, her fingers pulling absently on her long white
throat, supple as a seal, and begins to nod. She has an idea, a god's
idea, full of vengeance and wrath. She tells him, and his weeping
stops.

"He will do it?" Achilles asks, in wonder. He means Zeus, king of the gods, whose head is wreathed in clouds, whose hands can hold the thunderbolt itself.

"He will do it," Thetis says. "He is in my debt."

Zeus, the great balancer, will let go his scales. He will make the Greeks lose and lose and lose, until they are crushed against the sea, anchors and ropes tangling their feet, masts and prows splintering on their backs. And then they will see who they must beg for.

Thetis leans forward and kisses her son, a bright starfish of red, high on his cheek. Then she turns and is gone, slipped into the water like a stone, sinking to the bottom.

I let the pebbles tumble to the ground from my fingers, where they lie, haphazard or purposeful, an augury or an accident. If Chiron were here, he could read them, tell us our fortunes. But he is not here.

"What if he will not beg?" I ask.

"Then he will die. They will all die. I will not fight until he does." His chin juts, bracing for reproach.

I am worn out. My arm hurts where I cut it, and my skin feels coated with unwholesome sweat. I do not answer.

"Did you hear what I said?"

"I heard," I say. "Greeks will die."

Chiron had said once that nations were the most foolish of mortal inventions. "No man is worth more than another, wherever he is from."

"But what if he is your friend?" Achilles had asked him, feet kicked up on the wall of the rose-quartz cave. "Or your brother? Should you treat him the same as a stranger?"

"You ask a question that philosophers argue over," Chiron had said. "He is worth more to you, perhaps. But the stranger is someone else's friend and brother. So which life is more important?"

We had been silent. We were fourteen, and these things were too hard for us. Now that we are twenty-seven, they still feel too hard.

He is half of my soul, as the poets say. He will be dead soon, and his honor is all that will remain. It is his child, his dearest self. Should I reproach him for it? I have saved Briseis. I cannot save them all.

I know, now, how I would answer Chiron. I would say: there is no answer. Whichever you choose, you are wrong.

LATER THAT EVENING I go back to Agamemnon's camp. As I walk, I feel the eyes on me, curious and pitying. They look behind me, to see if Achilles is following. He is not.

When I told him where I was going, it seemed to cast him back into the shadows. "Tell her I am sorry," he said, his eyes down. I did not answer. Is he sorry because he has a better vengeance now? One that will strike down not just Agamemnon, but his whole ungrateful army? I do not let myself dwell on this thought. He is sorry. It is enough.

"Come in," she says, her voice strange. She is wearing a gold-threaded dress and a necklace of lapis lazuli. On her wrists are bracelets of engraved silver. She clinks when she stands, as though she's wearing armor.

She's embarrassed, I can see that. But we do not have time to speak, because Agamemnon himself is bulging through the narrow slit behind me.

"Do you see how well I keep her?" he says. "The whole camp will see in what esteem I hold Achilles. He only has to apologize, and I will heap the honors on him that he deserves. Truly it is unfortunate that one so young has so much pride."

The smug look on his face makes me angry. But what did I expect? I have done this. *Her safety for his honor.* "This is a credit to you, mighty king," I say.

"Tell Achilles," Agamemnon continues. "Tell him how well I treat her. You may come any time you like, to see her." He offers an unpleasant smile, then stands, watching us. He has no intention of leaving.

I turn to Briseis. I have learned a few pieces of her language, and I use them now.

"You are all right truly?"

"I am," she replies, in the sharp singsong of Anatolian. "How long will it be?"

"I don't know," I say. And I don't. How much heat does it take for iron to grow soft enough to bend? I lean forward and gently kiss her cheek. "I will be back again soon," I say in Greek.

She nods.

Agamemnon eyes me as I leave. I hear him say, "What did he say to you?"

I hear her answer, "He admired my dress."

THE NEXT MORNING, all the other kings march off with their armies to fight the Trojans; the army of Phthia does not follow. Achilles and I linger long over breakfast. Why should we not? There is nothing else for us to do. We may swim, if we like, or play at draughts or spend all day racing. We have not been at such utter leisure since Pelion.

Yet it does not feel like leisure. It feels like a held breath, like an eagle poised before the dive. My shoulders hunch, and I cannot stop myself from looking down the empty beach. We are waiting to see what the gods will do.

We do not have to wait long.

CHAPTER TWENTY-EIGHT

THAT NIGHT, PHOINIX COMES LIMPING UP THE SHORE
with news of a duel. As the armies rallied in the morning,
Paris had strutted along the Trojan line, golden armor
flashing. He offered a challenge: single combat, winner takes
Helen. The Greeks bellowed their approval. Which of them did not
want to leave that day? To wager Helen on a single fight and settle
it once and for all? And Paris looked an easy target, shining and
slight, slim-hipped as an unwed girl. But it was Menelaus, Phoinix
said, who came forward, roaring acceptance at the chance to regain
his honor and his beautiful wife in one.

The duel begins with spears and moves quickly to swords.
Paris is swifter than Menelaus had anticipated, no fighter but fast
on his feet. At last the Trojan prince missteps, and Menelaus seizes
him by his long horsehair crest and drags him down to the earth.
Paris' feet kick helplessly, his fingers scrabble at the choking chin-
strap. Then, suddenly, the helmet comes free in Menelaus' hand
and Paris is gone. Where the Trojan prince sprawled there is
only dusty ground. The armies squint and whisper: Where is he?
Menelaus squints with them, and so does not see the arrow, loosed
from a ibex-horn bow along the Trojan line, flying towards him. It
punches through his leather armor and buries itself in his stomach.

Blood pours down his legs and puddles at his feet. It is mostly a surface wound, but the Greeks do not know that yet. They scream and rush the Trojan ranks, enraged at the betrayal. A bloody melee begins.

"But what happened to Paris?" I ask.

Phoinix shakes his head. "I do not know."

THE TWO SIDES FOUGHT on through the afternoon until another trumpet blew. It was Hector, offering a second truce, a second duel to make right the dishonor of Paris' disappearance and the shooting of the arrow. He presented himself in his brother's place, to any man who dared answer. Menelaus, Phoinix says, would have stepped forward again, but Agamemnon prevented him. He did not want to see his brother die against the strongest of the Trojans.

The Greeks drew lots for who would fight with Hector. I imagine their tension, the silence before the helmet is shaken and the lot jumps out. Odysseus bends to the dusty earth to retrieve it. *Ajax.* There is collective relief: he is the only man who has a chance against the Trojan prince. The only man, that is, who fights today.

So Ajax and Hector fight, heaving stones at each other, and spears that shatter shields, until night falls and the heralds call an end. It is strangely civilized: the two armies part in peace, Hector and Ajax shaking hands as equals. The soldiers whisper—it would not have ended so if Achilles were here.

Discharged of his news, Phoinix gets wearily to his feet and limps on the arm of Automedon back to his tent. Achilles turns to me. He is breathing quickly, the tips of his ears pinking with excitement. He seizes my hand and crows to me of the day's events, of how his name was on everyone's lips, of the power of his absence, big as a Cyclops, walking heavily amongst the soldiers. The excitement of the day has flared through him, like flame in dry grass. For the first time, he dreams of killing: the stroke of glory, his inevitable spear through Hector's heart. My skin prickles to hear him say so.

"Do you see?" he says. "It is the beginning!"

I cannot escape the feeling that, below the surface, something is breaking.

THERE IS A TRUMPET the next morning at dawn. We rise, and climb the hill to see an army of horsemen riding for Troy from the East. Their horses are large and move with unnatural speed, drawing light-wheeled chariots behind them. At their head sits a huge man, larger even than Ajax. He wears his black hair long, like the Spartans do, oiled and swinging down his back. He carries a standard in the shape of a horse's head.

Phoinix has joined us. "The Lycians," he says. They are Anatolians, long allies of Troy. It has been a source of much wonder that they have not yet come to join the war. But now, as if summoned by Zeus himself, they are here.

"Who is that?" Achilles points to the giant, their leader.

"Sarpedon. A son of Zeus." The sun gleams off the man's shoulders, sweat-slick from the ride; his skin is dark gold.

The gates open, and the Trojans pour out to meet their allies. Hector and Sarpedon clasp hands, then lead their troops into the field. The Lycian weapons are strange: saw-toothed javelins and things that look like giant fishhooks, for ripping into flesh. All that day we hear their battle cries and the pounding hooves of their cavalry. There is a steady stream of Greek wounded into Machaon's tent.

Phoinix goes to the evening's council, the only member of our camp not in disgrace. When he returns, he looks sharply at Achilles. "Idomeneus is wounded, and the Lycians broke the left flank. Sarpedon and Hector will crush us between them."

Achilles does not notice Phoinix's disapproval. He turns to me in triumph. "Do you hear that?"

"I hear it," I say.

A day passes, and another. Rumors come thick as biting flies: tales of the Trojan army driving forward, unstoppable and bold in Achilles' absence. Of frantic councils, where our kings argue over desperate strategy: night raids, spies, ambushes. And then more, Hector ablaze in battle, burning through Greeks like a brush fire, and every day more dead than the day before. Finally: panicked runners, bringing news of retreats and wounds among the kings.

Achilles fingers this gossip, turning it this way and that. "It will not be long now," he says.

The funeral pyres burn through the night, their greasy smoke smeared across the moon. I try not to think how every one is a man I know. Knew.

ACHILLES IS PLAYING the lyre when they arrive. There are three of them—Phoinix first, and behind him Odysseus and Ajax.

I am sitting beside Achilles as they come; farther off is Automedon, carving the meat for supper. Achilles' head is lifted as he sings, his voice clear and sweet. I straighten, and my hand leaves his foot where it has been resting.

The trio approach us and stand on the other side of the fire, waiting for Achilles to finish. He puts down his lyre and rises.

"Welcome. You will stay for dinner, I hope?" He clasps their hands warmly, smiling through their stiffness.

I know why they have come. "I must see to the meal," I mumble. I feel Odysseus' eyes on my back as I go.

The strips of lamb drip and sear on the brazier's grill. Through the haze of smoke I watch them, seated around the fire as if they are friends. I cannot hear their words, but Achilles is smiling still, pushing past their grimness, pretending he does not see it. Then he calls for me, and I cannot stall any longer. Dutifully I bring the platters and take my seat beside him.

He is making desultory conversation of battles and helmets. While he talks he serves the meal, a fussing host who gives seconds to everyone and thirds to Ajax. They eat and let him talk. When they are finished, they wipe their mouths and put aside their plates. Everyone seems to know it is time. It is Odysseus, of course, who begins.

He talks first of *things,* casual words that he drops into our laps, one at a time. A list really. Twelve swift horses, and seven bronze tripods, and seven pretty girls, ten bars of gold, twenty cauldrons, and more—bowls, and goblets, and armor, and at last, the final gem held before us: Briseis' return. He smiles and spreads his hands with a guileless shrug I recognize from Scyros, from Aulis, and now from Troy.

Then a second list, almost as long as the first: the endless names of Greek dead. Achilles' jaw grows hard as Odysseus draws forth tablet after tablet, crammed to the margin with marks. Ajax looks down at his hands, scabbed from the splintering of shields and spears.

Then Odysseus tells us news that we do not know yet, that the Trojans are less than a thousand paces from our wall, encamped on newly won plain we could not take back before dusk. Would we like proof? We can probably see their watch-fires from the hill just beyond our camp. They will attack at dawn.

There is silence, a long moment of it, before Achilles speaks. "No," he says, shoving back treasure and guilt. His honor is not such a trifle that it can be returned in a night embassy, in a handful huddled around a campfire. It was taken before the entire host, witnessed by every last man.

The king of Ithaca pokes the fire that sits between them.

"She has not been harmed, you know. Briseis. God knows where Agamemnon found the restraint, but she is well kept and whole. She, and your honor, wait only for you to reclaim them."

"You make it sound as if I have abandoned my honor," Achilles says, his voice tart as raw wine. "Is that what you spin? Are you Agamemnon's spider, catching flies with that tale?"

"Very poetic," Odysseus says. "But tomorrow will not be a bard's song. Tomorrow, the Trojans will break through the wall and burn the ships. Will you stand by and do nothing?"

"That depends on Agamemnon. If he makes right the wrong he has done me, I will chase the Trojans to Persia, if you like."

"Tell me," Odysseus asks, "why is Hector not dead?" He holds up a hand. "I do not seek an answer, I merely repeat what all the men wish to know. In the last ten years, you could have killed him a thousand times over. Yet you have not. It makes a man wonder."

His tone tells us that he does not wonder. That he knows of the prophecy. I am glad that there is only Ajax with him, who will not understand the exchange.

"You have eked out ten more years of life, and I am glad for you. But the rest of us—" His mouth twists. "The rest of us are forced to wait for your leisure. You are holding us here, Achilles. You were given a choice and you chose. You must live by it now."

We stare at him. But he is not finished yet.

"You have made a fair run of blocking fate's path. But you cannot do it forever. The gods will not let you." He pauses, to let us hear each word of what he says. "The thread *will* run smooth, whether you choose it or not. I tell you as a friend, it is better to seek it on your own terms, to make it go at your pace, than theirs."

"That is what I am doing."

"Very well," Odysseus says. "I have said what I came to say."

Achilles stands. "Then it is time for you to leave."

"Not yet." It is Phoinix. "I, too, have something I wish to say." Slowly, caught between his pride and his respect for the old man, Achilles sits. Phoenix begins.

"When you were a boy, Achilles, your father gave you to me to raise. Your mother was long gone, and I was the only nurse you would have, cutting your meat and teaching you myself. Now you are a man, and still I strive to watch over you, to keep you safe, from spear, and sword, and folly."

My eyes lift to Achilles, and I see that he is tensed, wary. I understand what he fears—being played upon by the gentleness of this old man, being convinced by his words to give something up.

Worse, a sudden doubt—that perhaps, if Phoinix agrees with these men, he is wrong.

The old man holds up a hand, as if to stop the spin of such thoughts. "Whatever you do, I will stand with you, as I always have. But before you decide your course, there is a story you should hear."

He does not give Achilles time to object. "In the days of your father's father, there was a young hero Meleager, whose town of Calydon was besieged by a fierce people called the Curetes."

I know this story, I think. I heard Peleus tell it, long ago, while Achilles grinned at me from the shadows. There was no blood on his hands then, and no death sentence on his head. Another life.

"In the beginning the Curetes were losing, worn down by Meleager's skill in war," Phoinix continues. "Then one day there was an insult, a slight to his honor by his own people, and Meleager refused to fight any further on his city's behalf. The people offered him gifts and apologies, but he would not hear them. He stormed off to his room to lie with his wife, Cleopatra, and be comforted."

When he speaks her name, Phoinix's eyes flicker to me.

"At last, when her city was falling and her friends dying, Cleopatra could bear it no longer. She went to beg her husband to fight again. He loved her above all things and so agreed, and won a mighty victory for his people. But though he had saved them, he came too late. Too many lives had been lost to his pride. And so they gave him no gratitude, no gifts. Only their hatred for not having spared them sooner."

In the silence, I can hear Phoinix's breaths, labored with the exertion of speaking so long. I do not dare to speak or move; I am afraid that someone will see the thought that is plain on my face. It was not honor that made Meleager fight, or his friends, or victory, or revenge, or even his own life. It was Cleopatra, on her knees before him, her face streaked with tears. Here is Phoinix's craft: Cleopatra, Patroclus. Her name built from the same pieces as mine, only reversed.

If Achilles noticed, he does not show it. His voice is gentle for the old man's sake, but still he refuses. *Not until Agamemnon gives back the honor he has taken from me.* Even in the darkness I can see that Odysseus is not surprised. I can almost hear his report to the others, his hands spread in regret: *I tried.* If Achilles had agreed, all to the good. If he did not, his refusal in the face of prizes and apologies would only seem like madness, like fury or unreasonable pride. They will hate him, just as they hated Meleager.

My chest tightens in panic, in a quick desire to kneel before him and beg. But I do not. For like Phoinix I am declared already, decided. I am no longer to guide the course, merely to be carried, into darkness and beyond, with only Achilles' hands at the helm.

Ajax does not have Odysseus' equanimity—he glares, his face carved with anger. It has cost him much to be here, to beg for his own demotion. With Achilles not fighting, he is *Aristos Achaion*.

When they are gone, I stand and give my arm to Phoinix. He is tired tonight, I can see, and his steps are slow. By the time I leave him—old bones sighing onto his pallet—and return to our tent, Achilles is already asleep.

I am disappointed. I had hoped, perhaps, for conversation, for two bodies in one bed, for reassurance that the Achilles I saw at dinner was not the only one. But I do not rouse him; I slip from the tent and leave him to dream.

I CROUCH IN LOOSE SAND, in the shadow of a small tent.

"Briseis?" I call softly.

There is a silence, then I hear: "Patroclus?"

"Yes."

She tugs up the side of the tent and pulls me quickly inside. Her face is pinched with fear. "It is too dangerous for you to be here. Agamemnon is in a rage. He will kill you." Her words are a rushing whisper.

"Because Achilles refused the embassy?" I whisper back.

She nods, and in a swift motion snuffs out the tent's small lamp. "Agamemnon comes often to look in on me. You are not safe here." In the darkness I cannot see the worry on her face, but her voice is filled with it. "You must go."

"I will be quick. I have to speak with you."

"Then we must hide you. He comes without warning."

"Where?" The tent is small, bare of everything but pallet, pillows and blankets, and a few clothes.

"The bed."

She piles cushions around me and heaps blankets. She lies down beside me, pulling the cover over us both. I am surrounded by her scent, familiar and warm. I press my mouth to her ear, speaking barely louder than a breath. "Odysseus says that tomorrow the Trojans will break the wall and storm the camp. We must find a place to hide you. Among the Myrmidons or in the forest."

I feel her cheek moving against mine as she shakes her head. "I cannot. That is the first place he will look. It will only make more trouble. I will be all right here."

"But what if they take the camp?"

"I will surrender to Aeneas, Hector's cousin, if I can. He is known to be a pious man, and his father lived as a shepherd for a time near my village. If I cannot, I will find Hector or any of the sons of Priam."

I am shaking my head. "It is too dangerous. You must not expose yourself."

"I do not think they will hurt me. I am one of them, after all."

I feel suddenly foolish. The Trojans are liberators to her, not invaders. "Of course," I say quickly. "You will be free, then. You will want to be with your—"

"Briseis!" The tent flap is drawn backwards, and Agamemnon stands in the doorway.

"Yes?" She sits up, careful to keep the blanket over me.

"Were you speaking?"

"Praying, my lord."

"Lying down?"

Through the thick weave of wool I can see the glow of torchlight. His voice is loud, as if he is standing beside us. I will myself not to move. She will be punished if I am caught here.

"It is how my mother taught me, my lord. Is it not right?"

"You should have been taught better by now. Did not the godling correct you?"

"No, my lord."

"I offered you back to him tonight, but he did not want you." I can hear the ugly twist in his words. "If he keeps saying no, perhaps I will claim you for myself."

My fists clench. But Briseis only says, "Yes, my lord."

I hear the fall of cloth, and the light disappears. I do not move, nor breathe until Briseis returns beneath the covers.

"You cannot stay here," I say.

"It is all right. He only threatens. He likes to see me afraid."

The matter-of-factness in her tone horrifies me. How can I leave her to this, the leering, and lonely tent, and bracelets thick as manacles? But if I stay, she is in greater danger.

"I must go," I say.

"Wait." She touches my arm. "The men—" She hesitates. "They are angry with Achilles. They blame him for their losses. Agamemnon sends his people among them to stir up talk. They have almost forgotten about the plague. The longer he does not fight, the more they will hate him." It is my worst fear, Phoinix's story come to life. "Will he not fight?"

"Not until Agamemnon apologizes."

She bites her lip. "The Trojans, too. There is no one that they fear more, or hate more. They will kill him if they can tomorrow, and all who are dear to him. You must be careful."

"He will protect me."

"I know he will," she says, "as long as he lives. But even Achilles may not be able to fight Hector and Sarpedon both." She hesitates again. "If the camp falls, I will claim you as my husband. It may help some. You must not speak of what you were to him, though. It will be a death sentence." Her hand has tightened on my arm. "Promise me."

"Briseis," I say, "if he is dead, I will not be far behind."

She presses my hand to her cheek. "Then promise me something else," she says. "Promise me that whatever happens, you will not leave Troy without me. I know that you cannot—" She breaks off. "I would rather live as your sister than remain here."

"That is nothing that you have to bind me to," I say. "I would not leave you, if you wished to come. It grieved me beyond measure to think of the war ending tomorrow, and never seeing you again."

The smile is thick in her throat. "I am glad." I do not say that I do not think I will ever leave Troy.

I draw her to me, fill my arms with her. She lays her head upon my chest. For a moment we do not think of Agamemnon and danger and dying Greeks. There is only her small hand on my stomach, and the softness of her cheek as I stroke it. It is strange how well she fits there. How easily I touch my lips to her hair, soft and smelling of lavender. She sighs a little, nestles closer. Almost, I can imagine that this is my life, held in the sweet circle of her arms. I would marry her, and we would have a child.

Perhaps if I had never known Achilles.

"I should go," I say.

She draws down the blanket, releasing me into the air. She cups my face in her hands. "Be careful tomorrow," she says. "Best of men. Best of the Myrmidons." She places her fingers to my lips, stopping my objection. "It is truth," she says. "Let it stand, for once." Then she leads me to the side of her tent, helps me slip beneath the canvas. The last thing I feel is her hand, squeezing mine in farewell.

THAT NIGHT I LIE IN BED beside Achilles. His face is innocent, sleep-smoothed and sweetly boyish. I love to see it. This is his truest self, earnest and guileless, full of mischief but without malice. He is lost in Agamemnon and Odysseus' wily double meanings, their lies and games of power. They have confounded him, tied him to a stake and baited him. I stroke the soft skin of his forehead. I would untie him if I could. If he would let me.

CHAPTER TWENTY-NINE

W E WAKE TO SHOUTS AND THUNDER, A STORM THAT has burst from the blue of the sky. There is no rain, only the gray air, crackling and dry, and jagged streaks that strike like the clap of giant hands. We hurry to the tent door to look out. Smoke, acrid and dark, is drifting up the beach towards us, carrying the smell of lightning-detonated earth. The attack has begun, and Zeus is keeping his bargain, punctuating the Trojans' advance with celestial encouragement. We feel a pounding, deep in the ground—a charge of chariots, perhaps, led by huge Sarpedon.

Achilles' hand grips mine, his face stilled. This is the first time in ten years that the Trojans have ever threatened the gate, have ever pushed so far across the plain. If they break through the wall, they will burn the ships—our only way of getting home, the only thing that makes us an army instead of refugees. This is the moment that Achilles and his mother have summoned: the Greeks, routed and desperate, without him. The sudden, incontrovertible proof of his worth. But when will it be enough? When will he intervene?

"Never," he says, when I ask him. "Never until Agamemnon

begs my forgiveness or Hector himself walks into my camp and threatens what is dear to me. I have sworn I will not."

"What if Agamemnon is dead?"

"Bring me his body, and I will fight." His face is carved and unmovable, like the statue of a stern god.

"Do you not fear that the men will hate you?"

"They should hate Agamemnon. It is his pride that kills them."

And yours. But I know the look on his face, the dark reckless-ness of his eyes. He will not yield. He does not know how. I have lived eighteen years with him, and he has never backed down, never lost. What will happen if he is forced to? I am afraid for him, and for me, and for all of us.

We dress and eat, and Achilles speaks bravely of the future. He talks of tomorrow, when perhaps we will swim, or scramble up the bare trunks of sticky cypresses, or watch for the hatching of the sea-turtle eggs, even now incubating beneath the sun-warmed sand. But my mind keeps slipping from his words, dragged down-wards by the seeping gray of the sky, by the sand chilled and pallid as a corpse, and the distant, dying shrieks of men whom I know. How many more by day's end?

I watch him staring over the ocean. It is unnaturally still, as if Thetis is holding her breath. His eyes are dark and dilated by the dim overcast of the morning. The flame of his hair licks against his forehead.

"Who is that?" he asks, suddenly. Down the beach, a distant figure is being carried on a stretcher to the white tent. Someone important; there is a crowd around him.

I seize on the excuse for motion, distraction. "I will go see."

Outside the remove of our camp, the sounds of battle grow louder: piercing screams of horses impaled on the stakes of the trench, the desperate shouts of the commanders, the clangor of metal on metal.

Podalerius shoulders past me into the white tent. The air is thick with the smell of herbs and blood, fear and sweat. Nestor looms up at me from my right, his hand clamping around my shoulder, chilling through my tunic. He screeches, "We are lost! The wall is breaking!"

Behind him Machaon lies panting on a pallet, his leg a spreading pool of blood from the ragged prick of an arrow. Podalerius is bent over him, already working.

Machaon sees me. "Patroclus," he says, gasping a little.

I go to him. "Will you be all right?"

"Cannot tell yet. I think—" He breaks off, his eyes squeezed shut.

"Do not talk to him," Podalerius says, sharply. His hands are covered in his brother's blood.

Nestor's voice rushes onward, listing woe after woe: the wall splintering, and the ships in danger, and so many wounded kings—Diomedes, Agamemnon, Odysseus, strewn about the camp like crumpled tunics.

Machaon's eyes open. "Can you not speak to Achilles?" he says, hoarsely. "Please. For all of us."

"Yes! Phthia must come to our aid, or we are lost!" Nestor's fingers dig into my flesh, and my face is damp with the panicked spray of his lips.

My eyes close. I am remembering Phoinix's story, the image of the Calydonians kneeling before Cleopatra, covering her hands and feet with their tears. In my imagination she does not look at them, only lends them her hands as if perhaps they were cloths to wipe their streaming eyes. She is watching her husband Meleager for his answer, the set of his mouth that tells her what she must say: "No."

I yank myself from the old man's clinging fingers. I am desperate to escape the sour smell of fear that has settled like ash over everything. I turn from Machaon's pain-twisted face and the old man's outstretched hands and flee from the tent.

As I step outside there is a terrible cracking, like a ship's hull tearing apart, like a giant tree smashing to earth. *The wall.* Screams follow, of triumph and terror.

All around me are men carrying fallen comrades, limping on makeshift crutches, or crawling through the sand, dragging broken limbs behind them. I know them—their torsos full of scars my ointments have packed and sealed. Their flesh that my fingers have cleaned of iron and bronze and blood. Their faces that have joked, thanked, grimaced as I worked over them. Now these men are ruined again, pulpy with blood and split bone. Because of him. Because of me.

Ahead of me, a young man struggles to stand on an arrow-pierced leg. Eurypylus, prince of Thessaly.

I do not stop to think. I wind my arm under his shoulder and carry him to his tent. He is half-delirious with pain, but he knows me. "Patroclus," he manages.

I kneel before him, his leg in my hands. "Eurypylus," I say. "Can you speak?"

"Fucking Paris," he says. "My leg." The flesh is swollen and torn. I seize my dagger and begin to work.

He grits his teeth. "I don't know who I hate more, the Trojans or Achilles. Sarpedon tore the wall apart with his bare hands. Ajax held them off as long as he could. They're here now," he says, panting. "In the camp."

My chest clutches in panic at his words, and I fight the urge to bolt. I try to focus on what is before me: easing the arrow point from his leg, binding the wound.

"Hurry," he says, the word slurring. "I have to go back. They'll burn the ships."

"You cannot go out again," I say. "You have lost too much blood."

"No," he says. But his head slumps backwards; he is on the edge of unconsciousness. He will live, or not, by the will of the gods. I have done all I can. I take a breath and step outside.

Two ships are on fire, the long fingers of their masts lit by Trojan torches. Pressed against the hulls is a crush of men, screaming, desperate, leaping to the decks to beat at the flames. The only one I can recognize is Ajax, legs widespread on Agamemnon's prow, a massive shadow outlined against the sky. He ignores the fire, his spear stabbing downwards at the Trojan hands that swarm like feeding fish.

As I stand there, frozen and staring, I see a sudden hand, reaching above the melee to grip the sharp nose of a ship. And then the arm beneath it, sure and strong and dark, and the head, and the wide-shouldered torso breaks to air like dolphin-back from the boiling men beneath. And now Hector's whole brown body twists alone before the blankness of sea and sky, hung between air and earth. His face is smoothed, at peace, his eyes lifted—a man in prayer, a man seeking god. He hangs there a moment, the muscles in his arm knotted and flexed, his armor lifting on his shoulders, showing hip bones like the carved cornice of a temple. Then his other hand swings a bright torch towards the ship's wooden deck.

It is well thrown, landing amid old, rotting ropes and fallen sail. The flames catch immediately, skittering along the rope, then kindling the wood beneath. Hector smiles. And why should he not? He is winning.

Ajax screams in frustration—at another ship in flames, at the men that leap in panic from the charring decks, at Hector slithering out of reach, vanishing back into the crowd below. His strength is all that keeps the men from utterly breaking.

And then a spear point flashes up from beneath, silver as fish-scale in sunlight. It flickers, almost too fast to see, and suddenly Ajax's thigh blooms bright-red. I have worked long enough in Machaon's tent to know that it has sliced through muscle. His knees waver a moment, buckling slowly. He falls.

CHAPTER THIRTY

ACHILLES WATCHED ME APPROACH, RUNNING SO HARD my breaths carried the taste of blood onto my tongue. I wept, my chest shaking, my throat rubbed raw. He would be hated now. No one would remember his glory, or his honesty, or his beauty; all his gold would be turned to ashes and ruin.

"What has happened?" he asked. His brow was drawn deep in concern. *Did he truly not know?*

"They are dying," I choked out. "All of them. The Trojans are in the camp; they are burning the ships. Ajax is wounded, there is no one left but you to save them."

His face had gone cold as I spoke. "If they are dying, it is Agamemnon's fault. I told him what would happen if he took my honor."

"Last night he offered—"

He made a noise in his throat. "He offered nothing. Some tripods, some armor. Nothing to make right his insult, or to admit his wrong. I have saved him time and again, his army, his life." His voice was thick with barely restrained anger. "Odysseus may lick his boots, and Diomedes, and all the rest, but I will not."

"He is a disgrace." I clutched at him, like a child. "I know it, and all the men know it too. You must forget him. It is as you said; he will doom himself. But do not blame them for his fault. Do not let them die, because of his madness. They have loved you, and honored you."

"Honored me? Not one of them stood with me against Agamemnon. Not one of them spoke for me." The bitterness in his tone shocked me. "They stood by and let him insult me. As if he were right! I toiled for them for ten years, and their repayment is to discard me." His eyes had gone dark and distant. "They have made their choice. I shed no tears for them."

From down the beach the crack of a mast falling. The smoke was thicker now. More ships on fire. More men dead. They would be cursing him, damning him to the darkest chains of our under-world.

"They were foolish, yes, but they are still our people!"

"The Myrmidons are our people. The rest can save themselves." He would have walked away, but I held him to me.

"You are destroying yourself. You will not be loved for this, you will be hated, and cursed. Please, if you—"

"Patroclus." The word was sharp, as he had never spoken it. His eyes bore down on me, his voice like the judge's sentence. "I will not do this. Do not ask again."

I stared at him, straight as a spear stabbing the sky. I could not find the words that would reach him. Perhaps there were none. The gray sand, the gray sky, and my mouth, parched and bare. It felt like the end of all things. He would not fight. The men would die, and his honor with it. No mitigation, no mercy. Yet, still, my mind scrabbled in its corners, desperate, hoping to find the thing that might soften him.

I knelt, and pressed his hands to my face. My cheeks flowed with tears unending, like water over dark rock. "For me then," I said. "Save them for me. I know what I am asking of you. But I ask it. For me."

He looked down at me, and I saw the pull my words had on him, the struggle in his eyes. He swallowed.

"Anything else," he said. "Anything. But not this. I cannot."

I looked at the stone of his beautiful face, and despaired. "If you love me—"

"No!" His face was stiff with tension. "I cannot! If I yield, Agamemnon can dishonor me whenever he wishes. The kings will not respect me, nor the men!" He was breathless, as though he had run far. "Do you think I wish them all to die? But I cannot. I cannot! I will not let him take this from me!"

"Then do something else. Send the Myrmidons at least. Send me in your place. Put me in your armor, and I will lead the Myrmidons. They will think it is you." The words shocked us both. They seemed to come through me, not from me, as though spoken straight from a god's mouth. Yet I seized on them, as a drowning man. "Do you see? You will not have to break your oath, yet the Greeks will be saved."

He stared at me. "But you cannot fight," he said.

"I will not have to! They are so frightened of you, if I show myself, they will run."

"No," he said. "It is too dangerous."

"Please." I gripped him. "It isn't. I will be all right. I won't go near them. Automedon will be with me, and the rest of the Myrmidons. If you cannot fight, you cannot. But save them this way. Let me do this. You said you would grant me anything else."

"But—"

I did not let him answer. "Think! Agamemnon will know you defy him still, but the men will love you. There is no fame greater than this—you will prove to them all that your phantom is more powerful than Agamemnon's whole army."

He was listening.

"It will be your mighty name that saves them, not your spear arm. They will laugh at Agamemnon's weakness, then. Do you see?"

I watched his eyes, saw the reluctance giving way, inch by inch. He was imagining it, the Trojans fleeing from his armor, outflanking Agamemnon. The men, falling at his feet in gratitude.

He held up his hand. "Swear to me," he said. "Swear to me that if you go, you will not fight them. You will stay with Automedon in the chariot and let the Myrmidons go in front of you."

"Yes." I pressed my hand to his. "Of course. I am not mad. To frighten them, that is all." I was drenched and giddy. I had found a way through the endless corridors of his pride and fury. I would save the men; I would save him from himself. "You will let me?"

He hesitated another moment, his green eyes searching mine. Then, slowly, he nodded.

ACHILLES KNELT, buckling me in, his fingers so swift that I could not follow them, only feel the quick, pulling cinches of tightening belts. Bit by bit, he assembled me: the bronze breastplate and greaves, tight against my skin, the leather underskirt. As he worked, he instructed me in a voice that was low and quick and constant. I must not fight, I must not leave Automedon, nor the other Myrmidons. I was to stay in the chariot and flee at the first sign of danger; I could chase the Trojans back to Troy but not try to fight them there. And most of all, most of all, I must stay away from the walls of the city and the archers that perched there, ready to pick off Greeks who came too close.

"It will not be like before," he said. "When I am there."

"I know." I shifted my shoulders. The armor was stiff and heavy and unyielding. "I feel like Daphne," I told him, barked up in her new laurel skin. He did not laugh, only handed me two spears, points polished and gleaming. I took them, the blood beginning to rush in my ears. He was speaking again, more advice, but I did not hear it. I was listening to the drumbeat of my own impatient heart. "Hurry," I remember saying.

Last, the helmet to cover my dark hair. He turned a polished bronze mirror towards me. I stared at myself in armor I knew as well as my own hands, the crest on the helmet, the silvered sword hanging from the waist, the baldric of hammered gold. All of it unmistakable, and instantly recognizable. Only my eyes felt like my own, larger and darker than his. He kissed me, catching me up in a soft, opened warmth that breathed sweetness into my throat. Then he took my hand and we went outside to the Myrmidons.

They were lined up, armored and suddenly fearsome, their layers of metal flashing like the bright wings of cicadas. Achilles led me to the chariot already yoked to its three-horse team—*don't leave the chariot, don't throw your spears*—and I understood that he was afraid that I would give myself away if I actually fought. "I will be all right," I told him. And turned my back, to fit myself into the chariot, to settle my spears and set my feet.

Behind me, he spoke a moment to the Myrmidons, waving a hand over his shoulder at the smoking decks of ships, the black ash that swarmed upwards to the sky, and the roiling mass of bodies that tussled at their hulls. "Bring him back to me," he told them. They nodded and clattered their spears on their shields in approval. Automedon stepped in front of me, taking the reins. We all knew why the chariot was necessary. If I ran down the beach, my steps would never be mistaken for his.

The horses snorted and blew, feeling their charioteer behind them. The wheels gave a little lurch, and I staggered, my spears rattling. "Balance them," he told me. "It will be easier." Everyone waited as I awkwardly transferred one spear to my left hand, swiping my helmet askew as I did so. I reached up to fix it.

"I will be fine," I told him. Myself.

"Are you ready?" Automedon asked.

I took a last look at Achilles, standing by the side of the chariot, almost forlorn. I reached for his hand, and he gripped it. "Be careful," he said.

"I will."

There was more to say, but for once we did not say it. There would be other times for speaking, tonight and tomorrow and all the days after that. He let go of my hand.

I turned back to Automedon. "I'm ready," I told him. The chariot began to roll, Automedon guiding it towards the packed sand nearer the surf. I felt when we reached it, the wheels catching, the car smoothing out. We turned towards the ships, picking up speed. I felt the wind snatch at my crest, and I knew that the horsehair was streaming behind me. I lifted my spears.

Automedon crouched down low so that I would be seen first. Sand flew from our churning wheels, and the Myrmidons clattered behind us. My breaths had begun to come in gasps, and I gripped the spear-shafts till my fingers hurt. We flew past the empty tents of Idomeneus and Diomedes, around the beach's curve. And, finally, the first clumps of men. Their faces blurred by, but I heard their shouts of recognition and sudden joy. *"Achilles! It is Achilles!"* I felt a fierce and flooding relief. *It is working.*

Now, two hundred paces away, rushing towards me, were the ships and the armies, heads turning at the noise of our wheels and the Myrmidon feet beating in unison against the sand. I took a breath and squared my shoulders inside the grip of my—his— armor. And then, head tilted back, spear raised, feet braced against the sides of the chariot, praying that we would not hit a bump that would throw me, I screamed, a wild frenzied sound that shook my whole body. A thousand faces, Trojan and Greek, turned to me in frozen shock and joy. With a crash, we were among them.

I screamed again, his name boiling up out of my throat, and heard an answering cry from the embattled Greeks, an animal howl of hope. The Trojans began to break apart before me, scrambling backwards with gratifying terror. I bared my teeth in triumph, blood flooding my veins, the fierceness of my pleasure as I saw them run. But the Trojans were brave men, and not all of them ran. My hand lifted, hefting my spear in threat.

Perhaps it was the armor, molding me. Perhaps it was the years of watching him. But the position my shoulder found was not the old wobbling awkwardness. It was higher, stronger, a perfect balance. And then, before I could think about what I did, I threw—a long straight spiral into the breast of a Trojan. The torch that he had been waving at Idomeneus' ship slipped and guttered in the sand as his body pitched backwards. If he bled, if his skull split to show his brain, I did not see it. *Dead,* I thought.

Automedon's mouth was moving, his eyes wide. Achilles does not want you to fight, I guessed he was saying. But already my other spear hefted itself into my hand. *I can do this*. The horses veered again, and men scattered from our path. That feeling again, of pure balance, of the world poised and waiting. My eye caught on a Trojan, and I threw, feeling the swipe of wood against my thumb. He fell, pierced through the thigh in a blow I knew had shattered bone. Two. All around me men screamed Achilles' name.

I gripped Automedon's shoulder. "Another spear." He hesitated a moment, then pulled on the reins, slowing so I could lean over the side of the rattling chariot to claim one stuck in a body. The shaft seemed to leap into my hand. My eyes were already searching for the next face.

The Greeks began to rally—Menelaus killing a man beside me, one of Nestor's sons banging his spear against my chariot as if for luck before he threw at a Trojan prince's head. Desperately, the Trojans scrambled for their chariots, in full retreat. Hector ran among them, crying out for order. He gained his chariot, began to lead the men to the gate, and then over the narrow causeway that bridged the trench, and onto the plain beyond.

"Go! Follow them!"

Automedon's face was full of reluctance, but he obeyed, turning the horses in pursuit. I grabbed more spears from bodies— half-dragging a few corpses behind me before I could jerk the points free—and chased the Trojan chariots now choking the door. I saw their drivers looking back fearfully, frantically, at Achilles reborn phoenix-like from his sulking rage.

Not all the horses were as nimble as Hector's, and many panicked chariots skidded off the causeway to founder in the trench, leaving their drivers to flee on foot. We followed, Achilles' god-like horses racing with their legs outflung into the palm of the air. I might have stopped then, with the Trojans scattering back to their city. But there was a line of rallied Greeks behind me screaming my name. His name. I did not stop.

I pointed, and Automedon swept the horses out in an arc, lashing them onward. We passed the fleeing Trojans and curved around to meet them as they ran. My spears aimed, and aimed again, splitting open bellies and throats, lungs and hearts. I am relentless, unerring, skirting buckles and bronze to tear flesh that spills red like the jagged puncture of a wineskin. From my days in the white tent I know every frailty they have. It is so easy.

From the roiling melee bursts a chariot. The driver is huge, his long hair flying behind as he lashes his horses to foam and froth. His dark eyes are fixed on me, his mouth twisted in rage. His armor fits him like the skin fits the seal. It is Sarpedon.

His arm lifts, to aim his spear at my heart. Automedon screams something, yanks at the reins. There is a breath of wind over my shoulder. The spear's sharp point buries itself in the ground be-hind me.

Sarpedon shouts, curse or challenge I do not know. I heft my spear, as if in a dream. This is the man who has killed so many Greeks. It was his hands that tore open the gate.

"No!" Automedon catches at my arm. With his other hand he lashes the horses, and we tear up the field. Sarpedon turns his chariot, angling it away, and for a moment I think he has given up. Then he angles in again and lifts his spear.

The world explodes. The chariot bucks into the air, and the

horses scream. I am thrown onto the grass, and my head smacks the ground. My helmet falls forward into my eyes, and I shove it back. I see our horses, tangled in each other; one has fallen, pierced with a spear. I do not see Automedon.

From afar Sarpedon comes, his chariot driving relentlessly towards me. There is no time to flee; I stand to meet him. I lift my spear, gripping it as though it is a snake I will strangle. I imagine how Achilles would do it, feet planted to earth, back muscles twisting. He would see a gap in that impenetrable armor, or he would make one. But I am not Achilles. What I see is something else, my only chance. They are almost upon me. I cast the spear.

It hits his belly, where the armor plate is thick. But the ground is uneven, and I have thrown it with all of my strength. It does not pierce him, but it knocks him back a single step. It is enough. His weight tilts the chariot, and he tumbles from it. The horses plunge past me and leave him behind, motionless on the ground. I clutch my sword-hilt, terrified that he will rise and kill me; then I see the unnatural, broken angle of his neck.

I have killed a son of Zeus, but it is not enough. They must think it is Achilles who has done it. The dust has already settled on Sarpedon's long hair, like pollen on the underside of a bee. I retrieve my spear and stab it down with all my strength into his chest. The blood spurts, but weakly. There is no heartbeat to push it forward. When I pull the spear out, it dislodges slowly, like a bulb from cracking earth. That is what they will think has killed him.

I hear the shouts, men swarming towards me, in chariots and on foot. Lycians, who see the blood of their king on my spear. Automedon's hand seizes my shoulder, and he drags me onto the chariot. He has cut the dead horse free, righted the wheels. He is gasping, white with fear. "We must go."

Automedon gives the eager horses their head, and we race across the fields from the pursuing Lycians. There is a wild, iron taste in my mouth. I do not even notice how close I have come to death. My head buzzes with a red savagery, blooming like the blood from Sarpedon's chest.

In our escape, Automedon has driven us close to Troy. The walls loom up at me, huge cut stones, supposedly settled by the hands of gods, and the gates, giant and black with old bronze. Achilles had warned me to beware of archers on the towers, but the charge and rout has happened so quickly, no one has returned yet. Troy is utterly unguarded. A child could take it now.

The thought of Troy's fall pierces me with vicious pleasure. They deserve to lose their city. It is their fault, all of it. We have lost ten years, and so many men, and Achilles will die, because of them. *No more.*

I leap from the chariot and run to the walls. My fingers find slight hollows in the stone, like blind eye-sockets. *Climb.* My feet seek infinitesimal chips in the god-cut rocks. I am not graceful, but scrabbling, my hands clawing against the stone before they cling. Yet I am climbing. I will crack their uncrackable city, and capture Helen, the precious gold yolk within. I imagine dragging her out under my arm, dumping her before Menelaus. Done. No more men will have to die for her vanity.

Patroclus. A voice like music, above me. I look up to see a man leaning on the walls as if sunning, dark hair to his shoulders, a quiver and bow slung casually around his torso. Startled, I slip a little, my knees scraping the rock. He is piercingly beautiful, smooth skin and a finely cut face that glows with something more than human. Black eyes. *Apollo.*

He smiles, as if this was all he had wanted, my recognition. Then he reaches down, his arm impossibly spanning the long distance between my clinging form and his feet. I close my eyes and feel only this: a finger, hooking the back of my armor, plucking me off and dropping me below.

I land heavily, my armor clattering. My mind blurs a little from the impact, from the frustration of finding the ground so suddenly beneath me. I thought I was climbing. But there is the wall before me, stubbornly unclimbed. I set my jaw and begin again; I will not let it defeat me. I am delirious, fevered with my dream of Helen captive in my arms. The stones are like dark waters that flow ceaselessly over something I have dropped, that I want back. I forget about the god, why I have fallen, why my feet stick in the same crevices I have already climbed. Perhaps this is all I do, I think, demented—climb walls and fall from them. And this time when I look up, the god is not smiling. Fingers scoop the fabric of my tunic and hold me, dangling. Then let me fall.

MY HEAD CRACKS the ground again, leaving me stunned and breathless. Around me a blurring crowd of faces gathers. Have they come to help me? And then I feel: the prickling chill of air against my sweat-dampened forehead, the loosening of my dark hair, freed at last. *My helmet.* I see it beside me, overturned like an empty snail shell. My armor, too, has been shaken loose, all those straps that Achilles had tied, undone by the god. It falls from me, scattering the earth, the remnants of my split, spilt shell.

The frozen silence is broken by the hoarse, angry screams of Trojans. My mind startles to life: I am unarmed and alone, and they know I am only Patroclus.

Run. I lunge to my feet. A spear flashes out, just a breath too slow. It grazes the skin of my calf, marks it with a line of red. I twist away from a reaching hand, panic loose and banging in my chest. Through the haze of terror I see a man leveling a spear at my face. Somehow I am quick enough, and it passes over me, ruffling my hair like a lover's breath. A spear stabs towards my knees, meant to trip me. I leap it, shocked I am not dead already. I have never been so fast in all my life.

The spear that I do not see comes from behind. It pierces the skin of my back, breaks again to air beneath my ribs. I stumble, driven forward by the blow's force, by the shock of tearing pain and the burning numbness in my belly. I feel a tug, and the spear point is gone. The blood gushes hot on my chilled skin. I think I scream.

The Trojan faces waver, and I fall. My blood runs through my fingers and onto the grass. The crowd parts, and I see a man walking towards me. He seems to come from a great distance, to descend, somehow, as if I lay in the bottom of a deep ravine. I know him. Hip bones like the cornice of a temple, his brow furrowed and stern. He does not look at the men who surround him; he walks as if he were alone on the battlefield. He is coming to kill me. *Hector.*

My breaths are shallow gasps that feel like new wounds tearing. Remembrance drums in me, like the pulse-beat of blood in my ears. He cannot kill me. He must not. Achilles will not let him live if he does. And Hector must live, always; he must never die, not even when he is old, not even when he is so withered that his bones slide beneath his skin like loose rocks in a stream. He must live, because his life, I think as I scrape backwards over the grass, is the final dam before Achilles' own blood will flow.

Desperately, I turn to the men around me and scrabble at their knees. Please, I croak. Please.

But they will not look; they are watching their prince, Priam's eldest son, and his inexorable steps towards me. My head jerks back, and I see that he is close now, his spear raised. The only sound I hear is my own heaving lungs, air pumped into my chest and pushed from it. Hector's spear lifts over me, tipping like a pitcher. And then it falls, a spill of bright silver, towards me.

No. My hands flurry in the air like startled birds, trying to halt the spear's relentless movement towards my belly. But I am weak as a baby against Hector's strength, and my palms give way, unspooling in ribbons of red. The spearhead submerges in a sear of pain so great that my breath stops, a boil of agony that bursts over my whole stomach. My head drops back against the ground, and the last image I see is of Hector, leaning seriously over me, twisting his spear inside me as if he is stirring a pot. The last thing I think is: *Achilles.*

CHAPTER THIRTY-ONE

ACHILLES STANDS ON THE RIDGE WATCHING THE DARK shapes of battle moving across the field of Troy. He cannot make out faces or individual forms. The charge towards Troy looks like the tide coming in; the glint of swords and armor is fish-scale beneath the sun. The Greeks are routing the Trojans, as Patroclus had said. Soon he will return, and Agamemnon will kneel. They will be happy again.

But he cannot feel it. There is a numbness in him. The writhing field is like a gorgon's face, turning him slowly to stone. The snakes twist and twist before him, gathering into a dark knot at the base of Troy. A king has fallen, or a prince, and they are fighting for the body. Who? He shields his eyes, but no more is revealed. Patroclus will be able to tell him.

HE SEES THE THING IN PIECES. Men, coming down the beach towards the camp. Odysseus, limping beside the other kings. Menelaus has something in his arms. A grass-stained foot hangs loose. Locks of tousled hair have slipped from the makeshift shroud. The numbness now is merciful. A last few moments of it. Then, the fall.

He snatches for his sword to slash his throat. It is only when his hand comes up empty that he remembers: he gave the sword to me. Then Antilochus is seizing his wrists, and the men are all talking. All he can see is the bloodstained cloth. With a roar he throws Antilochus from him, knocks down Menelaus. He falls on the body. The knowledge rushes up in him, choking off breath. A scream comes, tearing its way out. And then another, and another. He seizes his hair in his hands and yanks it from his head. Golden strands fall onto the bloody corpse. Patroclus, he says, Patroclus. Patroclus. Over and over until it is sound only. Somewhere Odysseus is kneeling, urging food and drink. A fierce red rage comes, and he almost kills him there. But he would have to let go of me. He cannot. He holds me so tightly I can feel the faint beat of his chest, like the wings of a moth. An echo, the last bit of spirit still tethered to my body. A torment.

BRISEIS RUNS TOWARDS US, face contorted. She bends over the body, her lovely dark eyes spilling water warm as summer rain. She covers her face with her hands and wails. Achilles does not look at her. He does not even see her. He stands.

"Who did this?" His voice is a terrible thing, cracked and broken.

"Hector," Menelaus says. Achilles seizes his giant ash spear, and tries to tear free from the arms that hold him.

Odysseus grabs his shoulders. "Tomorrow," he says. "He has gone inside the city. Tomorrow. Listen to me, Pelides. Tomorrow you can kill him. I swear it. Now you must eat, and rest."

ACHILLES WEEPS. He cradles me, and will not eat, nor speak a word other than my name. I see his face as if through water, as a fish sees the sun. His tears fall, but I cannot wipe them away. This is my element now, the half-life of the unburied spirit.

His mother comes. I hear her, the sound of waves breaking on shore. If I disgusted her when I was alive, it is worse to find my corpse in her son's arms.

"He is dead," she says, in her flat voice.

"Hector is dead," he says. "Tomorrow."

"You have no armor."

"I do not need any." His teeth show; it is an effort to speak.

She reaches, pale and cool, to take his hands from me. "He did it to himself," she says.

"Do not touch me!"

She draws back, watching him cradle me in his arms.

"I will bring you armor," she says.

IT GOES LIKE THIS, on and on, the tent flap opening, the tentative face. Phoinix, or Automedon, or Machaon. At last Odysseus. "Agamemnon has come to see you, and return the girl." Achilles does not say, *She has already returned*. Perhaps he does not know.

The two men face each other in the flickering firelight. Agamemnon clears his throat. "It is time to forget the division between us. I come to bring you the girl, Achilles, unharmed and well." He pauses, as if expecting a rush of gratitude. There is only silence. "Truly, a god must have snatched our wits from us to set us so at odds. But that is over now, and we are allies once more." This last is said loudly, for the benefit of the watching men. Achilles does not respond. He is imagining killing Hector. It is all that keeps him standing.

Agamemnon hesitates. "Prince Achilles, I hear you will fight tomorrow?"

"Yes." The suddenness of his answer startles them.

"Very good, that is very good." Agamemnon waits another moment. "And you will fight after that, also?"

"If you wish," Achilles answers. "I do not care. I will be dead soon."

The watching men exchange glances. Agamemnon recovers.

"Well. We are settled then." He turns to go, stops. "I was sorry to hear of Patroclus' death. He fought bravely today. Did you hear he killed Sarpedon?"

Achilles' eyes lift. They are bloodshot and dead. "I wish he had let you all die."

Agamemnon is too shocked to answer. Odysseus steps into the silence. "We will leave you to mourn, Prince Achilles."

BRISEIS IS KNEELING by my body. She has brought water and cloth, and washes the blood and dirt from my skin. Her hands are gentle, as though she washes a baby, not a dead thing. Achilles opens the tent, and their eyes meet over my body.

"Get away from him," he says.

"I am almost finished. He does not deserve to lie in filth."

"I would not have your hands on him."

Her eyes are sharp with tears. "Do you think you are the only one who loved him?"

"Get out. Get out!"

"You care more for him in death than in life." Her voice is bitter with grief. "How could you have let him go? You knew he could not fight!"

Achilles screams, and shatters a serving bowl. "Get out!"

Briseis does not flinch. "Kill me. It will not bring him back. He was worth ten of you. Ten! And you sent him to his death!"

The sound that comes from him is hardly human. "I tried to stop him! I told him not to leave the beach!"

"You are the one who made him go." Briseis steps towards him. "He fought to save you, and your darling reputation. Because he could not bear to see you suffer!"

Achilles buries his face in his hands. But she does not relent. "You have never deserved him. I do not know why he ever loved you. You care only for yourself!"

Achilles' gaze lifts to meet hers. She is afraid, but does not draw back. "I hope that Hector kills you."

The breath rasps in his throat. "Do you think I do not hope the same?" he asks.

He weeps as he lifts me onto our bed. My corpse sags; it is warm in the tent, and the smell will come soon. He does not seem to care. He holds me all night long, pressing my cold hands to his mouth.

At dawn, his mother returns with a shield and sword and breastplate, newly minted from still-warm bronze. She watches him arm and does not try to speak to him.

HE DOES NOT WAIT for the Myrmidons, or Automedon. He runs up the beach, past the Greeks who have come out to see. They grab their arms and follow. They do not want to miss it.

"Hector!" he screams. "Hector!" He tears through the advancing Trojan ranks, shattering chests and faces, marking them with the meteor of his fury. He is gone before their bodies hit the ground. The grass, thinned from ten years of warfare, drinks the rich blood of princes and kings.

Yet Hector eludes him, weaving through the chariots and men with the luck of the gods. No one calls it cowardice that he runs. He will not live if he is caught. He is wearing Achilles' own armor, the unmistakable phoenix breastplate taken from beside my corpse. The men stare as the two pass: it looks, almost, as if Achilles is chasing himself.

Chest heaving, Hector races towards Troy's wide river, the Scamander. Its water glints a creamy gold, dyed by the stones in its riverbed, the yellow rock for which Troy is known.

The waters are not golden now, but a muddied, churning red, choked with corpses and armor. Hector lunges into the waves and swims, arms cutting through the helmets and rolling bodies. He gains the other shore; Achilles leaps to follow.

A figure rises from the river to bar his way. Filthy water sluices off the muscles of his shoulders, pours from his black beard. He is taller than the tallest mortal, and swollen with strength like creeks in spring. He loves Troy and its people. In summer, they pour wine for him as a sacrifice, and drop garlands to float upon his waters. Most pious of all is Hector, prince of Troy.

Achilles' face is spattered with blood. "You will not keep me from him."

The river god Scamander lifts a thick staff, large as a small tree-trunk. He does not need a blade; one strike with this would break bones, snap a neck. Achilles has only a sword. His spears are gone, buried in bodies.

"Is it worth your life?" the god says.

No. Please. But I have no voice to speak. Achilles steps into the river and lifts his sword.

With hands as large as a man's torso, the river god swings his staff. Achilles ducks and then rolls forward over the returning whistle of a second swing. He gains his feet and strikes, whipping towards the god's unprotected chest. Easily, almost casually, the god twists away. The sword's point passes harmlessly, as it has never done before.

The god attacks. His swings force Achilles backwards over the debris lining the river. He uses his staff like a hammer; wide arcs of spray leap from where it smashes against the river's surface. Achilles must spring away each time. The waters do not seem to drag at him as they might at another man.

Achilles' sword flashes faster than thought, but he cannot touch the god. Scamander catches every blow with his mighty staff, forcing him to be faster and then faster still. The god is old, old as the first melting of ice from the mountains, and he is wily. He has known every fight that was ever fought on these plains, and there is nothing new to him. Achilles begins to slow, worn out from the strain of holding back the god's strength with only a thin edge of metal. Chips of wood fly as the weapons meet, but the staff is thick as one of Scamander's legs; there is no hope that it will break. The god has begun to smile at how often now the man seeks to duck rather than meet his blows. Inexorably, he bears down. Achilles' face is contorted with effort and focus. He is fighting at the edge, the very edge of his power. He is not, after all, a god.

I see him gathering himself, preparing one final, desperate attack. He begins the pass, sword blurring towards the god's head. For a fraction of a second, Scamander must lean back to avoid it. That is the moment Achilles needs. I see his muscles tense for that last, single thrust; he leaps.

For the first time in all his life, he is not fast enough. The god catches the blow, and throws it violently aside. Achilles stumbles. It is so slight, just the smallest lurch off-balance, that I almost do not see it. But the god does. He lunges forward, vicious and victorious, in the pause, the small hitch of time that the stumble has made. The wood swings down in a killing arc.

He should have known better; I should have known. Those feet never stumbled, not once, in all the time I knew them. If a mistake had come, it would not be there, from the delicate bones and curving arches. Achilles has baited his hook with human failure, and the god has leapt for it.

As Scamander lunges, there is the opening, and Achilles' sword streaks towards it. A gash flowers in the god's side, and the river runs gold once more, stained with the ichor that spills from its master.

Scamander will not die. But he must limp away now, weakened and weary, to the mountains and the source of his waters, to stanch the wound and regain his strength. He sinks into his river and is gone.

Achilles' face is sweat-streaked, his breaths harsh. But he does not pause. "Hector!" he screams. And the hunt begins again.

Somewhere, the gods whisper:

He has beaten one of us.

What will happen if he attacks the city?

Troy is not meant to fall yet.

And I think: do not fear for Troy. It is only Hector that he wants. Hector, and Hector alone. When Hector is dead, he will stop.

THERE IS A GROVE at the base of Troy's high walls, home to a sacred, twisting laurel. It is there that Hector, at last, stops running. Beneath its branches, the two men face each other. One of them is dark, his feet like roots driving deep into soil. He wears a golden breastplate and helmet, burnished greaves. It fit me well enough, but he is bigger than I, broader. At his throat the metal gapes away from his skin.

The other man's face is twisted almost beyond recognition. His clothes are still damp from his fight in the river. He lifts his ashen spear.

No, I beg him. It is his own death he holds, his own blood that will spill. He does not hear me.

Hector's eyes are wide, but he will run no longer. He says, "Grant me this. Give my body to my family, when you have killed me."

Achilles makes a sound like choking. "There are no bargains between lions and men. I will kill you and eat you raw." His spear-point flies in a dark whirlwind, bright as the evening-star, to catch the hollow at Hector's throat.

ACHILLES RETURNS to the tent, where my body waits. He is red and red and rust-red, up to his elbows, his knees, his neck, as if he has swum in the vast dark chambers of a heart and emerged, just now, still dripping. He is dragging Hector's body behind him, pierced through its heels with a leather thong. The neat beard is matted with dirt, the face black with bloody dust. He has been pulling it behind his chariot as the horses run.

The kings of Greece are waiting for him.

"You have triumphed today, Achilles," Agamemnon says. "Bathe and rest yourself, and then we shall feast in your honor."

"I will have no feast." He pushes through them, dragging Hector after.

"HOKUMOROS," HIS MOTHER CALLS him in her softest voice. *Swift-fated.* "Will you not eat?"

"You know I will not."

She touches her hand to his cheek, as if to wipe away blood.

He flinches. "Stop," he says.

Her face goes blank for a second, so quickly he does not see. When she speaks, her voice is hard.

"It is time to return Hector's body to his family for burial. You have killed him and taken your vengeance. It is enough."

"It will never be enough," he says.

FOR THE FIRST TIME since my death, he falls into a fitful, trembling sleep.

Achilles. I cannot bear to see you grieving.

His limbs twitch and shudder.

Give us both peace. Burn me and bury me. I will wait for you among the shades. I will—

But already he is waking. "Patroclus! Wait! I am here!"

He shakes the body beside him. When I do not answer, he weeps again.

HE RISES AT DAWN to drag Hector's body around the walls of the city for all of Troy to see. He does it again at midday, and again at evening. He does not see the Greeks begin to avert their eyes from him. He does not see the lips thinning in disapproval as he passes. How long can this go on?

Thetis is waiting for him in the tent, tall and straight as a flame.

"What do you want?" He drops Hector's body by the door.

Her cheeks have spots of color, like blood spilled on marble. "You must stop this. Apollo is angry. He seeks vengeance upon you."

"Let him." He kneels, smooths back the hair on my forehead. I am wrapped in blankets, to muffle the smell.

"Achilles." She strides to him, seizes his chin. "Listen to me. You go too far in this. I will not be able to protect you from him."

He jerks his head from her and bares his teeth. "I do not need you to."

Her skin is whiter than I have ever seen it. "Do not be a fool. It is only my power that—"

"What does it matter?" He cuts her off, snarling. "He is dead. Can your power bring him back?"

"No," she says. "Nothing can."

He stands. "Do you think I cannot see your rejoicing? I know how you hated him. You have always hated him! If you had not gone to Zeus, he would be alive!"

"He is a mortal," she says. "And mortals die."

"I am a mortal!" he screams. "What good is godhead, if it cannot do this? What good are *you*?"

"I know you are mortal," she says. She places each cold word as a tile in a mosaic. "I know it better than anyone. I left you too long on Pelion. It has ruined you." She gestures, a flick, at his torn clothing, his tear-stained face. "This is not my son."

His chest heaves. "Then who is it, Mother? Am I not famous enough? I killed Hector. And who else? Send them before me. I will kill them all!"

Her face twists. "You act like a child. At twelve Pyrrhus is more of a man than you."

"Pyrrhus." The word is a gasp.

"He will come, and Troy will fall. The city cannot be taken without him, the Fates say." Her face glows.

Achilles stares. "You would bring him here?"

"He is the next *Aristos Achaion*."

"I am not dead yet."

"You may as well be." The words are a lash. "Do you know what I have borne to make you great? And now you would destroy it for this?" She points at my festering body, her face tight with disgust. "I am done. There is no more I can do to save you."

Her black eyes seem to contract, like dying stars. "I am glad that he is dead," she says.

It is the last thing she will ever say to him.

CHAPTER THIRTY-TWO

I N THE DEEPEST REACHES OF NIGHT, WHEN EVEN THE WILD dogs drowse and the owls are quiet, an old man comes to our tent. He is filthy, his clothing torn, his hair smeared with ashes and dirt. His robes are wet from swimming the river. Yet his eyes, when he speaks, are clear. "I have come for my son," he says.

The king of Troy moves across the room to kneel at Achilles' feet. He bows his white head. "Will you hear a father's prayer, mighty Prince of Phthia, Best of the Greeks?"

Achilles stares down at the man's shoulders as if in a trance. They are trembling with age, stooped with the burdens of grief. This man bore fifty sons and has lost all but a handful.

"I will hear you," he says.

"The blessings of the gods upon your kindness," Priam says. His hands are cool on Achilles' burning skin. "I have come far this night in hope." A shudder, involuntary, passes through him; the night's chill and the wet clothes. "I am sorry to appear so meanly before you."

The words seem to wake Achilles a little. "Do not kneel," he says. "Let me bring you food and drink." He offers his hand, and helps the old king to his feet. He gives him a dry cloak and the soft cushions that Phoinix likes best, and pours wine. Beside Priam's furrowed skin and slow steps he seems suddenly very young.

"Thank you for your hospitality," Priam says. His accent is strong, and he speaks slowly, but his Greek is good. "I have heard you are a noble man, and it is on your nobility that I throw myself. We are enemies, yet you have never been known as cruel. I beg you to return my son's body for burial, so his soul does not wander lost." As he speaks, he is careful not to let himself look at the shadow facedown in the corner.

Achilles is staring into the cupped darkness of his hands. "You show courage to come here alone," he says. "How did you get into the camp?"

"I was guided by the grace of the gods."

Achilles looks up at him. "How did you know I would not kill you?"

"I did not know," says Priam.

There is silence. The food and wine sit before them, but neither eats, nor drinks. I can see Achilles' ribs through his tunic.

Priam's eyes find the other body, mine, lying on the bed. He hesitates a moment. "That is—your friend?"

"*Philtatos*," Achilles says, sharply. Most beloved. "Best of men, and slaughtered by your son."

"I am sorry for your loss," Priam says. "And sorry that it was my son who took him from you. Yet I beg you to have mercy. In grief, men must help each other, though they are enemies."

"What if I will not?" His words have gone stiff.

"Then you will not."

There is silence a moment. "I could kill you still," Achilles says.

Achilles.

"I know." The king's voice is quiet, unafraid. "But it is worth my life, if there is a chance my son's soul may be at rest."

Achilles' eyes fill; he looks away so the old man will not see.

Priam's voice is gentle. "It is right to seek peace for the dead. You and I both know there is no peace for those who live after."

"No," Achilles whispers.

Nothing moves in the tent; time does not seem to pass. Then Achilles stands. "It is close to dawn, and I do not want you to be in danger as you travel home. I will have my servants prepare your son's body."

WHEN THEY ARE GONE, he slumps next to me, his face against my belly. My skin grows slippery under the steady fall of his tears.

The next day he carries me to the pyre. Briseis and the Myrmidons watch as he places me on the wood and strikes the flint. The flames surround me, and I feel myself slipping further from life, thinning to only the faintest shiver in the air. I yearn for the darkness and silence of the underworld, where I can rest.

He collects my ashes himself, though this is a woman's duty. He puts them in a golden urn, the finest in our camp, and turns to the watching Greeks.

"When I am dead, I charge you to mingle our ashes and bury us together."

HECTOR AND SARPEDON are dead, but other heroes come to take their place. Anatolia is rich with allies and those making common cause against invaders. First is Memnon, the son of rosy-fingered dawn, king of Aethiopia. A large man, dark and crowned, striding forward with an army of soldiers as dark as he, a burnished black. He stands, grinning expectantly. He has come for one man, and one man alone.

That man comes to meet him armed with only a spear. His breastplate is carelessly buckled, his once-bright hair hangs lank and unwashed. Memnon laughs. This will be easy. When he crumples, folded around a long ashen shaft, the smile is shaken from his face. Wearily, Achilles retrieves his spear.

Next come the horsewomen, breasts exposed, their skin glistening like oiled wood. Their hair is bound back, their arms are full of spears and bristling arrows. Curved shields hang from their saddles, crescent-shaped, as if coined from the moon. At their front is a single figure on a chestnut horse, hair loose, Anatolian eyes dark and curving and fierce—chips of stone that move restlessly over the army before her. Penthesilea.

She wears a cape, and it is this that undoes her—that allows her to be pulled, limbs light and poised as a cat, from her horse. She tumbles with easy grace, and one of her hands flashes for the spear tied to her saddle. She crouches in the dirt, bracing it. A face looms over her, grim, darkened, dulled. It wears no armor at all anymore, exposing all its skin to points and punctures. It is turned now, in hope, in wistfulness, towards her.

She stabs, and Achilles' body dodges the deadly point, impossibly lithe, endlessly agile. Always, its muscles betray it, seeking life instead of the peace that spears bring. She thrusts again, and he leaps over the point, drawn up like a frog, body light and loose. He makes a sound of grief. He had hoped, because she has killed so many. Because from her horse she seemed so like him, so quick and graceful, so relentless. But she is not. A single thrust crushes her to the ground, leaves her chest torn up like a field beneath the plow. Her women scream in anger, in grief, at his retreating, bowed, shoulders.

Last of all is a young boy, Troilus. They have kept him behind the wall as their security—the youngest son of Priam, the one they want to survive. It is his brother's death that has pulled him from the walls. He is brave and foolish and will not listen. I see him wrenching from the restraining hands of his older brothers, and leaping into his chariot. He flies headlong, like a loosed greyhound, seeking vengeance.

The spear-butt catches against his chest, just starting to widen with manhood. He falls, still holding the reins, and the frightened horses bolt, dragging him behind. His trailing spear-tip clicks against the stones, writing in the dust with its bronze fingernail.

At last he frees himself and stands, his legs, his back, scraped and crusted. He faces the older man who looms in front of him, the shadow that haunts the battlefield, the grisly face that wearily kills man after man. I see that he does not stand a chance, his bright eyes, his bravely lifted chin. The point catches the soft bulb of his throat, and liquid spills like ink, its color bled away by the dusk around me. The boy falls.

WITHIN THE WALLS OF TROY, a bow is strung quickly by rushing hands. An arrow is selected, and princely feet hurry up stairs to a tower that tilts over a battlefield of dead and dying. Where a god is waiting.

It is easy for Paris to find his target. The man moves slowly, like a lion grown wounded and sick, but his gold hair is unmistakable. Paris nocks his arrow.

"Where do I aim? I heard he was invulnerable. Except for—"

"He is a man," Apollo says. "Not a god. Shoot him and he will die."

Paris aims. The god touches his finger to the arrow's fletching. Then he breathes, a puff of air—as if to send dandelions flying, to push toy boats over water. And the arrow flies, straight and silent, in a curving, downward arc towards Achilles' back.

Achilles hears the faint hum of its passage a second before it strikes. He turns his head a little, as if to watch it come. He closes his eyes and feels its point push through his skin, parting thick muscle, worming its way past the interlacing fingers of his ribs. There, at last, is his heart. Blood spills between shoulder blades, dark and slick as oil. Achilles smiles as his face strikes the earth.

CHAPTER THIRTY-THREE

THE SEA-NYMPHS COME FOR THE BODY, TRAILING THEIR seafoam robes behind them. They wash him with rose oil and nectar, and weave flowers through his golden hair. The Myrmidons build him a pyre, and he is placed on it. The nymphs weep as the flames consume him. His beautiful body lost to bones and gray ash.

But many do not weep. Briseis, who stands watching until the last embers have gone out. Thetis, her spine straight, black hair loose and snaky in the wind. The men, kings and common. They gather at a distance, afraid of the eerie keening of the nymphs and Thetis' thunderbolt eyes. Closest to tears is Ajax, leg bandaged and healing. But perhaps he is just thinking of his own long-awaited promotion.

The pyre burns itself out. If the ashes are not gathered soon, they will be lost to the winds, but Thetis, whose office it is, does not move. At last, Odysseus is sent to speak with her.

He kneels. "Goddess, we would know your will. Shall we collect the ashes?"

She turns to look at him. Perhaps there is grief in her eyes; perhaps not. It is impossible to say.

"Collect them. Bury them. I have done all I will do."

He inclines his head. "Great Thetis, your son wished that his ashes be placed—"

"I know what he wished. Do as you please. It is not my concern."

SERVANT GIRLS ARE SENT to collect the ashes; they carry them to the golden urn where I rest. Will I feel his ashes as they fall against mine? I think of the snowflakes on Pelion, cold on our red cheeks. The yearning for him is like hunger, hollowing me. Somewhere his soul waits, but it is nowhere I can reach. *Bury us, and mark our names above. Let us be free.* His ashes settle among mine, and I feel nothing.

AGAMEMNON CALLS a council to discuss the tomb they will build.

"We should put it on the field where he fell," Nestor says.

Machaon shakes his head. "It will be more central on the beach, by the agora."

"That's the last thing we want. Tripping over it every day," Diomedes says.

"On the hill, I think. The ridge by their camp," Odysseus says.

Wherever, wherever, wherever.

"I have come to take my father's place." The clear voice cuts across the room.

The heads of the kings twist towards the tent flap. A boy stands framed in the tent's doorway. His hair is bright red, the color of the fire's crust; he is beautiful, but coldly so, a winter's morning. Only the dullest would not know which father he means. It is stamped on every line of his face, so close it tears at me. Just his chin is different, angling sharply down to a point as his mother's did.

"I am the son of Achilles," he announces.

The kings are staring. Most did not even know Achilles had a child. Only Odysseus has the wits to speak. "May we know the name of Achilles' son?"

"My name is Neoptolemus. Called Pyrrhus." *Fire*. But there is nothing of flame about him, beyond his hair. "Where is my father's seat?"

Idomeneus has taken it. He rises. "Here."

Pyrrhus' eyes rake over the Cretan king. "I pardon your presumption. You did not know I was coming." He sits. "Lord of Mycenae, Lord of Sparta." The slightest incline of his head. "I offer myself to your army."

Agamemnon's face is caught between disbelief and displeasure. He had thought he was done with Achilles. And the boy's affect is strange, unnerving.

"You do not seem old enough."

Twelve. He is twelve.

"I have lived with the gods beneath the sea," he says. "I have drunk their nectar and feasted on ambrosia. I come now to win the war for you. The Fates have said that Troy will not fall without me."

"What?" Agamemnon is aghast.

"If it is so, we are indeed glad to have you," Menelaus says. "We were talking of your father's tomb, and where to build it."

"On the hill," Odysseus says.

Menelaus nods. "A fitting place for them."

"Them?"

There is a slight pause.

"Your father and his companion. Patroclus."

"And why should this man be buried beside *Aristos Achaion*?"

The air is thick. They are all waiting to hear Menelaus' answer.

"It was your father's wish, Prince Neoptolemus, that their ashes be placed together. We cannot bury one without the other."

Pyrrhus lifts his sharp chin. "A slave has no place in his master's tomb. If the ashes are together, it cannot be undone, but I will not allow my father's fame to be diminished. The monument is for him, alone."

Do not let it be so. Do not leave me here without him.

The kings exchange glances.

"Very well," Agamemnon says. "It shall be as you say."

I am air and thought and can do nothing.

THE GREATER THE MONUMENT, the greater the man. The stone the Greeks quarry for his grave is huge and white, stretching up to the sky. A C H I L L E S, it reads. It will stand for him, and speak to all who pass: he lived and died, and lives again in memory.

PYRRHUS' BANNERS bear the emblem of Scyros, his mother's land, not Phthia. His soldiers, too, are from Scyros. Dutifully, Automedon lines up the Myrmidons and the women in welcome. They watch him make his way up the shore, his gleaming, new-minted troops, his red-gold hair like a flame against the blue of the sky.

"I am the son of Achilles," he tells them. "I claim you as my inheritance and birthright. Your loyalty is mine now." His eyes fix upon a woman who stands, eyes down, her hands folded. He goes to her and lifts her chin in his hand.

"What's your name?" he asks.

"Briseis."

"I've heard of you," he says. "You were the reason my father stopped fighting."

That night he sends his guards for her. They hold her arms as they walk her to the tent. Her head is bowed in submission, and she does not struggle.

The tent flap opens, and she is pushed through. Pyrrhus lounges in a chair, one leg dangling carelessly off the side. Achilles might have sat that way once. But his eyes were never like that, empty as the endless depths of black ocean, filled with nothing but the bloodless bodies of fish.

She kneels. "My lord."

"My father broke with the army for you. You must have been a good bed-slave."

Briseis' eyes are at their darkest and most veiled. "You honor me, my lord, to say so. But I do not believe it was for me he refused to fight."

"Why then? In your slave's opinion?" A precise eyebrow lifts. It is terrifying to watch him speak to her. He is like a snake; you do not know where he will strike.

"I was a war prize, and Agamemnon dishonored him in taking me. That is all."

"Were you not his bed-slave?"

"No, my lord."

"Enough." His voice is sharp. "Do not lie to me again. You are the best woman in the camp. You were his."

Her shoulders have crept up a little. "I would not have you think better of me than I deserve. I was never so fortunate."

"Why? What is wrong with you?"

She hesitates. "My lord, have you heard of the man who is buried with your father?"

His face goes flat. "Of course I have not heard of him. He is no one."

"Yet your father loved him well, and honored him. He would be well pleased to know they were buried together. He had no need of me."

Pyrrhus stares at her.

"My lord—"

"Silence." The word cracks over her like a lash. "I will teach you what it means to lie to *Aristos Achaion*." He stands. "Come here." He is only twelve, but he does not look it. He has the body of a man.

Her eyes are wide. "My lord, I am sorry I have displeased you. You may ask anyone, Phoinix or Automedon. They will say I am not lying."

"I have given you an order."

She stands, her hands fumbling in the folds of her dress. *Run*, I whisper. *Do not go to him*. But she goes.

"My lord, what would you have of me?"

He steps to her, eyes glittering. "Whatever I want."

I cannot see where the blade comes from. It is in her hand, and then it is swinging down on him. But she has never killed a man before. She does not know how hard you need to drive it, nor with what conviction. And he is quick, twisting away already. The blade splits the skin, scoring it in a jagged line, but does not sink. He smacks her viciously to the ground. She throws the knife at his face and runs.

She erupts from the tent, past the too-slow hands of the guards, down the beach and into the sea. Behind her is Pyrrhus, tunic gashed open, bleeding across his stomach. He stands beside the bewildered guards and calmly takes a spear from one of their hands.

"Throw it," a guard urges. For she is past the breakers now.

"A moment," Pyrrhus murmurs.

Her limbs lift into the gray waves like the steady beats of wings. She has always been the strongest swimmer of the three of us. She used to swear she'd gone to Tenedos once, two hours by boat. I feel wild triumph as she pulls farther and farther from shore. The only man whose spear could have reached her is dead. She is free.

The only man but that man's son.

The spear flies from the top of the beach, soundless and precise. Its point hits her back like a stone tossed onto a floating leaf. The gulp of black water swallows her whole.

Phoinix sends a man out, a diver, to look for her body, but he does not find it. Maybe her gods are kinder than ours, and she will find rest. I would give my life again to make it so.

THE PROPHECY TOLD TRULY. Now that Pyrrhus has come, Troy falls. He does not do it alone, of course. There is the horse, and Odysseus' plan, and a whole army besides. But he is the one who

kills Priam. He is the one who hunts down Hector's wife, Andromache, hiding in a cellar with her son. He plucks the child from
her arms and dashes his head against the stone of the walls, so hard
the skull shatters like a rotted fruit. Even Agamemnon blanched
when he heard.

The bones of the city are cracked and sucked dry. The Greek
kings stuff their holds with its gold columns and princesses.
Quicker than I could have imagined possible they pack the camp,
all the tents rolled and stowed, the food killed and stored. The
beach is stripped clean, like a well-picked carcass.

I haunt their dreams. *Do not leave,* I beg them. *Not until you
have given me peace.* But if anyone hears, they do not answer.

Pyrrhus wishes a final sacrifice for his father the evening before they sail. The kings gather by the tomb, and Pyrrhus pre-
sides, with his royal prisoners at his heels, Andromache and
Queen Hecuba and the young princess Polyxena. He trails them
everywhere he goes now, in perpetual triumph.

Calchas leads a white heifer to the tomb's base. But when he
reaches for the knife, Pyrrhus stops him. "A single heifer. Is this
all? The same you would do for any man? My father was *Aristos
Achaion.* He was the best of you, and his son has proven better
still. Yet you stint us?"

Pyrrhus' hand closes on the shapeless, blowing dress of the
princess Polyxena and yanks her towards the altar. "This is what
my father's soul deserves."

He will not. He dare not.

As if in answer, Pyrrhus smiles. "Achilles is pleased," he says,
and tears open her throat.

I can taste it still, the gush of salt and iron. It seeped into the grass where we are buried, and choked me. The dead are supposed to crave blood, but not like this. Not like this.

THE GREEKS LEAVE TOMORROW, and I am desperate.

Odysseus.

He sleeps lightly, eyelids fluttering.

Odysseus. Listen to me.

He twitches. Even in sleep he is not at rest.

When you came to him for help, I answered you. Will you not answer me now? You know what he was to me. You saw, before you brought us here. Our peace is on your head.

"MY APOLOGIES for bothering you so late, Prince Pyrrhus." He offers his easiest smile.

"I do not sleep," Pyrrhus says.

"How convenient. No wonder you get so much more done than the rest of us."

Pyrrhus watches him with narrowed eyes; he cannot tell if he is being mocked.

"Wine?" Odysseus holds up a skin.

"I suppose." Pyrrhus jerks his chin at two goblets. "Leave us," he says to Andromache. While she gathers her clothes, Odysseus pours.

"Well. You must be pleased with all you have done here. Hero by thirteen? Not many men can say so."

"No other men." The voice is cold. "What do you want?"

"I'm afraid I have been prompted by a rare stirring of guilt."

"Oh?"

"We sail tomorrow, and leave many Greek dead behind us. All of them are properly buried, with a name to mark their memory. All but one. I am not a pious man, but I do not like to think of souls wandering among the living. I like to take my ease unmolested by restless spirits."

Pyrrhus listens, his lips drawn back in faint, habitual distaste.

"I cannot say I was your father's friend, nor he mine. But I admired his skill and valued him as a soldier. And in ten years, you get to know a man, even if you don't wish to. So I can tell you now that I do not believe he would want Patroclus to be forgotten."

Pyrrhus stiffens. "Did he say so?"

"He asked that their ashes be placed together, he asked that they be buried as one. In the spirit of this, I think we can say he wished it." For the first time, I am grateful for his cleverness.

"I am his son. I am the one who says what his spirit wishes for."

"Which is why I came to you. I have no stake in this. I am only an honest man, who likes to see right done."

"Is it right that my father's fame should be diminished? Tainted by a commoner?"

"Patroclus was no commoner. He was born a prince and exiled. He served bravely in our army, and many men admired him. He killed Sarpedon, second only to Hector."

"In my father's armor. With my father's fame. He has none of his own."

Odysseus inclines his head. "True. But fame is a strange thing. Some men gain glory after they die, while others fade. What is admired in one generation is abhorred in another." He spread his broad hands. "We cannot say who will survive the holocaust of memory. Who knows?" He smiles. "Perhaps one day even I will be famous. Perhaps more famous than you."

"I doubt it."

Odysseus shrugs. "We cannot say. We are men only, a brief flare of the torch. Those to come may raise us or lower us as they please. Patroclus may be such as will rise in the future."

"He is not."

"Then it would be a good deed. A deed of charity and piety. To honor your father, and let a dead man rest."

"He is a blot on my father's honor, and a blot on mine. I will not allow it. Take your sour wine and go." Pyrrhus' words are sharp as breaking sticks.

Odysseus stands but does not go. "Do you have a wife?" he asks.

"Of course not."

"I have a wife. I have not seen her for ten years. I do not know if she is dead, or if I will die before I can return to her."

I had thought, always, that his wife was a joke, a fiction. But his voice is not mild now. Each word comes slowly, as if it must be brought from a great depth.

"My consolation is that we will be together in the underworld. That we will meet again there, if not in this life. I would not wish to be there without her."

"My father had no such wife," Pyrrhus says.

Odysseus looks at the young man's implacable face. "I have done my best," he says. "Let it be remembered I tried."

I remember.

THE GREEKS SAIL, and take my hope with them. I cannot follow. I am tied to this earth where my ashes lie. I curl myself around the stone obelisk of his tomb. Perhaps it is cool to the touch; perhaps warm. I cannot tell. A C H I L L E S, it says, and nothing more. He has gone to the underworld, and I am here.

PEOPLE COME TO SEE his grave. Some hang back, as if they are afraid his ghost will rise and challenge them. Others stand at the base to look at the scenes of his life carved on the stone. They are a little hastily done, but clear enough. Achilles killing Memnon, killing Hector, killing Penthesilea. Nothing but death. This is how Pyrrhus' tomb might look. Is this how he will be remembered?

Thetis comes. I watch her, withering the grass where she stands. I have not felt such hatred for her in a long time. She made Pyrrhus, and loved him more than Achilles.

She is looking at the scenes on the tomb, death after death. She reaches, as if she will touch them. I cannot bear it.

Thetis, I say.

Her hand jerks back. She vanishes.

Later she returns. *Thetis*. She does not react. Only stands, looking at her son's tomb.

I am buried here. In your son's grave.

She says nothing. Does nothing. She does not hear.

Every day she comes. She sits at the tomb's base, and it seems that I can feel her cold through the earth, the slight searing smell of salt. I cannot make her leave, but I can hate her.

You said that Chiron ruined him. You are a goddess, and cold, and know nothing. You are the one who ruined him. Look at how he will be remembered now. Killing Hector, killing Troilus. For things he did cruelly in his grief.

Her face is like stone itself. It does not move. The days rise and fall.

Perhaps such things pass for virtue among the gods. But how is there glory in taking a life? We die so easily. Would you make him another Pyrrhus? Let the stories of him be something more.

"What more?" she says.

For once I am not afraid. What else can she do to me?

Returning Hector's body to Priam, I say. *That should be remembered.*

She is silent for a long time. "And?"

His skill with the lyre. His beautiful voice.

She seems to be waiting.

The girls. He took them so that they would not suffer at another king's hands.

"That was your doing."

Why are you not with Pyrrhus?

Something flickers in her eyes. "He is dead."

I am fiercely glad. *How?* It is a command, almost.

"He was killed by Agamemnon's son."

For what?

She does not answer for some time. "He stole his bride and ravished her."

"Whatever I want," he said to Briseis. *Was this the son you preferred to Achilles?*

Her mouth tightens. "Have you no more memories?"

I am made of memories.

"Speak, then."

I ALMOST REFUSE. But the ache for him is stronger than my anger. I want to speak of something not dead or divine. I want him to live.

At first it is strange. I am used to keeping him from her, to hoarding him for myself. But the memories well up like spring-water, faster than I can hold them back. They do not come as words, but like dreams, rising as scent from the rain-wet earth. This, I say. This and this. The way his hair looked in summer sun. His face when he ran. His eyes, solemn as an owl at lessons. This and this and this. So many moments of happiness, crowding forward.

She closes her eyes. The skin over them is the color of sand in winter. She listens, and she too remembers.

She remembers standing on a beach, hair black and long as a horse's tail. Slate-gray waves smash against rocks. Then a mortal's hands, brutal and bruising on her polished skin. The sand scraping her raw, and the tearing inside. The gods, after, tying her to him.

She remembers feeling the child within her, luminous in the dark of her womb. She repeats to herself the prophecy that the three old women spoke to her: *your son will be greater than his father.*

The other gods had recoiled to hear it. They knew what powerful sons do to their fathers—Zeus' thunderbolts still smell of singed flesh and patricide. They gave her to a mortal, trying to shackle the child's power. Dilute him with humanity, diminish him.

She rests her hand on her stomach, feels him swimming within. It is her blood that will make him strong.

But not strong enough. *I am a mortal!* he screams at her, his face blotchy and sodden and dull.

WHY DO YOU *not go to him?*

"I cannot." The pain in her voice is like something tearing. "I cannot go beneath the earth." The underworld, with its cavernous gloom and fluttering souls, where only the dead may walk. "This is all that is left," she says, her eyes still fixed on the monument. An eternity of stone.

I conjure the boy I knew. Achilles, grinning as the figs blur in his hands. His green eyes laughing into mine. *Catch,* he says. Achilles, outlined against the sky, hanging from a branch over the river. The thick warmth of his sleepy breath against my ear. *If you have to go, I will go with you.* My fears forgotten in the golden harbor of his arms.

The memories come, and come. She listens, staring into the grain of the stone. We are all there, goddess and mortal and the boy who was both.

THE SUN IS SETTING over the sea, spilling its colors on the water's surface. She is beside me, silent in the blurry, creeping dusk. Her face is as unmarked as the first day I saw her. Her arms are crossed over her chest, as if to hold some thought to herself.

I have told her all. I have spared nothing, of any of us.

We watch the light sink into the grave of the western sky.

"I could not make him a god," she says. Her jagged voice, rich with grief.

But you made him.

She does not answer me for a long time, only sits, eyes shining with the last of the dying light.

"I have done it," she says. At first I do not understand. But then I see the tomb, and the marks she has made on the stone. A C H I L L E S, it reads. And beside it, P A T R O C L U S.

"Go," she says. "He waits for you."

IN THE DARKNESS, two shadows, reaching through the hopeless, heavy dusk. Their hands meet, and light spills in a flood like a hundred golden urns pouring out of the sun.

ACKNOWLEDGMENTS

Writing this novel was a ten-year-long journey, and I was fortunate enough to meet many more kindly deities than angry Cyclopes along the way. It would be impossible to thank everyone who offered me encouragement over the years—it would take a second book—but there are some divinities that need worshipping.

In particular, I want to thank my early readers, who gave me such loving and thoughtful responses: Carolyn Bell, Sarah Furlow, and Michael Bourret. I also want to thank my amazing godmother, Barbara Thornbrough, who has cheered me on the whole way, as well as the Drake family for their kind encouragement and for being expert consultants on wide-ranging matters. My heartfelt appreciation goes also to my teachers, especially Diane Dubois, Susan Melvoin, Kristin Jaffe, Judith Williams, and Jim Miller; and to my passionate and fabulous students, Shakespeareans and Latin scholars alike, for teaching me much more than I ever taught them.

I have been fortunate enough to have not one but three amazing mentors in Classics, teaching, and life: David Rich, Joseph Pucci, and Michael C. J. Putnam. I am grateful beyond measure to their kindness and erudition. Thanks also to the entire Brown University Classics Department. It goes without saying that all errors and distortions in this work are my own entirely, and not theirs.

Special thanks to Walter Kasinskas, and to the beautiful and talented Nora Pines, who has always believed I would be a writer despite reading a number of my early short stories.

Thanks and thanks and ever thanks to the inimitable, irre-
pressible, and outstanding Jonah Ramu Cohen, a fierce fiery
warrior who fought for this book every step of the way. I am so
grateful for your friendship.

A Mount Olympus of gratitude to the astounding Julie Barer,
best of all Agents, who swept me off my feet and into a miracle,
along with all the rest of her amazing team.

And of course thanks to my dynamic, fabulous editor, Lee
Boudreaux, and the whole group at Ecco, including Abigail Hol-
stein, Michael McKenzie, Heather Drucker, Rachel Bressler, and
everyone who took such excellent care of me and this work. I
would also like to thank the fantastic people at Bloomsbury UK—
the outstanding Alexandra Pringle, Katie Bond, David Mann, and
everyone else on their team for all their incredible work on my
book's behalf.

Finally, I want to thank my family, including my brother Bud,
who has put up with my stories of Achilles for his entire life, and
my wonderful stepfather, Gordon. Most of all, I thank my amazing mother, who has loved and supported me in all my endeavors,
and who inspired me to love reading as much as she does. I am so
blessed to be your daughter.

Last, but never least, thanks to Nathaniel, my Athena-in-
shining-armor, whose love, editing, and patience brought me
home.

CHARACTER GLOSSARY

Gods and Immortals

APHRODITE. The goddess of love and beauty, the mother of Aeneas, and a champion of the Trojans. She particularly favored Paris, and in Book 3 of the *Iliad* she intervened to save him from Menelaus.

APOLLO. The god of light and music, and a champion of the Trojans. He was responsible for sending the plague down upon the Greek army in Book 1 of the *Iliad*, and was instrumental in the deaths of both Achilles and Patroclus.

ARTEMIS. The twin sister of Apollo and the goddess of the hunt, the moon, and virginity. Angry about the bloodshed the Trojan War would cause, she stopped the winds from blowing, stranding the Greek fleet at Aulis. After the sacrifice of Iphigenia, she was appeased and the winds returned.

ATHENA. The powerful goddess of wisdom, weaving, and war arts. She was a fierce supporter of her beloved Greeks against the Trojans and a particular guardian of the wily Odysseus. She appears often in both the *Iliad* and the *Odyssey*.

CHIRON. The only "good" centaur, known as a teacher of the heroes Jason, Aesculapius, and Achilles, as well as the inventor of medicine and surgery.

HERA. The queen of the gods and the sister-wife of Zeus. Like Athena, she championed the Greeks and hated the Trojans. In Vergil's *Aeneid*, she is the principal antagonist, constantly harassing the Trojan hero Aeneas after Troy has fallen.

SCAMANDER. The god of the river Scamander near Troy and another champion of the Trojans. His famous battle with Achilles is told in Book 22 of the *Iliad*.

THETIS. A sea-nymph and shape-changer, and the mother of Achilles. The fates had prophesied that Thetis' son would be greater than his father, which frightened the god Zeus (who had previously desired her). He made sure to marry Thetis to a mortal, in order to limit the power of her son. In post-Homeric versions of the story she tries a number of ways to make Achilles immortal, including dipping him by his ankle in the river Styx and holding him in a fire to burn away his mortality.

ZEUS. The king of the gods and the father of many famous heroes, including Heracles and Perseus.

Mortals

ACHILLES. The son of the king Peleus and the sea-nymph Thetis, he was the greatest warrior of his generation, as well as the most beautiful. The *Iliad* calls him "swift-footed" and also praises his singing voice. He was raised by the kindly centaur Chiron and took the exiled prince Patroclus as his constant companion. As a teenager, he was famously offered a choice: a long life and obscurity or a short life and fame. He chose fame and sailed to Troy along with the other Greeks. However, in the ninth year of the war he quarreled with Agamemnon and refused to fight any longer, returning to battle only when his beloved Patroclus was killed by Hector. In a rage, he slew the great Trojan warrior and dragged his body around the walls of Troy in vengeance. He was eventually killed by the Trojan prince Paris, with the assistance of the god Apollo.

Achilles' most famous myth—his fatally vulnerable heel—is actually a very late story. In the *Iliad* and *Odyssey* Achilles isn't invincible, just extraordinarily gifted in battle. But in the years after Homer, myths began popping up to explain and elaborate upon Achilles' seeming invincibility. In one popular version, the goddess Thetis dips Achilles in the river Styx to try to make him immortal; it works, everywhere but the place on his heel where she holds him. Since the *Iliad* and *Odyssey* were my primary sources of inspiration, and since their interpretation seemed more realistic, I chose to follow the older tradition.

AENEAS. The son of the goddess Aphrodite and the mortal Anchises, the Trojan noble Aeneas was renowned for his piety. He fought bravely in the Trojan War but is best known for his adventures afterwards. As Vergil tells in the *Aeneid*, Aeneas escaped the fall of Troy and led a group of survivors to Italy, where he married a native princess and founded the Roman people.

AGAMEMNON. The brother of Menelaus, Agamemnon ruled Mycenae, the largest kingdom in Greece, and served as the over-general of the Greek expedition to Troy. During the war he often quarreled with Achilles, who refused to acknowledge Agamemnon's right to command him. Upon Agamemnon's return home after the war, he was murdered by his wife, Clytemnestra. Aeschylus depicts this incident and its aftermath in his famous tragic cycle the *Oresteia*.

AJAX. The king of Salamis and a descendent of Zeus, who was known for his enormous size and strength. He was the second greatest Greek warrior after Achilles, and memorably stood against the Trojans' attack on the Greek camp when Achilles refused to fight. However, after Achilles' death, when Agamemnon chose to honor Odysseus as the most valuable member of the Greek army, Ajax went mad with grief and rage, and killed himself. His story is movingly told in Sophocles' tragedy *Ajax*.

ANDROMACHE. Born a princess of Cilicia, near Troy, she became the loyal and loving wife of Hector. She hated Achilles, who had killed her family in a raid. During the sack of Troy, she was taken captive by Pyrrhus and carried back to Greece. After Pyrrhus' death, she and Helenus, Hector's brother, founded the city of Buthrotum, which they built to resemble the lost Troy. Vergil tells their story in Book 3 of the *Aeneid*.

AUTOMEDON. Achilles' charioteer, skilled at handling his divine, headstrong horses. After Achilles' death, he served his son Pyrrhus.

BRISEIS. Taken captive by the Greeks in their raids on the Trojan countryside, Briseis was given as a war-prize to Achilles. When Achilles defied him, Agamemnon confiscated her as a punishment. She was returned after Patroclus' death, and in Book 19 of the *Iliad*, she and the other women of the camp mourn over his body.

CALCHAS. A priest who advised the Greeks, encouraging Agamemnon to sacrifice his daughter Iphigenia and to return the captive slave-girl Chryseis to her father.

CHRYSES AND CHRYSEIS. Chryses was an Anatolian priest of Apollo. His daughter, Chryseis, was taken as a slave by Agamemnon. When Chryses came to retrieve her, offering a generous ransom, Agamemnon refused, then insulted him. Enraged, Chryses called upon his god Apollo to send a plague to punish the Greek army. When Achilles publicly urged Agamemnon to return Chryseis to her father, Agamemnon erupted, precipitating their dramatic rift.

DEIDAMEIA. The daughter of King Lycomedes and the princess of the island kingdom of Scyros. To keep him from the war, Thetis dressed Achilles as a girl and hid him among Deidameia's ladies-in-waiting. Deidameia discovered the trick and secretly married Achilles, conceiving the child Pyrrhus.

DIOMEDES. The king of Argos. Known for both his guile and his strength, Diomedes was one of the most valued warriors in the Greek army. Like Odysseus, he was a favorite of the goddess Athena, who in Book 5 of the *Iliad* grants him supernatural strength in battle.

HECTOR. The oldest son of Priam and the crown prince of Troy, Hector was known for his strength, nobility, and love of family. In Book 6 of the *Iliad*, Homer shows us a touching scene between Hector; his wife, Andromache; and their young son, Astyanax. He was killed by Achilles in the final year of the war.

HELEN. The legendary most beautiful woman in the world, Helen was a princess of Sparta, the daughter of the queen Leda and the god Zeus (in the form of a swan). Many men sought her hand in marriage, each swearing an oath to uphold her union with whoever prevailed. She was given to Menelaus, but later ran away with the Trojan prince Paris, setting in motion the Trojan War. After the war, she returned home with Menelaus to Sparta.

HERACLES. The son of Zeus and the most famous of Greek heroes. Known for his tremendous strength, Heracles was forced to perform twelve labors as penance to the goddess Hera, who hated him for being the product of one of Zeus' affairs. He died long before the Trojan War began.

IDOMENEUS. The king of Crete and grandson of King Minos, of Minotaur fame.

IPHIGENIA. The daughter of Agamemnon and Clytemnestra, promised in marriage to Achilles and brought to Aulis to appease the goddess Artemis. Her sacrifice made the winds blow again, so that the Greek fleet could sail to Troy. Her story is told in Euripides' tragedy *Iphigenia at Aulis*.

LYCOMEDES. The king of Scyros and the father of Deidameia. He unknowingly sheltered Achilles disguised as a girl in his court.

MENELAUS. The brother of Agamemnon and, after his marriage to Helen, the king of Sparta. When Helen was kidnapped by Paris, he invoked the oath sworn by all of her suitors and, with his brother, led an army to retrieve her. In Book 3 of the *Iliad* he dueled with Paris for possession of Helen, and was winning before the goddess Aphrodite intervened on Paris' behalf. After the war, he and Helen returned to Sparta.

NESTOR. The aged king of Pylos and the former companion of Heracles. He was too old to fight in the Trojan War but served as an important counselor to Agamemnon.

ODYSSEUS. The wily prince of Ithaca, beloved by the goddess Athena. He proposed the famous oath requiring all of Helen's suitors to swear a vow to uphold her marriage. As his reward, he claimed her clever cousin Penelope as his wife. During the Trojan War, he was one of Agamemnon's chief advisers, and later devised the trick of the Trojan horse. His voyage home, which lasted ten years, is the subject of Homer's *Odyssey*, which includes the famous tales of his encounters with the Cyclops, the witch Circe, Scylla and Charybdis, and the Sirens. Eventually Odysseus returned to Ithaca, where he was welcomed by his wife, Penelope, and grown son, Telemachus.

PARIS. The son of Priam who became the judge of the famous "beauty contest" between Hera, Athena, and Aphrodite, with the golden apple as a prize. Each goddess tried to bribe him: Hera with power, Athena with wisdom, and Aphrodite with the most beautiful woman in the world. He awarded the prize to Aphrodite, and she in turn helped him spirit Helen away from her husband, Menelaus, thus starting the Trojan War. Paris was known for his skill with a bow and, with Apollo's help, killed the mighty Achilles.

PATROCLUS. The son of King Menoitius. Exiled from his home for accidentally killing another boy, Patroclus found shelter in Peleus' court, where he was fostered with Achilles. He is a secondary character in the *Iliad*, but his fateful decision to try to save the Greeks by dressing in Achilles' armor sets in motion the final act of the story. When Patroclus is killed by Hector, Achilles is devastated and takes brutal vengeance upon the Trojans.

PELEUS. The king of Phthia and the father of Achilles by the sea-nymph Thetis. The story of Peleus overpowering the shape-changing Thetis in a wrestling match was a popular one in antiquity.

PHOINIX. A longtime friend and counselor of Peleus, who went with Achilles to Troy as his adviser. In Book 9 of the *Iliad*, Phoinix spoke of having cared for Achilles when he was a baby, and vainly tried to persuade him to yield and help the Greeks.

POLYXENA. The Trojan princess whom Pyrrhus sacrificed at his father's tomb, before leaving Troy for the voyage home.

PRIAM. The elderly king of Troy, who was renowned for his piety and his many children. In Book 24 of the *Iliad*, he bravely made his way into Achilles' tent to beg for his son Hector's body. During the sack of Troy, he was killed by Achilles' son, Pyrrhus.

PYRRHUS. Formally named Neoptolemus but called "Pyrrhus" for his fiery hair, he was the son of Achilles and the princess Deidameia. He joined the war after his father's death, participating in the trick of the Trojan horse and brutally murdering the old king of Troy, Priam. In Book 2 of the *Aeneid*, Vergil tells the story of Pyrrhus' role in the sack of Troy.